Kay Brellend is the bestselling author of The Campbell Road series, The Bittersweet Legacy trilogy, and The Workhouse to War trilogy. Kay never imagined she would become a writer, certainly not a writer of novels inspired by her own family. 'Writing has been an absorbing journey for me. I have learned much about my ancestors and their toughness and resilience and I feel pride in my roots in the worst street in north London.'

Please visit her website http://www.kaybrellend.com for news, upcoming titles and more.

By Kay Brellend

Women's War series

A Daughter's Heartbreak
East End Orphan
The Englishman's Daughter

The Bittersweet Legacy series

A Sister's Bond
A Lonely Heart
The Way Home

The Workhouse to War series

A Workhouse Christmas
Stray Angel
The Workhouse Sisters

THE ENGLISHMAN'S DAUGHTER

Kay Brellend

PIATKUS

PIATKUS

First published in Great Britain in 2025 by Piatkus

1 3 5 7 9 10 8 6 4 2

Copyright © 2025 by Kay Brellend

The moral right of the author has been asserted.

All characters and events in this publication, other than those clearly in the public domain, are fictitious and any resemblance to real persons, living or dead, is purely coincidental.

All rights reserved.
No part of this publication may be reproduced, stored in a retrieval system, or transmitted in any form or by any means, without the prior permission in writing of the publisher, nor be otherwise circulated in any form of binding or cover other than that in which it is published and without a similar condition including this condition being imposed on the subsequent purchaser.

A CIP catalogue record for this book
is available from the British Library.

ISBN 978-0-349-43558-9

Printed and bound in Great Britain by Clays Ltd, Elcograf S.p.A.

Papers used by Piatkus are from well-managed forests
and other responsible sources.

Piatkus	The authorised representative
An imprint of	in the EEA is
Little, Brown Book Group	Hachette Ireland
Carmelite House	8 Castlecourt Centre
50 Victoria Embankment	Dublin 15, D15 XTP3, Ireland
London EC4Y 0DZ	(email: info@hbgi.ie)

An Hachette UK Company
www.hachette.co.uk

www.littlebrown.co.uk

For the Thirteen
Yolande Beekman, Denise Bloch, Andree Borrel, Muriel Byck,
Madeleine Damerment, Noor Inayat Khan, Cecily Lefort,
Vera Leigh, Elaine Plewman, Lilian Rolfe, Diana Rowden,
Yvonne Rudellat, Violet Szabo.

Chapter One

31 May 1940, Northern France

Given a choice he would rather have died in England. But he'd left it too late to pick a side.

Had they set off for the coast yesterday they might have stood a chance of making it. But his children wouldn't leave. They'd thought he was overreacting. Nothing like that was about to happen. The Allies were strong and would protect them. Victory was imminent. *It would all be over soon, Papa,* they'd reassured him.

The problem with the young was they'd not been there the first time round. He had, and had heard it all before: enlist and it'll all be over by Christmas, they'd been told. Crafty buggers never said which Christmas.

Luc and Elise weren't kids to be carted off whether they liked it or not. They were young adults and knew their own minds. Sidney Cooper had never hesitated in saving his own skin in the past. For the first time in his life, he'd behaved as a good father would and stayed by them, for whatever use he proved to be.

At almost sixty years old he was paying for four decades

of debauchery and was tired and weak in body and mind. But he'd a gun, and if necessary he'd use it. And that was that.

He could hear them getting closer and his guts leaped and dived and gurgled in protest. Twenty-five-year-old memories flocked in his head: carrion shadows ... shrill whistles ... dawn sprints towards an enemy trench, never knowing if another second of life remained to him.

The inside of his mouth had dried out and he took a swig of wine. He'd immersed himself in the French custom of wine drinking but had already been a drunk before settling in France. His wives had tried to tame him for his own good: his first had been fifteen when they met in London's East End. Nine months and a shotgun wedding later they'd been parents. When Iris passed away during those war years, he'd been serving on the Western Front. Newly widowed, he'd abandoned London and his children and moved in with his French mistress. They'd never married but had lived together as though they were husband and wife. Sophie Bouchard had been buried in the village churchyard seven years ago, dead of pneumonia. He'd made an attempt at rearing their two children for a while but found the business too trying. His son and daughter had been despatched to their maternal grandmother and he'd bolted back over the Channel. Being so much older, his English kids were less of a bother.

He'd come back to suit himself rather than Luc and Elise, but since being reunited with them, a sense of duty, and his mortality, had been making itself known. Too many women and too much alcohol had pulled apart his health, leaving him little time left to put things right. He'd been a bad father to all of his six children but his regrets were with Luc and Elise, the youngest two.

He drained the glass of wine, wiped his mouth on the back of an unsteady hand, and listened.

The noise was the same: boots beating time, heavy equipment creaking. A tank division, possibly. No horses this time. The stamp and snort accompanying the rattle of the gun carriages and mess wagons had been everywhere in 1914. Snatches of soldiers' chanting drifted to him – bawdy songs no doubt, but he couldn't understand much German. French was a different matter. He was fluent, having lived here on and off for more than a quarter of a century. His daughter would giggle at his accent mangling the words. They spoke mainly in English though, and it made him smile to hear his French girl twanging like a Cockney sparrer. His beautiful little Elise, the image of her mother: hair almost black and eyes as grey as the slate on the roof above. He'd wasted precious time they could have spent together.

As though his thoughts had conjured her up, Elise hurtled in through the back door, startling him out of brooding and almost giving him a heart attack to finish him off. He would have happily gone that way.

'Papa ... you were right. Tanks are coming. The Nazis are everywhere in the village and Luc is still in the fields,' she panted out and rushed against his side to cling to him.

'Hush now and listen to me.' He stroked curls with the gloss of a raven's wing off her flushed cheeks. 'They might pass us by. But if somebody has told them an Englishman lives here they will stop. You must be prepared if I'm arrested—'

'No ...' she interrupted, swinging her head wildly away from his comfort.

'Hush ...' He cupped her face to still her agitated movements and gazed intently at her. 'They might not take me but if they do you must go and find your brother. You must both stay with your grandmother and never come back here until I do.'

'Nobody will betray you. They wouldn't be so mean. The Nazis will think you're French, Papa. You are French now,' she said and stamped her feet in a rage of fear.

'Yes, they might think that,' he soothed her. To comfort himself he touched the weight of the pistol hanging inside his trousers. A cord tied around his waist held it suspended between his thighs. The Luger was loaded with two bullets and had been relieved from the corpse of a dead German officer. A souvenir from the Great War. A poor description if ever there was one.

Elise ground her forehead against the flax of her father's shirt. 'I'm sorry, Papa, you were right. We should have left for the coast earlier in the week.' A spark of hope and determination lit her eyes. 'There is still time. We could go out the back way and hide in the fields. Then pick up Luc on the way ... Grandma too if she will come. There are lots of refugees already on the road.' She started pulling her father towards the door that gave access into the poppy-headed meadows.

For a second Sidney was tempted, fired by her youthful optimism that everything could come right. But it was too late to outrun misfortune as he had in the past. 'No, love, it would be worse to be caught fleeing. I was wrong, it wouldn't have been wise to leave last night. The roads are dangerous ... crowded with the retreating troops and their vehicles. It is safer for you here.' His seventeen-year-old daughter's beauty would attract the attention of soldiers of any flag. Her brother would try to protect her and put himself in jeopardy. At nineteen, tall and well built, Luc would be a target. He'd be rounded up as forced labour or sent to an internment camp. At least these flint walls provided some protection.

'If they stop and come in we'll play it by ear ... let me do the talking ... they might not have much French, these Boches.' He led her to a chair hoping she couldn't feel his hands quivering. 'Sit down and do your knitting. Act naturally.'

Her upturned gaze was pitilessly direct and glistening with unshed tears. Acting naturally was impossible.

'If they take you away will you come back here after you've answered their questions or stay with us at Grandma's?' She gnawed on her thumbnail while they waited in an agony of tension. The atmosphere rocked with the sound of marching and Elise's jaw ached from clenching her teeth. 'They will see you aren't a threat and let you go, won't they?' Her whispers became quieter as the noise grew deafening.

'I'll return here.'

'Why mustn't we come back here then, Papa?' She began to rise but he controlled her with an untouching hand that guided her back into her seat.

'Just don't,' Sidney said softly. 'When I'm sure it's over I'll fetch you from your grandmother's.'

He couldn't tell her that she mustn't be alone ... that she might end up like her mother. Sophie hadn't wanted to catch a German officer's eye in 1915 or be passed around his friends until she ended up diseased. Her distraught parents hadn't intervened when their only child started working in a brothel. It had been too late to undo a scandal, and inviting attention from the men involved wouldn't have been wise for Resistance fighters.

When Sidney met Sophie at the brothel she'd said she

was clean again, so he needn't worry. She'd said he was a gentleman in comparison to the others. It was the first time Sidney Cooper had received such praise. Women might tell him he was handsome but quite often followed it up by complaining he was a selfish pig. He couldn't deny treating most of them badly. Sophie had rarely nagged him and it had made her special. She'd told him her parents had been shunned by neighbours who believed Sophie Bouchard was a collaborator as well as a whore.

The invaders were back, jogging memories, and it terrified and enraged Sidney in equal part that his children might become the victims of decades' old grudges. Women were always at risk during war and soon he wouldn't be able to protect his daughter from a similar fate.

'I should fetch Luc. He'll look after us.' Elise couldn't sit still. She jumped up and went to the open back doorway to search the horizon for her brother. Luc worked on a neighbouring farm. By now he would know about the enemy's advance driving back the Allies. Everybody would know. Surely Luc would come home.

'Sit down, Elise; say nothing about your brother to them. They might search for him and take him too.' Their eyes clashed as several sets of footsteps became distinct from the rest.

'Will Luc know to stay away?' Elise hoped her brother would hide now rather than rush home to them.

'He's no fool.' Sidney's hissed reassurance was drowned out by a hammering on the cottage door.

It was burst open before Sidney could reach it. A German officer strode in, and behind him came two armed soldiers. His arrogant blue gaze flashed from the man with greying hair to the girl with defiance shining in her eyes.

A quiet ensued and Sidney noticed his daughter was drawing the most attention. 'What do you want, monsieur? We have little food or anything else to give you.'

'Are you the Englishman?'

Sidney felt as tense as a coiled spring. He'd not fooled the bastard. He'd spoken in French but the German had answered in English. Sidney sent his daughter a warning look. Elise reacted by barging in front of him.

'Of course he isn't English.' She gestured away the absurdity. 'My father's as French as I am.' She spoke her own language, but again the young officer smiled and answered in English.

'You understand English, Mam'selle.' He looked her up and down in a way that made her stomach squirm. 'Who taught you?'

'A schoolteacher. Who taught you?'

'My schoolteacher.' He removed his cap, revealing a neat head of blond hair. 'So . . . as we are such good students we will talk in English so everybody understands. My apologies. I should introduce myself. Hauptmann Konrad Stein at your service.' He extended a hand to her. She ignored it. With apparent reluctance, he turned his attention to Sidney. 'Come with us please, Mr Cooper.'

'No!' Elise launched herself forward as though to push Stein away.

Sidney yanked her back before she could touch him. 'You remember what I told you?' he murmured hoarsely.

She nodded, but refused to let go of his hands.

Sidney raised them to his lips, rubbed his cheek against their soft backs. 'Don't worry, I'll see you again soon, dear. And I love you, Elise.' He took his coat from the peg and shrugged into it.

She tried to follow but the soldiers blocked her way as her father went out with the officer. She watched from the open doorway, and listened to Stein shouting at his men in German.

Her father didn't look back, but his captor did, staring at her over the car roof before getting into the vehicle. Elise glared back through a blur of tears that magnified the furious loathing in her eyes.

'Papa! she cried as the car moved off. The brigade marched by watching her, not singing any more. She withdrew inside and leaned against the door, sobbing.

She knew now why her father had told her to go from here. Some of them might come back for her next time.

The Hauptmann didn't make much conversation as the vehicle bumped over the rutted road. They'd make him talk though, Sidney knew that, and they wouldn't accept he didn't know anything, even though he really didn't.

'You are English?' Stein sounded bored and surveyed the blooming hedgerows that were close enough in places to skim the car windows as they passed.

'Yes, from London.'

'Your daughter is also from London?'

'No ... she's French. Her mother was French.'

'Your wife is dead?'

'She died years ago.'

'Your daughter is all alone.' Stein smiled to himself. 'You will want to help us quickly then to return home to her. Pretty girls shouldn't be left alone.'

'I've nothing to tell you.'

'We will see. You were here the last time. I think you were a Tommy who fell for a Mam'selle.'

'I was. Now I'm too old for all of that.' He chuckled. 'I'm so old I need to pee all the time. In fact, I need to go now.' No lies so far.

'What?' The younger man swung him a glance of distaste.

'Got a bit of a problem with the old waterworks.' He rolled his eyes at his groin. 'If you don't stop the car I'll wee on the seat ... and your nice uniform will suffer.' He gazed at the grey thigh close to him and a highly polished boot. He'd enjoy pissing on that.

Stein gestured his disbelief but shot forward to clap the driver on the shoulder. He scrambled out before the vehicle had come to a complete stop, fearing he might be a laughing stock and soon stink of piss. He strode around to open the door and let his prisoner out, his teeth grinding on an easily identifiable German oath.

'Don't need no toilet paper, thanks,' said Sidney and suffered a cuff for his insolence and having his coat pockets searched. He hopped from foot to foot to show it was an emergency. The Hauptmann gave him a shove, sending him away. With a smirk, Sidney walked to the shrubbery at the side of the road. He stepped modestly in among the trees, fiddling with his trouser buttons.

Half an hour had passed, he judged, time for Elise to be a fair distance away from the cottage. There was nothing else he could do to help his children than this. But he wished there was another way ... turn back the clock and do things differently, be a better person ... a better father. He'd killed before and not just during the war. Death didn't bother him, it was the dying ...

He wasn't a spy; he was a coward. They would assume he was an English spy though, and he'd suffer for it. He slid his hand inside his trousers and pulled out the gun and his cock. Two bullets. It would be a shame to waste one of them. He began wetting the undergrowth in front of him as a drift of tobacco smoke reached him. He would have liked a final cigarette himself. He took a proper grip on the gun and let his leg get wet as he turned.

The first bullet hit Stein and spun him around, and Sidney felt a burst of elation that he could still do it. The second entered his own mouth before the driver had got his door fully open.

Chapter Two

'Your father's gone?' Mathilde Bouchard swung a horrified look between her grandchildren. Her son-in-law had abandoned these two in the past when things got difficult, but this time a more sinister reason than his selfishness was to blame for his absence.

'They took Papa away. He said we must come here and stay with you until they let him go.'

'He was right to do so.' Mathilde hastily ushered them inside, closing the door against prying eyes.

When Elise reached the farm Luc had been stowing the tractor in the barn, having heard the noise of the approaching army. He'd jumped down the moment he saw her and listened in dismay to her report of their father's arrest. His boss had been herding his poultry into the barns to keep it out of sight of scavenging soldiers. Luc had told him he'd no time to help with the chickens and they'd set off immediately for their grandmother's village north of Lille. The settlement comprised a cluster of whitewashed cottages on a narrow lane. At its eastern end it widened into a square around which sat a church, a forge and a bakery.

To avoid the troops they'd used short cuts over the fields

and along narrow winding paths offering some cover. Scouting parties would soon be infiltrating the countryside, though and they'd be stopped and interrogated.

'Why didn't you come and get me sooner? I wouldn't have let them take him!' Luc continued pacing to and fro, squinting at his sister. After the heat and glare of the midday sun the atmosphere inside seemed cool and shady.

'Papa forbade me and there was no time anyway. What shall we do?'

'I'm doing what I should've done before. I'm joining the army,' declared Luc. 'What's left of it.'

'If they've taken your father you should both keep your heads down here for a few days and see what happens,' their grandmother cautioned. 'Be quiet and stay inside until he comes for you. Did anybody see you arrive?'

'The lane was quiet, nobody was about,' said Luc.

'Good ... they're all still at the market I expect.' A weekly market in the neighbouring village drew most of the housewives away for the mornings. They'd be hurrying back now though to batten down the hatches at home. 'Nobody must know you're here with me,' said Mathilde. 'Why did you not heed your father and go to England?'

'It's my fault ... I didn't believe Papa when he said it would be bad for us.' Elise covered her guilty face with her hands.

'I wanted to stay put as well.' Luc embraced his distraught sister. 'Why's this happened to France, anyway? This isn't our fight. So much for Maginot and his line,' he spat in disgust. 'It's all mad.'

'War is mad. It always starts with some man's insanity.' Mathilde whirled an angry finger by her temple. 'Here, drink this.' She poured hot strong coffee from a metal pot and handed them a cup each. Before they'd tasted it a sound of strident conversation outside prompted Mathilde to shoo her grandchildren into the bedroom. She put a finger to her lips just as the door received a bang and a neighbour called to Mathilde to open up.

From their place behind the half-closed door they sipped coffee and listened intently to their grandmother being told about a calamity. The market had been alive with talk of a German officer having been shot by a local man. The advancing troops had halted not far away to deal with the incident. It was rumoured the assailant was English and had also been shot. Was it Mathilde's son-in-law? Where was Sidney Cooper? The woman demanded to know. And what about reprisals?

Luc stifled his sister's gasp of anguish with his hand. Quickly he put a comforting arm about her to prevent her bursting into the parlour. He'd picked up from his grandmother's behaviour that not even long-standing acquaintances should be trusted.

Mathilde denied knowing anything and got rid of the elderly widow, who rejoined the others outside. At intervals the little group turned around to stare at the cottage.

'Is she talking about Papa?' Elise whispered, coming out of the bedroom.

'I think so,' Mathilde answered on a sigh, turning from the narrow casement through which she'd been spying on the gossips. 'Do you know if your father had a gun?'

Elise shook her head in despair but Luc said, 'When I was a kid he showed me a German revolver from the Great War. I didn't think he still had it. I've not seen it in ages.' He gave his sister a little shake to liven her up. 'Could he have taken something like that with him, Elise?'

'I don't know ... possibly it was in his pocket. He took his coat from the peg.'

'If your father is responsible, you two aren't safe,' Mathilde interrupted. 'You mustn't go back to work, Elise. You will be easily found there.' Hastily, she got from the larder half a loaf and a wedge of cheese, wrapping it in a cloth. 'The town will be crawling with Boches.'

'Madame Laurent locked up and pulled down the shutters as soon as the first soldiers arrived.' The couturier where Elise worked sold gowns of fine silk and lace. Madame Laurent had told her that during the last occupation some soldiers – both Allies and enemy – had acted like swine when drunk. They stole her lovely clothes to give to their women back home. 'Somebody betrayed Papa. The Hauptmann knew his name was Cooper.'

'When people are frightened they think only of themselves. It was the same last time.' Mathilde pointed to the window through which the neighbours' rapid voices penetrated. 'She was widowed during the Great War. Your grandfather survived the fighting but never recovered from what went on. He knew he wouldn't make old bones. And so did I. Some people suffer their bitterness, others spread it around.' She approached her grandchildren and raised her hands to cup their faces. 'You two must think only of yourselves and travel to England somehow. You must shelter with your father's family in London. We can't be certain of his fate. But I know if he's able to, he will somehow get there to be with you.' She went to a drawer and found a tin, pulling out some folded banknotes. She halved the amount, holding out cash in both hands. 'Here, you will need this until you find work.' She pressed the notes on to them when they seemed reluctant to take her savings. 'If it's too risky to travel to Calais go south and hide among the refugees heading away from the fighting. Speak only French and keep to yourselves. Trust nobody.'

The voices outside became louder and Luc strode to peep through the window. Helmeted heads and grey torsos were all that was visible of the infantry approaching through the long meadow grass. The neighbours had spotted them and were dispersing indoors in a panic.

'A patrol's coming this way.' Luc swung back. 'It might be a coincidence.'

'It might,' said Mathilde. 'They scavenge for milk ... bread ... anything they can lay hands on.' She glanced at her white-faced grandchildren. 'You two must go quickly. They won't bother with an old woman. I'll find them some beer and send them on their way.' She gazed at her strapping grandson; they would find work for him. And Elise too would draw their interest. Mathilde pulled open the drawer again and withdrew a notebook. She tore out a page. 'Your father gave me this address after your mother passed away, so I could let his English family know if he was about to meet his maker. Even back then I think he knew he'd get there before I did.' She thrust the paper at Elise. 'Guard it. Sidney told me these Coopers are good people.' Her son-in-law had been a liar as well as all the rest. She'd believed him on that though. His other children had never visited him and Mathilde found that quite understandable. 'Good luck and God bless and keep you safe.' She gave Luc the wrapped food to put in his pocket.

'Come ... hurry ...' Luc caught his sister's arm then let her go in order to briefly hug his grandmother in farewell. Elise also embraced Mathilde and kissed her wrinkled forehead. She was returned a swift kiss then pushed away.

'Be brave, both of you.' Mathilde warded off her granddaughter's grasping hands. '*Vite!* There's no time to waste. I love you both. We'll see each other soon. God speed, my dears ...' The last was addressed to the door swaying on its hinges. She swiftly closed it without giving in to her yearning for a last look at them. She sank into a chair and put a thin hand to her forehead where her granddaughter's warm kiss lingered.

She heard them in the lane and got up to peek out of the window at a trio of soldiers working the water pump. They were jovially filling their bottles and tin helmets then pouring water over their sweaty faces. Mathilde turned away and shook a fist at the ceiling. 'Why?' she cried in despair. 'Only twenty years ... why this again already?'

No guttural voices had demanded they halt as they raced along the banks of the stream. This was the shortest route to the woodland that would give them protection on their journey north. Finally they reached the oaks and plunged thankfully beneath a cool green canopy of leaves, hurdling undergrowth and zigzagging between trees. Luc led the way and at intervals stopped to encourage his sister as brambles tore at her legs and arms and her harsh breathing penetrated his own gasps.

Working on the farm had built his strength but Elise was slender and shop work hadn't prepared her for this. He slowed down the second he glimpsed the road up ahead and within a minute Elise had caught him up. Luc turned and put his finger to his lips. Between pants she nodded that she understood. Close by, everything seemed still and quiet; in the distance though was the rumble of the German army and the intermittent crack of rifle fire as Allied troops skirmished with their pursuers.

They picked their way onwards until a few ancient trunks were all that lay between them and open space.

Luc grasped Elise's arm then turned to look at her. 'We're still in front of them but need to keep going.'

'Will you come to England with me?' Elise read her answer in his solemn gaze. Her black hair was wild about her shoulders and she gathered up a thick hank and wound the ribbon more securely around it. Her eyes darted here and there as the gunfire got louder and startled crows from the trees flapped and cawed overhead.

'I'm staying to fight, Elise. We must all fight or we'll never get rid of the bastards.' He touched her face, pink from exertion and scratched from a thorn. 'I'll stay with you until we reach the coast. Don't be frightened, I'll look after you.' He crept forward to the road, signalling for her to stay put. Having got his bearings, he darted back.

'We're about nine kilometres from Lille.'

Although they'd travelled a good distance north from their grandmother's house they were still far from the sea; there'd be no scent of brine to hearten them until late tomorrow.

A twig cracked somewhere close by. They ducked down in unison and strained to listen for another sound. There was nothing but the rustle of small creatures and the creak of timber.

Heavy running footsteps made them quickly conceal themselves behind a tree. Elise sent her brother an optimistic look. Luc had also heard somebody declaring himself 'bleeding knackered' in a London accent similar to their father's. He prevented his sister breaking cover nevertheless.

'English!' insisted Elise. She was keen to speak to the soldiers and find out everything they could about what was happening.

'Careful ... could be a trap ...' Luc refused to let go of her arm.

'Good advice ...' drawled a voice from behind. 'So who are you two?'

Luc jerked around and immediately put up his hands on seeing a man in khaki battledress pointing a rifle at him.

'Who are you?' Elise boldly took a step towards him.

'I asked first.' He gave her a half-smile.

'Luc and Elise Bouchard,' Luc hastily said, sending his sister a warning glance to mind her tongue. This Tommy with two stripes on his uniform sleeve could be a godsend ... or a danger.

'Who are *you*?' Elise insisted. 'Are there more of you?'

'Three of us; Middlesex Infantry.'

'Is that it?' she sounded disappointed.

'The others might be about somewhere. With Jerry too close for comfort and taking potshots, we got separated.' He studied them. They looked French with their dark hair and continental complexions. But that didn't make them friends yet. 'You speak good English.'

'Our father's English,' said Elise. 'He was taken by the Germans only a few hours ago.'

Luc frowned another warning at her not to say too much; he took up the conversation. 'We're not sure why they want him or what's happened to him. We've scarpered in case they come back looking for us.'

Elise was a daddy's girl but Luc saw his father for what he was: a parasite and a drunk. He'd hated him at times for disappearing then swanning back to pick up where he'd left off as though it was his right to treat them like that. If his father had found the gumption to shoot a German it would be out of character; a memory for his son to cherish.

'Your father's a British agent?' The Tommy lowered his rifle a fraction, looking dubious.

'No, of course not!' Elise butted in. 'He's a civilian. He's lived in France for years ... decades.'

The soldier's gun was lowered further. In the last village they'd passed through locals had been talking of a foreigner who'd shot a Nazi. They were raising a glass to the dead Englishman. 'Where are you heading then?' He didn't want to be the bringer of bad news, especially as it might be the wrong man.

'To the coast for a passage to England,' Elise said.

'Good luck with that.'

'What's that supposed to mean?' she asked sharply.

'There's a crowd in front of you wanting to get to England, miss. Most of them British army and they're royally ... browned off.' He remembered his manners at the last minute.

'I'll join your lot. I intend to stay in France and fight,' Luc declared.

'You'll be on your own then, mate. We're retreating to Dunkirk beach hoping to get picked up and ferried back. Trouble is Hitler ain't about to let us off the hook just like that.' He looked at Elise. 'If I was you, miss, I'd take your brother's route. Stay in France. Head the opposite way together or you'll end up right in the thick of it.' He paused. 'Maybe your father's safely home by now.'

'You're all giving up and going back to England?' Elise sounded disgusted.

'A lot of your French army's hoping to come along with

us...' A whistle from the road drew the soldier's eyes away from them. 'That's my lads. Best of luck then. Reckon we're all going to need it.' He gripped Luc's arm in farewell. 'Look after your sister.'

'She's in danger here.' Luc dashed in front of the corporal to halt him. 'The Nazis don't know me but some have seen Elise. They can identify her. If our father has killed one of their officers...' He couldn't speak his worst fear about the reprisals his family would suffer. 'Would you take her to Dunkirk... get her on a boat?' Luc pulled his sister towards the Tommy. 'We've family in London, you see. She'll be fine over there.'

'You said you'd stay with me,' Elise cried. 'You're only going back to be with Yvonne.'

'I'm not...' he said but blushed at the mention of his boss's daughter. 'I have to stay and fight. There'll be Resistance groups somewhere if the army's finished.'

'I'll stay as well then,' said Elise. 'We'll chance it together. This soldier's right; Papa might have been released. The shooting might be nothing to do with him.'

'You've heard about that trouble then?'

Luc nodded and was eager for more details. 'What do you know about it?'

'A Hauptmann got shot... the assassin got shot... that's all... nothing more specific.'

Luc saw his sister wince and cover her mouth with a hand. He recalled she'd said a Hauptmann had taken their father away. How much proof did they need? He knew this was bad but put an arm around her and encouraged, 'Nothing specific, see, Elise. The place is littered with Hauptmanns and assassins now this has all blown up. I'm joining the Resistance and that's it.' He'd fight in his father's memory, to honour Sidney Cooper. 'Do you know any people?' he asked the corporal.

'Wouldn't tell you if I did. Don't know you.'

Elise dried her eyes with her knuckles, thinking the Tommy had said something very sensible.

'Woss goin' on, Corp? They're gonna be up our arses in a moment if we don't get cracking ...' A short skinny private had loped into the trees, rifle leading the way. He gawped at the strangers, his eyes swivelling from the tall youth to admire the petite girl.

'French refugees, just asking questions. You 'n' Wilmot get going, and keep your eyes peeled, Evans. I'll catch you up in a sec.' He turned to Elise. 'I can't stop you tagging along if you want to. You'll be more of a target with British troops though and my advice would be to turn around. At Dunkirk you'll take your chance along with the rest of us.' He gazed at her, thinking she was far too young and pretty to be stuck with a crowd of angry and frustrated servicemen. Nobody wanted this humiliation: fleeing with their tails between their legs like whipped curs. 'If you say you're a nurse or something like that you might get put to the front of the queue.' He shrugged that he couldn't make any promises then started jogging after his comrade. 'Good luck,' he called back.

Luc hugged his sister then pushed her away. 'Go on. He seems an all right sort. It's your only chance of getting to England. You must take it.' He tilted up her chin so she'd see the urgency in his eyes. 'Once you get to the coast you might find a French fishing boat; the skipper might take you over to Kent. Papa told us about the hop fields there, didn't he? He would go hop picking with his mum and dad when he was a little kid. I bet you'd like it there, love.'

Elise knew her brother was trying to buck her up to keep her mind off the nightmarish reality of their situation. 'Come with me then, Luc,' she pleaded.

The English soldier was many yards away and almost out of the trees when a whistling sound sent him hurtling back, bawling at them to get down. He flattened Elise beneath him on the scratchy ground. The exploding shell sliced the crown off a tree close to the road and it toppled sideways with a groan. He jumped up and pulled her with him into the clearing, shouting at Luc, 'Get into the open or you'll risk getting brained.'

Ears ringing and hearts hammering, Luc and Elise pelted for the fields and waded into the paltry camouflage of thigh-high barley that slowed them down. The soldier's comrades were now far in the distance.

After a few minutes of driving themselves deeper into the crop Luc came to a stop and turned to his exhausted sister, straggling behind. 'I'll make a detour back to Lille, then on from there.' He embraced her, kissed her forehead. 'Keep safe. And remember Grandma said don't trust anybody.'

'What about him?' Elise jerked a nod at their guide many yards in front.

'He's one of us; he's helped us so far. You have to trust him, Elise. Who else is there?' Luc backed away. 'Love you. Good luck.'

'Don't go . . .' she pleaded.

Tears sprang to his eyes but he shook his head and continued stepping away from her. The moment she came after him he turned and made a push towards a field of tall grass that would provide cover on his journey south, back towards Lille.

Elise stood and watched him with silent sobs heaving

her chest. He was a good distance away when a crack of rifle fire startled her into darting looks around. She whipped her head back to see her brother's dark figure had disappeared.

'You can't help him.' The corporal had stopped to come back for her. 'We have to keep going.' He dragged her on, then when she fought him silently and savagely he pulled her down into the barley with him and gripped her face in his hand. 'You want to end up like your father and your brother, do you?'

'Luc might be alive. They both might be.' She tried to shove him off, weeping hysterically.

'He might. Or he might be dead. Or he might have taken a dive to protect himself. Your brother's no fool.'

'I'll go and see.' Elise pulled back and he unexpectedly let her go. She tumbled onto her posterior, her skirt rucked up about her thighs, but righted herself quickly and faced him on her hands and knees, looking ready to spring at him.

'If he's all right he doesn't need you. If he's dead he doesn't need you. If he's wounded he'll be seen to. He's French, in civvies. This lot on our tail's got more to do than bother with civilians roaming the countryside.'

'They bothered with my father, didn't they?' she said fiercely.

'I know and I'm sorry.' He shook his head in defeat. 'Your brother hoped you'd get to England. It's up to you though. Come with me or go after him but I can't wait. I'm not carrying you either. You need to keep going or I'll leave you.'

'I don't need you to carry me.'

'Good ...' His lips twitched at her spirited indignation.

'I don't know what's safest for you either way, miss. But if they recognise you as the Englishman's daughter, waiting here for them to catch up with you ain't the wisest choice.' He rose to a half-crouch and started off again.

Elise scrambled up and gazed at the place where she'd last seen her brother. She said a prayer for him and for her father, and as she followed the corporal, she said one for herself.

Chapter Three

'How far is it now to Dunkirk?'

'Half a day's march, maybe less.' Her guide consulted a compass then replaced it in his jacket.

'Can we stop for a while?' Elise had been dog-tired miles back but hadn't asked to rest. She felt guilty for slowing him down as it was. Having made it this far she didn't want to be left behind. He could have already outpaced her and disappeared over the horizon to catch up with his men. Instead, he'd sacrificed safety in numbers to stick by her. He'd said he wouldn't carry her but probably would try to if she collapsed, and then she'd feel even more of a wretched burden.

It seemed as though she'd been trailing in his wake for days yet she'd still been with her father that mid-morning. The low sun would disappear soon leaving a dark landscape more hostile than it already was.

'What time is it?' She attempted to speed up but only succeeded in stubbing her toes against a stone lodged in the grass.

'Nearly eight,' he said over a shoulder and kept going although he'd heard her curse of pain.

'Can we stop soon?' She hopped and rubbed her

throbbing foot. She had removed her shoes to carry them hours ago. The cool meadow grass had felt soothing against her blisters but there were hazards in going barefoot.

He halted, allowing her to catch up, then nodded at a distant white building on their left with adjacent outhouses. 'When we reach the farmhouse we'll find a place to shelter overnight. Start again at first light.' He surveyed the clouds in the sky. 'If we're lucky the rain'll hold off.'

The sun had vanished before they were skirting the farmyard, entering in clandestine fashion through the gate furthest from the house. All looked deserted. Then he noticed the hound's glittering eyes. It had spotted him and stiffened against its leash, about to bark. His low whistle distracted it while he pulled a strip of dried beef from his rations pack. He lobbed the meat, keeping the dog occupied while hurrying them out of sight.

Elise let out a sigh as she sank to a seated position on the lee of the barn. She drew her knees in and inspected her bleeding heels.

'Take a drink . . .' He took the cap off his water bottle and handed it to her then started unpacking his rations. 'You'll need to be hungry to want to eat those,' he said, offering her a couple of hardtack biscuits.

'I am hungry. Thank you.' She remembered the food her grandmother had prepared and put in Luc's pocket for them to share. She hoped he'd eaten every scrap of bread and cheese on his journey back to Lille. Elise blocked the memory of her last sighting of him; she'd only torment herself by brooding on it. There was nothing she could do other than trust in her brother and his ability to look after himself. To ease his own mind he would be thinking of her in the same way, believing her safe with her soldier escort.

She upended the metal bottle and the lukewarm water tasted sweet as milk in her parched mouth. She studied the main house about a hundred yards away. A single window showed a light. The people inside would be preparing to retire for the night, fretting over what the clatter in the distance would turn into tomorrow.

She was relieved they'd not alerted the farmer to their presence. Intelligence about retreating Allied troops would be interesting to the Germans. They might also ask about sightings of a young woman. Scared of consequences, the locals would speak up, and betray her as they had her father. Trust nobody ... it was the rule she reminded herself to stick to as she leaned her head back against planks of rough wood.

The lowing of resting cattle wasn't soothing. Freed from the pain of forcing her body to keep moving, a different agony was taking over. Images of her brother and her father were becoming impossible to shut out. She reminded herself that Luc was quick and clever. The moment he heard gunshot he would have sought cover. Her father's fate, though, was a different matter. She muffled a sob by taking a bite of dry biscuit, then washed it down with water before it choked her. Eating and resting were vital or she'd never finish this trek. Her body ached everywhere and her head felt ready to burst. Yet she was scared to go to sleep.

She ate one of the biscuits and gave him back the other and his water. 'You never told us your name,' she said through the fingers massaging weariness from her face. While waiting for his answer she rested her cheek against her palm and closed her eyes, hoping to doze.

'Corporal Nathaniel Hawkes, at your service, miss.' He swigged water then gave her a glance. His ironic tone had been lost on her. A tear was clearing a path through the dust on her face. She was a courageous little thing. Her father was dead, he was almost sure of that. Her brother ... he could still be alive, but if the Gestapo discovered he was the assassin's son he wouldn't want to be in Luc Bouchard's shoes. 'Where's your mother?'

'She passed away ... long time ago.' Elise had spoken without raising her eyelids. She didn't need to look at him to know he pitied her being a lonely orphan. 'I've my grandmother though ...' She sat up straight. 'And until I know differently I have my father and Luc.' She'd said it defiantly, but in seconds had started to cry. She turned her face from him, smearing away the tears and embracing herself to stop her shoulders jumping with sobs. He would leave her behind if she became a hopeless blubberer.

A dirty-nailed hand curled over her arm in comfort. 'You do have them, miss, until you know differently.' He shook the bottle to gauge how much water remained inside. 'Where's your family in England?'

Elise's memory was jogged to the precious address in her pocket. She swiped a hand over her wet face then withdrew the paper to discover where she'd find her half-siblings. She knew she had three sisters and a brother who were older than her. But she didn't know their names. Her father's reluctance to speak about them arose from his guilt at abandoning them, she'd assumed. He'd not deserted his first wife though. Her mother had told them that Sidney had been widowed during the last war, and Sophie Bouchard had never lied to her children.

Elise unfolded the paper and angled it until faint moonlight illuminated her grandmother's handwriting. 'Silvertown in East London. Silvertown ...' Elise repeated the place name. 'It sounds nice.'

Nathaniel Hawkes smiled up at the grey heavens. He knew Silvertown was a dump. Worse than the dockside area he called home. 'Makes us almost neighbours then,' he said. 'Poplar's my stamping ground.'

'You're from the East End?' She found the energy to scramble onto her knees to face him. 'Do you know any of my family?' she asked eagerly.

'Never heard of any Bouchards.'

'They're not Bouchards. My father's name was Sidney Cooper.' She dropped her chin, realising she'd used the past tense when talking about him.

'Ah, I see ...'

Out of respect he wouldn't ask, but she wasn't ashamed of being the daughter of an unmarried woman. Elise had been just ten when her mother died but even then she'd known why neighbours told their children to avoid Sophie Bouchard's bastards.

'I think our mother gave us her name because she knew there'd be a day when he wouldn't come back.' She turned to sit with her back against the barn, unsure why she'd told a stranger something very private.

The quiet lengthened and she looked at his profile. He had taken off his jacket and tin helmet and she had her first proper view of him through the dusk. He had fairish hair but not blond. His eyes she imagined might be blue, though it was too dark to see, and his lashes were lowered as he opened a cigarette packet. He offered them, taking one himself when she shook her head. He stood up and stretched out. He was tall and broad ... as well built as her brother. Sidney had been a big man too, but he'd shrivelled in recent years. In his prime he'd been brown-haired with a tanned complexion and the bluest of eyes; he'd looked as

French as any neighbour. Elise had been proud of her strong handsome father. But recently she'd noticed his clothes had seemed too big for him and his shoulders had curved inwards. The last time he came back after a trip to England he had seemed different: greyer and diminished by whatever had occurred while he'd been away.

'My parents weren't married either.' Nathaniel struck a match to the cigarette. He propped an elbow against the barn and stared over the shadowy countryside while he smoked. 'Hawkes is my father's name though, and unlike yours, he never did come back. How old are you, miss?'

'Eighteen later this month. What about you?'

'Twenty-three.'

'Are you a full-time soldier?'

'Nah ...' He flicked ash and chuckled. 'River worker.'

'What's that?'

'Unloading the ships on the Thames.'

'Bet you wish you still were doing that, don't you?'

He glanced at her with another sardonic smile thinning his mouth. 'Do I ...' he drawled ironically. 'Enlisting seemed like a good idea at the time. Before the phoney war weren't so phoney. Get out of the Smoke and see the world ...' He mocked himself and took a long drag on the cigarette. 'Real enough now, ain't it. Get some sleep, miss.'

'You can call me Elise if you like; I won't think you're being familiar. Shall I call you Nathaniel?'

'Nathan is what friends call me.'

'Nathan then ...' She smiled, pleased he thought of her as a friend. Elise wanted to rise and stand next to him, ask him lots of questions about London and in particular Silvertown. Too exhausted to push herself to her feet, she rested her head against the rough timber behind and reflected on how mundane her life had been only days ago.

She understood Nathan Hawke's wish to break away ... do something different and exciting. She'd been born in a village near Lille and had never travelled further than Paris in one direction and the Normandy coast in the other. When they'd had that summer holiday by the sea, she'd been about eight and her mother had still been alive. Her father had taken her and Luc down to the water's edge to paddle. Over there were white cliffs that could be seen from the middle of the ocean he'd said, pointing across the waves. She'd been eager to visit her father's homeland but he'd made it clear he couldn't take them. She'd not asked much about it after that but had remained curious about her English siblings. A few days ago, Sidney Cooper had changed his mind, insisting they must all move permanently to London. His warnings that France would become dangerous and overrun by Nazis had seemed exaggerated. Their whole lives had been spent in this country; why would she and Luc want to move to England, after all this time?

She pressed her regretful tears back behind her eyelids and listened to the muted night-time noises that seemed fraudulently melodic. German motorcycles had roared along the road earlier, forcing them to fall flat in the rye fields to avoid being seen. She'd be thought a spy if they were caught together. She understood why the corporal had told her at the start that it would be safer for her to turn back. But it was too late now. And she no longer wanted to. 'Have you a girl waiting for you?' She'd spoken aloud her thoughts and felt rude for doing so when he didn't immediately reply.

'After this?' He dropped the cigarette stub and stepped on it. 'Damned if I know.'

'Sorry, didn't mean to pry.'

'How about you? Got a boy back there?'

'Dad sees them off,' she said ruefully. There had been a boy she'd liked too but he'd lost interest after knocking on the door and repeatedly being told to go away by Sidney ... and not politely, either.

'He's been a good father then.'

The lump in her throat grew and she changed the subject before she started to cry again. 'What's happened to Evans and Wilmot?'

'Gawd knows ...'

His rough laughter didn't mean he was amused. Far from it. 'I'm sorry you got caught up in this ... it's our fault you lost touch with your comrades. Will you get into trouble for stopping and helping us?'

'There's worse trouble I could get into than helping refugees.'

'What sort of trouble?'

'Don't know yet ... trouble never sends a warning. Just lands on you. Try to sleep now. We'll start early in the morning.'

Elise smoothed two ragged edges of blue crepe over her calves. Madame Laurent expected her assistant to look very presentable. Elise had purchased an elegant dress at a generous discount, and a pair of fashionable shoes. The cost had been deducted from her wages over many weeks. She had left home smartly at seven-thirty and caught the bus to work preparing to serve customers in a lavender-scented shop. Now her dress was torn and her shoes worn down. And so was she: with terrible uncertainty. Nathan Hawkes was right: there was never any warning.

She drooped sideways and curled her legs into her chest.

When he dropped his jacket on top of her she didn't speak but gratefully snuggled into the musky-smelling blanket. She was going to say, 'good night' but it seemed daft somehow to do that.

The planes woke her before it was properly light. She came to with a jolt, but remained drugged by a dream of her mother dashing to meet her at the school gate. Sophie was late and all the other children had gone, even her brother. Her mother's comforting embrace was slipping away, transforming into the sensation of a hard body lying next to hers.

'Messerschmitts ... Luftwaffe ...' Nathaniel said, pushing up onto an elbow. 'Heading for the same place we are, I reckon.' He was soon on his feet, checking his rifle and gathering up his equipment.

Elise warded off her stupor to clumsily scramble up, holding onto the barn for support. She remembered where she was ... who he was. She rubbed sleep from her eyes then handed him his jacket, hanging off one of her shoulders. Together they watched the trio of fighter aircraft droning north.

'Ready to go?'

She nodded and found her shoes, wincing as she forced her feet into them. 'I'd better spend a penny first.' She licked her flaking lips. Her mouth tasted unpleasantly dry and dirty but she knew little water was left so didn't ask for a drink.

'Go round that side, away from the dog.' He'd noticed her looking for somewhere private. 'If it sees you it'll wake everyone up.'

'Was I talking in my sleep?' she asked, as they set off over the poppy fields side by side.

'You were ...' He chuckled. 'I've got used to that sort of thing in a barracks.' He glanced at her. 'Sweet dream was it?' He reckoned it was as she'd cuddled him and he'd not stopped her. He'd curved a protective arm across her. He'd told himself it was to keep them warm and dozing. His body had told him something else while he drowsed in the lavender scent of her hair.

'I dreamed about my mum.' A smile was in her voice.

'Worth holding onto those dreams,' he said and started to pull in front, setting the pace for their march.

Elise felt the papery poppy heads brushing her hands, their vivid colour dulled by grey dawn light. 'In Flanders fields the poppies blow, between the crosses, row on row ...'

'We learned that at school.' He'd heard her murmured recitation and commented in a similar resigned tone, but he didn't turn around and she didn't finish the war poem but sped up to walk again beside him.

By the time the sun was colouring in the horizon Nathan had one of his colleagues in his sights. He gave a whistle and Private Wilmot ducked then whipped around, rifle ready. He was a stocky auburn-haired fellow who gawped in surprise at his corporal and the dark-haired girl. They put on a spurt to join him.

'Got company then, Corp?'

'French nurse got separated from her unit. She's on her way to help evacuate the wounded at Dunkirk. Elise Bouchard's her name. She speaks good English and is tagging along with us.'

Elise exchanged a glance with Nathan. That was her story then, even for his comrades. Though how she'd explain away her lack of a nurse's uniform she wasn't sure.

She'd deal with it if it cropped up though, as she had with everything else.

She understood his need to protect himself as well as her. Escorting a French nurse to Dunkirk to help save Allied soldiers' lives was commendable; allowing a random mademoiselle to tag along like a camp follower wasn't. He'd land in trouble. She might have had few boyfriends – thanks to her father's strict vigilance after she turned thirteen – but she wasn't clueless about men and women. She knew what others would read into Corporal Hawkes' interest in her.

They'd be wrong; he'd been respectful at all times, even when knocking her flat and lying on her in the swaying grass, his hand on her mouth, while they waited for the enemy to pass by. Even while sharing an embrace that had got them through the blackest of nights.

'Where's Evans?'

'Dunno...' said Wilmot, rubbing a finger under his nose. 'He got restless and took off at first light towards Dunkirk; I said I'd hang back a bit for you to catch us up. Ain't seen the bugger since.' He blushed. 'Sorry, Miss Boo...'

'Bouchard,' Elise supplied and her smile caused him to colour up again beneath his freckles.

They set off together, Elise keeping behind Corporal Hawkes and in front of Private Wilmot. The hamlets they passed through looked deserted but they knew they were being watched from behind half-closed cottage doors. Some of the braver souls darted out and offered bread or cups of milk and muttered blessings for them. Pails of water had been left at the roadside for the retreating soldiers to drink from. Hawkes and Wilmot filled their bottles. But they didn't stop for long. The booming guns behind were encouragement enough to keep going, as were the motorbike scouts. At increasingly frequent intervals they diverted behind hedgerows to hide in fields of ripening wheat.

Elise would have liked to speak French to the villagers and ask them what they knew about the shooting yesterday. These communities had fast-working grapevines and the news would have spread. But she daren't; she would be wanted for questioning. The Gestapo might already have been back to her home looking for Sidney Cooper's children. Advertising her interest in the incident and her whereabouts would be foolish.

By the time the sun was high in the sky the tang of brine was in the air, and the noise of battle was coming from two different directions. Nathaniel grabbed hold of her arm, forcing her to trot with him towards the warehouse buildings and hotels lining the coastal road. Having passed those, they got a first glimpse of the sea, their view channelled along an elevated lane. Tanks ... trucks ... cars, all had been abandoned on these back roads by their crews. With renewed vigour they dodged the obstacles and ran out onto the esplanade. Their first sight of the beach caused them to stop and stare in shock and dismay.

Thousands of men were forming human jetties that spanned from the water's edge to fifty yards or so up the beach. Others crowded into the waves impatiently hailing the small boats riding the waves, imploring to be taken away. A landing stage to the left had a large vessel at anchor. It was flanked by servicemen jostling to embark. Stretcher bearers trotted towards the hospital ship, bawling at walking wounded to be let through with the less fortunate. Medical officers were on their knees attending to the casualties. The corpses were ignored and there were hundreds of them scattered on the sand as far as the eye could see.

'There's bloody Evans!' Wilmot pointed at the short fellow jogging purposefully towards a boat being rowed to shore. He gave him a shout, which was drowned out in the general uproar. The overloaded boat set off, Evans having failed to reach it in time.

'Find out if he's met up with any of the others.' Nathaniel took a look around. He'd not yet spotted any familiar faces from their platoon and wondered if they were the first to have made it this far. Once Wilmot had gone, Nathan's gaze returned to some hillocks at the back of the beach. 'If you're questioned, stick to the story that you're a nurse,' he said to Elise. 'I'll go and find out if that hospital ship'll take you on.'

'I'll come with you . . .'

'No, you need to keep out of it.' He jerked a nod at the sand dunes. 'Up there might be the best place for you to wait while I'm gone. And keep your head down.'

She wasn't keen on being left alone. The guns behind were getting louder. As they'd marched, she'd heard her companions talking about the Scots regiment tasked with holding off the advancing enemy so that others could escape. Those final battles now sounded ominously close. 'I'd rather come with you, Nathan, please let me . . .'

'No!' he said harshly. 'You shouldn't be here. It's bad enough for us lot. To cap it all, you're a girl of seventeen. And you're a civilian not a nurse.'

'I'm nearly eighteen.' She saw him roll his eyes. 'Sorry . . .' There was nothing else to say; he was right to be vexed. She wasn't sure what she'd been expecting when she got here but it wasn't anything as bad as this overwhelming chaos and stench. The rage and desperation of thousands of men fouled air already sulphurous with cordite.

A trio of infantrymen barged them apart, barking at one

another about their determination to get home. They were curious to see a female civilian though and sent backward glances as they ran on. With rifles held above their heads they waded into the waves that wrapped around and over them. They were almost up to their necks, and at the back of a queue to board a small craft. Anything that might ferry men to the ships at anchor further out to sea was being utilised. Jettisoned timbers and oil drums were held on to as makeshift floats by men intent on getting away. A few intrepid souls were making a swim for it, heads intermittently bobbing into view as they made for the lure of dangling rope ladders.

Elise gazed at all of it in utter disbelief.

'Stay close to me, or you'll get lost.' Nathaniel was back at her side, yelling to break into her daze. He pulled her with him along the beach and when they reached a clearer expanse of sand fronting an empty sea he began to climb up into the dunes.

'Ain't got time for that, pal, if you fancy getting out of here before Fritz blows us up.' A smirking soldier jogged past.

Nathan yanked Elise up behind him then pushed her down to sit in a hollow. 'Stay here. It's the safest place for you. I'll see what I can do. Ain't making promises though. Sorry, but it's worse than I imagined.'

She nodded her understanding, biting her lip to stop it wobbling. She knew what he really wanted to say was that if he'd known it'd be like this he wouldn't have allowed her to tag along. She felt quite terrified as he slid away from her onto compact ground. She separated the sharp grasses sprouting from the sand and watched him sprinting back the way they'd come. Keeping him in her sights was impossible. Eventually he was gone ... just another uniform in a mass of khaki. And she wished she'd followed him.

He couldn't make promises. He wouldn't come back. He'd taken her as far as he could. Done as much for her as he could. He had a home to get to in England as much as she did. More than she did. She'd no idea if she'd be welcomed or shunned on reaching Silvertown.

She didn't blame Corporal Nathaniel Hawkes for abandoning her. Her brother had. Her father had ... many times over the years. She'd look after herself somehow, she told herself as she crouched down with her hands clamped to her ears and her eyes screwed shut against fearful tears. She remained huddled like that, trying to make herself as small and invisible as possible, until the noise of aircraft penetrated through her fingers.

She opened her eyes and stared up at a formation of planes getting closer. She squinted, unsure if they were friend or foe. She peeked through reeds and discovered the answer from those on the beach. Lines of men toppled over like dominoes, hands over heads as a machine gun rat-a-tat was heard. The Luftwaffe whined away and became dots in the sky.

The men started picking themselves up, but not all of them.

Chapter Four

'You ain't pushing in, pal. Wait yer turn.'

'Not trying to push in,' Nathan snarled and shoved the sapper out of his way. 'There's a French nurse got separated from her unit. She could get on board here and help the doctors. Just need a say-so from somebody in charge.'

'Let him through you bloody fool; look at what's going on. The more nurses the better.' A Royal Army Medical Corp sergeant spoke up and elbowed the belligerent soldier aside. 'Where is the nurse, Corporal?' he demanded. 'I'll vouch for her.' He had a pencil hovering over the clipboard in his hand.

'Up there, away from the worst of it.' Nathan jerked a sideways nod. There was no time to say more. As a man, their faces turned skywards and they swore in unison too.

The Messerschmitts were back. The column of men on the jetty, unable to scatter, such was the crush of bodies, dipped in unison, a cobbled armour of helmets their only cover. The whine of a missile was heard followed by the spit of machine gun fire. Nathaniel leaped from the jetty and dragged himself up some minutes later with his hearing deadened by an explosion. He swung about to see smoke was coming from the hospital ship and men were jumping or falling overboard into the sea. He started to run along the shore, having spotted something that in the pandemonium others had so far missed. A small vessel was chugging up and he was first to wade out and reach it. He gripped its side and called out, 'Are you from England?'

'Broadstairs.' A fair-haired young woman shouted back. 'Getting on?' She hurried closer and offered her hand to help pull him in.

'A nurse wants passage. Will you take her with you? She's trying to get back to her family in London.'

The female sailor looked dubious, as though she'd heard likely stories from Tommies before.

'She's young ... a probationer nurse.' He cleared his face of brine as a roller smacked into him. 'She got separated from her colleagues and needs to get to safety. Can't leave her here alone.' He gestured at the scene behind. No words were needed to describe it.

'All right ... bring her up,' the woman shouted.

'I'll get her. Wait for us.' Nathaniel grinned his thanks and turned away. He began barging through the group of men fighting their way through the waves for a chance to secure a place on board.

During the second air attack Elise had been showered in sand blasted from the adjacent dune. She'd scrambled onto her knees and was brushing grit off her eyelids when the soldier who'd run past with a dirty remark appeared in front of her. She tried to struggle up, but he shoved her onto her back.

'Well, ain't you a sight for sore eyes.' He laughed at her trying to cover her bare thighs with her skirt.

'You'd better leave me alone. I'm a nurse. Corporal Hawkes is escorting me.' She lashed out at him with fist and foot, catching his knee with her shoe and making him stumble. She scrambled up, prepared to launch herself onto the beach, but he grabbed her leg and pulled her down beside him.

'Nurse are you? My eye. Reckon I know what you are.' The soldier rolled on top of her. 'Your corporal's probably a goner, love. Same as we all are. Just sitting ducks, waiting for Jerry to pick us off. Well, before he gets to me there's something I'd like to do for the last time,' he grunted.

Elise tried to pull his hand out from between her legs but a forearm was pinning her down by the neck and his eyes and teeth were gleaming at her. Then just as she feared she'd black out, his weight was gone.

She wheezed in a breath, then began coughing, vaguely conscious of Corporal Hawkes hitting the soldier in the face. Then he dropped to his knees to punch the man again until he lay still.

Nathan hauled Elise upright and for a moment they stood swaying on sinking sand, breathing hard.

'All right?'

She nodded.

'Come on; there's an English girl on a motor yacht; she'll take you over to Kent.' He grabbed her fingers and pulled her with him. Stumbling, they slid and slithered down the dune to the beach and pelted hand in hand to the shoreline.

The boat was full, preparing to leave, and he roared at the woman to get her attention. He waved and pointed at Elise, dragging her behind him into the sea.

'I can't swim, I can't, Nathan ...' she protested as he yanked her along and waves slapped into her and would have knocked her over but for his grip keeping her upright.

The water was under his armpits, but over her chin, and every further lurch forward filled her nose and mouth with its salty sting, making her gag.

'Get out the way,' he bawled at the men in front of him. He began shoving them aside. 'Nurse is coming through. She's got a place on board.'

'She ain't troops; don't reckon she's a nurse either. And if she is she should be helping, not scarpering,' grumbled a middle-aged man.

Nathan thrust him out of the way, sensing her fingers slipping from his. He hoisted Elise up into his arms as a wave rolled over her head. With a groan and a growl accompanying the effort, he heaved her over the side of the craft.

The female sailor helped Elise onto the floor of the boat and the cargo of Tommies already on board obligingly made room for another passenger.

'Look after her,' he bawled.

'I will.' The blonde woman nodded and gave him a reassuring thumbs up. 'Lady on board, you lot. Best behaviour,' she said while knocking Elise's back to help her bring up seawater.

Nathan nodded in thanks, too spent to speak, and watched as a signal was given for the craft to set off. The skipper of the boat was yelling that no more on board or the craft risked capsizing. The wizened fellow was apologising while prising fingers from the sides of the boat. The unlucky boys left behind began moving morosely back to shore. Nathan stayed where he was.

Elise crawled, snorting and choking, to the boat's edge, gripping it to pull herself up and see over the top of it.

She blinked at Nathan through the gritty sting in her

eyes splintering him into pieces. She could see his shoulders and chest pumping from the cost of saving her. She pulled a hand across her vision before using it to wave. 'Silvertown...' she croaked. She inhaled hard, rasping her throat with salt. 'Silvertown...' she shouted.

'I'll come and find you,' he called back and put up a hand in farewell.

She placed her shivery fingertips to her lips then pointed them at him.

He caught the kiss in a fist. She saw him smile. A proper smile, not sarcastic.

Neither of them turned away. He stood with the waves knocking him backwards and forwards; she rested her cheek on the edge of the boat and kept him in her sights until the swell of the sea made him vanish.

'Here ... put this on.' The female sailor was back holding out a lifejacket, and a towel.

Elise took the things with a teeth-chattering mumble of thanks as a blanket was draped around her shoulders.

'There ... you look less like a drowned rat now.' The blonde woman winked a bright blue eye. 'I'm making some tea; bet you could do with a cup.'

'I could do with one of them 'n' all,' chipped in a young private. He looked about Elise's age and doffed his cap at her. 'Ladies first though. I'll wait my turn.'

'There's enough for everybody. Who fancies bread 'n' jam?'

Hands shot up. The mention of food had reminded Elise her belly was empty but she didn't feel like eating.

'Is that where you live, miss?' asked the youth after the woman went to make tea. 'Silvertown?'

Elise stopped towelling her hair and nodded. 'My family's there. Do you know the East End?' His sing-song accent didn't sound anything like her father's rough dialect.

'Oh no. Never been to London. Port Talbot's where I hail from.'

'Welsh Fusiliers... that's us,' said the middle-aged fellow who'd complained at Elise being given a place on the boat. He seemed shamefaced and keen to be friendly.

Elise didn't blame any of them trying to save themselves. But she wished there had been room for one more. Corporal Nathaniel Hawkes could have been on his way home; instead he'd come back for her and sacrificed his safety for hers. She put her hands over her face, feeling wretched for having doubted him. He was a true friend and she already missed him.

The older Welshman bent down to pat her arm. 'It's all a bit much now, isn't it?' he said, having heard her muffled sob.

She kept her face lowered and nodded. When feeling composed, she glanced around at the men in sopping uniforms; she could count thirty from where she was crouching with her knees drawn into her chest. There were no seats. She guessed the boat's fittings had been removed to make more space. Nobody spoke much. Everybody appeared sombre and lost in their own thoughts while gazing at their boots, or back towards Dunkirk.

Elise didn't look back. He wouldn't want her moping over him; neither would her father or brother. They'd want her to cherish this chance they'd given her. She couldn't stop thinking about them though, or praying she would see them all again.

By standing she'd take up less room, so she gave a brisk

final rub to her hair then got unsteadily to her feet. She shook out her clammy skirt, wishing she was more serviceably dressed. The female sailor was kitted out in trousers and shirt and oilskin jerkin. Her fair hair was neatly clipped back. Elise knew she resembled a pitiable waif, but she could be of some practical use.

Sea water was dripping from the Welsh lad's limp fringe onto his nose. She handed him the towel then dropped the life jacket over her head and fastened it around her wet clothes. Men trod on one another's toes while courteously budging aside to let her pass through the crush.

'I'd like to help with the food.' Elise entered the boat's galley to find the blonde woman was already busy.

'Thanks, could do with another pair of hands. There's only a couple of us. More space for the boys with a skeleton crew.' The woman gave Elise's slender figure an envious glance. 'Bit of a tight squeeze in here but there's not much of you. I could do with losing a few pounds. Might've fitted in another little 'un if I'd lost a bit of this.' She smacked her buxom hip. 'The water's boiled. I've put tea in the pot. Fill it up, would you?' She pointed to the counter. 'Steady yourself against that; there's a few rollers out there this afternoon and don't want you scalding yourself before you've found your sea legs.'

Elise took that sensible advice, planting her feet apart for balance as the boat bucked and her stomach did likewise. She carefully used the kettle and stirred the teapot. 'I should introduce myself. I'm Elise Bouchard. I'm not a French nurse. I'm a refugee.'

'Didn't think you were a nurse, or French actually. You speak English as well as I do.'

'My dad's English . . . from London. My mum was French though.'

'Pleased to meet you, Miss Boosher. I'm Faith Yates.' After shaking hands, she jerked a nod at the middle-aged skipper sporting a leather cap. 'That's my dad, Ronald. We usually run this as a pleasure boat out of Broadstairs but our *Kentish Belle* got drafted in to help bring our lads home. Don't mind telling you it's the scariest thing I've done in my life.' She blew out her cheeks. 'Got strafed by a German Ju yesterday. Luckily, wasn't much damage, only a few cuts and grazes from splinters when the cabin took a hit.' She thumbed at the mangled joinery above their heads. 'You should have seen our lads when that Jerry put in an appearance. Every one of them who still had his rifle was shooting up at the rotten blighter. The air was blue, I can tell you.' She chuckled briefly before resuming, 'If it hadn't been for one of our Hurricanes bringing the bugger down I wouldn't be standing here talking to you.' She shook her head. 'Terrible to-do, isn't it?'

'It is ...' said Elise, thinking her own ordeal seemed less hair-raising after hearing that. 'It's all happened so horribly quickly as well. Yesterday morning I was in Lille with my father. Now ...' She was unable to describe what the invasion had done to her family. 'Thanks for waiting for me and letting me on just now.'

'Pleased to help, Miss Boosher, even if you don't know any more about nursing than I do.' Faith gave her arm a reassuring pat. 'The lads we've picked up seem in good shape. Let's hope we've a clear run ahead of us and no bandages needed.'

Elise had heard Faith struggling to get to grips with her French name. 'You can call me Elise if you like.'

'Righto. I will, if you call me Faith. So now we're pals I won't be being cheeky if I ask if he's your boyfriend.' She jerked her chin towards Dunkirk. 'The dishy corporal.'

'We met by chance on the road. Once he knew I was trying to get to England he let me tag along for safety's sake.'

'Wish I met fellows like that. What a gent.' Faith sighed dreamily then became brisk. 'Right, if you spread some of this bread with marge, I'll collect their tea mugs. They've mostly got their own on them unless they've lost stuff. Some poor souls have been arriving back with little more than a shirt on their back.'

'You're very brave to go back to Dunkirk after what you went through yesterday.'

'Couldn't not, after we saw what it was like. Thirty-two got on yesterday. Not sure how we managed it without towing a rubber dinghy for some to sit in.' She grinned. 'Only joking ... don't have a dinghy for a start. But the *Kentish Belle* is only supposed to take a dozen passengers including the crew.'

Elise chuckled at an image in her head of the small pleasure cruiser towing a dinghy full of Tommies taking aim at the sky.

'Yesterday's lot were mostly lads from Derbyshire. Coal miners. Thought today things might be better. Makes you wonder if it'll be us holding them off on our beaches next.' Faith ducked down to look inside a cupboard beneath the counter. 'I'm sure there's a pot of jam left from yesterday. We'll have to spread it thinly though.' She straightened up, displaying her find, and took the muslin top off it. 'You spoke of your dad ... where is he? And your mum?'

'My mum died when I was a child. Dad's in France and so's my brother.' Elise busily sawed at the loaf then opened the pack of Stork margarine. 'Luc's nineteen, a year and a bit older than me. He was driving a tractor but now wants to fight.' She refused to say that they might both have already perished.

'He's the same age as me then,' said Faith. 'I don't blame him wanting to fight the Nazis. I'm up for joining the war effort.'

'Think you already have,' said Elise admiringly.

'We didn't volunteer ... but everybody with a boat was glad to do their bit. Tourists won't be flocking to Broadstairs after this. Jerry might be sunbathing in our deckchairs by July.' She paused. 'Kent's known as the Garden of England. Soon it'll be harvest time. They'll need help to bring it in now labourers have started joining up.' Faith noticed her companion had become rather withdrawn after talking about her family. 'Fill that up for yourself,' she said, pushing a mug over the countertop. 'You'll feel better with a cuppa down you. I'll go and see the lads; they'll be wondering where the tea's got to.'

Elise did pour herself a drink and it warmed her, helping her forget about the damp dress and cardigan clinging to her beneath her blanket shawl. Once the teapot had been endlessly refilled and the jam pot was empty, the *Kentish Belle* was far out to sea. Above them was clear sky, although planes had droned past heading in the opposite direction. From the roar of support that went up Elise knew they were friendly. On the sea, more small boats passed them, heading for Dunkirk. Ronald Yates had clattered the bell in salute and the boys on board had cheered their appreciation to the crews.

When the food had been cleared away, Faith went to speak to her father. Elise fastened the cupboard doors as she'd been shown, then made her way up the wooden stairs, gripping the handrail as the boat rocked.

Through a light haze she could glimpse the outline of the chalk cliffs ahead of them that her father had told her about. Her emotions were kept in check by a churning in her stomach that had nothing to do with nostalgia. She focused on keeping her food down as the vessel plunged through the waves. She didn't want to bring up her bread and jam in front of everybody, so headed towards the skipper where there was slightly more room now Faith had gone to form a choir with the Welsh boys. The song sounded hauntingly melodic but it didn't tranquillise Elise's rolling guts. She inhaled deeply.

'Keep looking at the horizon. It seems to settle collywobbles.' Faith's father indicated the white cliffs. 'And isn't that a sweet sight to hold your eye?'

Elise managed a polite nod for the wiry fellow with sinewy brown arms who had a gaze as direct and blue as his daughter's.

She heeded his advice and kept her eyes fixed on the chalk face. But the next time the boat was tossed high she folded over at the middle and retched over the side.

'Never mind, dear,' said Mr Yates, patting her back with one hand and steering with the other. 'Not too much longer and you'll be on dry land. You'll be home.'

Chapter Five

'You should stay with us tonight; you can sort out your journey tomorrow,' was Faith's answer to Elise's enquiries about the train timetable to London and local boarding houses. 'It'll be nice to have some company.'

'It's very good of you but I don't want to be a nuisance.' Elise felt awkward accepting before Faith had spoken to her mum and dad.

'Honestly, you won't be a bother. You should sleep at ours and wait for a regular service to Victoria.' She chuckled. 'Mind you, hitching a ride on a troop train with a load of sex-starved Tommies might have benefits . . .'

'For goodness' sake, Faith,' scolded her mother. 'The young lady will think you're a baggage talking like that!'

The girls had entered through the garden gate in the twilight and Mrs Yates had heard the tail end of their conversation. It was after nine o'clock but the midsummer days were long and light. She took a washing peg from between her teeth to give the newcomer a smile.

'You are very welcome to stop the night, dear, if you'd like to.'

'You can have Graham's room,' Faith helpfully interjected.

'My brother's hardly ever home from London since he got a promotion at work.'

'What will happen after this defeat, though?' Mrs Yates sighed and continued taking sheets from the line to drop into a wicker basket. 'I hope our Mr Churchill has a plan.' She picked up the washing. 'What's your name, dear?'

'Elise Bouchard ... and thank you, I would like to stay, if you're sure it's no trouble.'

Faith butted in. 'She likes to be called Elise, and she's a French refugee. Her dad's still in France, although he's a Londoner.'

'Ah, that accounts for your good English, Elise,' said Mrs Yates, leading the way along the shingle path past a chicken coop and aromatic rosemary and lavender bushes that brushed against their legs. 'I'm glad you're all back safely. How was it today, Faith?' Mrs Yates asked over her shoulder.

'Better than yesterday,' her daughter succinctly replied.

'Has your father gone for a drink?' Mrs Yates knew he'd need a couple of rums to help him sleep. Her husband and daughter had seen and heard some ghastly things at Dunkirk yesterday. They had played down the hazards met to avoid worrying her. She wasn't a fool, though, and knew the boat hadn't been damaged by accident, but by enemy bullets. She'd not tried to stop them when they said they were going back. Everybody had to swallow their fears now and face up to the coming perils, including her.

'Dad said he was off to the Tar and Anchor once all the boys were safely disembarked at Dover.' The hostelry on the quayside was used by the skippers as a meeting place. Those who'd returned from France would have stories to tell tonight. 'I could do with a tot myself,' Faith muttered as they trooped in single file into the cottage. It was set a few streets back behind the harbour, on an incline. On a clear day the bedroom windows provided a scenic view across the sea to France.

Mrs Yates turned up the gas mantle to get a proper look at their unexpected guest. The girl's thick black hair was matted and glittering with dried salt. Her skin was pale and drawn with fatigue while her nice clothes looked ragged and creased. Despite her dishevelment she was a beautiful girl and Mrs Yates told her so. She followed up by saying, 'I'll get the kettle on; bet you two could do with a nice hot drink and some supper. I made some vegetable soup earlier that'll just need heating.' She jerked her head at the stairs at the back of the kitchen.

'Show Elise up to her room. She looks beat. There are some clean towels in the airing cupboard.'

'Thank you,' said Elise. The overwhelming relief of being safely on dry land in a cosy home brought on a yawn that she smothered with a hand.

'Mind your head, there's a low beam,' said Faith halfway up the narrow stairs.

Elise saw it, ducked and on reaching the top followed Faith along a short landing.

'Here we are then.' Faith opened the door and they entered a small neat room with a single bed covered in a patchwork quilt. Against the pale walls stood a few items of stocky dark furniture. 'Bet you could sleep the clock round, couldn't you?'

It was an English expression Elise wasn't familiar with but she grasped it meant 'have a good kip', as her father would have said. She nodded and sank down onto the edge of the bed with a sigh.

'Strange, I'm dog-tired but doubt I'll get much shut-eye. I

couldn't after the first Dunkirk run,' said Faith and drooped down beside Elise. 'Probably because I knew we'd be going back again at dawn. Didn't want to overdo it.'

'I hope all the men get back.' Elise's mind flashed back to when she'd hidden in the dunes and covered her ears against the sound of the fighting getting closer. Troops were still on the shore and on the east Mole breakwater when she'd been heading out to sea. Those soldiers would have been praying a good Samaritan from home would come and get them before the Germans did. Her good Samaritan had been among those left waiting for a miracle to happen.

'You've turned up in England with just the clothes on your back.' Faith looked at the crumpled blue dress with its limp lace collar and the slightly shrunken cardigan. 'You must've left home in a terrible rush. You were in danger, I suppose, as your dad's English.'

Elise nodded and bit her lip. 'He was arrested. He guessed he would be; he told us to flee in case the Nazis came back for us. I didn't stop to pack anything. I thought we'd all return home in a day or two.' She gestured hopelessness.

'I'm so sorry for what's happened to you, Elise.' Faith put a comforting arm around her. 'I hope your brother remains free. But your father will probably be interned.'

Elise didn't want to become tearful again from recounting that there was more to it and there had been a shooting. She would be relieved to know her father had been interned ... but doubted that was his fate.

'My boyfriend's a rear gunner in a Lancaster bomber,' said Faith. 'I worry every day that I'll get a letter from his mother saying ...' She paused. 'You know ... bad news,' she finished huskily.

Elise held Faith's hand and felt her fingers vibrating. 'What's his name?'

'Bob Pearson. Last time he wrote he asked me to marry him even though we've only been walking out a short time. I wasn't sure what to tell him. I think I'll say yes. I'd like to be a wife and mother. After this ... why wait? Who knows what might happen.'

'Your Mr Churchill might have a plan ... a very good one, too,' said Elise encouragingly.

'Please God you're right.' Faith stood up and rubbed a damp patch transferred to her trousers. 'Right, you'd better get out of those wet things; you'll catch a chill. The bathroom's next door if you want a wash and tidy up. I'll go and find you a nightdress to change into and a few other bits and pieces to make you comfortable.'

'Thank you. You've all been so good to me.'

"S'what friends are for,' said Faith. 'Once you're in your nightie, if you let me have your clothes, Mum'll smarten them up for you. She's a marvel with a pressing iron.' She gazed out of the undrawn window into darkness. 'Well, Elise Boosher, reckon you 'n' me are paid-up members of the Dunkirk Club now,' she said wryly. 'So let's drink to it.' She pulled a pewter flask from her pocket and took a swig. 'Brandy,' she said, smacking her lips before taking another glug. 'Mum doesn't mind me having a fortifying tipple but thinks it's unladylike to drink from a bottle.' She handed the flask to Elise. 'Members of the Dunkirk Club don't always get to act like ladies.'

'No, they don't,' agreed a rueful Elise, recalling her chin spattered in vomit during her journey to England. She'd washed her face with a handkerchief dipped into the briny. 'I'll drink to that as well.' She took a sip and managed to swallow the liquor without coughing. It coursed through her, dragging pleasant warmth in its wake.

'It's a bloody awful way to meet you.' Faith took back the flask for another mouthful before stowing it away in her pocket. 'But I'm glad I did.'

Elise rose to hug Faith, glad she was no longer trembling. They remained locked in an embrace for some minutes, lost in private thoughts. They'd only been acquainted for a short while but knew they had already formed an unbreakable bond of friendship.

There were no lights on the craft silhouetted against the harbour wall; a blackout was being observed in case the enemy planes flew over. A pale moon and a few stars were in the sky and every so often silver glints were visible in the distance as moonbeams betrayed the sea.

Elise drew the curtain and turned from the window before putting a match to the candle Faith had left for her on the chest of drawers. Also resting on its top were her French francs and the address her grandmother had given her. Her worldly goods.

She'd remembered to remove those things from her pocket before she'd handed over her clothes for ironing. She'd carefully unfolded the damp papers to allow them to dry. A bank would exchange the francs for English money, but she'd no idea how much it would amount to or if it would buy her a rail ticket to London. She guessed the Yateses would offer to cover the cost but Elise didn't want that when she'd no idea how or when she could repay them.

She looked at the Silvertown address; the writing was faded from being in the sea. She moved the paper closer to the candle and noticed something she had missed when reading it in moonlight. Beneath the address was a name: Clover Cooper. The word 'Cooper' had a line through it and 'Ryan' had been pencilled underneath.

Elise imagined Clover was one of her sisters and had married a Mr Ryan. Clover ... the person her father had chosen as his next-of-kin in the event of tragedies or emergencies. Elise feared both applied since the Germans had taken Sidney Cooper away and she had fled her home.

She returned to the window and sat down on the chair she'd used before when gazing out into the night. She blew out the candle then opened the curtain again. Planting her elbows on the windowsill and her chin on her palms, she stared across the sea towards her homeland and dwelled on those she loved.

She thought of Luc first, wondering where he was. He might have returned to Mathilde's but she doubted he'd stay long. He wouldn't risk drawing trouble to their grandmother's door. Mathilde Bouchard had never got on well with her son-in-law and all her neighbours knew it. Mathilde was a patriot through and through, and hadn't agreed with her grandchildren speaking more English than French. They never did when with her. Mathilde's dislike of Sidney Cooper might protect her from persecution. Elise was sure her brother was alive. Now France was about to fall, he would seek out others determined to resist the occupation. Her father ... she had no optimistic feelings and closed her eyes and prayed for him.

Then she thought of Corporal Nathaniel Hawkes and her eyes were raised again to the sparkles on the sea. Was he somewhere along the English coast, having got on board another vessel shortly after she'd departed? Or was he still on Dunkirk beach, lying with the soldiers the stretcher bearers stepped over?

She refused to consider it and stood up, closing the curtains. 'Stay alive!' she whispered furiously into the darkness. 'And you'd better not be married or have a girl waiting. I'm waiting!'

Elise had stayed longer with the Yateses than anticipated. She'd been out for the count until noon the following day and nobody had woken her, believing she obviously needed a good rest to recuperate from her ordeal. She did, but when she finally got up she was wobbly on her feet with a raging headache and a sore throat.

Mrs Yates had diagnosed a bad chill got from her sea soaking, and had sent her straight back to bed, saying she was in no fit state to travel to the end of the street let alone to London. Two days later, her temperature was almost back to normal and the vivid nightmares about her family and an army of fair-haired Nazis had stopped. She didn't dream about Nathan but he was constantly in her thoughts nonetheless.

The following day, she was able to get dressed and go downstairs. Plenty of rest and regular Beecham powders normally did the trick Mrs Yates had said while dishing up breakfast. The scrambled eggs were fresh from the chicken coop in the garden and piled atop hot buttered toast. The teapot was constantly on the go too. Sidney Cooper had introduced his children to tea drinking and would always bring a packet of Typhoo with him when he returned from England. Elise and Luc would make tea in preference to coffee to Sidney's delight.

Elise was relieved she'd not attempted to soldier on.

Turning up in Silvertown like a sickly waif wouldn't have been a promising start with her step-family.

While she'd been laid up, Mr Yates had kindly found out about the train timetable and ticket prices to London. An hour ago, Faith had walked with Elise to Broadstairs High Street.

They'd gone into the bank to exchange the French francs. Elise had been pleasantly surprised to have more cash than expected left over after purchasing a ticket to Victoria station. The train was due to leave in an hour so they browsed the shops, then sat in a café lingering over creamy strawberry milkshakes and a plate of biscuits. Some English coins Elise was familiar with; her father would show her and Luc the pennies and ha'pennies he had left in his pocket from his trips to England. He rarely had unspent silver so those were new to her.

Faith sorted various coins between the plates and named them: florin ... sixpence ... shilling and a half a crown. Elise also had two ten shilling notes; the booking office clerk had apologised for not having a pound note to give her instead. She was feeling confident she'd not starve before finding a job to pay her keep. She collected up her money and they pushed back their chairs ready to leave.

'Let me pay,' said Elise, keen to use some of her English money and to treat Faith after all the help she'd received from the Yates family.

'I will not.' Faith ignored her friend's handful of coins. 'It's lovely of you to offer but you'll need that in London, Elise. Everything costs more in the capital. Anyway, this is my little leaving present; you can pay next time we go to a caff.'

'I wish I could stay here with you. Broadstairs is lovely. But ... I have to go.'

'I know,' said Faith with an equally wistful smile. 'Don't forget to write to me, will you?'

They exited the café and turned once more in the direction of the railway station, linking arms as they strolled along. They could have been long-standing pals instead of people who'd known each other less than a full week.

'Of course I'll write. I'll write so often you'll get fed up with it. And I'll come back to Kent to see you again the moment I'm able to.'

'That'd be smashing. If I get a chance I'll come to London and we can meet up. Graham's working in the City so I can see you both at the same time. You'll like my brother, he's funny. We can go to the theatre or a dance ... something like that.'

'Oh, I'd love to,' Elise said as they proceeded into the station and along the platform. The train was already standing and people were elbowing past, peering into the carriages to locate the best seats.

'Would you say thank you again to your mum and dad for everything they've done for me? And for this.' Elise patted her pocket. She'd been given a pack of wrapped sandwiches for the journey. She had thanked Mrs Yates earlier and had received a farewell embrace. Ronald had been out since first light, she'd been told, seeing to business on the quayside but he also sent his best wishes to her for the future.

Carriage doors were being slammed and the guards began positioning themselves to get a view along the platform to sound the all-clear. The girls knew they couldn't delay their parting any longer.

'If I hear anything about a Corporal Hawkes coming ashore, I'll let you know,' Faith said. 'If he turns up in

Broadstairs looking for you I'll recognise him.' She winked. 'Couldn't forget somebody as gorgeous as him. I'll ask around. Most of the Tommies want to get straight on the train and head home. Could be you'll find he's got to London before you.'

'I hope so.'

Elise had enquired from her sick bed about the men returning from Dunkirk. She'd been told that the day after she arrived it was deemed too dangerous for any more evacuations to take place. The Germans were on Dunkirk beach and Allied soldiers left behind were either dead or prisoners of war.

'I'd better get on the train.' The platform was virtually empty and she was one of the last to board.

'S'pose you had,' Faith slipped her hand from her friend's arm.

Elise hugged her and stepped away then rushed back for a final embrace before climbing aboard. The guard slammed the door and she stood by it as the whistle shrilled and the train jerked into motion.

'Don't forget ...' Faith shouted and mimed writing on her palm.

Elise nodded vigorously and waved until her friend was out of sight before looking for a seat.

She sat down next to a middle-aged woman who had pulled wool and needles from her bag and started knitting something bottle green. They exchanged a polite smile as the train shuddered and jolted and picked up speed.

'That's a fine bit of sewing,' said the woman after they'd sat in companionable silence for some minutes. 'You're a good needlewoman.'

Elise noticed the woman's eyes were on the repair to her

skirt. 'It's not my work,' she said. 'A friend did it for me.' Elise smoothed her skirt over her knees. She was surprised the woman had noticed it as the stitches were almost invisible. Mrs Yates had repaired the rip in her dress and washed and pressed all of her clothes in readiness for her trip to London. Mr Yates had taken her shoes to be soled and heeled and they shone with black polish. Elise knew she had been extremely fortunate in the people she'd met so far. Even before stepping foot on foreign soil she'd had the kindness of strangers.

But Nathan wasn't a stranger now; she'd slept beneath the stars with him, eaten his food, and held his hand while racing across the Dunkirk sand to safety. She locked the memory away and her private smile faded. Where was he? Was he safe?

She silently said a prayer for him then turned her mind to practicalities.

England was her home now for the foreseeable future, and wouldn't be foreign for long. But France had her heart.

She settled back and unfolded the scrap of paper to read the names of the place and the people she was hoping to see. Clover was a nice name ... gentle and pretty, but her character might be quite different. She was Sidney Cooper's daughter too. Elise loved her father but he had a mean side.

Are you like him, Clover? she wondered, then she folded the paper and stared out at the green fields racing past.

Chapter Six

Her darning needle was woven in and out of the cotton in regular small movements despite Mathilde Bouchard's vision being bleary with tears. The Gestapo had questioned her that morning about Sidney Cooper. She wasn't afraid of them for herself; she'd seen their ennui at having to bother with an elderly widow. Strong idealistic youth was a different matter though; they were keen to find her grandchildren and worries about their whereabouts and their safety were constantly tormenting her.

She pricked a finger with the needle and reached for the lamp to turn up the light. Before she could do so she was startled into pushing herself to her feet. The sequence of soft taps was familiar to her, although she'd not heard it in a long time. Few people still alive knew that code; many who had, had perished during the last German occupation. Her grandchildren were aware of it: her late husband had demonstrated it when relating tales of the Great War to them when they were at primary school. Mathilde had made him promise not to do it again. He would gently mock her fears telling her it was all history. Those ghosts were best left in peace, she'd said. Dropping her sewing, she swiftly opened the door before the noise came again.

'They've been here looking for you,' she whispered in alarm. 'You can't stay long. They might return.' Quickly and quietly, she closed the door behind him.

Luc Bouchard had waited until dark to creep along the unlit lane to his grandmother's house. He'd not dared to call out but had known she'd understand his signal and let him in.

Once inside, he collapsed down behind the door, a hand clamped at the top of his arm. 'I'm sorry to come back, Grandma. I won't stay long I promise. I didn't want you to worry. I had to let you know we're all right. I would've come sooner but—'

'All right?' she interrupted. 'You don't look all right.' Mathilde crouched beside him, loosening his jacket to investigate what was causing him to grimace in pain. 'You're bleeding, Luc!' She'd noticed his stained shirt and suffocated a gasp with her knuckles. 'What happened? Where's Elise?'

'She's safe, I think.' He grasped his grandmother's hand in comfort and kissed the back of it. Keeping his voice to a murmur he spilled out everything that had occurred after they'd left this house heading for Dunkirk. He told her that he'd been shot while running through a meadow – probably by accident he reassured her – having been mistaken for an Allied soldier by a short-sighted Kraut. It had taken him a long time to get back to Lille. He'd had to rest often and hide, surviving on the kindness of villagers. If the Nazis had come across him they'd want to know his name and how he'd been wounded.

Mathilde listened intently while helping him out of his

jacket. 'You believe this English Tommy will look after Elise properly?'

'I do. I think he will have done his best to help her.' He gritted his teeth and eased his injured arm from its shirtsleeve.

Mathilde took the lamp from the table and placed it on the floor beside him. 'The bullet's gone through, you're lucky. But it's a mess.' She pushed herself to her feet and put the kettle on the stove. She began ripping up the linen she'd been mending to use as a bandage. As she did so, it brought back memories of assisting fugitives during the last war and she began remembering things she'd rather forget. She'd believed such times had gone forever but here she was again, quaking inside while dressing men's wounds. And it was worse this time because her beloved grandchildren rather than her husband and his compatriots were involved. Mathilde swallowed the lump in her throat and said matter-of-fact, 'I can try to stitch the wound if you can bear it, Luc.'

'No ... if I'm arrested they'll know somebody's helped me; they'll guess it's you. A bandage I can do myself. What did they say when they came here? Are we all in bad trouble?'

Mathilde crouched down again with a bowl of steaming water. She began to dab away dried blood, then her deft fingers pressed together ragged edges of flesh and secured the cloth tightly about his upper arm. 'I don't think it's infected. I'll find you one of your grandfather's old shirts. And wash the blood off your jacket. You don't want anybody seeing that.'

'What did they say, Grandma?'

Forlornly, she shook her head. 'I'm sorry to tell you that your father's dead, Luc. Sidney did have a gun; he shot the

Hauptmann, then himself. Maybe the Nazis killed him, but I don't think they would be shy of saying so.'

'Why did he do that! They might have only wanted a few questions answered. They might have interned him. He had no need to kill himself ...'

'Hush!' she cautioned as he raged in despair. 'I don't know why he did it.' Mathilde put a hand on her grandson's cheek and felt his warm tears slide beneath her palm. 'Perhaps it is better for him that they did not get to question him. I think that is how your father saw it.' She paused. 'They asked me where Sidney Cooper's children were to be found. I said I didn't know and hadn't seen you in ages. The neighbours agreed that nobody had seen you or your father in the village recently. They said they'd heard me arguing with Sidney when he came here last. I told him to stay away. It is true. We did argue. I didn't like him sponging off you and Elise. He wasn't too old to work.'

'He wasn't always well ...'

'Wasn't well! Wasn't sober, that was his trouble.' Mathilde waved an apology for being blunt. 'I won't speak ill of the dead but I can't pretend I liked your father, Luc. He did stay with you when you wouldn't go to England, though. He could have gone alone as he always did.'

'I wish we had all gone,' Luc cried into his muffling palms.

Mathilde put her hand on his bowed dark head. 'It is too late for regrets. We must prepare for the future now France has fallen.' She sighed. 'And what a future it will be. Five long years of this we suffered last time.' She pointed to the door. 'Did you take care not to be seen just now?'

He nodded.

Mathilde got up and went into the bedroom to find a clean

shirt. She dropped it onto her grandson's lap then cut some bread and ladled broth into a bowl for him. The boiled water left in the kettle was used to make him a mug of coffee.

'Did they bury him?' Luc raised his tear-stained face and took the drink. He hated to think of his father's body being at the mercy of scavenging animals.

'I don't think so. I said I would arrange it if they brought him here ... they didn't bother to answer me. I expect they left him where he fell close to Amiens; the locals might have buried him out of respect. Your father is talked of as a hero for shooting the German officer.'

'He was brave. I want to fight for France but the army's finished,' Luc said bitterly before taking a gulp of strong coffee. 'Pétain is a disgrace,' he spat in disgust. 'I'm joining the Resistance or De Gaulle's Free French ...'

'Shhh.' Mathilde put a finger to his lips to quieten him. 'It's too soon. It takes a while for people to organise themselves; it was the same last time. You might still get to England somehow. That would be best for you.' Mathilde tried to encourage him as he sat with his head clasped in his hands. 'Come, eat this.' She beckoned him and put his food on the table.

Luc gingerly pushed himself upright and sat on the stool. His grandfather would tell stories about the Resistance fighters who helped Allied soldiers escape from behind enemy lines to return home. His grandfather had shown him an edition of a newspaper that had been printed and distributed covertly during those years to encourage the fight for freedom. Luc had read it eagerly; even as a boy he'd known he would have joined those rebels.

'Do you know any Resistance from last time, Grandma? I'll contact them.' Luc tore off a chunk of bread with his teeth, chewing fast.

'That's dangerous talk, Luc,' she fiercely said. 'Why didn't you go with your sister and the Tommy? You'd have been in London with your other family by now.'

'They're not my family. I don't know them. You're my family: you and Elise. I'm joining the freedom fighters.' He dunked his bread into the broth and finished the food quickly. 'Grandpa was in the Resistance,' he said between swallows. 'So were you.'

'Yes ... it's true. But it was a long time ago that we had our secret war.' Mathilde sat beside him and took his hand in her trembling fingers. 'And they had their secret police.' She paused to watch him with adoring yet sad eyes. 'It wasn't all heroic, Luc. Dreadful things were done. The Germans were not fools then and they won't be now. Their spies worm into the underground groups ... pretend to be sympathisers. Neighbours and friends turn on one another to stay alive. The women weren't spared either.'

'I know, we learned in history lessons about Gabrielle Petit and the British nurse Edith Cavell being shot for helping Allied soldiers to escape.' Luc sounded buoyed by their heroism rather than deterred in his course of action.

'Well, if you paid attention you must know that many others were betrayed and executed for doing far less for the Allies.' Mathilde felt alarmed by his bravado.

'I know the dangers; I'm not a fool, Grandma.' He stood up, appearing more composed. 'It's a cause worth dying for. There will be other patriots who think as I do.'

Mathilde tore another strip from the sheet and wound it up into a ball to give to him. 'You'll need to change the bandage; keep it clean or it might get infected.' She used another rag to scrub blood from his coat, then helped him ease into his clean clothes, frowning as he winced. 'A village south of Hazebrouck has a church,' she said, straightening his collar. 'The priest was a young man last time – not much older than you. Father Pascal survived the war. Your grandfather knew and liked him. If he is still there I doubt his views have changed much.'

'Thank you, Grandma.' Luc carefully embraced Mathilde and gratefully took the remainder of the bread she pressed onto him.

'Have you still got the money I gave you?'

He nodded.

'Use it wisely until you have a job. Keep to yourself. Trust nobody until you're very sure ... even the priest.' Mathilde knew it was better to point her reckless grandson towards a trusted source than allow him to blunder into bad company.

'I'll try and let you know that I'm all right. I'll use a different name ...' He glanced about for inspiration and his eyes alighted on a picture on the wall of a country scene: a chestnut horse being led by its owner along a sunlit country lane. 'Marron,' he said and grinned at the idea of becoming Mr Chestnut.

She clasped his face in her palms and kissed both his cheeks. 'Remember what I've said, Monsieur Marron. Always be careful and keep safe.'

She opened the door an inch then closed it again and put a finger to her lips. Voices were heard and a lantern swung a light against the window as two men ambled home from the tavern situated on the road to Lille. When it was quiet and the darkness unbroken, Mathilde opened the door. After a quick look to and fro she beckoned her grandson.

He brushed past with a murmured farewell and was soon lost in shadows.

Chapter Seven

Silvertown, East London

'For safety's sake they must go, love.' Neil Ryan shoved a hand through his dark hair. 'It's worrying the life out of me knowing London could be bombed tomorrow.' He sighed. 'I can't put out of my mind what happened to the school in Poplar last time.'

'I worry too, you know,' his wife said. 'I haven't forgotten about that either. But let's wait and see. There's been no invasion, no bombing, no nothing.' She showed him two sets of crossed fingers. 'And please God there never will be.'

'The French waited to see what would happen; didn't work out well for them, or our lads, did it.' Neil gestured apology; bringing that up hadn't been kind when his wife was fretting about what her father was going through in France.

The Dunkirk evacuation was on everybody's mind, as was guessing what Hitler's next move would be now he had the upper hand. Nobody was under an illusion that France's capitulation had brought an end to it.

'I've been constantly thinking about Dad...'

'I know you have, love. But there's not much we can do other than wait to hear from him.'

There was a pram in the room and the toddler dozing in it had been woken by his parents' bickering. Clover jigged the handle until his whimpering quietened. Usually she liked seeing her husband at dinnertime. If he was working close to home he'd come in at around noon instead of eating in a cafe. Today she felt on edge and wanted to be alone to think. He understandably wanted to protect their children. So did she, and would do so with her life, if necessary. But Silvertown was their home, and after waiting so long to become parents she couldn't bear their family to be broken apart a second sooner than was necessary. 'You'd better get going hadn't you?' She glanced at the clock on the wall.

'Yeah. I'm running late. The guvnor wants the job finished before we knock off. Don't wait tea for me. I'll eat later.'

At forty-four Neil Ryan was four years older than his wife, and twenty years older than his boss. He didn't mind taking orders from somebody so much younger; Jake Harding was his wife's brother and an all-round decent bloke. 'Will you think about it, Clover?' Neil shrugged into his jacket. 'Please ...'

He had tried to persuade his wife to evacuate with their son and daughter earlier in the week. A rumour had started circulating that the local infants' school would be closing to encourage parents to send youngsters to the countryside. Things were serious then, was the consensus of opinion. The powers-that-be must know London was about to be bombed and an invasion was imminent.

'I'll never let Vicky and Jamie live with strangers.' Clover sounded exasperated by his persistence.

'I wouldn't want that either when they're still so young. You should go too. It'll be safer for all of you,' Neil said.

'I will if things take a turn for the worse. Nan and Grandad have already invited us to stay in Southend. It'll be a tight squeeze though with Dora and William already there.' Her brother's wife had readily upped sticks from the East End and relocated to the Essex coast with their three-year-old son. 'The more the merrier, I suppose.' Clover rocked the pram again as a rap on the door startled Jamie.

Elise had stood outside this rather shabby-looking house for several minutes before making her presence known. Silvertown, she'd disappointingly discovered, didn't live up to its promising name. With its abundance of smoke-belching factories and terraces of ugly red-brick cottages, it was an unappealing place. She'd guessed her father's family would be working-class folk reluctant to have another mouth to feed. None of that had made her hesitate though and neither had her nervousness. She'd been waiting for a pause in the argument, unwilling to awkwardly barge in on the couple. It was bad timing, but at least this was a civilised disagreement, unlike those her parents would have. Sophie Bouchard hadn't always backed down and occasionally her yelling had drawn tutting neighbours into the lane for a gossip.

If Elise had children she wouldn't want them evacuated away from their father so she understood the woman's point of view. But the man was right too: delays cost lives. Sidney Cooper had understood that but his children hadn't until it was too late ...

'Hello ... can I help you?'

Elise was jerked to attention as the door was abruptly

opened. The two women were conscious of a similarity in their looks as they stared at one another. Only Elise was aware of the reason for it. 'Are you Clover Cooper ... Ryan, I mean?' she corrected herself.

'I am. What can I do for you?' Clover's quizzical smile was fading as extraordinary coincidences occurred to her. Although her hair was darker and her eyes a different colour there was no denying this young woman looked rather like her younger sister Annie ... who resembled their father ... as did their brother Johnny. And she believed the visitor had a slight French accent in her perfectly polite English pronunciation. Which was odd, as her father was over there ...

'I'm Elise Bouchard. Might I speak privately to you?' Elise glanced along the road. Some chatting women had been taking an interest in the stranger in their midst. 'I've come from Lille in France.'

Clover looked over her shoulder at her husband in mounting excitement. Her father lived in Lille. When things hotted up over there she'd written, enquiring how he was and inviting him to stay. She'd received nothing back, but that wasn't unusual. Apart from his slapdash attitude to keeping in touch, France was occupied now and the postal service doubtless in disarray.

Neil had taken his fretful son from the pram and was nursing him. He'd overheard the conversation and his expression mirrored his wife's bafflement.

'Yes ... sorry ... please do come in.' Clover snapped out of her daze and ushered the visitor inside.

Elise looked from the tall handsome man with silvering hair at his temples to the woman with luxuriant auburn tresses and green eyes. Clover was older than she'd expected her to be, but attractive, and wearing a floral pinafore over a neat set of clothes. She didn't have Sidney Cooper's colouring, but his strong bones showed in her face. 'I'm your half-sister.' Unsure how to dress it up she'd come straight out with it. 'I'm Sidney Cooper's daughter.'

Clover continued to gawp at the girl who looked young enough to be her own daughter, let alone her father's. A wondrous smile crept over her face, then she rushed to embrace Elise. 'I'm so very pleased to meet you, Elise! Our dad didn't tell us much about his French children but we knew you and your brother existed.' Clover drew the newcomer towards the settee. 'Oh, what a lovely surprise. Please do sit down. This is my husband, Neil.'

Neil returned his son to the pram and approached, extending a hand to be shaken.

'I'll bet you could do with a nice cup of tea. And how is Dad? Did he come to London with you?' Clover chattered away, her heart racing with the thrill of this extraordinary development. Anxiety wasn't far away though. If her father had come to England, surely he'd be here now with his daughter. Her question about Sidney remained unanswered and Clover's uneasiness increased.

'Well, I'd love to hang on and find out all about it.' Neil filled the gap in conversation. 'But I have to get back to work. See you later then, and you can tell me all the news.' He pecked his wife's cheek. 'I'll be back as early as I can.' A significant look passed between the couple.

After her husband had gone Clover put the kettle on then hurried to sit next to Elise on the settee. 'Something's happened, hasn't it?' She wasn't one to beat about the bush. 'I don't just mean the war ... something's happened to Dad?

Elise nodded, dropping her chin as tears prickled her eyes. Her sister's spontaneous welcome had melted away her nervousness. Clover was all she could have hoped her to be. But she must upset her in revealing the next part of the story.

'Has Dad been interned? It must be dreadful over there.' Clover put a comforting arm around the girl's shoulders. 'I've been so worried about him since France has fallen. Is your brother with you?' Clover rolled her eyes. 'Sorry, I'm talking nineteen to the dozen and not letting you get a word in edgeways.'

'They're still in France and so is my grandmother,' Elise said. 'I've been in England for weeks. I stayed with a family in Kent for a while. They owned the boat that brought me across the Channel. Then a lady I met on the train to London employed me in her shop after I told her I wanted a job.'

By the time they'd reached Victoria station Elise and her spinster travelling companion had hit it off rather well. Miss Booth had been visiting her sister in Broadstairs and was eager to get back to her drapery in Battersea to open up the shop again. On discovering Elise had experience selling expensive dresses, she'd offered her temporary employment. Elise had grasped the chance to add to her dwindling pot of money, and to learn a bit about London life. She'd declined an offer to stay longer. She wanted to be in Silvertown if Corporal Hawkes came looking for her.

Elise gazed into a pair of questioning green eyes. 'I'd best start at the beginning,' she said gravely.

By the time she'd finished her tale they were both weeping and the tea had been forgotten.

'But you can't be certain Dad's dead? Or your brother?'

Clover took the whistling kettle off the hob and rushed back to sit beside Elise.

'No . . .' she gruffly replied. 'I believe Luc is still alive but not Papa.' Elise shook her head and pressed a hand to her heart. 'In here I know he's gone . . .'

'Thank goodness you escaped.' Clover cuddled Elise, comforting them both. Eventually, she gave a deep sigh and stood up. 'I'll make that tea.'

Elise got up as well and gazed into the pram. She stroked the fidgeting boy's cheek. 'What's his name?'

'That's your nephew, Jamie. He's fifteen months and a bit of a grump as he's cutting his back teeth.'

Elise picked him up and nursed him, murmuring his name and stroking his soft auburn curls. 'He looks like you.'

'Jamie does favour me; my mum and my gran were also redheads,' said Clover, setting cups and saucers. 'My sister Annie and brother Johnny are brunettes like their dad . . . our dad.' Clover turned and assessed the beautiful young woman with black hair and grey eyes balancing Jamie astride her slim hip. She was singing a lullaby in a sweet attempt to stop Jamie grizzling. 'I guess you got your mum's colouring, Elise.'

Elise stopped crooning 'Frere Jacques' and said, 'I am like her. Not so much in character though.'

Clover detected an undercurrent in that and felt comfortable enough with her new sister to speak bluntly. 'Did Sidney treat your mother well?'

Elise set the little boy on his feet as he wriggled to get down. 'No . . . not really. Did he treat your mother well?'

Clover grimaced a negative. 'There were lots of problems between them.' She paused. 'Looking back, I don't blame Dad for all of it but . . .' She let her shrug have the final word.

'We had lots of problems too; my mother was often sad because of him, and lonely. Then, when it was too late and she became ill and passed away, it was his turn to pine.'

'He wasn't an easy man to get along with.' Clover hadn't wanted to speak of him in the past tense. In common with Elise, intuition told her Sidney Cooper's luck had run out. She'd not seen him in over six years and in that time she'd received only a handful of letters from the father who'd just upped and left without giving any of them a reason or a goodbye.

Clover had believed he'd perished on a previous occasion. She had grieved for him then before learning he'd not been blown to bits after all during the Silvertown munitions' factory explosion. He'd simply chosen to disappear. In his own time he had turned up again after the first war like a bad penny, with fanciful tales of having been missing in action and suffering from amnesia. Nobody was fooled. They all knew he'd deserted to be with his French mistress ... Elise's mother. Clover had used up her tears where Sidney Cooper was concerned.

'Are you and your brother alike? Is he older than you? Sorry for all the questions but I'd love to know more about you both. Dad was tight-lipped about his other family, I'm afraid.'

'Likewise ...' replied a rueful Elise. 'Luc's nineteen, a year older than me. I'm just turned eighteen.'

While staying with Miss Booth, the woman had asked her age and when she found out a birthday was imminent had bought a small cake to celebrate on the day. She had treated her assistant to a nightdress and a petticoat when she discovered Elise had very few clothes with her.

'Luc's the image of Papa but quite different in character.

Luc couldn't be persuaded to come with me to Dunkirk; he was determined to stay in France and fight. He's very brave.'

To Clover that sounded more foolish than brave but she kept her thoughts to herself ... just as she had when her younger brother had told her he was enlisting. Johnny had joined the army not long after war was declared. She thought he was wrong to do so. But he was a married man and a father; more than old enough to make his own decisions. Her role as his surrogate mum after theirs died when he was twelve was over and done with. It was his wife's place to object rather than hers. Dora had gone along with Johnny's thinking: this war should be nipped in the bud or they might face five years of hell, as they had last time.

'Johnny was rescued from Dunkirk by a Cornish fishing boat. We were all so worried about him.' She smiled and said, 'It'll take you a while to remember all the names. There's a lot of us.' Clover turned from the teapot and counted off on her fingers with a teaspoon their siblings. 'Johnny's thirty-five ... or thirty-six, I lose track sometimes. He's your brother.' Another finger was tapped. 'Annie's twenty-five and she's your sister. She's a cook in a big posh house in Mayfair.' Another tap. 'Then there's my youngest brother, Jake Harding ... he's twenty-three and I might as well tell you that Sidney isn't his father.' She turned back to find the milk bottle. 'It's too long a story to go into now; suffice to say that us Coopers are a complicated lot.'

'So are we. If you're wondering why I'm Elise Bouchard it's because Sidney and my mum never got married.'

'I guessed as much.' Clover dismissed it with a gesture. 'Makes no difference to us, any of that. We'd plenty of skeletons in cupboards before you turned up, Elise.' She winked and began rattling the teaspoon in the teapot while stirring the brew. 'Your brothers and sisters are going to be so excited to meet you. And all the in-laws. Your sister-in-law Rebecca – that's Jake's wife - is quite a businesswoman and does the books for their building firm in Whitechapel. Your other sister-in-law Dora used to be a factory hand before becoming a mum. She's evacuated to Southend with her little boy, William. Johnny headed straight to see them when he got back from Dunkirk.' Clover paused. 'Anyway, they'll all want to tell you a bit about themselves without me doing it for them.'

'I can't wait to meet everybody,' said Elise, but her thoughts were with another soldier who'd been at Dunkirk. 'Has anybody been here looking for me?'

'Looking for you?' Clover frowned.

'The soldier I told you helped me to escape said he'd look me up when he got home. He lives in Poplar.'

'Well, that's not far,' exclaimed Clover. 'What's his name? Perhaps I know of him.'

'Corporal Nathaniel Hawkes.'

After some pondering Clover shook her head. 'Doesn't ring a bell and nobody's been here.' She brightened. 'Jake might know him. He takes on building work all over London. Neil might have bumped into your Nathaniel Hawkes as well. I'll ask him later.'

'Oh, it doesn't matter too much.' Elise subdued her disappointment. She didn't want to make a fuss in case Nathan was simply getting on with his life. Although she didn't believe he'd forgotten her any more than she had him. 'He didn't have much to go on: only the name Cooper and Silvertown. He might not find me.'

Clover gave her a knowing look. 'Sounds to me like you want him to though. Good looking, is he?'

Elise blushed. 'Yes ... I think so. If it hadn't been for him ... well, he saved my life. I'd like to properly thank him, that's all,' she said somewhat untruthfully. She wanted to see him again for a lot more than that.

Clover patted her arm. 'I'd like to thank him too for looking after my sister. So I'll keep my ear to the ground and let you know if anybody's spotted asking where the Coopers live.'

'I didn't find out much about him. He might be busy ... with his wife and children.' Nathan's cryptic remark about his love life could have meant anything ... or nothing. Elise fervently hoped he was alive and fortunate enough to be in England with his family, whoever they were. She made herself stop thinking about him and in doing so let slip she'd been eavesdropping earlier. 'Your husband spoke of your children; is the other one at school today?'

'You heard us arguing ...' Clover shrugged an apology. 'Yes, we have a daughter. Vicky's nearly five. She attends a nursery class a few times a week. You can come with me when I collect her later.'

'I'd like to. What happened to the school in Poplar that your husband mentioned?'

Clover's smile vanished.

'Sorry, I shouldn't have said anything. I didn't mean to pry or be rude.'

'You aren't,' Clover reassured. 'It's only ... it's a tragedy nobody likes to talk about. This war's dragging up some horrible memories of the last one. The school was bombed in 1917 and lots of children died – some barely older than Vicky. Just babies really.' Clover covered her face with her hands at the reminder of what the Great War did to the East End during that year: in January the Silvertown explosion ripped apart the neighbourhood and she lost her beloved grandmother, a munitions worker at the doomed factory. Only months later, while Silvertown was still picking up the pieces, German bombs were dropped on innocent schoolchildren barely a few miles away in Poplar.

'My grandmother told me about similar dreadful things that happened in France during the Great War,' Elise said.

'I know Neil's right about sending the children away to safety. But I want us all to stay together for as long as possible.' She frowned. 'Am I being selfish?'

'No! I'd want that as well. It's all so unfair!' Elise's anger erupted. 'Everybody's lives turned upside down! Papa dead! He didn't deserve to be taken away ... he was at home with me minding his own business. I'm glad he shot the German!' They clung together and when they'd no tears left, they hiccoughed themselves calm and moved apart.

'You'll stay with us, of course,' croaked Clover. 'There's a spare bedroom. We used to only rent the ground floor here but the landlord let us have the upstairs as well.' She sniffed and dabbed her eyes with a hanky. 'In return for a cheap rent Neil does the landlord's repairs.' Finally, a watery smile tilted her lips. 'He's a good carpenter.'

'You've a nice home.' It wasn't polite flummery; the exterior looked uninviting but the atmosphere inside this house radiated warmth and love. Despite her melancholy, Elise felt comfortable here ... almost a part of the family.

'We should have a party so you can meet everyone. We love a get-together. I'm sure Johnny and Dora will come back from Essex and bring Nan and Granddad with them.' Clover busied herself cutting some bread. 'You must be hungry and you're in luck. I was in the bakery queue before it opened and bought a couple of loaves. There's some ham for a sandwich.'

'You've a good heart, Clover,' said Elise as she watched her sister spreading marge on bread. 'I was worried you might not like having me here.'

'You're my blood. In this family we take care of one another.' Clover stopped what she was doing to put two capable hands on her youngest sister's shoulders. She'd thought she'd done with mothering younger siblings. And perhaps she had she told herself; this petite, solemn-eyed stranger was tougher than she looked in Clover's opinion. Nevertheless she offered Elise Bouchard what she would to any brother or sister. 'If there's anything you need: advice about work, or money ... or men ... just ask and I'll do whatever I can to help you sort it out.'

Chapter Eight

'You must've got quite a shock, mate, when you saw her.'

'Too right. No warning ... no nothing. Just opened the door and there she was.' Neil shook his head. 'Clover was knocked for six. She saw the resemblance straight away.'

'Girl with hair as black as yours, turning up out of the blue ... bet you thought your misspent youth had come back to haunt you, didn't you, Neil?' A chortling Johnny elbowed his brother-in-law in the ribs while tearing open a packet of cigarettes.

'She's a real looker; she can't be one of his kids.' Jake joined in the ribbing, aware Neil could handle a joke.

'Seriously though, I'm pleased as punch to have another sister,' said Johnny. 'And what a lovely kid she is.' He handed round the Woodbines and the others helped themselves, murmuring agreement to his comment about Elise's beauty in looks and character.

Johnny and his wife, Dora, had returned from Southend for this family get-together, bringing their little boy William to meet his new aunt. Their grandparents had decided against the journey and remained at their bungalow by the sea.

'I'm surprised Sidney didn't get out of France in good time,' said Neil. 'Never knew him well but Clover said he wasn't backwards in looking out for number one.'

The trio of men were standing outside the house on the front path, getting a breath of fresh air while the welcome party for Elise was in full swing inside. Johnny cupped a palm around a struck match and they lit their cigarettes before resuming the discussion.

'Dad was shrewd but he was slowing down. I noticed that the last time he came back.' Johnny had taken the news of their father's death as philosophically as his sisters. From when they were children they'd got used to his roving eyes and feet taking him away from them. Impetuous and belligerent, they'd accepted a time would come when Sidney Cooper was unable to outrun trouble and they'd never see him again. It seemed he'd met trouble head on though and surprised them all in bowing out heroically.

Jake only shared a mother with his siblings, so talk of Mr Cooper's demise didn't affect him as keenly as the others. 'Never met Sidney myself,' he said reflectively.

'Didn't miss much.' Johnny sounded resigned rather than bitter. 'He let his French kids down as well but did what he could to protect them at the end. So God rest him, I say.'

Three bottles of brown ale, perched on the front window ledge, were gathered up, clinked together and swigged from in a toast to Sidney.

'I hope the lad's all right over there. He's without family now, apart from his Grandma Bouchard,' said Neil. 'He'd better make sure he keeps one step ahead of the Nazis. They'll be after him.'

'Elise reckons her brother's got his head screwed on.' Johnny was also concerned about his half-brother. He felt he knew Luc already as Elise had spoken affectionately and at length about him earlier that day. 'The boy's got balls. He could've escaped to England with his sister but stayed to fight.'

'Speaking of fighting,' said Jake. 'There's something I've been meaning to say.' He flicked ash, looking thoughtful. 'I've had my papers so won't be around for much longer. Would you keep the business ticking over while I'm gone, Neil?'

"Course ... you don't need to ask me about that.' Neil gripped his boss's shoulder. 'Anyhow, you're a builder so might get an exemption. Once the bombing starts there'll be plenty of repair work around for the likes of us.'

Jake shook his head, grinding his cigarette butt underfoot. 'I'm enlisting; I don't want Adam growing up speaking German.' He plunged his hands into his pockets and stared up moodily at the sky. 'Us Brits are on our tods now the French are out of it so it's all hands on deck to stop an invasion.'

'Ain't joining the navy are you?' Johnny sounded indignant.

'Nah; can't swim for a start.' Jake smirked. 'Army'll do me.'

'Better get your sunhat sorted out then,' said Johnny. 'A bleedin' hot desert is where the likes of us'll be heading next. Libya's my guess. Or Egypt.'

'Got me hat, and a bucket 'n' spade for the sandcastles,' said Jake. 'Can't see it being much of a holiday though.'

'Me neither.' Johnny's memory was jogged to Dunkirk beach and his larky mood evaporated. He finished his cigarette in a long, savage drag.

With the noise of laughter and Bing Crosby crooning in

the background, the trio weren't immediately aware of a vibration in the atmosphere.

During the lull in their banter Jake had been contemplating the twilight on the horizon and was thus first to notice an irregular shadow approaching, then separating into individual aircraft. Enemy planes would be heading inland rather than towards the coast so he wasn't unduly worried. He drew his companions' attention to the sky with a pointing finger.

'That's a squadron of Spitfires looking ready for business,' said Johnny in an ominous tone.

Neil sighed and shook his head. Of them all, only he had been old enough to serve last time. He had the scars to show for it . . . and the nightmares that woke him trying to claw his way out of an eiderdown that clung like Somme mud. If it came to it, he would volunteer though, despite his age. He didn't want his kids growing up speaking German either.

They craned their necks to watch the formation pass overhead then continue south.

'Are they going to France?' Clover had appeared, holding the hands of her son and daughter. Vicky trotted to her dad and the dark-haired angel was lifted up to rest her head against his shoulder.

'Luftwaffe will be paying us a visit, not the other way around, is my guess.' Johnny answered his sister's question. 'Some of our Brylcreem Boys will be stationed nearer the coast, ready to meet them.'

Neil exchanged a bleak look with his wife; her nod of defeat told him she'd be accompanying Dora back to Southend with their children.

Elise had also been alerted by the drone of aeroplanes. She quit the warm room filled with beery fumes and gramophone music to come and stand by the open doorway. Her heart was in her mouth as she watched a second squadron of fighters following the first. Up and down the lane neighbours were emerging from doorways, faces tilted up as they muttered blessings for themselves and the pilots. The limbo after Dunkirk had come to an end, was what everybody was thinking. Elise was thinking of Luc and Mathilde.

'Come on you miserable lot, party's not finished yet.' Clover bucked them all up, urging them back inside. 'There's a big chocolate cake needs cutting.' She picked up her son and linked arms with her half-sister. 'Guest of honour gets to cut it, of course.'

'How d'you manage to get enough stuff for a smashing cake like this then, Clo? I can't save enough marge to make a bit of pastry now it's on ration.' Johnny's wife, Dora, came to admire the confection topped with piped butter icing.

'Not my doing.' Clover thumbed at her sister. 'Better ask Annie how she conjured up this marvel.'

'You naughty gel,' said Dora, wagging a finger at Annie. 'Have you pinched stuff out of your lady's larder?'

'No, I have not.' Annie tossed her chestnut brown curls in mock indignation. 'I would've, if I'd had to.' She winked. 'I didn't need to though. I told her that my sister had escaped from France and we were celebrating with a party. She was most impressed by Elise's bravery and said I could take whatever I needed for a chocolate gateau. I'd made one for her son's birthday last month, you see, and she thought it was the best she'd tasted. She can be a good soul sometimes but when she's not . . .' Annie pulled a gargoyle face.

Elise chuckled and tucked in to her cake. There were definitely hints of Sidney Cooper in his children, she thought.

The good, fun part that her father hadn't displayed often enough. 'Mmm ... this is delicious. You should open a patisserie ... a cake shop,' she translated.

'Might just do that 'n' all.' Annie stooped to kiss her new sister on the cheek. 'Glad you like it, sweetheart.' She ran an envious hand over Elise's ebony-dark hair. 'You're as pretty as Hedy Lamarr, y'know. Wish I had your film star looks ...'

'Stop fishing for compliments, you. And it's my turn to sit next to Elise.' Jake's wife, Rebecca, good-naturedly nudged her sister-in-law off the chair arm then perched in her place. 'Clover said a soldier from Poplar helped you escape from France. She told me his name but I've forgotten it.'

'Nathaniel Hawkes,' said Elise, wiping crumbs from her mouth with her hanky.

'I'll ask Jake if he knows him.'

'It's all right, Neil's already said he doesn't recognise the name ...' Elise was too late to stop Rebecca trotting off to fetch her husband.

He approached with a smile for the new sister he'd met in a rousing welcome earlier in the day. In Elise he'd recognised the bashfulness he'd felt when scooped up by this rowdy family five years ago. The Cooper welcome had been warm and sincere but he'd felt slightly apart from the others, being their mother's illegitimate son. Sometimes he still did feel an outsider although he would never mention it and upset any of them. Especially Clover, who was the hub of the family and unfailingly gracious and loyal to everybody.

'A soldier called Nathaniel Hawkes helped Elise get to England. He comes from Poplar and is about our age. Ring any bells, Jake?'

'Well ...' He frowned and scraped a hand through his fair

hair. 'I do recall a Nat Hawkes from when I was a school kid in Stepney. Not seen him since I was about fourteen.' Jake crossed his arms and considered. 'I got on all right with him actually. I heard he moved up north though. What does your Nathaniel Hawkes do in civvies?'

'He's a river worker,' Elise said. She relished going over their conversations and keeping Nathan alive in her mind. But whether choice or circumstance was keeping him away, pining for him wouldn't help. She'd been in England for over a month; if he was back she had to accept he might not look for her.

'Was I being pushy, mentioning him?' Rebecca sat down beside Elise on the sofa as her husband headed off to get another beer.

'Of course not.' Elise budged up to make room. 'Corporal Hawkes will find the Silvertown Coopers if he wants to. He got us to Dunkirk, though I'm not sure how when we made one diversion after another to keep the Nazis off our backs.'

'Must've been terrifying for you.' Rebecca shivered.

'There wasn't time to be afraid; we just had to keep going. I felt safe while Nathan was around, even on the beach. He looked after me.' She rejected the memory of the soldier who'd attacked her and concentrated on dashing across the sand with him to the *Kentish Belle*. She wouldn't accept that watching him being buffeted by the waves might be her final memory of him.

Annie was dancing with her brother Johnny and Elise began tapping a hand and foot in time to the music belting out of the gramophone. She determinedly cheered herself up and hummed along to 'In the Mood', but Glenn Miller's band couldn't block out a whine of dive bombers in her head.

'You'll get used to the noise.' Rebecca had leaned closer to whisper in Elise's ear, startling her. 'Sorry, didn't mean to make you jump. They're a boisterous lot.' She jerked a nod at the assembled Coopers. 'Salt of the earth though, and pretty normal compared to my family.' She rolled her deep brown eyes but didn't elaborate.

'I thought there was another sister,' said Elise. 'Dad told us he had a son and a daughter and twin girls. That was all Luc and I knew of the Coopers.'

'Ah ... you mean Annie's twin. Jake never knew that sister either. Rosie passed away when she was four; she went down with Spanish flu poor little love.'

Elise let that sad news sink in. Her father hadn't mentioned that one of his children had died; but then he wouldn't. The tragedy could explain why he had returned to France seeming depressed after his final visit to England.

'Jake was about your age when he found out he was part of this family,' said Rebecca. 'He'd been adopted as a baby, you see, by a Mr and Mrs Harding.' Rebecca gazed at her strapping blond husband. 'We got married about the same time and it was lovely to have a wedding reception with all of these people we hardly knew. They're a real hoot. Anyway, I expect Jake will tell you all about it one day.'

Elise stared at Jake, feeling a particular bond with him although they shared no blood at all. In looks they were poles apart too.

'Do you remember who this lady is?' Rebecca asked her five-year-old son as he squeezed in to sit beside her.

'Auntie Elise,' Adam said without hesitation.

His mother ruffled his fair hair in praise.

'You look just like your dad,' Elise said and received a shy smile.

'I think so too,' said Rebecca. 'Clover said you used to work in a dress shop in France. Will you look for similar work here?'

'I've a part-time job at the primary school at the moment. The headmistress wanted somebody to translate for the refugees and Clover put my name forward.' Elise smiled. 'I enjoy it there ... reading and writing with the youngsters and helping their parents to understand the forms that need filling in.' She paused. 'The school's closing at the end of the summer term though. I've applied to a munitions factory and have an interview next week ...' She broke off as a hand was rested on her shoulder.

'There's a man at the door asking for you, love. I did invite him in but ...' Clover indicated with a jerk of the head that the visitor remained in the hallway. 'It's not him, I'm afraid,' said Clover and rubbed Elise's cheek in comfort as the hope died in her eyes.

'This fellow's called Graham Yates.'

For a few seconds Elise was unsure why the name seemed familiar. 'Oh, I do know him. It's Faith's brother!' she exclaimed, jumping to her feet. She edged out of the packed room into the coolness of the corridor.

'He's welcome to come in and join the party if he can stand the noise and the crush,' Clover poked her head around the door to call after her.

The fellow had his army cap tucked beneath an arm. He raised the other to thank the hostess and let her know he was fine where he was.

'I would've guessed who you were.' Elise approached him with a smile of welcome. 'You and Faith are very alike.'

'You won't be friends with her for long, talking like that. She says she's much better looking than me.' He clasped

Elise's outstretched fingers. 'Faith told me you were beautiful. Usually my sister's prone to exaggeration. Not this time though.'

Elise clucked her tongue at his flattery but already felt at ease in his company. His wry sense of humour seemed similar to Faith's. 'How is she? And your parents? Have you seen them recently? I've not had a letter from Faith for a few weeks ...'

'I can help with that.' Graham released her and drew an envelope from his pocket. 'I've just got back from Broadstairs actually. Faith asked me to deliver this.' He sighed. 'Our parents are fine ... my sister's not so good.'

'What's happened?' Frowning, Elise took the letter. 'Isn't she well?'

'Her boyfriend's missing in action. The Lancaster was brought down about a week ago and no news of survivors so far.' He dipped his head at the letter. 'I expect she's told you in her own way about it. She's not given up hope. Bob could be a prisoner of war, or injured and trying to find a way back to England under his own steam.'

Elise dropped her hands away from her dismayed face. 'Poor Faith. How rotten for her.' Tears stung her eyes and she wished she wasn't so far away from Broadstairs so she could rush to comfort her friend. Bob Pearson might never know his marriage proposal had been accepted.

'It's all a bloody rotten business, 's'cuse my French,' said Graham flatly. 'Now, how have you settled into London life, Elise? You don't mind if I call you Elise, do you? And please call me Graham.' Without waiting for a reply he carried on, 'Must be strange for you being uprooted so suddenly. I expect you miss your family and France, don't you?'

'I do ... very much.' It was the first time she'd admitted that to anybody. She was utterly grateful to have this sanctuary and this family around her, but her thoughts were constantly with Luc and Mathilde, and whether they had been arrested.

In Silvertown she had been given a small bedroom of her own with furniture that smelled of beeswax polish. The sheets were crisp and clean and the single bed comfortable; but she rarely slept past the small hours. And that wasn't solely due to little Jamie often being fretful at night.

Her restless mind would fly to Lille and dart into secret places that only a few locals would be aware of. Luc could find those hideaways. She imagined him sleeping on cold hard ground with the smell of fetid water in his nostrils, listening for the enemy soldiers searching for him. They'd used that den as children. The 'dungeon', they'd called the cave-like space that was only big enough for a few people to hide inside. It had been dug beneath a road bridge spanning a rivulet that disappeared into the bowels of the earth.

From breakfast to dusk they would remain outside playing during summer's long holiday. Their camp was a favourite place despite the foul smell of the slow-moving water. It never put them off their bread and cheese lunches packed by their mother. They'd tuck in and listen to footsteps passing overhead. Their grandfather had told them about it but their grandmother had stopped him speaking of the fugitives who'd made the bolthole during the last occupation.

'Only if you want to, of course.'

'Oh, I'm sorry, I missed what you said.' Elise gestured apology that she'd been miles away.

'I wondered if you'd like to see a show and perhaps a bit of London. The west side of town's quite different to the East End: shops and theatres and bright lights,' said Graham. 'Might as well make the most of it before things get worse. That could be any day now, unfortunately.'

'You saw the Spitfires as well.'

'I did.' He seemed about to say more but returned to a pleasanter subject. 'What do you reckon, Elise? Fancy a night out on the town with me?' He put up his hands declaring his innocence. 'No strings attached. And please don't think you have to say yes to be polite.'

'Has Faith bullied you into looking after me?'

He blushed and poked a finger inside his collar. 'Well, she did ask me to call and make sure you're all right. But that's not the only reason I want to show you a bit of London. I've already taken to you; I'd like us to be friends, too.'

Elise knew she'd like that as well. Graham Yates seemed a sincere sort of chap. 'I'd love to see London with you. Thank you.' She paused. 'Do you live in that part ... in the bright lights?'

He nodded. 'In a flat just off Wardour Street. My employer rented it for me. Jolly decent of him too I thought even though parts of Soho are a dive and the flat is poky.'

Poky or not, it didn't sound like the sort of treatment a new recruit to the military would get. She judged him to be about twenty-three or twenty-four. He wasn't as fair as his sister; his hair was a sandy colour and his eyes a lighter blue than Faith's. He had his father's compact wiry build, but unlike Ronald Yates, Graham didn't seem a man used to working outdoors. His skin was pale and his hands soft and clean. 'Faith said you were training in London; I thought you'd just joined up.'

'I'm an army lieutenant but I have been training. I got shoved sideways into a different department after the Dunkirk fiasco. I'm based at the War Office.'

'Would you like a drink or something to eat? There's chocolate cake.' Elise indicated the room where the sound of the children could be heard. Adam was laughing and little Jamie grizzling. She'd noticed that William was the quietest of the bunch, quite content to sit on the sofa and play with his toy truck, which was odd considering his parents were the rowdiest of the lot. Vicky would sit with her cousin William, disapprovingly contemplating the noisy adults in the way small girls did. Elise had loved meeting her niece and nephews.

'Thanks, it all sounds a hoot.' Graham chuckled, cocking an ear to the general hubbub. 'But I'd better shove off. Got a few things to do, actually.' He rotated his cap in his hands. 'How about if we make a date for next Saturday? I'll find out what's showing at the theatres and pick you up about seven, if that's all right? We could have a bite to eat as well.'

'I'll look forward to it,' said Elise.

He gave her hands a farewell squeeze then leaned to peck her cheek. Before moving onto the front step he said, 'Those Spitfires and Hurricanes we saw ... there'll be dogfights soon over England. Things will hot up over here so take care, all of you.' He glanced into the hallway, listening to the sweet sounds of family life. 'Keep those blackout curtains in place. And it might be best to evacuate the children out of London.'

Elise had noticed the look that had passed between Clover and Neil. They knew London was no longer safe. She stepped onto the path to wave Graham off as he looked over a shoulder at her, tipping his cap in a salute.

About to go back inside, Elise noticed Jake was standing on the opposite pavement with a stranger. He didn't appear to be as happy to have a visitor as she'd been. Jake suddenly prodded the other fellow and she could hear raised voices although not what was being said. They'd noticed her silhouetted on the doorstep in a weak glow of light.

Her first reaction was to act normally and wave; her second was to acknowledge that the men seemed quite alike, although Jake was slimmer and taller. Elise stopped staring and retreated inside before they thought she'd been spying on their argument.

'My friend's brother came to see me ... the people I met in Broadstairs.' Elise blurted an explanation for why she'd been outside.

'My brother came to see me.' Jake had caught her up in the hallway. He lit a cigarette and offered her the pack, pocketing it when she declined.

'I thought you looked similar,' said Elise.

'We don't have the same birth parents. We were adopted by the Hardings.' Jake dragged on the cigarette. 'You probably noticed we don't get on.'

'That's a shame.' She sounded sympathetic. 'When I turned up here I was very nervous. I wasn't sure they'd like me being as their father left them to be with us in France. I've been luckier than I could have hoped for.'

'I felt the same when I found out the Coopers were my family and I was the illegitimate odd one out. Did you always know your real parents, Elise?'

'I did ... although Sidney would regularly go off and leave us when we were small. After my mother died, he left again and Grandma brought us up. He was gone a long while; we weren't expecting him to come back but he did.'

'At least you knew them both. I never knew my real mum and dad. Wish I had.'

'How old were you when you were adopted?'

'About nine months, I think.' He took a final drag on the cigarette and flicked the butt out of the open doorway. 'I was whipped off to a convent just after being born so Sidney Cooper wouldn't know his wife had been unfaithful.'

Elise's grimace showed her understanding of her father's nature, and of what the outcome would have been if he had found out. 'Who was your dad?'

'The real love of Iris Cooper's life, so Clover told me.' He smiled wryly. 'I don't think she said it to be kind or to excuse our mum's infidelity. I think it's the truth. I know who he was, and that he was also married with a family. Even if I'd wanted to meet him it'd be too late. He died when I was still a kid.' Jake had never felt the need to make himself known to the other side of his family. The Coopers were enough for him. And he had his beloved wife and son. 'Did you leave somebody special behind in France? Don't mean your family ... a man?'

'Yes,' she said simply, feeling she could talk to Jake about this. 'Nathan Hawkes. I know we only just met and I'm not sure how he feels about me ...' She paused and frowned. 'No, I do know. I mean something to him. Anyway, I hope he's home. It'll be my fault if he didn't make it. He looked after me ... gave up his place on the boat to me.'

Jake put a hand on her shoulder as she sorrowfully bowed her head. 'Sounds like you mean more than just something. I reckon you were special to him. If he's the Nat Hawkes I knew he would've acted like that. A gentleman in the making was Nat.' He said ruefully, 'The Barnardo's home must've done a better job on him than me.'

'You're a lovely man, and you know it, so don't go digging for compliments,' Elise said flatly, in the manner of a sister slapping down a brother.

Jake burst out laughing. 'No chance of getting a swollen head around you is there?'

'None whatsoever.' She giggled but her thoughts were soon back with Nathan. 'He spoke of his mum and dad. Nathan *was* illegitimate and his dad left them for good. He didn't mention an orphanage though ...'

'What're you two doing out here? Come on, we've opened the sparkling wine,' called Clover from the doorway.

'On me way then,' said a grinning Jake. He rubbed Elise's shoulder and gestured for her to go first.

She entered the warm room and was welcomed with a glass of bubbling wine and a rousing cheer.

'To Elise and her family in France and to all of us lot. And here's to keeping safe and getting this war over with toot sweet.' Neil's toast was loudly sanctioned by everybody.

Elise sipped her wine, wishing she'd been able to finish her talk to Jake and find out more about the orphanage. It wasn't just that though. Jake seemed troubled and because she already felt an affinity with him, she wanted to know why.

She smiled and joined in the conversation, but her mind was in France. Was Luc hiding under the bridge in their childhood den? Dunkirk would have similar wartime hideouts, relics from years ago. But Nathan Hawkes wouldn't find any without help from locals ... if he was still there and still alive.

Chapter Nine

'Move! Out of the way. *Schnell!*'

Luc Bouchard touched his uniform cap and got back into the ambulance. He let off the handbrake and the vehicle rolled over ruts down the sloping road. The Nazi who'd snarled at him in broken French continued glaring so he shrugged another apology. That seemed to do the trick; the soldier turned his attention, and his weapon, back on the work party, herding them towards an open-backed truck loaded with equipment. Luc pulled on the handbrake, surreptitiously watching what was going on.

The group of prisoners numbered about a dozen. They all looked sullen and exhausted and remained unresponsive to the big mouth's barked commands. He didn't like being ignored and rifle-butted the closest man. The others were more inclined to understand what they were being told to do after that. The felled British soldier lay still, blood welling on his temple. Luc clenched his fists in impotent rage. He would've liked to give the Nazi thug a taste of his own medicine but daren't intervene.

The Allied prisoners of war were wearing their filthy army uniforms: mostly French, but Luc counted another in

English battledress keeping the unconscious private company. Shovels were being issued along with directions for the rubble blocking the road ahead to be cleared into the ditches. Luc started counting again: three guards in all. One standing on the back of the truck and two patrolling with machine pistols.

After he'd left his grandmother's house he had secretly dossed down for the night in his employer's barn before heading across country towards Hazebrouck. The perilous journey hiding from the enemy took him weeks, and by that time his wound was hot and throbbing and so was his head. He'd located the church and thankfully the priest his grandmother had told him about. By then he was out on his feet and Father Pascal had brought a retired nurse from the village to attend to him. She had applied a poultice, redressed his infected arm and told him he had a fever. The woman was a trustworthy friend from the old days the priest had assured him.

After a week's convalescence hidden in the church, he'd told these new friends he'd soon be well enough to work and earn some money. He needed to move to his own lodging and set up a new identity; if the priest was discovered hiding somebody in the church his cover would be blown and a fledgling network of dissidents dismantled before it had properly been established.

The nurse suggested Luc apply to the convent hospital as an ambulance driver as he could drive a tractor. Use of a vehicle always came in handy, the priest had told him, rubbing his hands in anticipation. Luc did some training and got the job. He'd surprised himself by meeting their requirements for driving and first aid. Not that he'd admitted to being a teenage farm hand; he was now Louis

Marron, twenty-one years old, and newly unemployed as his pharmacist boss had fled France with his family. The nurse had said the chemist angle might help him get a foot in the door of a hospital. Better than admitting his experience of things medical was limited to dosing cattle with wormer, in any event. She had coached him on the names and uses of common drugs but luckily he wasn't asked too many questions.

The hospital's patients were mostly civilians but there were a couple of wounded Germans occupying beds. Yesterday a Luftwaffe pilot had been brought in. His bullet-holed Messerschmitt had limped back to land in France after a dogfight. Luc had avidly eavesdropped on the staff gossiping about the air battles over Britain that the RAF were winning. It was surprising how much these men boasted about their missions when being nursed by a young nun with soft hands. These women seemed against the occupation but Luc kept his opinions strictly to himself; it was impossible to tell who might be a rotten apple.

His brooding was curtailed by an impatient banging and some gruff complaints. His passenger was demanding to know when he intended to free her. He hopped out of the ambulance and hastily opened the back doors. Distracted by his thoughts, he'd forgotten about the elderly patient he was bringing home. The spinster had suffered a heart attack at the beginning of the week but had been deemed healthy enough to be discharged after a few days. She'd announced to the Sisters – and to Luc on the journey – that she'd rather curl up her toes in her own bed than stay in hospital an hour longer breathing the same air as the Boches. A sight of the detested enemy yards away started her muttering beneath her breath. Luc got her down and hurried her towards her cottage, but not speedily enough to prevent her aiming spittle at the Nazis.

He politely refused the old girl's offer of a drink of beer before he left. She was quite steady on her feet and becoming increasingly vociferous about her dislike of the Germans so he quickly closed the door. He strode back to the ambulance and from behind the raised clipboard shielding his features watched the prisoners through the windscreen. The gun-butted private was still on the ground and Luc didn't think he was putting it on. He was a short thin fellow and seemed familiar, but it was difficult to get a good look at him beneath his bush of whiskers. The thuggish soldier turned around, doubtless wondering why he'd not driven off.

Luc made a show of ticking off names on his clipboard then stowed it on the passenger seat and tried the ignition ... but not too skilfully, in case the engine started. He gestured his frustration and got out, a rag in one hand and a spanner in the other, to tinker with the engine while covertly watching the prisoners. He made mental notes of what he saw to report back to the priest later. Father Pascal deemed all intelligence about the enemy's movements useful.

The private on the ground had stirred and made an effort to rise. His British comrade tried to assist him up despite a gun gesturing him back into line. The outstretched arm had a corporal's insignia on the sleeve.

A surge of excitement made Luc clumsy and he almost dropped the spanner into the van's innards. He began bashing it against the Citroën's radiator in the hope the corporal would pay attention and give Luc a better view of his face. He was breathing hard, sure that beneath a covering of dirt and matted beard was the corporal he'd entrusted Elise to. That would make the injured man Evans, the short fusilier they'd also met in the forest. Luc was desperate to discover what had happened to his sister.

A pair of sunken eyes in hollows beneath heavy brows was looking his way. Luc removed his cap and stared intently for no more than a second for fear of drawing the wrong attention. The cap was soon back on his head and adjusted to conceal his features. He resumed tightening nuts and bolts, hoping his meaning had been clear enough. He peeped up and saw one side of the Tommy's mouth pull aslant, followed by an imperceptible nod. Grimy knuckles were scraped to and fro on a bristly cheek with the thumb pointing most definitely upwards.

Luc felt his chest expand in joyous relief. He used the spanner to casually point at the back of the ambulance. Getting the corporal inside it was going to be no easy task, but he would leave the doors unfastened in case fate dealt them a decent hand in the next few seconds. He couldn't leave the man behind after what he'd done for them. Luc wiped grease off the spanner with the rag and swung himself up behind the wheel before the thuggish guard came to investigate.

Evans had struggled onto his knees, halfway to standing up. He made it to his feet but couldn't find his balance and staggered backwards into the ambulance's path. Luc unintentionally knocked him flat again. The accident distracted the Nazis. They started bellowing abuse at Luc, who wound down his window and protested his innocence with much gesticulation, blaming the clumsy idiot. Two of the French prisoners seized the opportunity to make a run for it. Immediately the soldiers were after them and shots were fired when they refused to heed orders to halt. One man collapsed to the ground, the other made it into the trees. The pandemonium encouraged others to try their luck.

And so was Luc determined to make the most of it while two of the guards were mobilising the truck to pursue the French absconders disappearing into the woods. The youngest Nazi had a gun pointed at the less courageous prisoners, bellowing encouragement for their comrades and jeers for their captors. The youth looked nervous, as though wishing his colleagues would return to back him up.

After pulling on the handbrake, Luc jumped out of the vehicle and flung open the rear doors. The injured man was bundled into the back of the Citroën when the corporal refused to leave him. The doors were slammed on both the Tommies and Luc leaped into his seat and set off.

Nobody bothered with the ambulance as it jogged up and down on potholes then picked up speed. Neither did they notice that the injured man and his English comrade had vanished.

Although in a state of panic, Luc instinctively headed towards the church on the outskirts of the town, forcing himself to drive normally. The gunfire had sounded an alert and German vehicles were speeding towards him in the distance. None of the troops roaring past took much notice of the ambulance courteously pulling onto the verge to allow them right of way.

When the final motorcyclist had skidded past and the road was clear, Luc stamped on the accelerator, and ten minutes later veered off onto a dirt track, bringing the ambulance to a halt when he judged they were out of sight of the main road.

He jumped down and rushed to open the back doors.

'Right, what's next?' Nathan said in black humour as he leaped out, easing his weary shoulder muscles.

'Did Elise get away?' Luc embraced the corporal as though he was family. He knew the question was unnecessary. He'd understood the subtle smile and thumbs-up signal.

'She did. On a boat bound for Kent. Have you heard from her?'

'Not yet; I don't know if she'll write. A letter from England might endanger my grandmother. Maybe she'll try to contact us another way.' He shrugged. 'I've been gone from Lille for ages now. I couldn't risk staying there.'

'Your sister was worried you'd copped it.'

'I nearly did.' Luc undulated his shoulder, easing the stiffness that remained in his upper arm. 'Bullet passed straight through and the wound's finally healing well.'

'You were lucky. Your father?'

'Not so lucky,' said Luc, grimly shaking his head.

Nathan gripped his shoulder in sympathy and looked at the meandering line of a bridleway that wound away into the undergrowth. It was marked with horses' hooves and clods of manure. It was a well-screened spot, but obviously not isolated, so they couldn't hang around here. 'Have you a lodging we can go to? Somewhere quiet to rest up for a while?'

Luc snorted a denial. 'I rent a room in a house close to the hospital where I work. I couldn't get you in there without you being seen and I don't know the others well enough to trust them. Gestapo will already be looking for you lot. Those prisoners that weren't shot that is,' he added bleakly.

'Did you make contact with the Resistance?'

Luc nodded and a glimmer of a smile brightened his face.

'A priest. We'll have to wait until dark before approaching the church though. Can't risk blowing the Father's cover.'

A groan from the back of the ambulance drew them towards the injured man. 'He's badly concussed,' said Luc, having briefly examined Evans' head wound. He'd not done more than nudge the fellow over. The damage had been inflicted by the guard's rifle butt.

'Would you take Evans to hospital? You could say you found him staggering about in a meadow. He's in no fit state to deny it. He stands a better chance in a POW camp than being dragged around with a fractured skull.' Nathan frowned, wishing now he'd left his comrade behind for his own good. 'I'll stay out of sight here and make my own way to the church. If the priest can't help, I'll head south—'

'You must be joking,' Luc interrupted. 'I can't go back to the hospital now. The Krauts will already have worked out where you two disappeared to. They'll be waiting to ambush me. Then ...' Luc drew a forefinger across his throat. 'I've been using an alias since I left Lille.' He extended an ironic hand. 'Louis Marron, and pleased to meet you.' He paused. 'You'd better tell me your name.'

'Nathan Hawkes ... pleased to meet you, and thanks for breaking me out. We were due to get transported to a camp in Germany. I didn't fancy spending the rest of the war there.'

'You're welcome. And thanks for looking after Elise.' Luc knew he owed this man more than he could ever repay. He didn't need to ask to know that his sister's safety had stolen this man's liberty. After shaking hands, Luc glanced up at the sky. A depressing amount of blue was visible through the leaves. 'Won't be nightfall for hours yet,' he said gruffly.

'This needs some camouflage.' Nathan began breaking foliage off trees to drape over the Citroën's coachwork.

'Come on. Lend a hand, and get it further under cover,' he said when the younger man seemed sunk in a daze. 'Let's hope nobody comes this way until after we've gone.'

Luc jerked himself into action. He was Resistance now. Not theorising about sabotage, but doing it. And risking dreadful punishment if caught. There was no going back.

'We've a trek in front of us to the church but I daren't drive closer. The Gestapo will raid the place if they see the ambulance close by.' Luc got in and edged the vehicle between the trees, then helped Nathan pile branches on its bonnet and against its doors. The green coachwork helpfully added its own camouflage.

Luc was grateful to Father Pascal for what he'd done for him. The priest had been suspicious of his tale at first, but after a thorough interrogation he'd welcomed in his old comrade Bouchard's grandson. This was different though; the priest wouldn't like this unexpected development. 'The villagers mustn't see us. It's hard to know who to trust. We'll have to move after dark. Maybe your friend Evans will come round by then.'

'Maybe,' said Nathan with little optimism.

It didn't matter that he couldn't understand a word of the rapid French being spoken. From the priest's tone of voice Nathan could tell they weren't welcome. A crouching figure began running back towards them through the shadowy graveyard. Luc Bouchard dropped to a knee behind the massive stone angel where Nathan was hiding with Evans.

'He'll take you in.'

'Are you sure? He didn't sound happy. Can you trust him?'

'With my life I think, and yours. Father Pascal's old school. He was Resistance last time with my grandfather.'

Luc gestured his understanding of the priest's reluctance. 'We've turned up at a bad time. He's already got people in there; they're due to be moved out tonight. Trust takes time but the network needs recruits or nothing will get done.' He paused. 'The courier will get rattled if he spots strangers hanging about. He'll abort the mission.'

'Best get cracking then before he turns up.' Nathan started to pull Evans upright. Luc took the semi-conscious man's other arm. Between them they half dragged, half carried the mumbling private over the bumpy grass and around the tilting headstones then up the step and through the heavy black door of the church, left ajar.

Mon Dieu.' The priest scrutinised the filthy, unshaven soldiers. 'They will need clean clothes,' he said in heavily accented English.

'He'll need a doctor first, Father,' said Nathan.

The priest looked at the fellow with his head hanging low between his shoulders. He spread his hands in defeat. 'I'll try to arrange something. Come this way. You'll want some food and washing water.'

They descended stone stairs worn concave in the centre. In the crypt were two men seated around a small table, silently playing cards. They were dressed in civilian clothes and sent suspicious glances at the new arrivals until the priest turned up the oil lamp and they recognised British uniform.

'Polish pilots,' explained the priest. 'En route to England tonight to help with your air battles.'

'By boat?' asked Nathan immediately. 'Is there room for all of us?' He included Luc in his encompassing gaze. 'You should get out now,' he told him. 'Go to London and stay with your sister.'

Luc shook his head. 'I'm staying to fight.'

Nathan sighed but respect lit his eyes and the dour Poles managed to break a smile.

The priest gave a fierce finger wag. 'The planning is done. Only two bicycles will be available to travel, and the boat is small, already hidden in the dunes.'

Nathan's smile was private as his mind returned to thoughts of sand dunes and Elise. 'We'll wait then,' he said quietly. 'Thank you.'

'We heard shots earlier.' The priest frowned an enquiry.

'That was us. Some French soldiers made a break for it as well.'

'You've disturbed a hornets' nest then,' said Father Pascal bleakly. 'Gestapo will be everywhere, stopping everyone.' He turned to the Polish pilots. 'The courier might not come after this. If he does, will you risk it?'

They nodded in unison and seemed to lack any resentment at their escape being jeopardised by these newcomers. In fact they stood up offering their seats and their cups, filled with coffee poured from a pot on the table.

'My friend might be able to help the poor fellow.' Father Pascal sighed and gazed at Evans. 'But she's not a doctor, and from the look of him, he needs one.'

Nathan took a cup of coffee then sank down onto the stone floor. Evans had been placed on his back on a woollen rug. Nathan wobbled his shoulder to rouse him, hoping to get him to take a sip. One of the pilots knelt down and put his head close to Evans's chest. He felt inside his collar then inside his jacket before staring at Nathan.

'He won't want coffee or a doctor; your friend's dead,' he said.

Chapter Ten

'You little fibber. You told me you'd never make a dancer!'

'I didn't think I would,' said Elise as her partner steered her neatly between the couples gliding over parquet. She promptly trod on Graham's foot, making them both burst out laughing.

The closing chords of 'Moonlight Serenade' faded into polite applause for the band. 'Saved by the bell ... I shan't cripple you after all.'

'I'd suffer any pain to keep you in my arms, my darling.' Graham roguishly twiddled an imaginary moustache.

'Oh, do give over, love,' said Elise, who'd got used to his flirtatious teasing, and to adopting Clover's blunt sayings.

They'd been out together numerous times to a variety of theatres and nightclubs. He'd taught her to waltz and fox-trot beneath dimmed globe lights in sultry atmospheres of cigarette smoke and gin fumes. In France, Elise's social life had been limited to gatherings in the village hall or summer fetes on the green. Those jigs were casual country affairs. But Paris could rival London for sophisticated nightspots. It was just that she'd never had a chance to grow up and visit any before the war ejected her from her homeland. She was enjoying these first experiences of the high life with an urbane gentleman. She felt like a proper adult ... a woman rather than a girl.

With his hand lightly on her elbow they strolled towards their table. Chatting people were holding them up by dawdling in front of them, and Graham turned to her to say, 'I should warn you that Faith seems reluctant to speak about Bob.' His manner had turned serious. 'I tried to bring the subject up when I collected her from the station earlier but she said she was tired and wanted to rest.' He shrugged. 'Perhaps I'm being insensitive and it's all too soon and too painful. Faith might prefer to talk woman to woman with you. I'd let her break the ice though.'

Elise nodded in understanding. There hadn't been an opportunity for the girls to have a proper heart-to-heart yet. Graham and Faith had turned up in a taxi to collect her for an evening out. After a hug it was on with the journey to the West End's bright lights. Questions and answers had been batted back and forth about respective family members, and how Elise liked her job in a munitions factory. She did, although it was noisy, dirty work. Elise in turn had been glad to hear that her friends' parents were both well. After that, their conversation had centred on the hellishly persistent bombardment being inflicted on the country, and on the capital in particular. Londoners were constantly alert to the air raid sirens while attempting to carry on as normally as possible.

Elise had wondered if she'd imagined Faith seemed different. Her brother had noticed it too, though. There was less of the intimacy between them that had existed immediately after Dunkirk. But then those extraordinary times had overruled expectations of stiff upper lips; people had gladly clung to one another for comfort. Months had passed since: the summer had turned into autumn, bringing with it no mellow fruitfulness but endless destruction and numerous civilian casualties. The Spitfires had driven off the Messerschmitt fighter planes, winning that battle for Britain, but now the German Heinkels came instead, relentlessly bombing British cities and the East End of London in particular.

Elise and Graham had been encouraged to dance by Faith, who'd insisted she didn't mind sitting alone. She wasn't alone now. The couples blocking the edge of the dance floor had dispersed, giving them a view of their table and of a louche-looking individual propping himself against it. He appeared to be flirting with Faith while lighting her cigarette. She must have spotted them and warned him they were to have company. He snapped the flame back into the gold case and strolled away.

Graham muttered something beneath his breath about lounge lizards before saying he was off to fetch fresh drinks.

'This is a beauty, and suits your colouring.' Faith caressed the lemon-coloured chiffon skirt of Elise's dress. 'Where are you doing your shopping in London?'

'Second-hand market stalls,' said Elise, settling into her chair. She ironically brushed non-existent specks from her shoulder. 'My sisters know all the best places to go to pick up bargains. I bought it out of my first munitions' pay packet.'

'I could do with something snazzy to wear for nights out in London. You'll have to take me along next time, Elise.'

'I will ... your dress is lovely too. The shade matches your blue eyes. How long are you staying in London?' Elise was grateful to Graham for diplomatically leaving them to have a private chat.

'I'm not sure. No need to rush back to Broadstairs. Dad's not going out on the boat so much now, and neither am I. Things changed for us after Dunkirk. The boat's repaired and he still loves the sea ... so do I but ...' Faith sighed. 'It's hard to describe what it did to us. I expect all the crews feel the same ... those that came back.'

'Dunkirk Club blues, that's what it is, *chérie*. I get them as well.' Elise squeezed Faith's hand resting on the table. 'Sometimes I wonder if it really happened, or was it simply a bad dream. Apart from the part where I met you, of course. And Corporal Hawkes ... I'd go through it again just for that.'

'I'll drink to that,' said Faith and raised her glass.

Elise chinked her port and lemon against the gin in a toast.

'You wanted him to come and find you, didn't you? *Really* wanted him to.'

'I did ...' Elise sighed. 'I can't dwell on it. Or my family. When I do it drives me mad with worry. And guilt. I'm safe, and I don't know if any of them are. That's the worst of it, but there's nothing I can do from here.' Her voice had sharpened, drawing glances from the people at the next table.

'Sorry, love ...' Faith parked her cigarette in the ashtray and half rose from her chair to hug her friend. 'Should've kept my bloody mouth shut.'

'It's all right. Have you heard anything about Bob?' Elise didn't regret blurting it out despite Graham's caution to tread carefully. She'd rather be told to shut up than appear careless of Faith's hurt. 'If you don't want to talk about him, I'll understand.'

Faith retrieved her cigarette and took a hefty drag before saying, 'His mother promised to keep me up to date. She's not been in touch for over a month. The poor woman. I feel so sorry for her. The not knowing keeps hope alive, and hope's cruel and I can't be doing with it.' She ran a finger around the rim of her empty glass. 'I wish everyday Bob hadn't been shot down. I know he's bought it and won't be coming back. I feel rotten, but no point pretending that I'm absolutely heartbroken that we won't be getting married after all.' She paused. 'I wasn't sure it was love. We just drifted together after war was declared. I'd known him for ages as he lived down the road in Ramsgate when he was a kid. After he enlisted he asked me to write to him and I thought it'd be nice to have a boyfriend in the services.' She grimaced ruefulness. 'And Mum was pleased that I seemed settled with a steady dependable bloke. Trouble is, I'm not sure steady and dependable is what I'm after any more. Life's too short to put up with being bored.' She sighed and pushed a blonde curl behind her ear. 'Sound like a bitch, don't I?'

'You do not,' Elise said emphatically. 'You sound like somebody being honest.'

'I can't tell Graham what I've told you. Bob was his best friend when they were at school.'

'I won't repeat anything to your brother.'

'He likes you, you know.' Faith gave a cheeky smile. 'You make a nice couple.'

'I like him,' said Elise. 'He's taught me to dance. Well, after a fashion,' she qualified on a giggle. 'I always make mincemeat of his toes.'

'We can practise foxtrotting around Graham's flat if you like.' Faith leaned forward, elbows on the table and chin propped in her hands. 'Seriously though, you'd make me the best sister-in-law.'

'We are like sisters already,' said Elise. 'Even before I met my stepfamily I thought, well, if they don't like me it won't matter. I've got Faith.'

'I'm glad they're nice people and you've settled in well.'

'I miss Clover since she evacuated with the children,' Elise paused. 'I'm relieved she did though. The end of our lane took a hit last week. Luckily everybody was out. Nobody was killed.' She shook her head. 'When I got back from work the firemen were busy. I felt horribly selfish running past praying it hadn't been us as well.'

'I would've felt the same. Everybody feels the same.' Faith rubbed her friend's arm in sympathy. 'Now London's being blitzed you must feel as though you're out of the frying pan into the fire.'

'At least the Nazis aren't marching down the streets here.' The comment brought Konrad Stein's arrogant face into her mind. It infuriated Elise that she could easily remember what he looked like when images of the people she loved were difficult to hold on to. When pegging out washing or sweeping leaves in the back yard she would break off stalks of rosemary and breathe in their scent to conjure up her grandmother. Likewise, a sight of the dairyman's horse and cart travelling the streets trailing manure could evoke a reminder of Luc on the farm. Her father she remembered clearly; Sidney Cooper's children had gone away from Silvertown though and she was no longer jolted into recognition of his features when with them.

There was no tang of briny water here, only the sour smell of the River Thames. During those final hours together on Dunkirk beach the overcast light of the morning had allowed her a good look at Nathan Hawkes. His image washed away in seconds, however hard she tried to hold on to it. She reminded herself he had hair the colour of caramel and eyes of honey brown. When out shopping, or when walking to and from her factory shifts she would search the crowds for a tall man like that. She'd gone to Poplar and traipsed through markets and peered in through pub windows. Nothing. Nobody compared to him. She despaired that he would remain undiscovered somewhere in France.

'Graham's taking his time with the drinks.' Faith ran a finger inside her glass and licked gin residue.

Glancing around Elise located not Graham but the fellow who'd been with Faith earlier. 'You've got an admirer.' She discreetly tipped her head at the man propped against the bar watching them. 'We saw him lighting your cigarette.'

Faith's smile was smugly content. 'Toby Winters is still hanging around is he? I won't say no if he asks me out. Graham's not keen on him though. They avoid one another socially.'

'Oh, you know him. I thought he was a stranger chatting you up.' Elise took another quick look at him. 'I think I've seen him before.'

'He's a regular in the clubs. High roller.' Faith rubbed together thumb and fingers. 'You might have noticed him when you've been out with Graham. Good-looking, isn't he? He's usually got a pretty girl hanging on his arm ... Ah ... here's the fellow I've been waiting for.' She beamed as Graham arrived and put down three filled glasses.

'Take it easy.' Her brother had watched her picking up the gin almost before it hit the table. 'I'm not carrying you home.'

'Spoilsport,' said Faith and took a gulp.

Elise sensed tension between them but knew what it was to have an older brother lecturing you. She'd never again complain about Luc being a pain in the neck. All she wanted was to have the chance to hug him.

'I hope you're going to introduce me to the ladies, Yates.'

Graham's scowl showed what he thought of the person butting in. He shoved his chair backwards, dislodging the individual leaning on its rail. Once on his feet, he swung around with aggressive speed. 'You know my sister Faith; this is her friend.' He glanced at Elise. 'A work colleague, and I'm sorry he's bothering us ...' was the sum of his introduction.

'Her name's Elise—' Faith began to supply the missing information.

'Elise ...' The man interrupted in a protracted drawl. 'A pretty French name for a beautiful lady.' He bowed. 'As Graham's acting churlish and isn't going to introduce me properly I'll do it myself. Toby Winters at your service. Would you do me the honour of dancing with me, Mademoiselle?' He held out a hand and tipped his head at the dance floor.

'If you like ...' It seemed easier to dance than endure a scene, although Winters was a bit too smooth and cocksure for her liking. The start of a snarl was lifting Graham's top lip, as though he were itching to send the man packing. 'You'll regret asking me though, sir,' she said as she stood up. 'I've just broken Graham's toes.'

'Poor fellow,' Toby purred, extending an indolent hand to her. 'I hope he didn't snivel.'

Elise wanted to give Faith a sisterly smile to let her know she wasn't interested in her high roller but couldn't catch her eye. Faith was watching her fingers grinding out her cigarette in the ashtray.

'I thought it was you.' Winters whirled Elise towards him the moment they reached the edge of the dance floor.

He deftly caught her about the waist, moving them easily through the throng in an accomplished manner that rendered Graham's skill clumsy in comparison.

'Thought it was me?' Elise queried, rather giddy with the speed at which she was being swept along.

'You're my brother's French sister. I wasn't certain until just now when I heard your name.'

Elise was so taken aback she stumbled and trod twice on his foot in quick succession.

'You weren't joking, were you, about your ability to put a fellow on crutches?' He chuckled. 'You should've let me teach you to dance instead of that buffoon Yates.'

'I like Graham very much,' she said forcefully. 'So please don't run him down in my company, Mr Winters.'

'Noted,' he said in a careless fashion.

Elise cocked her head and studied his face, recognising him then as the person who'd been arguing with Jake in the street on the night of her welcome party. There was a definite likeness in the men's features. She wouldn't have made the connection, though, had it not been brought to her attention. In some ways the brothers were chalk and cheese. Toby Winters had a cut-glass accent, whereas Jake spoke like an East-Ender. Elise's handsome blond stepbrother was funny and kind and she already adored him and his wife and child, while Toby Winters had an overindulged, overconfident air she found off-putting; she could understand why Jake didn't get on with him.

'What's the verdict?' he asked drily as she continued studying him. 'Do you recall me from months ago?'

'Just about,' she said.

'I wasn't trying to gatecrash the party. Not that I needed to ... I could hear the jollies from outside.'

His attitude made her hackles rise. He thought himself a cut above Jake, and her too she suspected. Jake had said they'd had the same adoptive parents and had lived together when small; she was curious to know what had happened after that to turn them into such different characters. She wouldn't ask him though. She'd find out from Jake when he was good and ready to tell her. That might not be for some time: he'd done his military training and had been posted to north Africa alongside Johnny. She'd no idea when she could expect to see either of her brothers home on leave.

She allowed a pause to develop so he'd know she'd no intention of rising to his bait. 'We had a marvellous time that evening,' she said lightly. 'You missed out on chocolate gateau. My sister Annie is a wonderful cook.'

'Marvellous times and chocolate cake I can get anywhere, at any time. I would have liked to come in though. I knew you'd be there. You escaped France through Dunkirk. And your father died a hero, so I heard. Exciting stuff for a girl of eighteen.'

'News travels fast in London.' Elise wasn't sure she was happy with her business being so widely known.

He negotiated a path through the waltzing couples and led her off the dance floor out of sight of her friends on the opposite side of the room. Before she could stop him, he'd got her backed against the wall with an arm barring her escape route.

'I saw you speaking to Yates that night. Quite a weird coincidence us having his mutual acquaintance. How did you meet him?'

'Through his sister. Faith and her father have a pleasure boat business and were involved in the Dunkirk rescue. But I expect you already know that.' Elise moved forward, letting him know she was done talking to him. He didn't budge and she stepped back, regretting bumping against his chest.

'I'd like to get to know you better, Elise,' he said. 'Strictly above board, of course. I'm not getting fresh with you. You're a lovely girl ... but a girl all the same. Too young for me.' He brushed a finger over her cheek. 'Put me in my place if you want but I think of you as my family as well as Jake's. He and I have had our differences over the years but we have things in common. How could we not when we spent many years together as brothers?' He gazed at her. 'Jake wouldn't deny that there's an awful lot we do share.'

Elise sensed an undercurrent she didn't understand in his final statement and she'd had enough of being penned in. 'Will you escort me back to my friends, Mr Winters?' She pushed his imprisoning arm down quite roughly. 'I don't mind going back alone if you'd rather steer clear of Graham.'

'Of course I'll take you back,' he said. 'If you'll promise to call me Toby. I've just said I think of you as my extended family ... cousins or something like that. There's no formality needed, surely?'

Elise didn't want to be impolite and say she'd rather he didn't think of her in that way as she didn't reciprocate his feelings. She simply gave him a non-committal smile.

'And please don't think I'm scared of Graham Yates. I can handle him. Would you come out with me so we can get to know one another? We could have tea at the Ritz. Something like that.' When she didn't immediately answer he added, 'Look, I know Graham doesn't like me. Nothing sinister. We're work rivals. Office politics, that's all it is.' He chuckled. 'He resents me paying attention to his sister as well.'

'Were you flirting with Faith just to annoy him?' She suspected this man would do something like that.

'I flirt with everybody, sweetheart.' Toby chuckled. 'It's just my way. No need for jealousy.'

Elise rolled her eyes at his conceit. Unfortunately though, she imagined Faith might be feeling a twinge of needless jealousy. 'I'm going back now. Thank you for the dance.'

He drew her arm through his and they began to walk around the perimeter of the dancefloor towards her friends. After barely covering a yard the wail of air-raid sirens was heard, then seconds later all the lights went out. Grunts and mumbled apologies abounded as people bumped into one another in the gloom while trying to find the exit. Disembodied voices called out, seeking companions. The band members could be heard downing instruments in preparation to quit the podium. A fire escape door just behind them was thrown open and fresh November night air flooded in. People began surging towards the limey light of a full moon illuminating blacked-out streets. Elise and Toby were herded along with them. In that moment she felt as though she were back on Dunkirk beach; being pushed and shoved by men yelling to one another. This wasn't the person she'd had by her side then and in whom she'd willingly put her trust. Elise pulled free of Toby to fight her way back to her friends. 'I can't leave them behind. I have to go and find Graham and Faith,' she yelled over her shoulder.

His response was drowned out by the sound of an explosion coming from the street. Those who'd elbowed themselves to the front, to be first out of the building, were hit by a whoosh of hot air that knocked them into the crowd behind. Drinks left unattended on the tables were sent flying, adding to the pandemonium. The barmen were standing arms outstretched to prevent bottles falling off the shelves. They soon gave that up as an impossible job following a showering in glass from another tremor. They scrambled over the counter out of immediate danger.

'There's no sense in going back inside,' Toby shouted and grabbed her arm. 'You won't get through in any case. Come on... this way. We'll find them in the shelter I expect. Goodge Street Underground is closest.'

With a small cry of frustration, Elise squirmed around to face him. She'd made little progress going against the flow and had received insults for impeding others' escape. Toby propelled her outside into the midst of crowds exiting other nightspots. People were heading pell-mell towards the shelters, away from the bombed buildings that had started to blaze.

'Damn idiots were too late sounding the sirens,' muttered Toby. 'Those Heinkels aren't done yet.' He yanked on her hand, urging her to keep up with him. 'The Underground stations will be jammed to the rafters. I don't fancy an all-nighter in one of those cesspits. I know somewhere better we can go. It's not far ... don't worry, I'll look after you, Elise.'

Chapter Eleven

Overhead, the German bombers were glinting in the moonlight like malevolent moths. Their heavy drone was descanted by the whine of smaller craft engaged in dogfights. The chill in the autumn night had been burned away and the air reeked of Bonfire Night. But that had passed weeks ago. Crashes of falling masonry intermittently penetrated the thump of blood in Elise's ears as she was propelled up a flight of stone steps.

The place she'd arrived at after a five-minute dash turned out to be a house rather than an air-raid shelter. In fact despite the chaos Elise noticed that it was more of a mansion than a house. She had little breath left to demand to know why he'd brought her somewhere like this.

Despite the dangers, Elise was tempted to turn for home. But attempting to reach the East End on foot on such a night would be extremely foolish. Those taxis and buses still in use would be crammed with passengers. Joining forces with her friends wasn't an option either; it would be easier to find a needle in a haystack than Faith and Graham in an overcrowded Underground shelter. She hoped they had stopped searching for her and saved themselves, trusting she would do the same.

Toby used his keys and urged her to enter the gloomy hallway. Suppressing her misgivings, she went inside with him. While he locked up she squinted into blackness, then the flame of his cigarette lighter outlined a torch on a console table. Grabbing it up and with its thin beam wavering before them, he guided her past a wide stairway, their footsteps echoing on the pale marble underfoot.

'Don't be frightened, Elise,' he said in a calm, earnest way quite different from his earlier cavalier manner. 'This shelter has all the comforts of home.' He'd stopped by some wood panelling behind the stairs and she wondered what on earth he was doing until a section of it was opened inwards. Taking her hand, he led the way down some gloomy stone steps. At the bottom, he switched on a light, revealing that they were on the threshold of a large furnished basement room. Chairs were positioned around an Oriental floor rug and a billiards table and a cocktail cabinet were stationed nearby.

'There's our escape route should the worst happen.' He pointed to a side door and beckoned her towards it. 'A path leads around the side of the house and steps go up to the street. Even if the house is hit, we'll be all right.' He drew her towards a sofa. 'Sit down. Make yourself at home,' he said with an easy smile and went to the drinks cabinet. 'What's your poison?'

'I don't want a drink, thanks,' she said but did sit down, sinking into soft chenille upholstery with a sigh. Her court shoes weren't made for sprinting through the streets. She eased one off to rub her sore heel.

He mixed himself a Scotch and soda and turned to look at her. 'That's it, make yourself comfortable. Feeling better?'

She smiled to let him know she was. 'Is this your house?'

There was no need to see the rest of it to know it was a large property in an exclusive part of London.

'It is.' He took a sip of his drink then gestured with the glass. 'My childhood home. Jake's too. We would play down here as kids. We were pirates sailing the seas and this was our hideaway. We'd stash our spoils of war in the ottoman. It used to be over there against the wall.' He indicated the place now occupied by the cocktail cabinet. 'Back then the foe to outwit was the cook and the swag amounted to goodies pilfered from her kitchen. If she guessed where the cakes on the cooling tray went to, she never let on. I expect she knew it was us,' he mused. 'We weren't particularly adept at deceit back then.'

'And now?' Elise asked after a pause.

She didn't get a reply. The chandelier swung, diverting their attention. They waited to see if the vibrating ceiling might shed some plaster.

After some seconds had passed and nothing fell on their heads Toby smiled triumphantly. 'Told you ... safe as houses.' He took the seat opposite her. 'Tell me a bit about yourself while we wait for Fritz to clear off. What have you been up to since arriving? Have you a job?'

'I work at the Royal Arsenal at Woolwich.'

'I say! A bomb girl, are you, Elise?'

'I'm only doing packing ... nothing clever.'

'Maybe in time though you will be. You strike me as a very sharp young lady. Your English is perfect and only a faint trace of a French accent.'

'Thank you.'

'Your father taught you, I suppose.'

'He spoke English to us every day when he was around.'

'Tell me a bit about your job. Are you kept very busy with production?'

'Non-stop,' she said bluntly. 'Overtime is always on offer and it pays well. I'm on nightshift tomorrow.'

'The factory observes a blackout though?'

'Of course they take every precaution with security. And the air defence teams are always set up.'

'Where are those then? By the factory itself?'

She shrugged. 'I've not been there long enough to know much about it. When I arrived in England I took a job assisting at the local school my niece attended. Then it closed down. Most of the children have evacuated.'

'Ah, your niece must be Clover Ryan's daughter.'

'That's right.'

'Tell me a bit about all of the Coopers. Jake's never very forthcoming about them. For a start, the girl who bakes the cakes. I imagine she's older than you are.'

'Yes, she is.' Elise smiled at the reminder of Annie Cooper, who she liked very much. 'My sister Annie's twenty-five and a live-in head cook in a big house. She said she'd show me the square it's on next time she gets a day off. Sometimes she accompanies her employers to their country estate. Her boyfriend works for the same family, although Anthony used to be in service across the road. Now when work takes them out of London they can still see one another.'

'That's a cosy arrangement. I discovered your brother Johnny used to be a bit of a scallywag ... as did Jake, of course.'

'I don't care about that.' Elise's Gallic shrug made him chuckle. 'It runs in the family. My father used to be a bit of a scallywag too.' Clover had already informed her with a wink that her brothers had somewhat misspent youths but were now reformed characters and doting husbands and fathers.

'You're a loyal little thing, aren't you?' Toby said and gazed at her over the steeple he'd made of his fingers.

'Oh, I am,' she said. 'Very.'

'And your family in France? Jake said you were orphaned and turned up out of the blue without your brother.'

She was grateful for his attempt to take their minds off the chaos outside. She'd rather not dwell on it either, although as the rumbling went on it was hard not to wonder what damage might be revealed when dawn broke. She was sure this would turn out to be the worst air raid so far. Selfish though it might seem, she'd sooner the West End took the brunt of it for a change than the East End.

'My brother remained in France.' She was aware he had leaned towards her, trying to catch her eye and put a stop to her brooding. 'Luc wanted to stay and fight.'

'How can he if the French surrendered?'

'Not everybody surrendered, even if the army did.' She sounded proud and made no attempt to hide her disgust for the Vichy French authorities now in charge and kowtowing to Hitler. 'There will be others like Luc who won't give up so easily. They'll remain loyal to de Gaulle.'

'Ah ... Resistance fighters you mean.' Toby settled back, his expression displaying his interest in the topic under discussion. 'Are networks already set up that you know of around Lille?' He paused. 'That is where you lived, isn't it?'

'In a village close by, but my brother won't hang around there now.'

'Where will he go?'

'I'm not sure. I haven't been in touch with Luc since I came to England. I wish very much that I could contact him; I've no idea if he and my grandmother are all right.' Elise chewed her lower lip and blinked back her tears. 'Do you live here alone?' A reverberation from the continuing bombardment was penetrating the walls but the house itself seemed perfectly serene.

'I do, apart from the staff, and there aren't many of those. The housekeeper is going deaf; she's a curmudgeonly old girl but a decent cook. She's probably in her room. She won't let the Luftwaffe disturb her routine. A cleaning lady comes in during the week. I don't need much help as I'm rarely here for meals and don't make much mess.'

Elise digested that; it seemed odd to live in a mansion and hardly use it. Jake had told her that his brother was younger than he was by a few months. She knew little else about Toby Winters other than he seemed to inspire few people to like him. She guessed he wasn't married as he described himself as a flirt. But then you never knew with some men – like her father – whether or not they were careless adulterers. So she decided to ask. 'It's a big house for just you. I thought maybe your wife or parents lived with you.'

'God no! I'm far too young to be married and far too old to be living with my parents even if I had one of them still alive. I'm twenty-three and my mother and father died years ago.'

'Oh, I'm sorry to hear that.'

'No need to be,' he said blithely. 'The only one of them I liked died when I was six or seven . . . too long ago for me to remember much about Rupert Harding. My mother remarried and had a sprog. The boy's at boarding school now. She was pushing it a bit getting pregnant for a second time in her late forties. It didn't go well and that was the end of her and my new sister. About six years ago, that was.'

Elise was taken aback that he could recall the tragedy so

unemotionally. He hadn't been a youngster when he lost his mother; he would have been seventeen by her calculation. 'Do you see your little stepbrother?'

'Thankfully not. When the brat's home from school he lives with his father and stepmother. Ian Winters was married again before his wife was cold in her grave. I never wanted his name. I didn't get on with him and still think of myself as a Harding.'

'Jake kept that name.'

'Jake was long gone by the time Ian Winters arrived on the scene. My brother was sent back to an orphanage when he was just a kid. Didn't he tell you?'

'He did tell me he was a Barnardo's boy.' The memory of having a heart-to-heart with Jake in turn reminded her they'd spoken about Nathan Hawkes. She felt a pang of emotion tighten her belly as she thought of him. The passing months hadn't mellowed her longing to know what had happened to him ... where he was ... whether he thought of her as constantly as she thought of him.

'I missed Jake at first when he went away.' Toby swirled the whisky in his glass.

'I expect your mother did too,' Elise said. 'It must have been horrible for her to have to give one of you up.'

'I'm not sure she had to; rather she chose to, to keep up appearances and continue living here. Violet Harding could be a cold fish.'

Elise bit her tongue on saying it took one to know one. She was happy to let him kill time reminiscing about his and Jake's history while they waited for the all-clear.

'It was our father's idea to adopt orphans, not hers,' said Toby. 'Jake ended up back where he started after Rupert Harding was robbed and murdered in the street. Mother claimed she couldn't afford to keep two of us.' Toby finished his drink in a gulp. 'Anyway, I won the raffle and stayed in Mayfair. I attended public school and Cambridge University then was offered a job in the City by one my stepfather's friends. Jake went to Stepney and at fourteen was living on his wits after he left the Barnardo's home.' Toby abruptly ended his confessional by standing up and going to the cocktail cabinet for a refill.

'Maybe Jake was the lucky one,' said Elise, surprised he had divulged so much about himself to somebody he barely knew. For all his privileges and swagger, Toby Winters didn't seem half as content as Jake.

'Maybe he was lucky at that,' Toby agreed sourly. 'Certainly he was fortunate in missing having Winters as a stepfather.' He didn't expound on it, but instead he said, 'Most people are shocked to hear our father was murdered. You took it in your stride.'

'I already knew about that. Clover explained a good deal to me about the various family histories before she went away. I miss her very much, and our chats.'

'What else did she tell you about Jake and me, and our ... differences?'

'Nothing that I can recall. Clover's not a gossip. She said very personal things are best left to the people concerned to reveal when they're ready.'

An expectant pause followed but he didn't say anything else about himself – rather he turned the spotlight onto her. 'Your father also came to a sticky end.'

'He did,' she said and left it at that.

'Sorry, didn't mean to upset you.' Toby placed a hand on her shoulder. 'It seems we have suffered similar woes, you and I: losing our fathers violently and being separated from our brothers.' He shot back the whisky and put down his glass. 'Right, then ...' He began prowling to and fro with his hands dug into his pockets, ruining the line of his evening jacket. 'I'm feeling rather peckish,' he said with a boyish smile.

In that moment he looked appealingly bashful despite his suave get-up. She had a glimpse of the lad who would enjoy feasts of pilfered cakes down here with his brother.

'I'll go and see what's on offer in the kitchen and have a gander outside to check the lie of the land. Once we get the all-clear I'll take you home.'

'Thank you; I should get back as soon as possible.' Elise put her shoe back on and stood up. Approaching the side door, she went onto tiptoes to peer out through the fanlight. Things seemed quieter outside but she couldn't see much at all through the taped glass. 'My brother-in-law will be worried about me.'

Toby drew her back against him with an arm around her waist. 'Don't do that.' His throaty voice was close to her ear. 'You might get glass in your beautiful grey eyes if a bomb goes off nearby.'

She eased herself free with a forced smile. So much for his declaration that he wouldn't try to seduce her. She recognised a fondling hand when she felt one.

'I thought you lived alone since the Ryans evacuated.'

'Clover and the children went to Essex. Neil stayed in London to keep Jake's business ticking over while he's away fighting.' She cocked her head. 'Will you volunteer for active service?'

He looked surprised by the question before shrugging. 'I doubt it ... I work in a reserved occupation in the City. It's all a bit hush-hush so don't ask me what I do.' He chuckled.

'I could tell you ... but then I'd have to kill you. And what a waste that would be.'

She smiled, although she didn't think it a particularly funny thing to say. She felt uneasy again. 'Neil Ryan is a lovely man,' she picked up their previous conversation. 'He's a good carpenter and serves part-time in the Home Guard. After tonight he'll not have much time for volunteering; he'll be run off his feet putting houses back together. I don't know how he'll cope with the paperwork after Rebecca's gone. I'll offer to help but I can't type—'

'Where's Rebecca going?' he interrupted.

'To stay with relatives. And not before time. She's been answering telephone calls and dealing with invoices and so on but has decided to take Adam out of London.' Since the Blitz started Jake had been writing to his wife to persuade her to drop everything and travel to her mother's.

'Where are they based ... these relatives?'

His tone had become interrogatory, almost bullying. Rebecca's mother lived in Cambridge, but Elise intuitively knew Jake wouldn't thank her for telling his brother about his family's business. She shrugged and went on the offensive. 'Why were you arguing with Jake that night?'

'You'd better ask him about it.'

Again, that suppressed aggression. 'Sorry, wasn't prying, just making conversation.'

'I'm the one who should apologise.' He thrust a hand through his hair in frustration. 'This damn war's getting to everybody. But that's no excuse for snapping.' He nodded at the sofa. 'Sit down and I'll go on manoeuvres to find us something nice to eat. Who knows? Might even turn up some caviar in the larder. There's probably a bottle of Bollinger about the place to go with it.'

Her expression showed she wasn't impressed. 'A custard cream biscuit and a cup of tea would be nice.'

He laughed in genuine amusement and brushed her cheek with a finger as he passed by on his way to the stairs. 'You're priceless. A mademoiselle who prefers tea to champagne.'

When he had gone Elise took a closer look at her surroundings. She'd been brought up in a cottage with rustic functional furniture, very different from the showy mahogany in here. She wandered to the billiard table and placed her hands on the polished side, frowning while dwelling on the conversation she'd just had with Toby. He seemed bitter when speaking about his parents and his brother. There was something odd about the antagonism between him and Jake that went deeper than the difference in their stations in life. Elise couldn't put her finger on what it was. She gently bowled one of the billiard balls into a side pocket and told herself it wasn't really her business to know about it. But she was curious to know why Toby Winters worked in a government office if he could afford to live like this. He didn't seem a conscientious type, toiling for king and country. So she might ask him, although that wasn't really her business either.

When he hadn't returned after fifteen minutes she grew restless and went up the stairs. She opened the door and stepped into the hallway, looking to and fro. A wall sconce had been lit; its glow puddled yellow on the marble floor and put a glitter in a crystal chandelier suspended from the ceiling. She started to walk along the hall, straining her ears for any sound of aircraft overhead. It seemed quieter outside apart from the clattering bells of the emergency services. But she'd not yet heard the all-clear sounded.

She guessed it must be past midnight and she was eager to go home. She didn't need or want him to take her. Weighing everything up, she realised she'd not felt very comfortable with Toby Winters and wouldn't be sad to lose his company. It was only right to say goodbye though, rather than to simply disappear. She called his name but got no answer. She opened one door of a pair and poked her head inside; the echoing silence in the dark room led her to believe it was a large sitting room. She proceeded further along, looking up, down, and all around at the grandeur ... or perhaps it was just her innocent eye that made it seem so. Hearing the sound of a male voice, she hurried towards it, thinking he must be talking to his housekeeper. He'd probably roused the poor woman to prepare some food for them. Elise wished he'd not done that for her benefit.

She reached a door and put her ear to it. Satisfied he was inside talking to somebody she was about to open it but hesitated and inclined close to the panel again. Within seconds her features froze and she snatched her hand away from the brass doorknob as though it had scalded her. She didn't move her head though; she listened intently, realising he must be alone and using a telephone as his was the only voice and at intervals there was silence while he listened.

She backed away and headed quickly towards the exit. She hadn't heard German spoken since Konrad Stein barked orders at his men on the last day of her father's life. She'd learned elementary German at school and knew *die Französin* translated as the French girl. She suspected Toby Winters had been talking about her.

'You weren't leaving me without saying goodbye, were you?'

She was struggling to turn the iron key in the large front door when she was startled into whirling around. Her legs felt wobbly and her heart was battering at her ribs but somehow she managed to act naturally. 'I did call out but you didn't reply. I imagined you were tucking into caviar in the kitchen. I wasn't sure which way to go to find you so decided to leave you in peace.'

'Is that so?' he drawled and gave her a thoughtful smile. 'Little Elise ... ever the diplomat. You could do my job, I suspect. Perhaps we should swap places and I'll make munitions.'

'You'd be a disaster; the overalls wouldn't suit you.'

He threw back his head and guffawed. 'You're delightful to be around, you know. I'll show you some more of the house, if you like. Then next time you'll know where to find me. Or ... better still ... how about I give you a thrashing?' He allowed a pause to develop before tipping his head at the cellar door. 'At billiards.'

'You wouldn't win. I know how to play ... my father taught me and he said I'm good. But, alas, no thank you, not tonight. I must get going before my brother-in-law sends out a search party. And then there's Graham too; he'll realise I'm still with you when I'm not found at home. He'll come here to find me, I expect.'

'You're a lucky girl to be so far from home and have so many friends looking out for you.'

'I know I am,' she said and her steady grey gaze held his narrowed eyes.

The silence that followed was broken by the wail of the all-clear and Elise had to stop herself from sighing in relief.

'Right ... come on then ... let's see if we can find a taxi,' he said cheerily, and savagely turned the stiff key in the lock as though regretting having left it there. But with gentlemanly charm he half bowed and held out an arm, inviting her to proceed him down the front steps.

Chapter Twelve

'Thank God you're all right. What happened to you last night? We searched for you for ages.' Faith ushered Elise into the flat and the two young women immediately hugged in relief to find they'd both survived the bombing unscathed.

'I'm glad you got home safely as well. I was worried sick that you might endanger yourselves looking for me.'

'Graham would've carried on all night but I told him you'd more sense than to wander about outside and risk getting blown to bits. I dragged him down into the Tube station in the end. We couldn't find you there either but I reassured him that Toby would look after you.'

'Yes, he did.'

'Which station did you go to?'

'He took me to his house ... we stayed in the cellar.'

Faith's jaw dropped and so did her hands, away from Elise. 'He took you home with him?' she said with a mixture of awe and envy.

'Nothing like that,' Elise quickly reassured her. 'He was quite a gentleman. We just sat it out down there talking. Then he took me back to Silvertown in a taxi. There weren't many about and we had to go on a tour to avoid the bomb sites. It was almost two o'clock when I eventually got in. Neil had been searching for me after the all-clear. He saw the state of Soho and was in a bit of a panic when he got back and found me still not home. He would have tried the hospitals next, he said. Luckily I turned up in the nick of time.'

Elise didn't believe all the diversions en route to the East End had been strictly necessary. She suspected Toby had directed the driver to waste time so he could continue probing to find out what she might know. By that point she'd been tired out but had somehow kept her wits about her and hadn't let him trip her up and admit she'd overheard something she shouldn't have.

'You got off lightly, Elise,' Faith said. 'We were crushed in with hundreds of others down Tottenham Court Road Tube. The whole place reeked of wee. Kids were crying, dogs were barking...' Faith groaned. 'I couldn't wait to get out of there. In Broadstairs during a raid we just dig in at the pub, have a sing-song, and hope for the best.'

'That does sound more civilised. Where's Graham? I'd like to thank him for trying to find me.'

'He set off early for work. He said he couldn't sleep last night for worrying about what might have happened to you. He was going to call at your house first to see if you were back. You can't have missed one another by much. Aren't you at work today?'

'I'm on late shift at the factory ... if it's still standing, of course.' Elise gave a hopeless shake of her head. 'The damage out there is awful. Some roads are impassable. People are clambering over the wreckage of their houses, searching for something to salvage.'

'I guessed it must be bad,' Faith sighed. 'We could hear the explosions and feel the ground shake down in the shelter. It seemed to go on for ages. Graham wants me to go home to Broadstairs where it's safer. I suppose I ought to, really.'

'It's sensible advice; I'll miss you though, and it's such a shame when you've only just turned up.'

'I suppose it was foolish to come; I hoped the blitz on London would let up, just for me.' Faith rolled her eyes in self-mockery. 'So you two just chatted then?' She reverted to her favourite subject, leading the way into the sitting room. 'What did you find to talk about with Toby Winters? Roulette ... the opera?' She giggled.

'Family, mostly,' said Elise. 'You might not know this but we share family members. I told you I thought he seemed familiar and he reminded me why that was: he'd visited Clover's house and I spotted him speaking to his brother Jake outside. He said he'd like to think of me as his cousin.'

Faith had disappeared into the kitchen to fill the kettle and make a pot of tea. She reappeared, kettle in hand, and gawped at Elise. 'You two are *related*?' she choked out.

'Not by blood. My stepbrother Jake is Toby's brother. They were adopted by a rich couple and grew up together until they were separated after their father died suddenly. They lived in that big house of his in Mayfair.'

'Well, I never did!'

'The Coopers, I've discovered, are a melting pot of complicated scandals and tragedies.' Elise added with heavy irony, 'So I fit right in.'

'So it seems.' Faith's eyes had widened in amazement. 'Toby Winters didn't try it on with you then?' Still holding the kettle, she sat down next to Elise and plonked it on her lap. 'If I'd known you'd end up on your own with him I would've warned you he's an incurable womaniser. Did he try to kiss you?'

'No! He'd be wasting his time with me. I don't like him.'

'I thought you said he was a gentleman.' Faith gave Elise a piercing look.

'He was, but I suspect it was an act.'

'What's he done to make you say that, love?' Faith put the kettle onto the table and took her friend's hands, giving them a squeeze. 'What's happened?'

'Oh, nothing really. Call it women's intuition.' She paused. 'Do you know what he does at work? He says it's hush-hush.'

'He used to work with Graham, then Graham got promoted after the war started.' Faith shrugged. 'Now my brother's at the Ministry of Economic Warfare, whatever that is when it's at home. I asked him what he actually does but he's never forthcoming about his work; understandable, I suppose. Walls have ears, and all that.'

'Toby works for the government, though?' Elise didn't want to overreact to last night's events. There could be an innocent explanation for what she'd overheard.

'As far as I know he does. Why d'you ask?'

'Oh, no particular reason, it's only ... I found out he can speak German.'

'He speaks French as well, and Latin. He spouts lines from classics sometimes. He was privately educated and likes to impress people.'

Elise knew he'd not been showing off last night ... at least, not about being skilled in languages. He'd been unaware of her listening outside the door. Faith could be right to brush it off though. Toby Winters might deal with all sorts of foreign diplomats in his line of work. German families had migrated to Britain, just as English people lived in France. Those unfortunates had been caught out by the war and now found themselves in the wrong place at the wrong time.

'Graham!' Elise's pondering was curtailed by a welcome sight. The new arrival ignored her outstretched hands and caught her to him in a bear hug.

'I've been damned frantic over you, you know.'

'Faith told me so. I was worried about both of you as well.'

'I just spoke to your brother-in-law. He told me you'd arrived home in the early hours and had gone out again after only a short sleep to make sure we'd got home safely.' Graham cleared his throat and let her go, appearing rather bashful after his demonstration of affection. 'Neil Ryan seems a nice chap.'

'Well then...' said Faith with a knowing look veering between the couple. 'I'm off to the shop for some milk for tea. And if they've any eggs I'll get some for breakfast; if not it'll be toast and jam, I'm afraid.' She grinned at her brother. 'If I'd thought of it I could've brought a couple of bantams with me from Broadstairs. You could do with keeping chickens, Graham, what with all this rationing malarkey.'

Once Faith had gone out, her brother turned to Elise with a shrug. 'It's not a bad idea, but where in the devil does she think I'll put the damn things, living in an upstairs flat?'

Elise chuckled. 'I wouldn't ask her that... knowing Faith, she might tell you.'

Graham burst out laughing; a moment later he thrust his hand through his untidy hair. 'What a night that was.'

'Indeed it was.'

Sensing her stare, and something unspoken straining

the atmosphere, Graham frowned. 'What is it?' His eyes raked over her face and his jaw hardened. 'Is this to do with Winters? Your brother-in-law told me you sheltered with him in his cellar.'

'I did, and firstly I must say I'm not about to accuse him of any assault or anything else for that matter. I have got something to tell you though, and to ask you.' Graham had worked with Toby and knew him well. He also held a similar opinion to her own of Toby Winters. She'd decided he was the best person to confide in.

She recounted everything that had happened after they got separated in the club, while observing Graham's reaction. He looked as surprised as his sister had been to learn about the family connection to Winters, but he didn't interrupt and continued listening intently. When she got to the end of the tale, Elise realised she might have been right to feel uneasy. Not that Graham seemed angry. His expression had taken on a weird look of triumphant satisfaction.

'So ... Winters doesn't know you overheard him talking German?'

'He might have guessed, but he didn't get a chance to ask me outright. I would have denied it anyway. I distracted him by saying I could beat him at billiards. He has a table you know, down in the cellar.'

'You did well, Elise.' Graham's tone rang with praise and admiration.

'What's going on though? Does he have German friends?'

'Very possibly,' said Graham with an odd inflection. He turned away from her and, tilting back his head, studied the ceiling for some seconds. 'Did Toby ask to see you again?'

'He asked me to have tea at the Ritz with him later in the

week. I said I'd need to check my work shifts first as I got out of the taxi. I'll avoid him if anything. There's something about him I don't trust.' She paused. 'He looks quite like Jake but he's not got any part of his lovely character.'

'If I asked you to have tea with Winters, would you?'

Elise frowned. 'Why would you do that?'

'I'd like you to find out a few things then report back to me.' He rubbed his chin. 'I think you've an aptitude for this sort of thing.'

'What sort of thing?'

'Information gathering.'

'I'm not sure I have, Graham,' Elise said ruefully. 'And I don't want to cause trouble in my family by being underhand. I love Jake, and Toby is his brother. They must have a fondness for one another even if they are—' she whirled a hand while trying to find an appropriate English phrase —at loggerheads,' she burst out as her father's voice echoed in her mind.

'What's that all about then? Jealousy?'

'Not on Jake's part. He doesn't seem bothered about his brother's wealth. He's the happier of the two of them. I tried to find out what's eating at Toby but he wouldn't say.'

Graham grinned. 'See, you are a natural at this sort of thing. I bet you'd like another go at finding out, wouldn't you?'

Her impish smile let him know she was unable to deny it.

'Did you tell Faith about these suspicions?'

'Not exactly. I said I knew Toby spoke German. She imagined he'd told me himself because he likes to brag about his education.'

'He does,' said Graham. 'He boasts about everything he thinks makes him superior to the rest of us.' He continued criss-crossing the rug from door to mantelpiece, frowning in concentration.

Elise was also mulling things over and concluded that Graham had credited her with being cleverer than she was. She feared she might have been very stupid indeed. 'Toby asked me about my family, my brother in particular, and whether I knew if any Resistance groups had been set up in France around Lille.'

'And do you? What did you tell him?' Graham approached her and placed his hands on her shoulders.

Elise nibbled a thumbnail while trying to recall the flow of their conversation. 'I said that Luc and other patriots like him wouldn't surrender even though the French army had. I said I didn't know about any networks ... it's the truth, I don't.' Her hands sprang to grip Graham's forearms and give him an urgent little shake. 'Have I put Luc in danger?' The blood drained from her complexion. 'Is Toby Winters some sort of traitor?'

'Don't be upset. You haven't said anything harmful. As for Winters, I can't comment on that yet.'

'Why would somebody like him be a traitor?' Elise pivoted away in agitation. 'It's absurd to think so when he has a good life in England.'

'There are some here who are sympathetic to the Nazis. France has similar people, I'm sure. Oswald Mosley is a prominent English Fascist. Have you heard of him?'

'I think my father might have mentioned his name ... something about rallies, years ago when I was still at school.'

'There were Fascist marches and some turned violent. Mosley's been interned now but there are others like him. Toby Winters' stepfather was once a friend and supporter of Mosley's. He seems to have turned his back on all that though. After being widowed, Ian Winters married an heiress; he's apparently been living a blameless life in Yorkshire for many years.'

'Toby hates him; he told me so. He must have still been a student during the rallies so shouldn't be tarred with the same brush as his stepfather.'

'That's true,' Graham said. 'Nevertheless, I brought the connection between the Winters and the Fascists to the attention of our superiors. They already knew of it, but there's a certain lackadaisical attitude among the Old Boy network. Careless,' he enlightened her having seen her puzzlement. 'Anyway, the outcome was that I made a fuss and Toby was denied a promotion to a position that deals with quite sensitive matters. As I saw it, it was a wise precaution. Obviously he didn't see it that way.'

'That's why you two don't get on, isn't it? Because you went behind his back.'

'I'd put it differently. But I've definitely rubbed him up the wrong way, perhaps unnecessarily. Better to be safe than sorry though when we're at war.' He gave her an apologetic look. 'I appreciate you're in a rather awkward position now this family connection has come up. I don't want you to think badly of me. There's no personal vendetta involved on my part. That doesn't alter the fact that, like you, I don't trust that man.' He paused. 'I'll do anything to help the Allies win this damnable war and put an end to the hell we find ourselves in.'

'I feel the same way,' she said forcefully. 'It's all I want, and to be back in France with my family.' Her chest heaved with emotion. 'I don't think badly of you; without people like you we'll never defeat Hitler.' She fell quiet for several seconds. 'This war has already killed my father. I'll do whatever I can to try and stop it killing what's left of my family in France.'

'Faith told me about your father. I'm so sorry, Elise.'

'I will have tea with Toby Winters.' She impatiently rubbed incipient tears from her eyes. 'He might think it odd if I look too keen though. He's not daft, and knew I wasn't charmed by his company.'

'That's a thought.' Graham tapped his lips while concentrating. 'You could use the family connection angle: say it'd be nice to swap notes about skeletons in closets.' He grunted in dry amusement. 'He might not bother questioning why you've warmed to him. His ego's big enough to come up with reasons for it.'

'He'd want to talk about family; Jake and Rebecca in particular.'

'We're on then. If nothing comes of it, Elise, at least you'll get a nice tea out of him.'

Elise would like to visit the London Ritz hotel. There was a Ritz in France as well. On a trip to Paris with her mother and grandparents and Luc – an occasion when Sidney Cooper had been absent in England – the family group had stood outside the grand building and decided that they would save up enough to go inside and have tea next time. There had never been another trip for them all, and never would be now her mother and grandfather had passed away.

'Are you due at the factory today?'

'I am.' A mention of the Royal Arsenal had brought something worrying to mind. 'Toby seemed interested in my work. Possibly he was only making conversation but he asked about production and if I knew where the defence batteries were set up. I don't and told him so.'

'Curiouser and curiouser. You'll know to be cautious in your answers if any similar questions come your way. Don't let him suspect you're on to him, though, or he'll dry up.'

'You're taking this seriously, aren't you, Graham?'

'I am. I'll make a point of bumping into him to say I appreciate him looking after you and that I know you're keen to thank him personally for getting you home safely ...' Graham broke off, putting a finger to his lips before pointing it at the door. Swiftly, he took a fountain pen and a notebook from his breast pocket. He scrawled on a leaf and ripped it out. 'My office telephone number so you can contact me quickly if you need to. And don't tell anybody about this. Keep Faith in the dark,' he hissed. 'The little fool likes Winters, and now she's turning into a drunk she could blab and ruin everything. I hope she'll go back to Broadstairs actually.'

Elise didn't like the idea of deception; more worryingly she'd been ignoring the fact that Faith was drinking more than was sensible. She wished Graham had seemed a little more concerned than judgemental about his sister though.

'Success!' Faith entered the flat, wobbling an egg carton in her hand. She put the groceries on the table, seemingly oblivious to tension in the atmosphere. 'Popped into the baker's for a nice fresh loaf as well. Right, what's it to be? Fried, boiled or scrambled?'

Chapter Thirteen

'Sorry I'm late home, love. The family wants to move back in tomorrow so I stayed to get it finished for them.' Neil Ryan had bowled into the parlour bringing crisp winter air with him. He flipped his cap off his head and dragged his fingers through his flattened hair. Having hooked his hat and coat up behind the door, he rubbed together his grubby palms. 'Gawd it's taters out there ... frost's coming down. You'd better wrap yourself up warm.'

He had been working on a property that had suffered a smashed front door and window in an air raid. His customers had been camping with in-laws while the repairs were being done. They had been luckier than their neighbours, who'd lost most of their roof slates. With no relative available to put them up, the family of seven were crammed, shivering, into two downstairs rooms, praying it wouldn't snow and that their tight-fist of a landlord would get the job done this side of Christmas. Nevertheless, they were thankful not to be one of the families whose house had been reduced to rubble. Those displaced folk in turn pitied the people who rushed from hospital to hospital seeking missing relatives, while dreading being pointed in the direction of the mortuary.

'If I get a move on I'll make it to the factory in time to clock on,' said Elise. 'I've left your dinner in the oven.'

Neil opened the oven door, liberating a mouth-watering waft of gravy. 'Smells nice.'

'Sausage and mash in onion gravy,' said Elise pulling on her coat. 'My dad liked bangers and mash. He would get my mum to make it for him. Our sausages are spicier but after a while he got used to French *saucissons* . . .' A nostalgic smile tilted her mouth.

'Good old British grub is bangers 'n' mash,' said Neil. 'Shall I save you some?'

'I had mine with Adam a little while ago.' Elise turned to the boy sitting quietly at the table. To keep him occupied while his mum was out shopping, she'd taught him some French words. Next to his writing he'd drawn his version of a cat and dog, which were really rather good for a child of five. 'You've been good, *chéri*, haven't you?' Elise ruffled his hair.

He nodded. 'Is mum coming back soon?'

'She won't be long. She's buying things for your trip to see your nan. You'll like a holiday in the countryside, won't you?'

'S'pose so,' he said glumly. 'I'll miss my friend though, Auntie Elise. And my new teacher.'

'I'm sure you'll make lots of new friends at the village school, and have a nice teacher as well,' Elise encouraged him while buttoning up her coat. 'And you'll see lots of animals: cows and sheep and horses. My brother used to work on a farm where there were lots of those. And he drove a tractor.'

'What's that?'

'It's a sort of big lorry the farmer uses to move heavy

things like hay. And he uses it to plough the fields. It's got huge wheels.' Elise spread her arms to demonstrate.

Adam brightened up. 'I'd like to drive a tractor. Will I see one when I live at my nan's house?'

'I expect so.'

He didn't seem completely convinced. 'I'd rather go and stay with Vicky and Auntie Clover by the seaside.'

Elise and Neil exchanged a glance knowing the Coopers' Essex retreat already had a full quota of lodgers. 'We'll all get together at Christmas, son,' said Neil. 'You'll see all your cousins then. And in the meanwhile you'll have a bedroom all to yourself in your nan's house.' He washed his hands in a bowl of warm water then gave his nephew a wink while drying them. 'Reckon there's time for a biscuit before your mum gets back. Bet you know where the tin is, don't you?'

Adam nodded, got down from the table, and trotted to the sideboard.

Before Rebecca had gone shopping she'd said her son had had a tantrum because he wanted to remain close to his best friend. The boy lived next door to them in Whitechapel and his mother was adamant they were all staying put, no matter what Hitler threw at them. Rebecca had seemed upset by her son's defiance, which was understandable, Elise thought, after hearing some other, rather lovely news. Rebecca had confided that she was in the early months of another pregnancy. She hadn't written to Jake about it and didn't know whether to yet in case she suffered a miscarriage as she had last year.

Neil had been extracting his scarf from his coat pocket and a letter he'd also stuffed in there came out with the length of wool. 'Oh, sorry, love.' He retrieved it from the floor and held it out. 'This came for you yesterday. The postman caught me along the street. I meant to leave it on the table for you this morning before I went out.'

Elise understood why he'd forgotten. They passed like ships in the night most of the time. Usually she'd left for the factory before Neil arrived home from work in the evening. A manly black script was on the envelope but it wasn't Luc's writing. Her heart sank as it always did when days came and went, the postman came and went, and there was no news from France. She imagined letters to and from England were intercepted and scrutinised, especially if addressed to people under surveillance. She hadn't written to her grandmother, fearing putting her family in jeopardy. Her yearning to know what was happening to them both never let up. The passage of time hadn't lessened the pain of separation.

Having said her goodbyes and left the house, she walked swiftly up the dark lane. She always crossed the road before passing the bomb site close to the corner. She avoided looking into the gaping hole that exposed charred timbers and wilting wallpaper flapping eerily in the breeze. Turning towards the factory, she pulled up her coat collar against the icy atmosphere and dug her hands into her pockets. It was the first week of December; Christmas would be here before she knew it: her first without a living parent, and Luc and Mathilde at her side. She blinked away the tears stinging her eyes and bucked herself up. It would be a miserable time for them all but they'd make the best of it like everybody else missing their loved ones.

The letter was banging temptingly against her fingers and although she knew reading it would delay her she drew it from her pocket. She halted by a house to study the thick inky script, recognising it as the work of Graham's fountain pen. She'd not yet used the telephone number he'd written down for her over a week ago. She'd not heard a peep from Toby Winters and wondered if Graham hadn't had that talk with him after all. Having torn open the envelope flap, she read the one-line message by the weak light escaping between wonky blackout curtains. Graham advised her to shortly expect to have that nice outing they'd spoken about. The spare instruction, devoid of names, impressed on her that this wasn't a game she was embarking upon, and that he was taking precautions to protect them both. He had done his part, and soon it would be time to do hers.

Elise folded the paper and scoured the gloomy road, about to cross over and take a short cut through back alleys to arrive at Woolwich in the fastest time. A tooting car horn made her quickly step back onto the pavement but the dark saloon didn't pass by; it glided to a halt at the kerb. Right on cue, Toby Winters sprang from it to smile lazily at her over the car's roof. He would only be slumming it in Silvertown to see her. As much as she wanted to assist Graham in his investigation she felt irritated at the prospect of encouraging this man's company.

'I was on my way to speak to you. I hoped to catch you in,' he announced.

'I'm on my way to work.' She forced herself to give him a smile.

'Oh, of course. I forgot about you working night shifts. I'll give you a lift and we can have a natter on the way. How have you been? Have you heard from Jake? Any idea what my brother's up to in north Africa?'

'Heaven only knows.' Elise quickly hid the letter in her pocket. He seemed as arrogant as ever but she'd overlook it on this occasion, as she'd a date to make. 'I'd like a lift, thanks, as I'm running a bit late. I've been childminding for Rebecca.'

He came round to open the passenger door for her before striding back to get in beside her.

'I'm sorry I missed catching you at home in that case. I haven't seen the boy in ages. How is Adam?' He sent her a glance while steering away from the kerb.

'A bit grumpy actually. He's not happy about going to stay with his grandmother. He's got a new schoolteacher he likes very much. Rebecca isn't so keen on the young woman though.'

'Oh, why's that?'

'Rebecca thinks she lets the children get away with too much, for an easy life.' Elise chuckled. 'I suppose that's why the kids like her.'

'Rebecca's definitely quitting London then?'

'Yes, and not before time,' Elise said.

'Is Jake due home on leave soon?'

'Rebecca's not mentioned it and he sends her regular letters. It would be nice if both my brothers were able to spend Christmas with their wives and kids.'

Elise had been expecting some usual cocky banter but he continued to brood on what she'd told him about family members. In a few minutes more they would reach the factory. She had limited time to keep her promise to Graham.

'I wanted to thank you for looking after me during the bad bombing, Mr Winters. And I hope you haven't forgotten about treating me to tea at the Ritz.'

'Of course I haven't.' He flashed her a smile in the car's dim interior. 'But I might change my mind if you won't call me Toby in exchange for a few cucumber sandwiches.'

'That sounds like a reasonable deal.'

'How about Sunday afternoon, then if you aren't working? Shall I ask Faith if she'd like to come as well?'

'She might be busy packing,' Elise quickly replied. 'She's going back to Broadstairs for Christmas.' Faith's hope – everybody's hope – that the air raids would peter out had unfortunately come to nothing. The capital was still under constant attack. Ruins were piling up everywhere, but mainly in the East End, the location of a sizeable industry fuelling the British war effort. Faith had decided to return home and intended to apply for a job in the Land Army now her seafaring was on hold.

Toby didn't appear to be listening any more; without warning, he suddenly tooted the car horn and slowed down, doffing his hat in an odd manner.

The target of his mockery was Rebecca. She was hurrying along in the dark carrying shopping bags. She dropped one but her shocked expression revealed that the people in the car rather than the blaring noise had startled her. Elise waved but her sister-in-law grabbed the bag and rushed on without even a smile in response.

Elise was disturbed by the snub. Since the majority of the Cooper clan had dispersed elsewhere she'd believed they'd become close friends. They visited one another for tea and for a moan about the Blitz on London and life in general. It wasn't the first time Elise had looked after Adam while Rebecca was busy. Jake had admitted to bad blood existing between him and his brother but his wife hadn't made any complaints. In fact, Elise couldn't recall Rebecca ever mentioning Toby Winters' name.

'When is Rebecca leaving town?' Toby asked as the vehicle picked up speed and turned into the Woolwich Road.

His brusqueness reminded Elise of his attitude on

the night of the bombing. He'd apologised for his mood then. He didn't this time and gazed sharply at her for her answer.

There was no reason not to tell him, she reasoned and she needed to keep him sweet. 'Early next week. Monday, I think, if the trains are running as normal.'

He pulled up outside the factory gate and was back to his breezy self. 'Well, Elise, Sunday tea at the Ritz sounds charming. Wear that lovely yellow dress again and a pair of dancing shoes.' He lifted her fingers to his lips then got out to come and open the car door for her.

"Bye then,' she said and walked away, discreetly rubbing the feel of his lips off her skin.

'Why were you in Toby Winters' car yesterday?'

'He spotted me in the street and gave me a lift to work.' Elise refused to sound defensive and was unhappy about the accusation in Rebecca's voice. 'I was glad of the offer actually, as I was late.' She sighed. 'What's wrong, Becky?'

Elise had not long ago arrived home from her night shift, tired and hungry. She'd taken off her work clothes and put on her dressing gown then made herself some tea and toast, intending to go to bed after she'd eaten. She found it difficult to drop off during the day but knew she should rest as she'd another night shift in front of her. She'd been sitting at the kitchen table when Rebecca banged on the door. Even before she'd ushered her agitated-looking sister-in-law inside she'd known something was wrong.

'Did Toby ask about me and my son?'

'Yes, he did. He asked about Jake, too. I think he's concerned about you all.'

'Concerned! He's not concerned about us,' Rebecca snorted.

'Well ... interested, then ...' Elise gestured that she might have chosen a wrong English word. 'Come and sit down, Becky.' Elise pulled out a chair. 'I'll get you a cup of tea. It's freshly made.'

Rebecca did sit down and planted her elbows onto the table and her forehead against her clenched fists. 'I saw you laughing together as though you like him. You don't, do you?' she demanded.

'Not much.' Elise wrinkled her nose. 'He's a bit smarmy.' She poured the tea and brought it to the table. 'What's this all about?'

Rebecca slumped back in her chair and gulped at her tea. 'Jake told you he doesn't like his brother, so why are you hanging about with him? Because he's rich, is that it?'

'No, of course not.' Elise felt hurt that Rebecca would say such a thing. 'I've not tried to become acquainted with Toby. He introduced himself in a nightclub when I was with some mutual friends from Kent—'

'Neil told me all about that when I collected Adam yesterday,' interrupted Rebecca. 'He said it was the night of the bad air raid and that you sheltered in Toby's house with him. You wouldn't have done that if you knew him, bombs or no bombs.'

Elise deduced Neil hadn't volunteered the information but had been interrogated about what he knew. More than sibling rivalry was causing a family rift and it occurred to Elise that the Fascist connection might be playing a part. She'd been warned to keep mum, but a few casual questions couldn't hurt if they turned up useful information. 'Did you know Toby's stepfather?' She eased carefully into the conversation.

'Why d'you want to know that?'

'Toby said he didn't like the man. I wondered if it was a clash of personalities ... or politics ... something like that.'

'They don't get on because they're too alike, both wrong 'uns.' Rebecca stood up. 'Well, thanks for tea. For everybody's sake, yours included, I'd ask you not to have anything more to do with him.'

'Don't go like this, Becky.' Elise affectionately squeezed her sister-in-law's hands. 'What's wrong? I'd like to help.'

'You can help. Just stay away from him and don't ever discuss my business with him.'

Elise wanted a better answer than that, but was thwarted in pursuing the matter when Neil burst in.

'I thought I might find you here, Becky. Is Adam with you?' He swung a look around.

'He's at school. Why?' Rebecca's eyes widened in apprehensiveness.

Neil glanced between the two young women, sensing an atmosphere. 'The headmaster came round to your house and found me working in the yard. Adam's new teacher had told him your husband turned up and took Adam home. The fellow wanted to know why. I said I didn't think your husband was home on leave. Is he? Did Jake come back last night?'

Rebecca violently shook her head. 'I dropped Adam off and didn't leave until the bell was rung. He was queuing up in the playground to go into class with his friends.' She covered her mouth with a hand. 'It's Toby. He's taken him. I know he has.'

'No ... he wouldn't do that!' Elise tried to put a comforting arm about her sister-in-law but was roughly shaken off.

'This is your fault! What did you tell him?' Rebecca demanded. 'You told him about the new teacher, didn't you?

He's gone to the school pretending to be my husband. That dozy woman wouldn't bother questioning it.'

'I did tell him ... but ...' Elise felt confused, unsure what she'd done wrong.

'Did you also tell him we're leaving London?' Becky looked horrified and ready to lash out.

'I did ... yes ...'

'Go home now, Becky.' Neil positioned himself in front of the distraught mother, anticipating a blow being landed. 'I'll go and find them.'

'*I'll* go and find them,' Becky screamed. 'And when I do I'll kill Toby Winters if he's taken my son.'

Neil put his arms around his hysterical sister-in-law. 'Now listen to me,' he crooned, holding her still as she struggled to free herself. 'Adam might be waiting for you indoors by now. I'll go to Winters' house and if Adam is there, I'll not come out without him. I promise you that.'

Rebecca jerked a nod of agreement and wrenched herself free. With a blistering glare for Elise, she was gone.

Silence followed, then the slamming of the street door drew together the eyes of the two people left in the room. Neil shoved a hand through his hair then gripped Elise's shoulder as silent tears dripped down her cheeks. 'It's not your fault, dear,' he said kindly. 'You weren't to know just how big the trouble is in that family.'

'What have I done? *Pourquoi* ...?' She began to speak in French in her distress but Neil didn't understand and she gestured in despair. 'I'll come with you. I want to.' Elise smeared away her tears and followed him to the door. 'Wait while I get dressed ... please.'

'I'll go alone. And you have to stay out of it.' He turned back to give her a weary smile. 'I know you mean well but if he's got Adam there'll be bad trouble and I don't want you caught up in it.' He sighed up at the ceiling. 'It's as well Jake's not here. He'd create merry hell and ask questions later. And he's a fellow not given to temper on the whole. Except where protecting his family's concerned.'

Elise still wanted to accompany him, but ceded the argument. Whatever she said would make no difference. She'd already lost one friend and didn't want to lose another.

After Neil left, she sat down; only seconds passed before she was back on her feet, pacing to and fro. She had judged Toby Winters as an unpleasant character, but not as downright evil, and he would need to be to kidnap his brother's child. She couldn't just wait here, feeling like a caged animal. On impulse, she went upstairs to her bedroom and hastily pulled on the clothes she'd recently taken off then returned to the parlour, dragging a brush through her hair. That was cast onto the table and she grabbed her coat from the peg. She hurried out into the street, buttoning it up, ignoring a nagging voice in her head telling her to obey Neil's command not to meddle. She'd been accused of causing trouble and in her eyes that made her involved. She decided against heading to Whitechapel to apologise to Rebecca. She wasn't sure what she had to be sorry for; besides, she'd only make things worse. Rebecca wouldn't want her comfort.

At the top of the road she caught a bus to the West End. She sat squashed up against the window by a large woman with a florid face who was taking up most of the seat next to her. Elise kept her eyes averted to the street scene and ignored the chatter of the housewives around her. The women were chewing over who knew what about last night's air raid, while counting their blessings that they'd been spared the worst of it.

Elise and a few others alighted at the same stop and busily dispersed in different directions. Elise walked swiftly towards a familiar avenue lined with white stucco villas and turned into it. She headed for a property diagonally across the road from the one she was interested in and took up position behind a screen of privet hedging. She prayed nobody would come out of the house and ask her what she thought she was doing. She stared fixedly at the large double-fronted residence she'd been inside, thinking it didn't appear quite so grand with daylight revealing its grubby paintwork. She waited and waited. Her hands felt frozen and she plunged them deeper into her pockets. It was a frosty morning and she'd come out in a rush without her gloves. She marched her feet up and down as quietly as she could on the paving, trying to move the sluggish blood in her toes. After fifteen minutes of peering intently at Toby's mansion she believed she'd arrived too late and Neil had been and gone. The only way to discover if Adam had been found would be to go back to the East End.

She was on the point of emerging from the shrubbery when the door of Toby's house was opened and a woman's angry voice could be heard.

Elise shrank back to watch a black-clad servant flapping her hand to shoo somebody on their way. A grim-faced Neil nimbly descended the steps and set off at a run along the road.

Elise's heart was hammering in her throat as she watched him. He was alone. She guessed he'd insisted on searching the house against the housekeeper's will. Something else became clear: Toby Winters wasn't at home, or he'd be ejecting Neil Ryan himself.

'Have you lost something?'

Elise spun about to see a maid clutching two bottles of milk taken from the step.

'What're you doing?' The frowning woman descended a step as though to come and investigate.

'Sorry ... didn't mean to bother you,' said Elise and lifted her coat and skirt a few inches to fiddle underneath. 'My suspender's snapped. I think that's got it though.' She smoothed down her clothes and hurried off with a nervous smile. She knew she was under observation and hoped the servant didn't notice she wasn't wearing any stockings. She'd quit the house in too much of a rush to bother with dressing herself properly.

Chapter Fourteen

A bus soon arrived to take Elise back to the East End. The same passenger that had sat beside her on the outward journey hauled herself aboard as the vehicle jerked into motion. The woman's face appeared even ruddier from her last-minute dash. She plonked down next to Elise once more, with much heavy breathing, then started a conversation as though they were old friends.

'Don't want me today, does she,' she puffed. 'That's how they are, though, the posh ones, ain't it? No bleedin' consideration for the likes of us.'

Elise surfaced from her anxious thoughts about Adam's whereabouts. 'Pardon?' She glanced at a pursed-lipped profile.

'Me lady ... she don't want no charring done today.' The woman sniffed. 'Expecting guests over she said and don't want no cleaners in the way. Well, thanks very much, I says, and I won't be coming back here no more to waste me time 'n' bus fare.' She looked Elise over. 'You got put off 'n' all, did yer? Can't say you've the look of a daily, love.'

'No ... I'm not actually. Sorry ... excuse me ...' Elise stood up and wriggled past the woman's stout knees to yank on the bell.

The bus had almost reached its next stop and the moment it slowed down enough to do so Elise jumped off and began running back the way she'd come. She was being daft, she told herself, as her breath formed clouds in front of her. She'd watched the house for fifteen minutes. Neil had been inside long enough to make a thorough search. If Adam was in there he surely would have found him.

But he wouldn't have spotted the door in the panelling any more than she had. She imagined that was the point: the cellar's entrance was camouflaged so the room remained private.

There wasn't a maid scrubbing the step as was present at some of the other properties. Had there been she would have had an opportunity to strike up a conversation and slip inside an open doorway. She avoided the neighbour's garden she'd used as a hide, and stayed on the right side of the street. A gate guarded the side entrance to Toby's house and she cast a casual glance through ornamental ironwork on proceeding quickly past. On reaching the corner, she carried on around it, her chest still heaving from her sprint back here. Having taken a calming breath, she turned and retraced her steps.

Approaching the gate once more she noticed there was no padlock and the latch wasn't securely in place. It looked as though it had been recently used. She pushed at it, causing it to creak, but she speedily closed it then hurried down the steps to the lower-ground level, glancing behind for any sign of pursuit. It didn't take long to locate the cellar door and she immediately tried the handle. It wouldn't yield to her fingers or to the pressure of her hip banging against it. She stood on tiptoe to try to see through the fanlight but couldn't. Her ear was pressed to the panel, but nothing other than her own racing heartbeat was audible.

Glumly, she realised she'd have to knock on the front door after all if she were to get inside. And then her eye alighted on the large stone planter with nothing in it, shoved against the wall.

Her father would return from England after a year or more away and rouse them at midnight to let him in. Luc had started to leave a key under the flowerpot for Sidney to use when he mislaid his own and rolled home drunk. Her brother had soon seen a benefit for himself in the trick: mainly on those nights he disappeared for a dalliance with the farmer's daughter. Toby Winters wasn't a stranger to a dalliance or a drunken escapade either, Elise reckoned. And he'd be aware his deaf housekeeper wouldn't respond to his summons in the small hours.

Crouching down, she gave the massive urn a shove that jolted her arm bones back into their shoulder sockets. It didn't budge. Gritting her teeth she tried again and after much manoeuvring she eventually swivelled the pot sideways, revealing a piece of dull metal and a family of woodlice.

Then she heard something that made her shrink into a ball with her arms up over her head to conceal herself. A car door had been slammed and masculine boots were running up the steps. Soon after came the sound of the housekeeper's agitated voice and of a heavy door being shut.

Elise rose stealthily with the key gripped in her hand. She listened at the cellar door and again the sound of shoe leather hitting stairs reached her. So he had gone straight down into the cellar. It seemed an odd place to head unless something of importance was in there. Elise had overheard the housekeeper babbling about a man barging inside while he was out. The woman hadn't mentioned a child. If he'd smuggled the boy in this way his housekeeper might be in the dark over all of it. He'd want to satisfy himself that his captive was safe though. Elise remained perfectly still, straining to listen despite a fine sleet starting to web her hair and face with ice crystals. There were no voices, but she did hear footsteps on stairs and then a door being closed.

Dithering was of no use she told herself as the key in her hand remained hovering close to the lock. If Adam was in there he wouldn't be for much longer. Toby would move him elsewhere now he knew the boy had been missed and he was suspected of kidnapping him. She pushed the key home. It turned smoothly and she opened the door inwards, dreading being challenged. All remained quiet so she whipped inside, leaving her escape route open.

The cellar was unlit but for the grey daylight she'd let into it. The smell was familiar: alcohol and cigarettes and a woody masculine cologne. The vibration in the atmosphere she didn't remember though, or perhaps it was caused by the nervous energy buzzing in her head. She smeared sleet from her eyelashes while creeping forward and her searching gaze alighted on a crumpled blanket on the sofa. She rushed to yank off the cover and reveal the sleeping boy. Adam's face felt cold and she began rubbing his cheek. He stirred but began to doze off again. 'Come on, *cheri*, wake up.' She urgently wobbled his arm. 'Time to go home.' She managed to rouse him once more and received a slack smile of recognition. 'Let's go and find your mum.' She placed a finger to his lips as he tried to slur a few words. 'You have to be very quiet.'

Adam nodded and his heavy eyelids lifted as though he knew the reason for secrecy. She managed to get him to his feet and felt him sway against her for support. A savage hatred replaced her previous animosity towards Toby Winters. Adam wasn't simply tired; he'd been drugged with something. She guided him carefully towards the exit, hoping exercise would liven him up. He was a small boy but no easy weight to carry up the steps to the street and speed was crucial if they were to escape.

'You really are becoming a thorn in my side, Miss Bouchard.' A growling voice and the thud of long strides on the rug made her whirl around. She ducked, sure the approaching fist would hit her, but it shot over her head, ramming the door shut and cutting off the light.

She kept Adam behind her, out of his reach. 'Stay away from us both or I'll scream and bring the whole street running.' The threat reverberated in blackness.

'Go ahead. Nobody will come.' A strike of a match was heard before a candle flame painted their gigantic shadows on the walls. 'This room's quite soundproof, you silly girl.' He lobbed the matches down next to the fancy candelabra on the drinks cabinet then made a crafty grab for Adam, causing the boy to squeak and cling to Elise.

She was prepared for these tricks and kicked out, catching him a blow from her work boot that cracked against his shin, making him yelp and drop the holdall he was carrying.

'You bloody bitch,' he snarled. 'I suppose it was you sent Neil Ryan here to ransack the place. Well, he had no luck, and neither will you.'

'Stay away or you'll get your face scratched next,' she threatened. 'What have you given Adam to make him groggy?'

'A dose of laudanum to help him relax; stop making a fuss.'

Elise had believed she'd be terrified to be caught skulking in his house. She felt nothing of the sort, though. Toby Winters was a coward – probably more wary of her than she was of him. Bullying children might come easily to him but he wouldn't find her a pushover. 'Stay there and don't move, all right?' She cupped Adam's white cheek in comfort.

He nodded, biting his wobbling lip.

'I'm taking Adam home to his mother.' She started towards Toby with her chin up and her eyes brilliant with defiance.

'You're not, you know. He's coming with me to a better life.'

'The only place he's going is home. I'm not afraid of you. I've faced up to the Gestapo – a Hauptmann with a pistol at that – and came out on the winning side.' She noticed a glimmer of reluctant admiration in his eyes. 'I remember you joked about having to kill me when we were in this room before. It's not a joke now. That's what you'll need to do to stop me taking Adam home. And I don't think you want a corpse on your hands, do you?'

His muttered oath competed for her attention with the background humming as it transformed into a discordant crackling. Her eyes darted to the billiard table where a small suitcase was lying on the baize with the lid half closed. The noise seemed to be issuing from within. It wasn't like any radio she'd seen before, but she knew that's what it was. A muffled voice could be heard and though the words spoken were indistinct she guessed the language to be German. Swiftly, he strode and turned off the apparatus and positioned himself to hide it from view.

'If you insist on being heroic, Elise, your demise will have to be arranged.' He cocked his head, his expression regretful. 'A wasteful end for an audacious little beauty. I'd enjoy taming you. It's not an empty boast. Ask Rebecca.' He smirked. 'But back to the point. Nobody would be able to prove me responsible if your lifeless body was discovered beneath rubble on a bomb site.' He inched slyly closer to her. 'I'll wager you took pains to prevent yourself being seen breaking in. You could simply disappear, courtesy of some friends of mine.'

A stubby cue was lying on the baize alongside the suitcase. 'Some friends of yours?' she queried, moving towards the billiard table. 'Would those be the English Fascists or the German ones?'

He stopped stalking her, and a look of defeat replaced his insolent smile. 'So you were snooping that night. I had my suspicions. You shouldn't have told me and sealed your fate.'

'So did I have suspicions about you. I know all about your stepfather and Mosley and the rest of your chums. If you're sensible and let me take Adam back to his family without any trouble I'll keep quiet about what I know.'

'The boy is with his family,' he snapped.

'Don't try to be clever. You know what I mean.'

'Don't you be dense,' he snarled. 'You know nothing about this. Why do you think my brother and I hate one another? Why do you think I came to the house that night?'

'You knew I'd be there.'

'You? You're not important. I knew my son would be there and thought I might get a chance to see him on neutral territory.'

Elise didn't scoff or tell him he was talking rot. She'd already begun to question why a vain self-centred man would bother with a nephew not of his blood. The answer, of course, was he believed Adam was his blood.

'He's Jake and Rebecca's child.'

'You're not surprised, are you?' He sounded triumphant. 'She's told you, I suppose, about our sordid love triangle?'

'No, she hasn't. But I'll tell you this: I'm taking her son back to her.' Elise lunged for the cue and brandished it two-handed while taking crab-like steps towards the child.

'Don't be ridiculous,' Toby hooted in derision at her makeshift weapon. 'I can have that off you.'

'Maybe, but I'll do some serious damage with it first. Your bashed-up face won't be easy to explain away.' She jabbed with the cue, making him rear back. 'The police will be here soon. Rebecca's gone to Leman Street station to report you for abduction.' Elise didn't know that to be true but the threat worked. His face had taken on a furious colour and he seemed alarmed by the idea. 'You won't want the authorities poking around in your affairs, will you?' The cue was used to indicate the contraption on the table before it again hovered in mid-air close to his chest. 'And you won't want to explain what that radio's for.'

There wouldn't be a better moment to press home her advantage and negotiate Adam's release. In a way she was glad the boy was too woozy to properly understand what was being said. He might be only five but was a bright child and a primal revelation could blight his future happiness. 'Let me take Adam home now without any further trouble. In return I'll say there's been a misunderstanding, and you only intended to treat your nephew to a day out in town. The police might leave you alone. It'll give you some time to escape with the evidence, in any case.'

'You've got it all worked out, haven't you? No doubt with

some help from our friend Lieutenant Yates. Well, sorry, Cinderella. I'm not taking orders from an orphaned French refugee living on her sister's charity.'

He'd wounded her with that sneering comment, although she refused to let him see how much. She raised her eyebrows in faint disgust then went back on the attack. 'If you truly cared about Adam you'd let him go. Look at what you've done to him! He's hardly able to stand up. That's not a father's love.'

'I'm keeping him safe,' he roared. 'He'll have the best of everything with me. He shouldn't be living in the blasted East End, choking in factory smoke and bomb dust. He deserves better.' Toby felt savagely frustrated. But for Elise Bouchard poking her nose in, he would be on his way to Scotland with the boy. He'd been to collect his car from a nearby garage and had been ready to leave after packing a few belongings. From there, he'd planned to travel on by boat to Germany, the future hub of Europe ... the world; a place where blond, blue-eyed children were revered and assured of success.

He'd been planning this since Jake had gone to fight, leaving the coast clear. Toby hadn't been ready to strike yet but finding out Rebecca intended evacuating from London had forced his hand. He wanted Adam to have every advantage he'd been given in childhood but had later squandered to hedonism.

Both he and Jake had been illegitimate foundlings; spawned in Silvertown then dumped as newborns at an orphanage. An infertile fellow had adopted them and when older they had discovered they weren't true brothers, but were nevertheless related by blood. Toby had no ties to the Coopers; they were solely Jake's family. The Randalls were his kin and they could at least claim a modest prosperity in having owned a linen drapery.

Jake's sire was the link between them. Bruce Randall had a legitimate daughter of Clover Cooper's age. Henrietta Randall had given birth when still in her teens, but the man responsible wouldn't marry her. Such a predictably sordid tale Toby had thought when he found out about his natural parents. He'd decided he was glad he'd been rejected at birth. Being brought up to earn a living selling needles and thread sounded like hell to him.

Anybody who cared to ask was told he was the son of a City bigwig. His birth parents had married later on in life and had gone on to have other children. Toby had sisters but had never felt any inclination to discover if they knew he existed and couldn't have told you where they were now. But he knew the whole family had sold up the business and quit London. As for his grandfather – the man who had started the merry-go-round and farcically made Jake his uncle – he had been in the graveyard for decades.

The clatter of a police car's bell snapped Toby out of his brooding and into noticing that Elise was again at Adam's side and had a supportive arm about the boy.

'Cavalry's arrived.' Elise had received a much-needed piece of luck and knew to act on it. Abruptly, she hurled the cue, making Toby grunt as it struck his face and sent him teetering backwards. She didn't hang around to see what damage she'd inflicted; she yanked open the door and half carried Adam outside. The little lad made a valiant effort to mount the steps but stumbled on the icy surface. Elise carried him up the final few treads, aware of Toby surging out of the cellar in pursuit. She crashed the gate shut and glimpsed his contorted, bleeding face through the bars as he took the steps two at a time. A dark saloon car that she recognised was parked at the kerb. She'd ridden in it. She hurried Adam past it and across the wet road, lifting him up again when his sedated body wouldn't move fast enough.

The police car had halted at the corner by a bomb-damaged house. On both sides of the street servants were peering out of windows or emerging onto their employers' steps to discover what the excitement was about. Nobody took any notice of the young woman carrying the child along the sleety street. Elise glanced back. Toby had dashed after them but halted in the middle of the road. His expression was filled with fury. He knew he couldn't do anything to stop her with so many witnesses about.

When closer to the disturbance, it became clear what had happened: a sullen-faced fellow, loudly protesting his innocence, was being handcuffed for looting from the bomb-damaged property. The neighbour making the case for the prosecution was having her statement taken down in a notebook by a poker-faced constable. There was an opportunity for Elise to report another crime and to beg for help.

Toby had cottoned on to her reason for slowing down. He began to move backwards then swung around and loped towards his house. Elise watched him flee with great relief and satisfaction. His prime concern would be saving his own skin rather than getting revenge on her. If she accused him of abduction, questions and delays would follow. She put Adam down, gazing at the little chap gripping her hand and bravely holding in his tears. He wanted him mum, not justice for what he'd been put through. And how would his mother like her dirty laundry aired in public? Motives for the crime would be probed for in an investigation;

thus it must be for Rebecca to pursue this, not her. Elise guessed she wouldn't though if a secret surrounded Adam's parentage.

A bus was pulling in at the stop and the queue of people was shuffling forward.

The looter who'd been caught red-handed gave her a scowl for stopping to be nosy. She gave him a sympathetic smile; without him her drama would have ended differently.

'Come on, Adam, let's go home.' She buttoned up his coat against the chill, took his hand, then on they walked to join the others boarding the bus for Whitechapel.

Chapter Fifteen

'I've got to take me hat off to you, love. You've shown gumption and that's a fact.' Neil solemnly emphasised his praise by shaking his head.

Adam's mother and uncle had been shocked to realise they might never have seen the boy again if Elise hadn't courageously thwarted Toby Winters' kidnap plot in the nick of time.

'It was a fluke; I was fortunate to know about the cellar.'

Neil was battling his guilt at having failed to find the child himself but Elise wasn't being falsely modest or underplaying it for his sake. From discovering the key, to getting away under the noses of the policemen, Lady Luck had been on her side. The thanks she really wanted was from Adam's mother. So far Rebecca had found it hard even to meet her eyes. A few moments ago she had taken her son upstairs to quieten both their tears in private, leaving Elise alone with Neil. A silence developed between them as they retreated into their own thoughts. Elise roused herself to ask, 'Will you report Toby Winters to the police?'

Neil expelled a deep sigh. 'It's for Becky to say what

comes next.' He patted Elise's shoulder. 'We've all had a bad scare. Thanks to you it's turned out right in the end.'

'What's for me to say?' Having tucked her son up in bed Rebecca had returned to the kitchen. Her fierce brown eyes darted from one to the other of them.

'Will you set the police on him?' Neil asked.

'No need for any of that now Adam's back.' Rebecca's sharp voice impressed on them her ruling. She took a cigarette from a packet and lit it with shaking hands. Following a hefty drag, she offered the pack to the others.

Neil helped himself, and unusually, so did Elise. He lit their cigarettes and they stood quietly while a smoky haze added to the barrier between them.

'Will you write to Jake about this?' Neil ventured.

'No ... and you mustn't either.' Rebecca jabbed her cigarette's glowing tip at him. 'He needs to concentrate on dodging bullets, not on finding a way to go AWOL. And he will desert if he gets wind of this. So keep this to yourselves or there'll be even more trouble I can do without.' Another abrasive glance was swung between them.

'Yes ... of course,' Elise murmured while Neil nodded. They both knew Rebecca was feeling an emotional wreck, liable to explode, and they could understand why that was.

'Anybody want tea?' Rebecca reluctantly remembered her manners when nobody made a move to leave.

'No thanks, love; I'd best be getting off to work. Are you sure there's nothing else to be done?'

Rebecca shook her head. 'Thanks for what you did, Neil.'

'Should've done more,' he said bluntly and stuck the cigarette between his downturned lips.

'Tea?' Rebecca asked Elise after he'd gone.

'Thanks all the same, but I'd better be going too.' Elise

would have liked to stay for mutual comfort, but knew Rebecca didn't really want her company. 'How is Adam? Is he asleep?' She stubbed out her half-finished cigarette in the ashtray.

Rebecca nodded. 'He's been tearful but he'll get over it once we're away from here.' She paced aimlessly, smoking the cigarette in frantic spurts. 'Toby promised to let Adam stay in London with his friend. The lying conniving pig.' She swung herself to a standstill and formed fists that trembled in rage. 'I should have gone with you and killed him with my bare hands.'

Elise hung her head. She felt wretched for having been a catalyst to this pain. 'I'm so sorry, Becky, if I'd known I would never have told him—'

'Known what? What did he tell you about us?' Rebecca interrupted. 'What did that bastard say about me?' She grabbed the packet of Embassy and sucked into life another cigarette lit from the stub snatched from her mouth.

'It doesn't matter,' Elise soothed. 'I wouldn't believe a word he says. He's a criminal and a . . .' Elise stopped herself calling him a spy and resorted to grimacing in disgust. Graham was the only person she could talk to about that side to Toby Winters' villainy. Even at a time like this such secrets had to be kept. The outcome of the war could be affected; liberating France and returning there to her family was her beacon of light.

'He's a coward! That's what he is!' Rebecca snorted. 'He wouldn't have dared do this if Jake was around.' She weighed up whether to confide in Elise while darting glances at her. Decision made, she blurted, 'Don't suppose he told you he raped me? Years ago, it was, before I married Jake.'

'He didn't tell me.' Elise paused. 'He wouldn't. He hasn't got the courage to admit to that sort of truth. But I guessed something like that had happened.'

'I was seventeen, living at home still. My late father took me to the Winters' house with him one evening. Toby was back from university ... feeling bored. Just my luck, eh? He was never usually at home.' Rebecca savagely ground out her cigarette. 'My father held the same political views as them. He wasn't a very nice man, so naturally he got on like a house on fire with Fascist sympathisers.' She turned away, but Elise had already seen tears glossing her eyes.

'I'm so sorry, Becky. You don't need to say any more.'

'I will though,' Rebecca said forcefully, swinging back to face Elise. 'I warned you to steer clear of Toby Winters for your own good. Now you know what he's capable of, perhaps you'll make sure you do so in future.'

'I will,' said Elise to calm her down. It was unlikely he'd hang around in London, though, now she'd seen his radio equipment. With any luck she might never clap eyes on Toby Winters again.

'I've only told you this because you would've worked it out anyway,' Rebecca said. 'And you'll only be around for a short while. You'll go back home as soon as this blasted war's over. Gawd help us, I wish it would end today.'

It couldn't have been made any clearer that Rebecca would be relieved when the French girl left London and took bad memories with her. 'I want that too,' said a wistful Elise.

'Clover's guessed what's behind the bad blood between Jake and his brother,' said Rebecca. 'She and Neil have never pried but they knew I was pregnant when I got married. After this they'll have even more reason to be suspicious about Toby Winters' part in Adam's life.' Her shrug was jerky and defiant. 'They can all think what they like. The only explanation they'll get is that he took Adam without asking to be a troublemaking bastard as usual. I'd be obliged if you'd remember that when questions crop up.'

'I will.'

'Thanks,' Rebecca croaked and picked up the cigarettes. She didn't light up again but dropped the pack back onto the table. 'We don't need help or pity. We just want to be left alone to raise Adam. He's my husband's son. And nobody'd better say any different or they'll have me and Jake to answer to. These things get round even by accident. Adam's not growing up with name calling and finger pointing in the playground. We won't have it. So that's that.'

'That is that,' Elise said gently. 'Adam's a Harding like his dad. That's real.'

Rebecca jerked a nod of appreciation. 'I'll always be grateful to you for bringing Adam back.'

'It was the least I could do.'

'Yeah ... there is that to it.' Rebecca blushed, ashamed of being sarcastic. 'Well I won't keep you. I expect you're busy.'

'I do have a few things to do before I go to work later. I'll be off then.' Elise knew she was being asked to leave. She was ready to go, too. The atmosphere in the parlour had become stifling and it wasn't just due to an abundance of tobacco smoke. She'd never be completely forgiven for what had happened today. The terror in Rebecca had run too deep and nothing said or done could disperse it. Elise knew that in her shoes she'd react in the same way.

Eventually it would get round in this big sprawling family that Adam had been put in jeopardy by Sidney Cooper's French daughter speaking out of turn.

In a cruel twist of fate that left a rotten taste in her mouth, she'd gained something from this calamity: she'd found out what Graham wanted to know about Toby Winters' treachery, no tea at the Ritz required.

When outside in Rook Street, she set off towards the sounds of Whitechapel market with the sleet once more sandpapering her face. She felt in her pocket and found the piece of paper Graham had given her with a telephone number on it. There was a phone box on the opposite side of the street and she crossed over to use it, sorting some coins in her hand. As she walked on clutching those coppers, she hunched into her coat, tucking her chin into her collar and thinking she had never before felt as cold and lonely, or as homesick as she did right now.

'I won't let you miss out on afternoon tea at the Ritz. I'll take you myself in the New Year.'

Graham Yates was holding the door open for Elise as they entered a teashop. He threaded a path between occupied tables and found a vacant one by the window. Having pulled out a chair for her, he settled down opposite.

'I think I'm more of a Lyons Corner House girl,' said Elise ruefully, stripping off her gloves. 'But thank you for the offer.'

Graham leaned across the table to take her warm hands in his. He gazed at her; her grey eyes were sparkling and her complexion flushed from the frosty air that had left its lustre in her black hair. 'You, my dear, are the loveliest, classiest young lady and suit the Ritz better than anybody I know. Even if you do tend to scuff a chap's dancing pumps.' He chuckled while she groaned at his flattery. 'I know what you mean though: nothing beats these cosy places.' He glanced about at the other diners. Children, delighted to be treated to a Christmas shopping trip with a special tea thrown in, were assisting their mothers to deposit bulging bags beneath the tables before sitting up straight on their best behaviour.

It was the day before Christmas Eve and the Corner House had been decorated with colourful paper chains that danced in the draught, and stars that spiralled and sparkled as people came and went. There was a cheerful atmosphere and if one didn't notice the taped window glass it was possible to believe there wasn't a war on.

The Nippies, as the Corner House waitresses were known, were living up to their names, darting from table to table with notepads poised or tea trays balanced in capable hands. One cheerful soul with a sprig of tinsel pinned to her neat pinafore presented herself by them with a grin. Having given their order for a pot of tea and some crumpets, off she scooted. Graham turned his attention back to Elise, and he was looking rather serious.

'I wish we'd been able to meet up sooner. It's been pretty hectic though, as you might imagine. I'll bring you up to date with everything that's gone on after the bad business. And on a lighter note, I've an invitation to extend to you. Not the Ritz this time.' He smiled. 'Something far less glamorous, but I think you should accept.' He paused, conscious Elise seemed preoccupied.

She had been gazing out of the window at the Oxford Street shoppers while thinking of Nathan. She'd not dwelled on him at length for a while. But last night, out of the blue, she'd dreamed of him. It had been such a vivid, alarming dream that it had woken her up, and even now, hours later, she could recall springing upright in bed with her heart thudding and his face imprinted on the darkness before her eyes. She'd been convinced he was still alive and still in danger. And that had led to her fretting about her family. Was Luc safe, and Mathilde? Would they be able to spend Christmas together?

'Hey, daydreamer ... penny for them.' Graham shook her arm to gain her attention.

'Oh, sorry, I was thinking of the people at home.'

He sighed. 'I know it's a terrible to-do for your family. What a scare for the boy's poor mother. Winters must be deranged to abduct his own nephew. Perhaps he'll plead insanity in court.'

Elise didn't say that it wasn't the English side of her family troubling her mind. She felt rather remote from the Coopers now and the physical distance between them wasn't the only thing affecting her. Elise was now alone in the house and had only her factory colleagues and Graham for company.

'You seem rather solemn today, Elise. Not your usual self. I know you've been put through the wringer and I'd like to throttle Toby Winters for what he's done. They won't let me near him though.'

Elise's ears pricked up; she planted her elbows on the table and leaned closer. 'You got him then?' she whispered.

'He was apprehended last week on the Great North Road just outside Cumbria.' Graham mirrored her pose, until only inches separated them and they looked like lovers gazing into one another's eyes rather than people discussing treachery. 'Obviously it's not something I could have written to tell you about.' Graham kept his voice low, conscious of where they were. 'Winters was motoring towards Scotland but was forced to break his journey at a pub after getting a punctured tyre. A local garage had been called in to fix it. We think he also needed a base to—' his voice was barely a murmur '—transmit messages. Of course, he's clammed up. Won't explain how he came by that suitcase or who he had planned a rendezvous with north of the border.'

'I'm glad you got him. And I hope he's punished for whatever it is he's been up to. Where is he now?' she hissed.

'In custody ... that's all I can say. You know how it is. They don't tell me everything either.' They both sat upright in their chairs as the waitress returned and gave a discreet little cough. The middle-aged woman winked at Elise as she unloaded from the tray onto the table their tea and crumpets and some butter and jams.

'Mmm.' Graham growled his appreciation, having dived straight in, spreading a liberal amount of butter on the crumpet and biting into it. 'Delicious: fresh and springy.' He nodded at her untouched plate. 'Tuck in, don't want to let them go cold.' He upended the teapot into the cups, saying, 'I'll be mother.'

'What's this invitation you have for me then?' Elise sipped at her hot strong tea in between spreading her crumpets with blackcurrant jam.

'It's from my boss. He'd like to meet you to thank you personally for what you did to help.' Graham thumbed melted butter from his chin then licked it off. 'It's no exaggeration to say that without you we wouldn't have collared him. I told my boss you kept a cool head on the previous occasion you were in his house and managed to overhear ... what you did.' Graham continued to be careful in what he said.

'I didn't plan that – I was looking for an escape route at the time.'

'That's the point; you dealt with a tricky situation off the cuff, without knowing what you might be up against. That's not an easy thing to do.' He patted her arm in praise. 'Old Venables was impressed too. He's not been so forthcoming with telling me I was right all along about that man.' Graham gulped some tea then sat back with his arms crossed. 'Anyway, praise where it's due, Elise, and don't be too modest to take it.' He chuckled. 'Can't promise the old tight-fist will run to a reward though. It's a job getting a docket for paperclips out of him.'

'I don't want a reward.' Elise tutted in amusement. 'And I don't want any fuss, so thank him for the offer, but it's all finished as far as I'm concerned. I was scared stiff both times ... hardly a heroine.' She wiped her lips on a hanky. 'You're right, these crumpets are tasty. Almost as good as a freshly baked croissant.'

'Maybe you were scared, but I'll wager he didn't know it either time you were up against him.' Graham hadn't given up on getting her the recognition he believed she deserved. 'You carried it off and that's what counts.' His expression turned quizzical. 'What's a croissant when it's at home?'

'Come to France when this is all over and I'll show you. I'll introduce you to our lovely cakes and pastries: eclairs, madeleines, millefeuilles ...' Elise sighed nostalgically and turned to the window as a choir of carol singers with lanterns took up position outside in the dusk.

Inside the restaurant the chatter and clatter began to recede while everybody stopped what they were doing to appreciate the rendition of 'O Come, All Ye Faithful'. Polite applause broke out at the end and some wet eyes were dabbed with hankies as the final choral strains died away.

'Will you spend Christmas with your dad's family?'

Graham asked as the band of singers moved off to another location, their lanterns striping yellow onto the pavements.

'Unfortunately, I can't; nobody will be in London.'

'What, none of them at all?' he asked in surprise.

'Nobody,' she repeated with a wistful headshake. 'Neil's gone to Southend to be with Clover and the kids. He's staying until the New Year. Rebecca immediately took Adam to Cambridge. She won't be coming back. My sister Annie is in the countryside at her employer's estate.'

'Surely somebody invited you to spend the holiday with them?' Graham sounded shocked and not a little indignant.

'Yes, they did,' she said truthfully. 'Clover wrote to invite me to Southend and Neil insisted I should go with him or he'd stay behind. I told him not to be daft. I know they're overcrowded in the bungalow and besides . . .' She shrugged. 'I don't mind staying here in London. I've been offered overtime at the factory if I want it and . . .'

'And nothing,' Graham said firmly. 'You're spending Christmas with me. In fact, we're spending Christmas in Broadstairs. With my lot.' He gazed at Elise with intense sympathy. She'd been put in a rotten predicament because of him. 'I know you're feeling bad about the boy being taken. It wasn't your fault though, it was mine. I asked you to cosy up to Winters in the hope he'd betray himself. You would have avoided him like the plague if I hadn't done that.' He shoved a hand through his sandy hair and sighed. 'Then none of this would have happened, and you wouldn't be feeling awkward with your family. Look, I'll own up to it and tell them it was a silly game I pushed you into. Oh, I don't know . . .' He dropped back his head and contemplated the Christmas decorations while concentrating on finding a way to explain something that must remain confidential.

Elise remained loyal to the Coopers and didn't want him to think they were mean people who had shunned her. They were fair and decent. But she'd upset them and put one of their precious children in jeopardy. She understood why they were disappointed in her, perhaps making excuses for her as being weak and greedy like her father. But Toby Winters' riches had never been of interest, even if she were indeed an orphaned French refugee living on her stepfamily's charity. She'd chosen not to go to Southend and have her company tolerated and her character judged behind her back.

Graham sat forward to rap a knuckle on the table, having found a pertinent point in his defence. 'Winters would have tried to claim the boy sooner or later in any case. He says he's his father—'

'Well, he's not,' Elise interrupted. 'Adam is Jake's son.' She tapped her temple. 'Toby's jealous of his brother's happiness and it's affected him up here.'

'I have to say that crossed my mind as well. Let's talk about Christmas and forget all about him for now.' Graham drained his tea and returned the cup to its saucer. 'Will you come to Broadstairs with me tomorrow? There's a train from Victoria leaving at noon. Faith will be delighted to see you. She's already saying she's bored stiff and wishes she'd not chickened out and left London.' He frowned. 'I've heard from my mother as well. She's worried about Faith.' He looked optimistically at Elise. 'If anybody can make her see sense about her boozing, maybe you can. My sister always liked a drink, even as a kid. When our grandparents were alive we'd spend Christmas around the corner at their house. All the cousins and aunts and uncles would be invited. We'd all cram in their little back room round a dining table that went off in all directions.' He paused to reflect and smile nostalgically while indicating the haphazard tables with this hands. 'Us kids would get half a glass of Sauterne with our roast chicken as a treat. Faith was always after a refill.' His smile faded as the recollections got darker. 'Mum said after Dunkirk Faith started carrying a hip flask all the time. The bad news with Bob made everything worse.' He sighed. 'I know she's suffered recently but so have lots of people in this damned war.'

'I'll have a word with her.' Elise squeezed Graham's hand in comfort. 'I would love to see Faith and your mum and dad. So thank you, I'd like to come to Broadstairs if I can arrange it. I'm due in work this evening so better get moving and ask my supervisor nicely for some leave.'

'You and Faith hit it off straight away, didn't you?' he said while signalling to their waitress for the bill.

'Yes, we did ...'

'I've been around her for twenty years yet you seem to have got to know her better than me in just six months. I don't really understand what's got into my sister.'

'If you'd been at Dunkirk, you would, Graham,' said Elise quietly.

As he paid the bill, she turned to the window, buttoning up her coat. The dusk had become darkness while they'd been inside. The paper chains and sparkling stars were there in the glass but instead of her own reflection she saw a rolling sea and Nathan Hawkes stranded in it, gazing at her with fierce eyes.

Chapter Sixteen

Spring 1941, Tarbes, France

'What in hell's happened? Why are you back?'

'There's a traitor and I'd damn well like to know who it is and turn this on them.' A bloodied hand brandished a pistol used to bash on the door. The weapon was stuffed in his pocket and Nathan Hawkes quickly supported the man sagging against the flint wall.

Luc Bouchard assisted in dragging the wounded fellow inside. Before closing the door he peered nervously into the gloom; all seemed still in the shadowy landscape silvered by a misshapen moon. Even the owls were quiet.

'I'm pretty sure we weren't followed,' Nathan said.

Luc helped the unconscious airman to droop onto the floor while Nathan struggled out of his jacket to use it as a blanket.

'How far did you get?' There was no immediate response; Nathan had knelt beside the pilot to cover him and then succumbed to his exhaustion. His chin was low, almost touching his chest. When agitated, Luc reverted to his mother tongue and he expelled some French obscenities.

'We reached the river,' Nathan bucked himself up to answer. 'Were almost halfway across when they opened fire. Two black saloon cars were hidden in undergrowth and four Gestapo in them. I managed to shoot out their headlights and we hid in the rushes until they gave up. With luck they thought we'd made it to the other side or were dead in the water.' He swung around to face Luc. 'They weren't there by accident.' The next words were gritted out through his teeth. 'They were waiting for us.'

Nathan and the British pilot had left yesterday at twilight with the intention of crossing the border at an isolated spot. Once the other side of the river they faced another trek: over the mountains with a local guide, then onwards by sea towards home. Only none of the good bit on the Spanish side had happened. They were still in France and in a worse predicament than before. But they'd known the risks involved in trying, and failing, to escape.

'Let's hope the Gestapo think they finished you off, or they'll be crawling all over this place before long.' Luc had put into words his friend's fears. He hunkered down beside Nathan to peer at the airman's deathly pallor. A huge dark stain on the man's clothing was hard to miss. 'By the looks of it they have eliminated one of you. He's really bought it.' He gently disturbed the bloodied coat. 'Where's he been hit?'

'In his side. I think the bullet's still in there. It's not just that: the cold's done for him.' Nathan sank back onto his haunches and rushed a hand through his long matted hair. He closed his eyes, rocking on his heels in tiredness. His unruly mind though wouldn't let go of the memory of bullets being fired into the water while pencil-thin torchlight penetrated the reeds to find them. For what had seemed like an eternity he'd prayed the trigger-happy bunch would give up and drive off before his chattering teeth gave the game away. Eventually, he'd sluggishly crawled out, hauling the shot man with him. Minutes more and they'd both have frozen to death. 'God knows how he managed to keep moving on the way back, but he did and that probably saved his life.'

'You saved his life. But not for long, I'd say,' said Luc bluntly.

'We need to keep him warm and find him a doctor.' Nathan's shivering fingers beckoned. 'Give me your coat and anything else you can find to cover him.'

Luc did as he was asked before surging upright and urgently stirring the fire into life with a stick. He could tell that his friend was also perishing cold and close to collapse. He threw on a handful of kindling, tending the blaze with mesmeric attention. 'We can't help him, you know.' He dropped the poker and swung around. 'He's lost too much blood. You should have left him and kept going. You'd be on your way home by now.'

It was dim in the cottage: two burning candles and the flames in the grate provided the light. The pilot's sunken black eye sockets were obvious nonetheless. 'You should have left him behind,' Luc repeated harshly and banged a kettle down to boil on a primus stove. 'If you'd reached the opposite bank of the river the mission wouldn't have been a complete disaster.'

'We weren't close to the Spanish side. We were practically hiding under their boots when they searched the riverbank downstream. And we don't leave wounded men behind.'

'Well, we do! It's the rules. He'll slow us down. Put all of us in danger.'

Nathan gave a defeated chuckle. 'We're already in danger, mate; have been since long before we met him.' Nathan stood up, wincing at his stiffness. 'Your Resistance people have a rotten apple. I'm telling you those Krauts knew we were coming.'

Luc anxiously swiped a hand around his bristly face. It wasn't the first time they'd had a close shave; bad luck ... coincidence ... those excuses had worn too thin now.

'Has the courier been got at, d'you think?' Nathan brought to mind the girl who had been their contact. She was a solemn little thing of about twenty. A go-between in a nearby village had told them she was a seamstress with a toddler daughter. As well as ferrying messages and fugitives the seamstress donated old clothes she spruced up for re-use. Allied servicemen awaiting a chance to escape were glad of these to wear over their uniforms. Nathan had dressed as a civilian since the early days when Father Pascal gave him some labourer's clothes. When out, Luc did the talking. Nathan had picked up some French; not nearly enough to get him by on his own though.

'Paulette's husband was one of the first to be arrested after the fuel dump was blown up. He's been sent to a camp.' Luc had considered the girl's likely guilt and gave his verdict. 'She hates the Nazis. I think she's sound. Don't you trust her?'

The sardonic look in Nathan's eyes spoke for him. Nobody could be completely trusted. The Resistance groups were becoming skilled in sabotage. As well as fuel dumps, telegraph poles and railway lines were put out of action; French factories that had been commandeered to make German munitions had spanners thrown in the works, grinding them to a halt for months. In retaliation, punishments were becoming increasingly savage for those caught. Some prisoners broke and betrayed comrades, not always to save themselves, but their families.

'The farmer might know of a sympathetic doctor for our RAF pal. I'll go and speak to him.'

'Don't be too hasty. We need to think about this for a moment.' Luc grabbed his friend's arm. 'The old sod's jittery and doesn't want us on his land for long.' Luc poured two mugs of coffee and gave one to Nathan. 'He thinks we'll be gone by now, not setting up home in this bog-hole.'

'Stop moaning. It's got a roof.' Nathan almost smiled as he gulped the drink and felt its heat course through him. Back home he'd seen people living in East End slums worse than this. Silvertown ... the place Elise had gone to, taking his heart with her ... had many crumbling ruins after the Great War. In Poplar he'd played on bomb sites as a child, before he'd been sent to the orphanage.

Brooding on home was depressing. He and Private Evans had planned to escape from the moment they'd been captured. They'd talked of having a celebratory pint in a pub and a fish-and-chip supper the moment they hit London. Most of all Nathan longed to see Elise and hoped after all this time she would want to see him. His mind turned to the night he'd held her in his arms, but he blocked the memory after seconds. It only made things worse. 'We need to find a doctor,' he gruffly told her brother. 'Get moving, Luc. It's almost light. The farmer will already be up.'

'I know he will; I used to be a farm labourer,' Luc muttered. 'I'll talk to him when I've finished this.' He swallowed scalding coffee; his surliness stemmed from his frustration that the carefully planned escape had come to nothing.

He'd never been a regular soldier who'd bonded with

comrades, and thus found stubborn loyalty incomprehensible when it became suicidal. They'd become close though over the months of living and fighting the enemy together and Luc was indebted to Nathan Hawkes for saving his sister. He guessed his friend would be remembering the pal he'd served with for years and had left behind in the graveyard at Hazebrouck.

The pilot began mumbling in delirium, drawing their eyes as he threw off their covering jackets and struggled to sit up. The jerky movement made him groan in pain and collapse back.

Paulette had brought the pilot in yesterday evening not long before the planned departure. The preparations had been too frantic to bother with proper introductions. The new arrival had told them he was a fighter pilot from Oxford, shot down when chasing a Messerschmitt back to France last autumn. He'd spent the intervening months hiding and existing on well-wishers' charity while moving from place to place. Luc and Nathan had been doing much the same thing. If they'd made it into neutral territory Nathan would have shown an interest in getting to know the pilot better. In France, it was wise not to ask too much or to tell too little. It would be easy to resent the burden he'd become, but Nathan willed him to live. He'd sacrificed his liberty to give him a chance and didn't want it to be for nothing. He could have made it across the river on his own. He put down his half-finished coffee as the man cried out in pain. 'I'm not waiting any longer. We need a doctor. Spitfire needs that bullet out of him before infection sets in.'

'I'll go.' Luc swooped on his coat and shoved his arms into it. 'Your French isn't that good. Anyway, he's used to dealing with me and might be more obliging to one of his own kinsmen. I'll remind him of his patriotic duty.' Luc glanced around the derelict cottage as he pulled on his woollen balaclava.

The early spring had been cold. The portable cooking stove, the fire grate and a few meagre provisions provided by Paulette were the only comforts. They'd not prepared for a lengthy stay. Luc had intended to journey back to Lille and lie low once Nathan was on his way to England with a letter for Elise in his pocket.

He opened the door, scouring the countryside and sky before slipping outside. Nathan threw the last of the wood onto the embers and poked it into life. He shrugged into his coat, weighty with river water, and followed the younger man into the pale and frosty dawn to collect fuel. Building up the fire might help Spitfire sweat out a fever and at least get him back onto his feet so they could move him elsewhere. Staying here, close to the border with Spain, was asking for trouble.

The insipid light barely provided him with a glimpse of Luc's dark figure, running at a crouch through the icy meadow. A dog started barking, possibly having picked up his scent. But Nathan could see that Luc wasn't convinced about that either, and had slowed down to cautiously proceed. A candle began to burn at an upstairs window. The weight of the pistol in his pocket was welcome, but after last night it was almost empty of bullets. Their weapons would be useless soon if they couldn't get their hands on more ammunition. He heard the shouting, faint at this distance, but Luc was closer and more aware of what was going on. He had thrown himself to the ground the moment he noticed the warning signal's wavering flame.

Car doors slammed, and then came the sound of

guttural voices. The Gestapo hadn't spotted Luc; they were banging on the farmhouse door. A woman's shrieked protestations echoed on the still air. Nathan watched as the officers barged inside while the troopers remained by the vehicle. Nathan guessed it was one of the Daimlers from last night.

Luc shoved himself onto his knees, preparing to retreat. A melodic whistle, which might have been birdsong but he knew was not, drew no interest from the guards; they continued to mooch against the car and share a crafty cigarette, oblivious to movement in the meadow. He had a distance to cover to reach the thicket in which his friend was concealed but imminent danger lent him frantic energy. 'I nearly ... walked straight ... into that,' he wheezed out through a throat that felt as raw as his elbows. He'd pulled himself along keeping his body low in frost-wilted grass. He jumped panting to his feet to stand beside Nathan. 'You won't need that.' He looked at an armful of kindling. 'You can't go back to the cottage now. Nothing can be done for Spitfire. They can't be sure that you're alive but they've tracked where you came from.'

Nathan didn't need that spelled out. The Gestapo had come out of the house with the farmer. He was bundled into the back of the car and the officers got into the front. The infantrymen loped behind the moving vehicle as it set off in the direction of the cottage.

As the car drew closer, somebody else became visible in the back of it. A woman's small dark head was bowed in defeat. 'Paulette ...' said Nathan, feeling pity rather than anger for the young Frenchwoman. A toddler daughter and a husband in detention were powerful leverage.

'You were right about her then,' Luc said grimly as the

car bumped down the track to the derelict whitewashed building. 'Have you left anything important in there?'

'A fighter pilot.'

'You can't help him now.' Luc let his friend's sarcasm wash over him.

'I know. Spitfire's helped us though,' said Nathan roughly. 'We'd both still be in there if not for him.' He dropped the kindling to the peaty ground.

'Come on. We've got to go, before they search for us.' Luc tugged on his friend's arm.

Nathan retreated further beneath the sheltering trees, pulling Luc with him. He jerked a nod. The two foot soldiers, supporting Spitfire between them, had emerged from the cottage. The farmer was turfed out of the car to make room for the pilot to take his place. With a soldier on either running board the vehicle drove off, leaving the farmer behind.

'They'll be back for him and come mob-handed to scour the area.' Nathan turned to Luc. 'Our local Resistance friends need to be warned to expect a visit.'

'First, I'm going back to the cottage for the bread and cheese. It's too risky now to stop anywhere and buy food.'

'Quick as you can then,' said Nathan.

Luc hared towards the cottage, keeping out of sight of the farmer. Nathan watched the wailing fellow trudging towards home, gesticulating at the heavens. He knew he was trapped. He had no time to flee and only an agony of waiting in front of him until the men in black uniforms came for him. Nathan shook his head and expelled a long sigh. He was feeling guilty despite the man having volunteered to shelter them. A bottle of wine or two had been involved and toasts of 'viva la France!', Luc had said when merrily reporting that he and the go-between had sorted out somewhere for them to stay for a few nights.

'I doubt Spitfire'll survive long enough to talk; even so you'll be safer on your own,' said Nathan as they loped through the trees. Anybody caught assisting an escaped prisoner of war risked being shot and Luc was Elise's brother. He was a constant reminder of her in looks and Nathan felt obliged to do his best to protect him.

'I'd rather we stick it out together.' The idea of them splitting up alarmed Luc. Nathan was an asset despite his inability to pass himself off as a Frenchman on his own. He was a trained soldier, skilled in the use of weapons, and had a military cunning that Luc lacked. Being older and wiser, he had a cooler head and urged caution when Luc would have rushed headlong into a trap on occasion. They'd had to kill enemy soldiers already to stay alive in a slow and perilous trek south. There would be more of that to come now the Gestapo was closing in on them.

They approached a clearing and a muddy path that led to a cluster of houses surrounding a green. The hamlet reminded Luc of the place outside Lille where his grandmother lived. 'I'll tell him what's happened. He'll have to spread the word to the others.' Keeping to the treeline, he darted away to inform the go-between of the ambush and arrests.

Nathan hunkered down with his back against an oak to wait. He felt in his pocket for his share of the salvaged bread. He bit into it and after a couple of swallows it stopped his empty stomach rolling. His wallet had come out with the food and inside it, carefully folded, was Luc's letter to Elise. Nathan looked at the damp envelope with its smudged ink.

He'd badly wanted to see her. Even now, almost a year on, he could recall the summer scent of her.

'He was full of questions ... wanted to know about Paulette's part in it.' Luc had returned quickly to disturb Nathan's pleasant reminiscence. 'I said he knows more than I do and I couldn't stop to chew things over. He'll have to investigate the leak himself and cut out all the rot. And he'd better act fast before the whole lot of them are rounded up.' He rummaged in his pocket. 'I told him we needed money and ammunition. He coughed up without trouble.' He handed half of the francs and bullets to Nathan, who led the way onwards.

Soon, the sun was up, warming the atmosphere and glinting on the rail tracks glimpsed through branches unfurling their leaves. On the edge of the woods they settled down in undergrowth within striking distance of the line. The train would slow at this point where the track hit a bend, giving them a chance to get into one of the goods' wagons.

'I'm going back to Lille,' said Luc, tucking into a stale crust as though it were manna from heaven. He broke a lump of cheese off a small wedge to give to Nathan and finished off the other piece himself. 'Come with me,' he said through a mouthful of Brie. 'I need to see my grandmother and make sure she's safe. And find out if she's heard from Elise.'

Nathan finished eating and turned onto his back to let the sun filter through the canopy of foliage onto his face. His damp clothes began to dry and he watched the steam rising from his body. He wasn't relaxed; he was straining for the sound of pursuit or a train that might yet save them from the enemy not far behind.

'Well? What d'you say?' Luc stretched out beside him.

'We'll have to cross the border back into the Occupied Zone. It won't be any easier getting in than it was getting out.' They had paid a black-marketeer to hide them in his cart. The fellow was used to doing the crossing and knew which border guards to bribe with cigarettes. 'But might as well go that way,' Nathan said. 'The southern route's proved a dead loss.'

'The northern coastline is alive with Jerry,' Luc pessimistically pointed out.

'Maybe they'll not expect an escaped POW to be stupid enough to try slipping past them.' Nathan chuckled. 'Could work in my favour.' He folded up to a seated position and gazed into the distance. A faint sound became identifiable and the sun glanced off steel as the train approached. 'You fit?'

'As I'll ever be,' said Luc, using one of his father's expressions. A wistful smile accompanied his thoughts of Sidney Cooper. His father had dropped his children in it, going out with a bang like that. Luc felt proud of him though. He wasn't envious of Elise getting away to the safety of England. He was glad he'd stayed. 'Passenger train.' He squinted into the glare and grimaced disappointment. The train was likely to have Nazis on board as well as civilians.

'It's not,' said Nathan with a grin as a cloud curtained the sun, giving him a better view. 'It's a goods train.' He held out a hand to pull Luc to his feet.

They concealed themselves and waited, primed to run when the carriages reached the right spot.

Spitfire, the Resistance girl with the toddler, the weeping farmer ... all were forgotten as adrenaline surged through Nathan. Nothing mattered any more but getting onto the train. This rattling contraption was their best hope of outrunning capture. They'd barely make a few miles before being picked up if continuing on foot. Begging lifts or shelter was risky; they couldn't be sure those they met weren't collaborators. Even if they weren't, more innocent people would be jeopardised by associating with them now the enemy was hot on their tail. He gripped Luc's shoulder, holding him back as the younger man's impatience got the better of him, and he would've broken cover. Timing it right was imperative: not too early or they'd risk being spotted by the driver or guard, not too late or they'd be unable to reach the train as it picked up speed.

'Now.' He shoved Luc forward. They pelted from beneath the trees and headed for the final swaying wagon. Nathan pulled himself up using the bar on the door and worked it free of its hasp to force it open. Luc was charging alongside, keeping up but tiring, his arms and legs windmilling. Nathan held out his hand, gripped Luc's frantic fingers and twisted his own into them. The train was accelerating as it straightened out. With a final growling effort Nathan pulled and Luc sprung. They both rolled onto the floor of the carriage, and when they had breath enough to do so started to laugh.

Chapter Seventeen

'If only I could stay right here in paradise forever.'

Elise had been in Kent for months but the landscape's blissful tranquillity seemed more intense today. The scented air and ripening barley fields made it easy to believe rural Broadstairs must lie in a different country to Silvertown rather than a neighbouring county. Bees feasting on nearby wildflowers droned a soporific lullaby and the midday heat was tempered by a gentle breeze. The terrain opposite the cereal crop had an apple orchard clinging to its sloping ground. The gnarled trees had hung on to a smattering of blossom but the last of the fading flowers were being gathered up and sprinkled like confetti.

'There is a way you can stay forever, you know.' Faith was stretched out in the shade with her hands pillowing her head. Her eyelids remained closed against the dazzling June light. 'A nice husband and a brood of kids around your ankles would do the trick. You'll soon forget all about going back to London or to France.' She rolled over to prop her chin on her fists. 'I might be able to recommend a suitable local chap who would be happy to oblige.'

'That wouldn't be a certain Graham Yates, would it?' Elise

asked wryly. She was seated with her knees drawn up and her arms wrapped around her trousered shins. Her back was resting against the massive trunk of a walnut tree, its tangy lemony leaves rustling on low boughs. By her side was a wicker basket that had contained their midday meal. A limp gingham cloth was empty of cheese sandwiches and the tea flask had been drained.

'He's not going to give up so you might as well encourage him to propose. My brother hasn't shown this much interest in any girl since he was twelve and chasing Valerie Jiggins round the playground in a game of kiss chase.'

'Is Valerie still available?'

'Heavens no! She married a hotelier's son and moved to Brighton years ago. Graham was always a bit of a swot and she wasn't. She was a flirt. He had grown out of her before they left school. He had a few girlfriends at university. But now he's got his eye on you, love.'

'Graham deserves a better wife than me,' said Elise seriously.

'Why, what's wrong with you?'

I won't ever have the right feelings for him, Elise could have said, but didn't. Faith would be upset and ask why that was. Faith loved the idea of them being sisters-in-law. Elise did too. But it wouldn't be fair to encourage Graham when her heart wasn't in it ... when she wasn't even sure where her heart was because she'd no idea where Nathan Hawkes was, or whether he was still alive and wanted her. Until she did, she couldn't test whether her feelings for him were real. He'd selflessly protected her, probably saved her life and so began a girlish infatuation with her gallant hero. She wasn't that girl now but the longing for him remained; she'd turned nineteen and over a year had passed since she'd blown him a kiss goodbye and said hello to Faith Yates. Two people who were important to her, one gained and one lost within minutes of one another.

'Look, love, you must know he's probably bought it ... same as Bob did.' Faith sat up and put a comforting arm around her friend's shoulders. She'd guessed the cause of the stumbling block to her matchmaking. 'You just can't forget him, can you?'

'No,' Elise croaked.

'True love then,' Faith sighed. 'But in time you'll get over him. The not knowing's the worst, isn't it? When this damned war's at an end, you'll know for certain. You'll be able to lock him away in your mind and set your heart free.' She sighed. 'That's what us Dunkirk Club girls do.'

Elise let her head droop onto Faith's shoulder, aware her friend was being brutally blunt to be kind. 'I know it's more than likely going to be bad news. I'll go back to France anyway as soon as I can. I have to. I miss Luc and my grandmother dreadfully and it's driving me mad not knowing if they're all right.' She straightened up with a sigh. 'First, I'm off to London. I've been meaning to tell you, I'm heading back to Silvertown next week.'

'What? Why?' The startling news brought Faith swivelling to face her friend. 'You've got a job and a place to stay here in Kent. You know my mum and dad like having you.' Faith grimaced. 'I think they prefer having you around to me.'

'Don't be daft, your parents dote on you.' Elise pushed herself to her feet and stretched her arms over her head. The straw hat she'd discarded onto the grass earlier was swooped on and dusted against her knee. 'I adore being here but the last letter Clover sent didn't come from Essex.

She's moved back to London now the Blitz seems to be over. She's asked me to go home. She said she misses me and has things to talk about.'

'I'll miss you and I've got things to talk about.' Faith took the chewed blade of grass from her mouth and discarded it. 'I'll be bored stiff here without you.'

'Come with me then. We could still work together. The munitions factory said they'd give me back my job when I returned to town.'

'That was six months ago. Don't suppose they imagined your extended Christmas holiday would end in June.'

'Neither did I.' Elise chuckled as she put on her sunhat. She'd intended to stay only an extra few days with the Yateses and return to London with Graham during the first week of January at the end of his leave. Her hosts had invited her to stay on; Faith had begged her to. With nothing to go back to other than factory smoke and her brother-in-law's sporadic company it had been easy for Elise to agree. But her favourite sister was back and things were different. Clover had been like a mum to her since she'd turned up waif-like on her doorstep and been heartily welcomed by folk who reminded her of home. It was hard to deny the pull of the Coopers when they resembled Luc and her father.

There was more to it than that though: Elise had become restless without understanding why. She also felt that she'd badly outstayed her welcome with the Yateses. She was paying her way but even so felt awkward to still be using Graham's room or sharing Faith's bed when he came on a visit to his parents. Admittedly he'd only done so once since Christmas. At Easter he'd arrived with chocolate eggs and had made a point of telling her he missed her being in

London. She missed him too, but not in the way he wanted. She had questions to ask him about Toby Winters.

The sound of a shrill whistle drew a groan from Faith. Elise extended a hand to her friend and pulled her to her feet. 'Come on, lazybones, time's up.'

They brushed down their khaki drill breeches and utility shirts. Elise picked up the wicker basket and arm-in-arm they started down the grassy incline to join the other land girls finishing up their meals.

'I will come to London with you,' Faith declared as they strolled on with the sun scorching their backs.

'Really?' Elise turned to her with a delighted grin.

'Really.' Faith gave a firm nod. 'I'm ready for another taste of West End razzle-dazzle. Don't worry,' she said, on hearing her friend's mocking groan. 'You have my permission to send me straight home if I chase after any Toby Winters types.' She frowned. 'I hope he ended up in prison after trying to kidnap your nephew. Very strange to-do. Graham brushes over it when I bring it up. I'm sure my brother knows more about it than he's letting on.' Faith sent Elise an enquiring look.

'I don't know what happened to him after he was arrested,' she truthfully said. 'The others never mention Jake's brother in their letters. I haven't heard from Becky Harding since Easter when she wrote about taking Adam to see his cousins at the seaside. She said it was the last trip she'd make as the baby was due in a couple of months.' Elise had replied but not yet received anything back. Becky probably had her hands full with the new arrival, due right about now.

Faith took her screwed-up hat from her pocket and punched the crown into shape before seesawing it onto her fair hair. 'He must be weird, snatching a kid to pass off as his own. Don't know why I ever thought him attractive.'

'Pie-eyed ...' Elise used one of her father's expressions then ducked a friendly slap. She didn't avoid mentioning Faith's liking for a drink. In fact a good-natured joke now and then seemed to work better than a lecture.

Elise trotted the remaining yards to join their colleagues, avoiding any further mention of Toby Winters. Elements of that man's fantastic tales were true, but nobody would hear her say so. Even Graham. In turn, she knew Graham had information about Toby's treason that he'd never divulge to her. Nevertheless, they shared enough confidential knowledge to be bound together in a way that made her feel rather uncomfortable. She didn't like to have to dodge questions from friends and family about that episode. The heartache Becky had suffered – Jake too, for it must have been dreadful to know his brother was rotten to the core and had raped the woman he loved – wounded Elise. She'd grown fond of the couple, and their dear little boy.

'Oi ... can I have a bit of your Nivea Creme?' the girl from Bermondsey called out. 'I'm peeling.' She tapped her sunburnt nose.

'Here ... catch ...' Faith pulled a small tin from her pocket and lobbed it.

It was deftly caught by the girl seated on a cart that had been pulled into a patch of shade. There were two others with her; they were all similarly attired in twill dungarees with knotted scarves binding their hair. While one rubbed a liberal amount of Nivea into her red face the other two screwed lids onto Thermos flasks, preparing to resume work. A girl with freckles took a cigarette from her lips and stubbed it out on the cart. Her headscarf was adjusted for the butt to be lodged behind her ear.

Pitchforks and scythes that had been abandoned on the verges were collected up and the team of five trooped back to their positions to start gathering hay and clearing ditches that edged the meadow. An adjacent square parcel of land had been left fallow to enrich the soil for the crop to follow. In a few months the plough would be preparing the ground for sowing but Elise would be gone by then. Faith, too, if she stuck to her word and went to London.

At six o'clock, they knocked off, by which time Elise's flushed cheeks were striped with sweaty strands of black hair. The work was strenuous but she had become stronger and more able to cope with it over the months of being a land girl. She'd grabbed the chance to learn to drive the tractor when the farmer asked for volunteers. She'd always envied Luc up high on his perch on his boss's tractor in Lille. During the February snows the farmer had taken to his bed with a debilitating cough. He'd asked Elise and Freckles, who'd also learned to drive, to unblock the lanes with a plough attachment. They had taken turns forcing snow aside so livestock could be moved and provisions brought in. Faith had steered clear; saying piloting a boat was more her thing.

The Bermondsey girl and her friend from Peckham had been provided with accommodation in the farmhouse. They trudged off towards it, spades over shoulders, calling out their goodbyes. Freckles was a local. She was older than the rest of the team at twenty-six, and engaged to a leading aircraftman stationed in Scotland. She joined Elise and Faith in sitting on the cart, oohing and aahing as strained muscles began to twinge. Their boss watched over his shoulder as they settled down. They gave him the thumbs-up, signalling they were ready to get going. The tractor jerked the cart into motion.

The home-time songs varied from Vera Lynn ballads to Ginger Rogers show numbers; today Freckles struck up with 'Ten Green Bottles', beating time on the planks with a hand. After about a mile travelled, she was first to hop off the cart with a wave. The dog-end was retrieved from behind her ear and she ambled down the rutted lane trailing cigarette smoke. The other two carried on with another verse. They gave up on the bottles before they'd all fallen. They continued swinging their legs, sitting on the edge of the planked timbers, with the wicker basket rocking between them and discussed how Faith's mum and dad would take knowing they were leaving for London next week.

'You two are getting pretty lights in your hair where the sun's caught it,' was Mrs Yates' greeting as they trooped in through the kitchen door and took off their hats. She put down the potato peeler and looked the tired girls over with maternal pride. It was easy to think of them as sisters, although they couldn't have been more dissimilar in looks. She felt genuine affection for Elise. As well as being a beauty their French guest was charming and polite. Her main attribute in Mrs Yates' eyes was an ability to exercise a good influence over Faith. Her daughter wasn't drinking as much since her friend had come to stay.

Faith inspected her reflection in the mirror on the wall. 'I think I suit a suntan.'

'The summers always give you a healthy glow, dear, but make sure you moisturise or you'll spoil your complexion.' Mrs Yates touched her creased cheek. 'I took for granted I'd always look good without much effort. I had lovely skin at your age.' She didn't sound regretful; in fact, she missed those early married years when she'd accompanied her husband skippering the boat before the children came along to keep her indoors.

It was a worry of Faith's that sailing in all weathers might make her look old before her time. The Nivea was taken from her pocket and her face was massaged with a scoop of it.

Elise placed the empty basket under the table. 'Something smells good, Mrs Yates.'

'I've made a minced beef and onion pie,' said the woman turning her attention back to the pots on the stove. 'The butcher didn't have much but he did have mince and sausages. I'll boil potatoes for mash and there are a few runner beans from the garden too.'

'Good. I'm ravenous,' said Faith. 'What's for pudding?'

'Rhubarb crumble and custard,' her mother said with a glance at her daughter's trim figure. 'Just as well you're working off all the food you eat or you'd look like Bessie Bunter.'

'Got to have some enjoyment in life, haven't I?'

Elise's glance swung between mother and daughter, sensing the atmosphere becoming sparky.

'Your father had a party of tourists booked in for a trip to Bournemouth this afternoon, Faith.' Mrs Yates blithely changed the subject. 'This good weather is bringing people out to enjoy it while they can.' She sighed. 'Let's hope the rotten lot don't come back for another go at us and spoil the summer.' She gazed out of the window at the skies. During the worst of the Blitz, the horizon would appear thundery with approaching fleets of enemy bombers.

'I'm off upstairs to wash and change.' Elise diplomatically

allowed Faith to break the news privately to her mother about leaving home.

In her room, she stripped off to her underclothes, abandoning her work uniform where it fell. She lay down on the bed to rest her weary limbs and was close to dozing off when there was a tap on the door. She sat up, expecting to see Faith but Mrs Yates poked her head into the room before venturing inside.

'Faith's told me your plans.'

Elise stood up, wondering if she was about to be scolded for putting ideas in Faith's head.

'I'm pleased she's going to be with you,' Mrs Yates reassured, having read the girl's uncertainty. 'I knew you wouldn't stay here forever. How could you when your family's elsewhere? Family's everything, isn't it?'

'It is,' said Elise. 'But I've loved every minute of being here in Broadstairs with you all. I can never thank you enough for what you've done for me.'

Mrs Yates approached to take her hands. 'You don't have to thank me, dear. You've helped Faith stay sober and that's enough for me and her father. She wants to spend time with you because she knows you'll be gone for good soon. I hope you'll come back and see us again before you leave.'

'I will. When this is all over, I'm going back to France but I won't leave without saying goodbye.'

Mrs Yates cupped Elise's cheek with a chapped palm. 'You deserve to be happy wherever you are.' She paused. 'But I will ask you to keep an eye on Faith while she's in London, if you would. I don't want to burden you; I'd ask her brother and Graham would do his best, but she doesn't listen to him about the boozing, you see. They've always batted against one another, but the love's there.'

Elise smiled wryly, thinking of her and Luc bickering as they grew up. Then, exasperating; now a memory to cherish. She could tell Mrs Yates wanted to say more but was holding it in for fear of being thought rude. On impulse, Elise pecked the woman's wrinkled cheek. 'I will do my best to look after her. I have to; she means an awful lot to me. She looked after me at Dunkirk.'

'I'm so glad you got away.' Mrs Yates embraced Elise then sniffed and composed herself. 'Well, didn't mean to barge in.' She busily wiped potato stains from her fingers onto her pinafore then folded up Elise's crumpled trousers and shirt and put them on the end of the bed. 'Have a little nap, dear. Dinner's going to be ready at about seven-thirty.'

'Oh, you do look well!' Clover had been listening for the key to strike the lock. The moment it did, she rushed out of the living room to greet her sister in the hallway.

Before Elise had a chance to put down her suitcase, she was enclosed in two warm welcoming arms. 'So do you,' she finally replied when Clover relaxed her bear hug. The older woman certainly looked a picture of health. 'Sea air agrees with you, Clover. Bet you didn't want to come back to the smoke, did you?'

'Not really; but can't live on fresh air. That's the thing. Jake's business is our livelihood as well. Neil's been doing his best on his own but he needs some help with the paperwork before he's snowed under.' She linked arms with Elise as they walked towards the sitting room. 'We promised Jake we'd keep things ticking over for him while he's away fighting, and we will.'

There was a pregnant pause and Elise bit the bullet and

brought the matter up. 'Is Becky coming back to London to help out? Is she still angry with me?'

Clover put the kettle on the stove to make tea. She smiled to herself. No beating about the bush. Straight to it. Elise was definitely a Cooper. Clover saw something of herself in the girl's character; she'd always been one to meet trouble head on rather than brood on it. So she'd answer in the same vein.

'Becky's settled in the countryside with her mum and Adam's got used to his new school ... and his new sister. Becky's got her hands full.'

'A girl? Oh, how lovely for them all,' Elise exclaimed. 'What's the baby's name?

'Peggy. She was named after somebody Jake was very close to in his youth.' Clover paused. 'Anyway, if Becky is still angry, she's no right to be in my opinion. Neil's told me what happened and the others know as well. Nobody blames you, Elise. And I don't believe Becky does either.' She sighed. 'The poor woman wasn't thinking straight. Any mother in that situation would panic and let her tongue run away with her.'

'Does Jake know his brother kidnapped Adam?'

Clover nodded. 'Jake turned up unexpectedly in Southend. It was a wonderful surprise, having him back on leave for Easter. Especially for his wife and son.' She smiled while reminiscing. 'Becky had to tell him, but wisely played it down. Even so it's lucky for Toby Winters that he's been out of reach behind bars; Jake would have killed him if he'd got his hands on him. There's more to his imprisonment than meets the eye, if you ask me.' She raised an eyebrow at Elise who shrugged her bafflement.

'We'll leave it at that then.' Clover gave her sister an

old-fashioned look. 'Jake told us his brother worked for the government like your friend Graham Yates. So maybe prying's not wise. Anyway, far from blaming you, Jake calls you a heroine. We all do. Even Becky, I suspect, now she's feeling better.'

During her journey to London, Elise had felt a niggling anxiety about this meeting, as though she were breaking the ice with the Coopers all over again. There had been no need to fret after all.

'Speaking of Graham, you mentioned in your letter his sister might accompany you to London.'

'She did. We both came up on the train. Faith's travelled on to the West End. She's lodging with Graham but we hope to get jobs together.'

'She's a sailor, isn't she?'

Elise nodded. 'We won't be heading to the docks for work.' She chuckled. 'We could dig allotments though if all else fails.'

'The outdoor life suits you. You look very fit.' Clover recalled Elise had been a willowy little thing on turning up a year ago; her sister now had an attractively well-developed figure. 'Did you take to being a land girl?'

'I did, but the winter was tough going. We all got chilblains and our fingers were so numb we didn't feel the blackthorns stabbing us through our gloves.' She flexed her fingers at the memory of the painful scratches. 'Faith told us to stop moaning as it was nothing to being caught out on the boat during a blizzard.'

'I'd love to meet her; she sounds fun. We should have another party. Do you think she'd come?'

'Oh, definitely. Faith loves a party ... a bit too much, actually.' Elise sank onto the settee.

'Sounds like my sort of girl,' said Clover, pouring the tea.

'Are both the children at school?' Elise had become alert to the strangely quiet house.

'They're still in Southend. I miss them terribly but they're in the right place.' Clover handed Elise her tea and sat down beside her. 'After what's gone on in London ...' She shook her head despairingly. 'I couldn't believe my eyes when we arrived back in the East End. Neil had written about the bomb damage but a person needs to see it to believe it. I feel guilty that I didn't evacuate the children sooner. I won't risk it again. Anyway, they love being by the seaside. All the kids are spoiled rotten by their great-grandparents.' She smiled ruefully. 'I thought they'd cry for me to stay with them but they seemed quite happy waving me off.'

'I like the sea,' said Elise. 'Faith's a good sailor. We've been out on her dad's boat during the good weather.'

Since the bombing raids had petered out the *Kentish Belle* had been put back into use. If no weekend tourists were booked on the pleasure cruiser they'd enjoyed a lazy afternoon on the waters off the south coast. They'd never ventured very far from land though, in case a German flag hove into view.

'You must come with us to Southend. Our grandparents would love to meet you,' Clover enthused. 'They're both lovely people. Although there is a story involved – as usual, with us Coopers: neither of them is actually a blood relative. Bill Lewis was my grandmother's second husband. Some years after she passed away he married Lucy Dare, who would you believe it, had once been one of our dad's girlfriends.' Clover's lips were compressed over a giggle.

'I can't keep up with all of this.' Elise made a mock complaint. 'You lot really are the limit with your scandals.'

'I know, but we wouldn't have it any other way, would we, love?' They both burst out laughing and finally, when settling back wiping away mirthful tears, Clover clinked her teacup against her sister's. 'It's good to have you back.'

'It's good to be back,' Elise said.

Chapter Eighteen

Mathilde Bouchard had been married to a good man. She'd loved him. Nevertheless she was glad he'd died before the Germans returned. He'd survived the Great War but it had killed him all the same. Bernard had been a fervent patriot, incapable of turning a blind eye to leave the fight for another day. If he'd been alive, he would have been almost seventy. If he'd been here with her now he'd be in bad trouble. He wouldn't have forgotten the beatings that had broken his bones but would intervene anyway, and be another body bleeding on the ground.

Mathilde hadn't handled a gun in almost twenty-five years; she'd never wanted to use one again. She wasn't a coward and her rage was like acid burning her ribs but she didn't act. She was too old and tired to defeat several armed soldiers. She unclenched her fingers, kept her face averted and counted out centimes. The neighbour behind her in the queue snaking out of the bakery nudged her in the back.

'*Réseau* ...' The elderly widow had hissed the word through a few broken teeth and glanced from beneath the black headscarf pulled low on her brow.

Mathilde shrugged that the Resistance fighters' plight

seemed hopeless but she didn't speak. When at last it was her turn to be served, she stepped to the counter, put down her centimes, then quickly set off home with her bread. The line of people stretched for yards along the street. She knew most of them but muttered monosyllabic replies to any greetings. She wasn't in the mood for a chat and doubted anybody else was either. Her route would take her past the captured man, sprawled unconscious on the ground. Another prisoner was face front against a wall, hands above his head with a machine pistol jabbed against his spine. She kept as far away as possible and didn't look at the men or the black saloon car.

The soldiers ignored the elderly woman as she hurried past with a loaf under her arm. She sensed the officer's stare but didn't meet it. She'd recognised him; it was hard not to. He had been the second Gestapo officer to question her after her son-in-law shot the Hauptmann. The first one had been a Leutnant. Then came this Oberst. When a higher-ranking fellow turned up she'd hoped it didn't mean their interest in her and her grandchildren had increased.

Nobody had been back in months; but he had recognised her too. She prayed this ill-timed meeting wouldn't jog him into paying another visit. She sped up, keeping her head down. Luckily, an armoured car arrived from the opposite direction, sending up dust as it braked sharply. The new arrivals saluted and a barked conversation began.

Mathilde exhaled in relief as she reached the track that led to the cottages. Before she'd turned onto it, the armoured car drove past and she saw the backs of the prisoners' heads. She muttered a prayer for them as she continued on her way, past the forge. The blacksmith was shaping iron on the anvil. Their eyes briefly met and he shook his head. No words were needed but he resumed his work harder and faster. When her house was in sight her shoulders relaxed back into place.

She'd been out since dawn; every morning when a flour delivery was spotted, the bakery queue began to form early in the village. It was fully light now but overcast. Unsettled by the arrests, she didn't notice the back window of the cottage was ajar and creaking in the breeze. She entered and closed the door then dropped her bread in shock. Old habits died hard and she swallowed a scream.

'Luc!' she whispered and rushed to hug him, barely aware of another fellow picking up her bread and putting it onto the table.

'How have you been, Grandma?' Luc cupped her face and kissed both of her soft cheeks. 'I've been worried about you. I wanted to come back sooner but ...'

'You must go.' Mathilde struggled free, her rapid heartbeat making her feel faint. 'Go now. Gestapo are here in the village.' She pointed a frantic finger. 'They're making arrests.' She gripped him tightly by the arms, unsure how she had recognised her once strong, handsome grandson. He was bearded and smelled grimy. Beneath his clothes he felt thin. 'I've missed you. Where have you been? Has your arm healed?' She ran testing fingers up and down on his sleeve.

'Yes, all better ... I'm fine. We've been here, there, everywhere; on the move most of the time. Doing some work when we can get it. Farm labouring and so on.' Luc didn't tell her anything specific about places or people, unwilling to jeopardise her or them. 'Have you been questioned about me or Elise?'

Mathilde nodded vigorously. 'Several times. Months ago.

I think they've accepted I was not close to you and don't know your whereabouts. I tell them we didn't get on, to protect us all.'

'How many Gestapo in the village?' Nathan hadn't understood all of the fluent French spoken between grandmother and grandson. He'd picked up enough though to know they were in trouble.

'Who is this?' Mathilde frowned on hearing an English voice. The man sounded eerily like her son-in-law. 'You're from London?' she asked in accented English, looking intrigued.

'He's the Tommy who saved Elise. He was captured after Dunkirk but escaped. He's heading back to England.'

'He's taking his time about it,' she pithily pointed out.

'It's not been easy,' said Nathan with rueful understatement.

'Thank you for what you did for my granddaughter.' Mathilde grabbed the stranger's hands and brought them to her lips. 'You could have saved yourself, I think. So without you ...' She'd spoken in English again. 'It is Elise they want to question the most, you see. Because she was with Sidney when they came for him. A girl as beautiful as she is—' She broke off, unable to voice her fears. 'What's your name?'

'Better if you don't know.' Nathan gently disengaged himself. 'How many of them?'

'One ... maybe two officers and a few soldiers. I tried not to pay too much attention.'

Nathan approached the door and opened it a crack to peer out.

'Nobody saw you come in?' she demanded.

'It was barely light when we got here. We made sure nobody was about,' Luc reassured her.

'Where will you go?' Mathilde began to cut the loaf she'd

bought and the room was filled with an appetising yeasty aroma. She spooned some lukewarm broth from a pan into bowls.

They thanked her and ate hungrily, standing up. Nathan remained vigilantly close to the door, sending Luc warning glances. They should leave, but he understood the younger man's need to have this meeting.

'Where will you go?' she demanded.

'The priest helped us. He will again.' They were hoping they'd not be turned away. They'd been sleeping rough in barns and beneath hedgerows, scrounging or earning what they could along the way. But the summer would end soon and they'd need proper shelter. 'Have you heard from Elise, Grandma?' Luc asked before she could pry too deeply.

Mathilde sadly shook her head. 'Have you?' She looked from one to the other of them; it was unlikely if they were on the move all the time.

'No,' Nathan said. 'She'll be safe in London though.'

Mathilde felt a surge of affection for this Englishman with his cockney voice and quiet manner. He was as dishevelled as Luc but beneath it she knew he was handsome.

Nathan's head jerked at the door, impressing on Luc the need to leave. He put down his empty bowl. 'We can't stop Grandma. You'll be in bad trouble if we're found here. I only came to see how you are and ask about Elise.'

'Here, take this.' She opened a drawer and found some francs to thrust at him.

'You'll need money yourself,' he protested.

'Take it,' she insisted. 'I sold some things I didn't need. An old woman like me doesn't need much—'

'Car's coming,' Nathan interrupted in a hiss and fully closed the door.

'Quick ... this way ...' Mathilde stuffed the banknotes into her grandson's pocket and pushed him towards the kitchen door. 'The officer recognised me. He's the one who came here last time. Watch out for him. *Cicatrice.*' She drew a finger down her cheek. I could kill your father for what he did. He really started something.'

'The Boches started something.' Luc said and the pride for his father was back. 'We'll finish it. You'll see.' He gave his grandmother a hug and slipped outside.

'*Bonne chance. Vive La France,*' she murmured.

'Wash those and put them away.' Nathan pointed at the empty soup bowls before quickly following Luc.

'I knew what to do at times like these,' she said drily, picking up a dishcloth, 'before you were a twinkle in your father's eye, Tommy.'

They rounded the cottage, keeping flat against its walls, then crept along behind the high hedge, aware of the car coming to a halt on the other side of it. Seconds later, a banging on the door was heard.

'You have had guests, Madame Bouchard?'

'I never have guests, M'sieur.'

'You are very hungry then?'

'Of course. Who isn't these days?' Mathilde wiped her hands on the scarlet teacloth she'd used on the bowls seconds ago. She realised he'd noticed the loaf already half eaten. 'When there is bread available I buy it and eat it fresh in case tomorrow there is none.'

'Have you seen your grandchildren? Luc and Elise, I recall are their names.'

'I have told you before, sir, they don't keep in touch and that suits me.' She grimaced and made a spitting sound through her teeth. 'Too like their father.'

'Yet, you wished to arrange your son-in-law's funeral.'

'Out of respect for my dead daughter. I hated him; she loved him.' Mathilde shrugged. 'She was a good person. If the children had been more like her they would have been nicer people.' She turned away, feeling stiff with tension. She wished he would leave, but he continued to stroll from table to window to armchair with his hands clasped behind his back. She knew he was searching for a clue that proved somebody had been here and had eaten the bread, so he could arrest her.

'Hmmm...' He passed a thumb to and fro on his mouth, pulled askew by puckered skin. 'She was a good daughter you say yet I have heard Sophie Bouchard was a whore. Maybe you are wrong, maybe her daughter is like her, not her father.'

Mathilde felt her hands clenching again. She wanted to rip the smirk off his lips with her fingernails. 'Sophie was a good daughter,' she said quietly. 'A girl who caught the eye of a German officer last time... she couldn't help being beautiful.'

'Ah, indeed ... we German fellows have a liking for French mesdemoiselles. Her daughter Elise resembles her, I think.'

'She does,' said Mathilde with defiant pride.

'So ... why would your grandchildren disappear? Just like that.'

'To escape the shame of it, sir.'

'Shame? Are we again talking about their whore of a mother?'

'Their father caused bad trouble,' Mathilde snapped but pointed to a chair, inviting him to use it. She wouldn't let him see he'd succeeded in riling her; besides she now saw the sense in delaying him so Luc and the English Tommy had time to get away. 'People talk. They say life is hard enough as it is without fools making it worse. Sidney Cooper was weak. He would run away when things turned difficult and leave my daughter to cope alone.' The disgust in her voice was sincere and she saw the fellow believed her even though he'd ignored her offer to be seated. She watched him closely. He might once have been a fine-looking young man. He had a mother . . . a grandmother . . . crying for him she'd no doubt. 'The world is a rotten mess, isn't it?' she said. He didn't reply but she noticed him touching his disfigured face.

'I'm not leaving until I know she's safe.' Luc rested, panting, against a tree. They had sprinted from the village to the woods, keeping undercover as much as possible. While fleeing, they'd unfortunately met two men en route but neither stopped to talk. The one herding a few goats had nodded and they'd heard his rumbling chuckle. He'd known what they were. The other riding a bicycle with a suitcase strapped to the back had kept his eyes grimly on the road. Nobody had spoken. News travelled fast though and the recent arrests would already be common knowledge. From where they were sheltering they could still just about see Mathilde's cottage in the distance.

Nathan sank down to rest and shoved his hands through his hair. 'Bad luck turning up just as the local Resistance get busy.'

Luc shrugged. 'They're busy everywhere, my friend. We just don't always know it.'

'She's a cool one, your nan.' Nathan chuckled. 'No hysterics.'

'If you'd known my grandfather you'd understand why she's that way. One of them had to use this.' Luc tapped his head. 'They were Resistance last time. Grandpa was brave as a lion ...' His proud voice tailed away and he continued peering around the tree at the cottage. 'If everything's all right she'll give me a sign. She knows I'll hang around until I'm sure she's not been arrested.'

Nathan stood up and pointed at a car roof glimpsed at intervals where the hedging and walling undulated with the lie of the land. 'They're going. We need to get moving and let's hope the priest is glad to see us.' It was impossible to get a view inside the car at this distance and it was soon lost from sight.

'She could have been with them. Arrested. She'll let me know if she's all right,' Luc said obstinately. The minutes wore on and he kept watch.

Just as Nathan was about to drag him away, a figure emerged from the house. In seconds, three things were hanging on the clothes line. A blue tablecloth, a white nightdress and a red tea towel. Then Mathilde disappeared back inside with the washing basket. Luc chuckled and began humming 'La Marseillaise'. '*Vive La France*, Grand-Mère,' he murmured. Then to Nathan, 'Right, let's go.'

'It's too dark to tell if it's the same man. If you're right, though, he must've followed us.'

'It's him,' Nathan muttered while checking his pistol for ammunition. 'But he can't have followed us. He's showed up here first and I don't think he's aware he's been spotted. If he's an enemy agent, he's not a very good one.'

They peeked over the churchyard wall and watched a short stocky fellow get off a bicycle and lean it against a headstone. Then he took the suitcase from the bike, and with a scouting look about, hurried towards the church.

'Father Pascal must be expecting him. Could be he's one of ours.'

'Maybe,' said Nathan. 'On the other hand, if he's an assassin he could have a gun in that case, not a radio. Come on...'

They darted towards the church and when Father Pascal opened up they were right behind the cyclist they'd passed when leaving Mathilde Bouchard's cottage. The stranger felt the pistol in his back and spun about in surprise but was shoved inside. Nathan and Luc followed and quickly closed the door.

'Sorry to barge in, Father,' said Nathan. 'We're hoping you can help us again.'

The priest squinted at them. He smacked his cassocked thigh in recognition of faces behind beards. 'Ah, *oui*. Do come in then,' he said drily.

'You're English!' the cyclist burst out in surprise, and got a better grip on the case he'd nearly dropped during his rough handling.

'So are you by the sound of it.' Nathan barked a laugh and lowered his gun. 'We passed you outside Lille a few days ago.'

'Ah, I remember you now. Got a bit hairy, didn't it?' The man sucked his teeth. 'I'd been holed up in an attic but when it all kicked off I couldn't risk hanging about to help the others. HQ wouldn't have liked losing me or this.' He waggled the case and sighed his regret. 'You two were involved in nobbling the ball-bearing factory last week, were you?'

'If we'd been in the area, we would have been,' boasted Luc.

'Our boys in the RAF dropped some explosives after I let it be known they'd come in handy. It'll take Fritz months to get that place functioning again.'

'He's a wireless operator,' Father Pascal interrupted. He grabbed the case impatiently, fiddling with the catches to reveal the contents.

Nathan and Luc understood the Father's excitement. A wireless operator was a godsend to a Resistance circuit.

'I've urgent messages for you to send to London,' the priest said.

The fellow proprietorially reclaimed his equipment and looked around at the disappointingly thick stone walls. 'Could really do with somewhere high up to get a signal in this place.'

'Bell tower.' The priest grinned and jerked his eyes heavenward.

'Would you send a message to London for us?' Nathan eagerly asked. He and Luc knew the BBC French service broadcast to agents in the field. The Gestapo knew it too and would listen in to try and decode the messages.

'That's what I'm here for, squire,' said the wireless operator. 'To communicate with the bigwigs pulling the strings over there.'

Chapter Nineteen

'How time flies. It's hard to believe it's been a year since we sat here in this very spot listening to Christmas carols. Now, down to business, Elise. Will you come to Broadstairs for the holiday? I intend to nag you until you say yes. It won't take you two ticks to pack a few things.'

'Oh, I'd love to Graham. But I can't. My brothers are both back on leave and Clover's planned a big party. I did tell Faith yesterday.'

He tutted in exasperation. 'She's not said a word to me. Your party sounds good fun, though.' Graham spooned sugar into his tea. 'It'll be just me and Faith catching the train tomorrow then. D'you know, I think I'd rather stay in London with you and gatecrash your party.'

'You wouldn't need to; you'd be welcome to come along. Clover says the more the merrier. In fact . . .' She glanced at him with a pained expression. 'I think Faith's decided to stay here in town and spend Christmas with us. I take it she's not said anything?'

'No, she has not. The little so-and-so.' He put down his cup with a clatter. 'She's been saying for weeks that we have to be dutiful children and spend Christmas with our parents. I bet she's not let them know she's backed out. She'll leave that to me.'

Elise grimaced another apology. It wasn't the first time she'd been caught in the middle of one of their squabbles. Having had to deal with bad feeling in her own family she'd rather not be drawn into their spats.

He patted her hand, idle on the table. 'It's not your fault, love. Of course you must see your brothers when they're on leave. Anyway, it's only fair the Coopers have you, as you came to us last year.' He began to tap a teaspoon against a saucer, mimicking the beat of 'Jingle Bells' being enthusiastically belted out by the choir outside the Corner House teashop. 'I'll head home tomorrow on my own then; they'll be rightly upset if nobody turns up to eat the fatted calf. Well, I expect it'll be a goose but you get my drift.'

'I do,' she said with a sympathetic smile. 'I've a gift for your mum and dad. Would you take it with you, please?' Elise took a colourfully wrapped box and a Christmas card from her shopping bag, stowed by her chair. 'It's only chocolates.'

'*Only* chocolates?' He smacked his lips. 'Go down a treat those will after the plum pud.' He leaned across the table to tickle her cheek with his finger. 'You are a dear.' He wedged the box into the pocket of his coat, hanging on the chair rail. 'Right. Ready for the off? I'd better throw some things in a suitcase. The train leaves Victoria before nine in the morning.' After the bill was paid they went out of the warm bright restaurant into the sharp dark afternoon.

'There is one other thing,' said Graham, drawing her arm through his as they walked on past a fiery brazier filling the air with the aroma of roasting chestnuts.

Elise glanced up at his dear familiar face, thinking it

would be easy to settle down with this man by the fireside in the evening, even if a fire never ignited in her heart. But she'd be cosy with him ... maybe content, in time. 'What is the other thing,' she prompted when he continued frowning into the distance.

'My boss asked if you'd agree to come and see him. I don't know what's made Venables bring this up again. He wasn't very forthcoming when I asked. Probably because I made it clear I thought it bad manners to persist as you'd said no before.' He glanced down at her. 'I said I'd put it to you but I'll tell him no if you want.'

'Is it to do with Toby Winters, d'you think?'

'Possibly ... Venables can be tight-lipped when he wants to be.' He glanced at her. 'I don't suppose I'll be giving much away by telling you a French section's been set up in the department. Being as you've lived in France until recently he might want to pick your brains on certain matters.'

'What sort of matters?' asked Elise, intrigued. She was sure these government departments had maps of France and knew the lie of the occupied land.

'Maybe about industry around Lille – train depots, telephone exchanges, that sort of thing.' He shrugged. 'I'm too junior to be told much.'

It seemed to Elise that Lieutenant Yates knew more than he was letting on. 'I'll happily tell him what I can if it'll help win this war and get me home,' she said. 'So ... yes; you may say, I'll come in the New Year and speak to him.'

They had arrived at the Underground station where they were to part company. Graham would walk on to Soho and Elise catch the Tube to the East End.

He gave her a hug then dipped his head and kissed her

on the cheek. She returned him the same salute. 'Joyeux Noël, Graham, and remember me to your mum and dad.'

'I will, and Happy Christmas from me to you and all your family. I'll speak to my crafty sister when she gets in from work,' he said then stood awkwardly for a moment. 'I have something for you.' He withdrew a small package wrapped in red paper from an inside pocket of his jacket. He opened her hand and put the gift on her palm before closing her fingers around it.

'Oh, Graham, you shouldn't have,' she said. 'We agreed not to buy each other presents.'

'I know we did ... but, well, I bought a nice silk scarf for Faith. She would've created merry hell if I hadn't given her something, whatever we'd agreed. I saw this and thought of you. I wanted you to have it.' He cleared his throat, looking bashful. 'Well, I'll be off now. Take care of yourself. And my best wishes to your brothers when they go back over there.' He stepped away, and after covering a few yards, turned and blew her a kiss. 'See you in the New Year,' he called.

Elise watched him striding away, feeling rotten that she'd had nothing to give him in return. She was tempted to open the present, but didn't. Its size and shape made her wonder if it was jewellery. She descended the stairs to the Underground, the rush of warm air from the bowels of the station fluttering her hair about her face.

She felt disappointed in Faith today; her friend had been invited to come along to the Corner House for tea but had taken an extra shift at the munitions factory instead. She didn't much like the work and Elise suspected she'd decided to dodge being present when Graham discovered he'd be the only one spending Christmas in Broadstairs. She gave her matchmaking friend the benefit of the doubt:

Faith might have known about Graham's jewellery shop gift and decided 'three's a crowd' so had discreetly absented herself.

Having bought her Tube ticket, Elise dropped it in her pocket then curled her fingers around the gift box, hoping it didn't contain an engagement ring.

'You look exceptionally well, Jake.' Elise looked her stepbrother over from his shiny blond head to his polished shoes. He had quite a suntan from his stint in north Africa and looked very debonair in his army uniform.

'So do you, Elise.' He enclosed her in a hug. 'Thanks for what you did, bringing Adam back home.' He planted a smacker against her forehead.

'Do you mind if we don't talk about it?' She glanced up into his warm green eyes. 'I'd rather try to forget about that episode.'

'So would I, although I doubt I ever shall. I couldn't let it pass without a mention. Becky and I will always be grateful to you . . .' He cleared his throat, turned to the sideboard and refilled his glass with beer.

'Peggy is a beautiful little thing. She's as fair as you and Adam. I had a cuddle earlier.' She glanced at the pram that Rebecca was jigging in an attempt to get the baby off to sleep.

'She's a handful though and certainly exercises her lungs ... mostly at night,' he added ruefully. 'I bet my mother-in-law's glad she's finally got a week of undisturbed kip in front of her before I take them all back there.'

Jake and his family had been last to turn up to the afternoon party at Clover and Neil's house. They had been in Cambridge with Rebecca's mother until early afternoon then had set out after dinner in the works' van for London to spend the rest of the holiday with the Coopers.

'So, let's hear what you've been up to since I last saw you,' Jake said.

Elise began by telling him about her work at the factory in Woolwich then described her life as a land girl in Kent, making him guffaw at some of the crew's escapades and her mishaps driving the tractor into a ditch where it got stuck.

'That's your friend from Kent, isn't it?' He was watching his sister Annie doing a version of the jitterbug with the only fair-haired woman in the room. His sisters, and sister-in-law Dora, and his wife, were all brunettes of one shade or another.

'That's Faith, all right,' confirmed a rueful Elise. She hadn't nagged her friend to lay off the booze. It was Christmas after all; a time for everybody to enjoy themselves. But she could see Faith had already had too much to drink and was staggering into the furniture.

'Life and soul of the party, that one,' Jake chuckled.

'Only hoping she doesn't bring up her turkey,' said Elise, not wholly joking.

Faith had been invited to eat a Christmas dinner with them earlier. Clover had put on a lovely festive meal for family and friends: a huge turkey had taken pride of place on the table, and had been carved by Neil. Surrounding the platter on which sat the huge bronzed bird stuffed with sage and onion had been dishes piled high with roast potatoes, parsnips, carrots and sprouts and of course there was plenty of gravy to top it off. Annie and her boyfriend Anthony plus all the children and their parents had sat around the tables with Elise and Faith. The settee and armchairs had been moved against the walls and the sitting room transformed into a dining hall. Decorators' trestles – of which there were plenty at the firm's yard – had been pushed together then covered with pristine tablecloths. Extra chairs had been borrowed from neighbours. The children had all been brought back to their roots for an East End Christmas and had sat feeling excited, but on their best behaviour, knowing there would be new toys for good children to play with once everything was cleared away. Their great grandparents in Essex would have a well-earned rest, Dora had said, while pulling crackers and settling paper hats on small heads. Then in the New Year, back they would go to the seaside. If anything was certain in this rotten war it was that London would bear the brunt of any further attacks. Nobody was risking being caught in the middle of another East End Blitz.

'That's a pretty brooch,' said Becky, who'd come to join her husband and Elise.

The atmosphere between the women was almost back to normal and Elise felt very comfortable with everybody. 'Faith's brother Graham bought it for me for Christmas.' She touched the silver ballerina pinned to the lapel of her dress. 'It's a little joke between us that I'm not a very graceful dancer and always tread on his feet.' In the box had been a note from Graham that she was as light on her toes as Giselle in his opinion. Elise had gasped in delight on opening it and finding the brooch; she'd felt relieved too that it hadn't been a ring.

'What a smashing gift. Are you and Graham ... you know?' Becky mischievously quirked an eyebrow.

'He's a dear friend, that's all,' said Elise but blushed and changed the subject. 'Adam's come out of his shell, I see.'

Becky glanced fondly at her son, running around with his cousins. Toy guns and swords had been unwrapped earlier. Even Victoria, usually a prim little thing, was getting into the swing of it. Their uncle Johnny, ever the clown, was joining in the fun.

'Who's ready for a turkey sandwich?' called Clover.

Lots of hands shot up. 'And Christmas cake,' shouted Johnny, mid-tussle, with the kids all piled on top of him.

'I'll give you a hand, Clo,' said Becky and she went off to butter bread.

'You look gorgeous in that dress, Elise,' said Annie, who'd come for a rest and left Dora to take over jitterbugging with an energetic Faith. 'Did you get it down Roman Road?' She smoothed a hand on a blue velvet sleeve.

'I did; off the stall you told me about.'

'Let me top you up.' Johnny had bowled over, hair standing on end, sherry bottle in hand. He poured a good measure into Elise's depleted glass then filled his sister's when Annie put it under his nose.

'Got any fags, Johnny?' asked Annie, taking a glug of sherry. 'Could do with a breather outside in the air. Crikey, it's hot in here.'

After brother and sister had disappeared into the hallway Jake turned to Elise. 'That's a nice gift from Graham. Are you keen on him?' He quickly added, 'I'm not being nosy, it's only that I found out something about Nat Hawkes. I remember you seemed fond of him and keen to know what had happened but I'll leave it if you've forgotten him now ...'

'Don't you dare. I've not forgotten him.' Elise's glass of sherry was put down so abruptly that some slopped over the side. 'You've got news of Nathan for me?' she whispered with a look of joyous yearning in her eyes.

'Well, it's not much. After our regiment turned up in

Tripoli I asked around about him. A bloke in a bar said he knew somebody by that name. He'd heard that three of Nat's platoon were missing in action after Dunkirk. He didn't know the names but I imagine one of them might be Nathan.'

'There were three of them together. Nathan and Wilmot and Evans. He's alive then?' she whispered.

'Can't say for sure,' Jake said gently.

'He didn't come back to Poplar and forget about me.'

'He didn't,' said Jake. 'My guess is he's a prisoner of war. Probably in a camp in Germany. Don't suppose that's of much comfort to you though...'

'It is ... oh, it is,' she choked out and dipped her chin as tears smarted her eyes.

He put a comforting hand on her shoulder. 'Reckon I've just given you a better Christmas present than Graham.' He sighed. 'Poor bloke.'

'Turkey sandwich or Christmas cake anybody?' Clover came over with a heaped plate in each hand.

Jake took a sandwich then set off towards his son who had been a bit too heavy-handed with his toy sword and made William cry.

'Come and dance with me,' slurred Faith, intercepting him. She put her arms around his neck and gazed into his handsome face. 'You look like that film star ... whassisname ... .the gorgeous fair-haired one ... rides a horse ...' Her head flopped against his shoulder and she fondled his nape.

'Oh, *merde* ...' Horrified, Elise softly swore in French and clattered down her half-eaten cake. She glanced at Becky who'd also noticed Faith flirting outrageously with her husband. Elise didn't want another falling-out with this family now things seemed back on an even keel. 'She's had too many,' Elise mouthed, miming lifting a glass.

"S'all right.' Becky came over, nursing her daughter. 'I'm used to him getting the eye. Luckily, I'm not the jealous type.'

'No need to be jealous, have you,' Clover said bluntly, putting the sandwiches onto the sideboard. 'He thinks the sun shines out of you, love.' She chuckled. 'I'm glad Faith's enjoyed herself. I'll make her a nice strong cup of tea. Spark her up a bit. And maybe hide the gin bottle for a while. She can go and lie down in the bedroom for half an hour if she wants. Get her second wind.'

'Thanks, Clover.' Elise was grateful for the offer but declined. 'I'll take her home. She can sleep it off there. She's going to have a sore head in the morning.'

Elise could no longer deny that her friend's drinking had worsened since she'd returned to London. They had gone out to a club last week and Faith had got drunk and upset their table of drinks. Graham had got angry with her and frogmarched her outside for a talking-to. Then after finishing her work shift on Christmas Eve, Faith had gone to the pub with some colleagues. She'd overslept this morning and almost missed her Christmas dinner. She'd turned up, hungover and apologetic, just as the food was hitting the table.

'Maybe it would be best for her to head home,' said Clover. 'I'll get Neil to fetch a taxi.' She beckoned her husband who'd just entered from the backyard where he'd been emptying rubbish into the dustbin.

Elise helped Faith to sit down then found the sozzled girl's coat and bag while Neil went in search of a cab.

Clover made Faith a strong tea but she didn't get a sip

of it as a car horn was heard outside. Elise grabbed her own coat and put it on, calling out her goodbyes, then with Neil's help Faith was walked outside and settled in the vehicle.

'Come back with Faith at New Year and we'll do it all again,' Neil said in his wry Irish tone before giving her a big brotherly hug and heading indoors.

'Sorry about that...'

Jake had strolled out to join them. He waved away Elise's apology. 'Faith brought you back from Dunkirk, didn't she?'

Elise nodded, then quickly got into the cab, hoping her friend wouldn't be sick.

Jake crouched down to look at them huddled together. 'She's a brave girl, one of the best in my book. Sleep tight both of you.' He stood up and closed the car door.

Faith laid her head on Elise's shoulder and started to snore as the taxi moved through the quiet almost-deserted streets. On this magical evening the pavements glistened with frost and twinkles of festivities could be glimpsed from behind wonky blackout curtains. Nathan Hawkes was alive. Elise repeated it several times in her head. She savoured the wonderful news, eyes closed, mind closed to any other explanation for him not coming back than he was a prisoner of war. It was better than she'd dared hope.

When they got to Soho the driver obligingly helped Elise get Faith up the stairs to the apartment.

'Your friend's had a good night by the looks of it.' He chuckled and refused the coins she held out saying the fellow had paid him already.

Elise unlocked the door. With one arm around Faith, she guided her inside and straight into the bedroom.

'Don't leave me.' Faith rolled onto her side on the bed.

'Where's Graham? Don't like the dark ... there's planes in it.' She lifted a limp hand as though swatting something away.

'I'm going to stay with you, love. I told Clover I wouldn't be back tonight.' Elise started to slip off her friend's shoes and carried on carefully undressing her until Faith was in her underwear. She covered her up with the eiderdown and sat down beside her, easing off her own shoes with a sigh. Before she'd finished folding up their clothes she heard Faith retch and the bedsprings groan as she leaned over the side to be sick. Elise found a towel to clean up. Crouching down, she noticed the beautiful Liberty scarf Graham had bought his sister for Christmas, covered in vomit.

'I'm sorry ... you hate me, don't you? I'm a disgrace, aren't I?' Faith mumbled and started to cry.

Elise stroked her friend's matted hair, pushing it back from her cheeks. "Course I don't hate you, Faith, I love you. And you're not a disgrace. You can't be. You're a Dunkirk Club girl. So am I. No matter what happens we always stick together, don't we?'

Faith nodded, and burrowed her head further into the pillow. By the time Elise lay down beside her, Faith was asleep.

Chapter Twenty

'Do come in. Let me take your wet coat. Filthy weather, isn't it? All these showers aren't what we expect at this time of year.'

Elise slipped out of her mac and handed it to the smartly uniformed fellow sporting horn-rimmed glasses. He in turn gave it to his secretary to hang up on a stand that was already home to his cap and overcoat. He dealt with her dripping umbrella, poking it in the metal rack beside his own larger one.

'Major Teddy Venables, at your service, Miss Bouchard.' He approached to extend a hand. 'Please, sit down. I'm very pleased to meet you after all this time.'

'Thank you, and I'm pleased to meet you too, sir.' Elise took the chair indicated. She sensed this cordial fellow wanted to hear a reason for the delay in her turning up to see him. She knew Graham had already made her excuses but nevertheless added her own. 'I would have liked to come sooner but I've been staying with friends in Broadstairs since the New Year.'

'Ah, yes, the Yateses family. Their daughter is unwell, isn't she? What's ailing the poor girl?'

'Nothing, I'm glad to say. She's on the mend now,' said Elise. 'Graham – Lieutenant Yates – said I might be of some assistance. So here I am at last and happy to answer any questions as far as I can.' She avoided discussing the reason for her accompanying Faith home to her parents.

Her best friend had been quite ill, close to a breakdown the doctor had said, and suggested a sanatorium stay. Faith wouldn't hear of it though. Her father's ultimatum that she stop drinking and remain quietly at home, or be admitted, brought the matter to a head. She opted to spend time with her parents and Elise, if her friend would stay with her in Kent for a while. Elise gladly agreed; she would have done anything to help.

They went sailing or walking in the countryside during the day when weather permitted. Evenings were spent playing cards or board games. They always listened to the wireless; the *messages personnels* broadcast by the BBC to France was a particular favourite programme. Elise had translated for the Yateses the French phrases that sounded like double Dutch to anybody but the people they were intended for. British agents and French freedom fighters crouched by their radios across the Channel knew what 'the onion is ready for the pot' or similar such riddles actually meant. It kept Elise and Faith occupied, guessing the codes' meanings. As well as these simple activities something else had resulted in an improvement in Faith's health.

Her father had brought home a dog, not particularly as company for his sad daughter, but to save its life. The pub landlord's mongrel had given birth. The runt of the litter had been unclaimed by any customer and the landlord didn't want more than one animal. Mr Yates' soft heart wouldn't allow him to see the puppy destroyed. Faith had taken to the timid bundle of brown fur straight away and let him sleep on her bed.

Nobody, though, saw her as cured. Neither did Faith herself. She'd accepted she had a horrible problem and that her best friend couldn't keep her company forever. Elise had to return to London or lose her job at the factory for good this time. She'd been told by her boss after another lengthy unpaid absence that there was no further leeway. Graham had been helping his family financially while his sister was unable to work. Elise insisted on paying her keep to Mrs Yates, but her savings had dwindled and she refused to accept charity, or let Graham support her, which he had generously offered to do.

Venables had allowed a silence to develop to see if Miss Bouchard would fill it by talking about her friend's addiction. She didn't; she waited for him to speak. 'Lots of coughs and sneezes about it seems.' He ambled behind his desk and settled into his chair.

It was his business to know about his staff's backgrounds, even those who didn't serve overseas. He knew Lieutenant Yates' sister was an alcoholic, even though the fellow was tight-lipped about it himself. He'd noted the way Elise Bouchard had sidestepped his question and protected her friends' privacy. She'd outflanked Toby Winters – a slippery rival – and he could see how. 'Would you like tea and biscuits, Miss Bouchard?'

'Thank you,' said Elise then wished she'd not put him to the trouble of hoisting himself again from his chair to summon back his secretary.

'It's been a while since you first came to my notice through the Winters' escapade. What a rascal he is.' Venables re-seated himself.

'Will he be sent to jail for a long time?'

'If he's lucky ...'

Elise hadn't before given proper consideration to the possibility of Toby being executed. Whenever she'd asked Graham about this he'd glossed over things, no doubt to save her feelings. Toby was related to her extended family after all. He'd known the risks he was taking engaging in high treason. There was no reason for her to feel guilty of dropping him in it, especially when her nephew's safety had been at stake. Nevertheless, a chill rolled up her arms making her absently rub at them.

'Let's turn this up a bit.' Venables had noticed her shiver. He switched on another bar on the electric fire roasting their ankles. 'Tell me, how did you meet our Lieutenant Yates and his family?'

'Through his sister. We became friends after she and her father brought a rescue vessel to Dunkirk.'

'Fine, brave people, all of those skippers.' Venables spoke with gravel-voiced sincerity.

Elise was sure he knew all of this and wondered why he was testing her. He had a half-smile pulling at his lips as though he'd read her thoughts. She decided to cut to the chase. It was a miserable May afternoon and she'd rather not be out longer than necessary. She had shopping to do. 'I've made a list of factories and utilities and so on. Lieutenant Yates said such a thing might be beneficial.' She'd spent the afternoon writing down everything she could remember about the locations of industry in the towns and villages surrounding Lille.

He took the proffered paper and scanned it with a nod of appreciation. 'This is certainly the sort of thing we're after. Well done, Miss Bouchard.'

'I'm glad to be able to help.' She definitely was, but wished she'd not agreed to have tea with him. She didn't want to kill time and put herself on the spot fielding more questions now she'd handed in her work.

'There's something else I'd like you to help with and I will soon get to the crux of it.' He'd noticed her shifting on her seat as though to rise and grab her coat. 'Allow me to compliment you. You handled Toby Winters exceptionally well. He wasn't a complete stranger though, was he?'

'He's my stepbrother's kin. My English father's side of the family is rather complicated.'

The tea tray was brought in and the secretary started to pour but he dismissed her saying he'd do it himself. Not very successfully in the event. He slopped tea into the saucer and tutted at his clumsiness. 'I'm making a mess of it.' He put down the pot and gave her a winning smile.

She took over, but left the milk jug and sugar bowl in front of him so he could do that himself.

He offered her the plate of biscuits. 'I like the custard creams,' he said, eyeing the two among the selection on the plate.

'So do I. One each then.' She picked up hers and took a bite.

He chuckled and munched on the other. 'How old are you, young lady? Lieutenant Yates said you were nineteen but you look younger.'

'Do I? Well I'm twenty next month,' she said.

'And your brother? The French one?'

Elise put down her cup. There was a subtle change in his attitude from jovial to businesslike. 'Luc's twenty-one ... almost twenty-two.'

'You're a bright young woman; I won't treat you as less

than that.' Venables was already impressed by this attractive young Frenchwoman. 'I imagine you've guessed our work here at the Special Operations Executive involves military intelligence. At Baker Street we run the French Section which is self-explanatory. Initially, I only had to thank you for helping our people apprehend a traitor. More recently there's been another reason for wanting to meet you and hope you can assist us.'

'Does it concern Luc in France?' She was ahead of him. The mention of her brother hadn't been pointless small talk. She rather fancied Major Venables didn't actually bother with it, despite chat about the weather and her friends. He was analysing her every word and action. Even down to her having denied him both custard cream biscuits. 'Do you know how my brother is?' She moved forward on her seat, put her tea on his desk and waited impatiently for an answer. 'I know he's French Resistance, so you won't be betraying any secrets telling me that,' she prompted. 'I hoped Luc would escape with me to England. He stayed to fight. And now I wish I'd done the same. Our grandparents were Resistance during the Great War and my father shot a German officer before being killed himself.' She paused to study his inscrutable expression. 'You know all this about us, I'm sure. But I'll tell you anyway that the Bouchards have always been patriots. We want France liberated.' She drew a breath after her impassioned speech.

'Liberating France is a goal we're all working towards. In the doing of it, one of our people in France crossed paths with your brother.'

Elise shot to her feet, arms raised to the heavens and gave a muted shout of thankfulness. This was the first news she'd had of her family since leaving her homeland almost two years ago. Her fingers gripped the edge of his desk and she leaned towards him. 'Where is Luc? Somewhere close to Lille? Is he well?'

'He is well, and rather a useful fellow. As you say, he is Resistance. It would be good to know for sure though that he is who he says he is. And his friend.'

'Luc had friends, lots of them ... Jacques, Etienne ... Pierre ... others too he kept in touch with from school,' she eagerly vouched for him.

'This other fellow claims to be English – an escaped prisoner of war. Says his name is Corporal Nathaniel Hawkes.' He watched her shock slowly transform into a wondrous smile. 'You know the name and the man, I think.'

'I do,' she said huskily. 'He saved my life at Dunkirk.'

'Now for the bad news. Unfortunately, some of our circuits have been infiltrated by enemy agents.' He drummed his fingers on his notepad. 'What I ask of you, Miss Bouchard, is this: please provide me with a fact only known to your brother and to this Hawkes fellow, to test whether they are who they claim to be.' He paused. 'It is possible, of course, they'll be transmitting under duress. But it's the best we can do in the circumstances.'

Elise quickly sat down again, her heart pumping erratically. 'You think the Nazis might have them and try to force them to pass false information?'

'It is a concerning possibility. Most trained agents will send a clue in a message that they have a gun pointed at them. A deliberate error that we can pick up on.' His fingers resumed tapping on the notepad. 'But your brother and friend aren't trained in intelligence.'

'Neither of them are fools though,' she said proudly. 'Ask Luc to tell you who showed us the dungeon.' She dropped her chin, closed her eyes and reflected on her brief time with Nathan. When doing so, and she did often, her mind always travelled first to the memory of sleeping in his arms. 'The corporal knows who it was I dreamed about,' she said quietly and raised her face. 'That's all you need to ask them. If it's them, they'll understand.'

He scribbled down what she'd said on the pad then swivelled the paper towards her. 'Please supply the answers to the questions.'

She wrote the two words quickly: 'grandfather', 'mother', then pushed the pad back.

Venables gazed at her with increasingly thoughtful admiration. 'We have a sked ... a message slot scheduled with our wireless operator this evening.'

'I'll come back later and talk to them myself then,' she said excitedly.

'Heavens, no, we can't have that. We communicate in code. And only briefly. Wireless signals are a dead giveaway to where our people are holed up.'

From wanting to get going, Elise now wished to stay and learn more. But he was up and out of his chair, moving towards the coat stand to fetch her mac.

'If you can get me home to France, Major Venables, I'll join the Resistance and work for you.'

'That's not possible. You're only nineteen. I'll let you know what response we have to the message.' He shook out the gabardine and politely held it for her to slip her arms into the sleeves. 'If it's positive that'll be a comfort for you, won't it? There's a very good chance then that your brother and friend are alive and well.'

She put on her coat but continued to scour her mind for ways to persuade him. 'If I was in France I could get my old job back with the couturier. Madame Laurent told me that during the last war German officers came in to buy gifts for their wives. The men would gossip and be indiscreet. She said she heard things she shouldn't have about their military plans. If I was spying for you, I'd be able to let you know all of this.'

Venables shook his head. 'It's not possible.'

'You got this fellow with the wireless into France.'

'Precisely. He'd been trained to transmit messages and speaks excellent fluent French.'

'I speak excellent fluent French and will soon learn to use a transmitter.' She replied in her mother tongue with an undeniably authentic accent. He answered that he couldn't argue with that and drew a smile from her when she realised he was also fluent in French.

'You have a marvellous spirit, young lady,' he reverted to English. 'But you are young and the work isn't pleasant. Even the strongest sometimes succumb to despair. An average life expectancy of an operative is six weeks. Once captured ...' He gazed at the beautiful girl with defiance shining in her grey eyes. 'The treatment is not good. Often a swift end like your brave father had is a blessing.'

'Thank you for telling me. But I know all that, sir. I saw my grandfather's scars from the previous occupation. Nothing's changed but the date. I'm a woman, that's the problem, isn't it?'

'There are some who believe women unsuited to the work and oppose their recruitment. But not I. It's dangerous ... often lonely work that requires great courage. A woman of the right calibre could fit the bill remarkably well.'

'Every French person whether Resistance or collaborator lives with danger since the Nazis came. And loneliness is not so hard to bear. I often feel that way, even with kind people around me.'

She was sure he was wavering, but they were interrupted. The door was opened and his secretary beckoned him to the threshold to hand him a note.

'Well, that's a blow,' he said, stuffing the paper in his pocket. 'But rather extraordinary timing that you should be here at the precise moment I find this out.' He paused. 'Our Mr Winters has apparently broken out of the detention centre.'

Elise frowned in alarm. 'I'll warn my sister-in-law straight away. She's in Cambridge but ...'

He patted her arm. 'No need for that. My guess is he'll try and make a dash straight for Germany. Unless we can apprehend him first he'll pal up with like-minded types who'll assist in his escape.' Venables neatly replaced the used crockery on the tea tray. 'On the point of family, I doubt I need say that our conversation this afternoon must remain strictly confidential; please don't repeat any of it to your Coopers.'

'I won't speak of it, I promise. Will you get me home to France?'

'Winters won't come for you, my dear. He wouldn't risk it; he knows we'll have you and others under observation.'

'I didn't mean that.'

Venables plunged his hands into his pockets and remained quiet for some minutes. 'It's not solely up to me. My superior heads this department and has the final say. There's also the chap who deals with the recruiting of our agents. I will admit they hold similar views to my own on equal suitability of the sexes. We're also in agreement on the importance of training. You would never be let loose without first passing every rigorous test. That takes very many months. For example, how do you feel about parachuting from an aeroplane? Not always necessary, sometimes a reconnaissance aircraft can land, but if the Lysander cannot . . .' He shrugged. 'Apart from the obvious perils in that, there is weapons training, combat skills. You must be prepared to kill or be killed. And if that weren't enough, things have changed in France since you were there. You have no identity papers and there are rules in place regarding curfews and so on that you are unaware of. You wouldn't last five minutes before being picked up by the Gestapo.'

'Teach me what I need to know then.' She spoke calmly but he had brought to her attention that she had only sketchy knowledge of occupied France. Neither had she any experience of the Milice, the Vichy France police who worked with the Nazis. Frenchmen who joined the Milice were traitors to their country in Elise's opinion.

'An agent can never discuss the nature of their work with their family. Long absences from home beg an explanation though. For example, a young woman might tell her family that she's volunteered for the First Aid Nursing Yeomanry and will be away much of the time.' He paused. 'The deceit is necessary. Details would be finalised nearer the time but it is as well you are aware of expectations at the outset. For now, you'll want to go away and carefully consider all we've spoken about.'

'I've been thinking about ways to get back home for almost as long as I've been in England. I don't need to think about it any more. But if you consider it necessary, I will.'

'Your attitude is impressive but overconfidence is rarely a good trait for an agent if not allied with others. Precision, caution, madcap instinct and courage ... all play a part. Getting the balance right isn't easy.'

'I understand.'

'The training an agent undergoes is not only to keep themselves safe in the field but to protect their colleagues. A simple slip-up can result in a far-reaching calamity. An agent who fails the training shouldn't go.'

'I won't fail.' She paused. 'I have a request to make about when I'm dropped in France.' His eyebrows shot towards his hairline but she carried on calmly, despite her brazen display of overconfidence. 'When I get there, if the plane can land, please arrange for Corporal Hawkes to be waiting and brought back in my place.'

'He means something to you? A love affair, perhaps.'

She shook her head, knowing to admit to anything else would hinder her cause, and his. 'Corporal Hawkes gave up his place on a rescue vessel to me at Dunkirk. He's been away from his family for a long time. And I'm to blame.' She paused. 'I owe him a return favour, that's all.'

'I'll bear it in mind,' said Venables. 'For obvious reasons, agents rarely use their own names in the field. You'll need a code name. If you go. No harm in choosing it early on.'

Elise continued buttoning her coat and her fingers touched the ballerina brooch pinned to her lapel. 'Giselle,' she almost said, but didn't. She thought of Toby Winters, on the run somewhere in England full of vengeful wrath, she was sure. The battle of wills in his basement came sharply to mind, as did his insults. He'd called her a refugee and an orphan. 'Orpheline,' she said.

'Ah ... yes, very apt for you, my dear. The word sounds better in French. Pretty. Good choice.'

*

'I would never have passed on your message if I'd known you'd try to recruit her. You said you'd thank her, and ask about industry around Lille. That's all.'

'Dear fellow, I have not made any such attempt. And please remember to whom you're speaking.' Major Venables addressed his florid-faced subordinate. 'Miss Bouchard hasn't disappointed; she's provided us with some useful information.' He indicated the paper bearing her neat handwriting.

Graham Yates barely glanced at it but continued to prowl to and fro. 'Did you tell her that her brother's been in contact?' Graham had known this for some time but hadn't spoken of it to Elise in case the information proved false. It would break her heart to know Luc had been captured and the Gestapo had extracted enough information from him to impersonate him and fool his sister. 'If it is Luc Bouchard, he won't want her sent back there. He and the corporal risked their lives getting her out through Dunkirk in the first place.'

'She explained that.' Venables paused. 'Churchill wants Europe set ablaze. He hasn't opposed the recruitment of women. You know as well as I do, Lieutenant Yates, that here in my office this afternoon was an ideal candidate for training. What's more, she's begged me to allow her to go. I made it clear to her that so far nothing is arranged.'

'She's simply homesick, missing her family, it's only natural.' Desperation harshened Graham's voice.

'She's a patriot and a freedom fighter like the rest of her family, she says. She's bilingual and has a job possibility that would give her access to some officer class Nazis and their loose tongues. A girl like that could charm the birds from the trees.'

Graham swung about and stared at Venables. 'What are we now? Pimps?'

'Don't be ridiculous! Elise Bouchard won't do a thing she doesn't want to do for me or for you. She'd slip back into France and fit in straight away.' He sighed at his thunder-faced subordinate. 'Now come along, Yates, you know as well as I that if we are to get France back an Allied invasion's necessary. To do that we need our people in there, preparing the ground. It's damnably perilous work and we don't have volunteers queuing up to do it.'

'She's nineteen!' Graham exploded into his boss's speech.

'Nearly twenty – she made sure I knew that. If she successfully finishes training, she'll be closer to twenty-one.'

'The Free French won't like it,' Graham warned in desperation. 'De Gaulle wants his own people working for him, not for British Intelligence.'

'Her father's English, and was her last surviving parent. That gives us first dibs on her, I'd say,' said a pragmatic Venables. He gestured dismissively. 'We're all working towards the same end, in any case.'

'She's not going. And that's final.' Graham beat a fist on the desktop, making the tea things rattle.

'She says she will. I know it's not what you want to hear, Lieutenant Yates, but I fear neither of us could stop her if we tried. She'll find a way.' He crossed his arms over his chest and surveyed the irate chap. 'Are you in love with her?' Venables pitied the boy if he was; it had been obvious to him that Miss Bouchard had feelings for the corporal stuck in France who'd risked his life for her.

Graham blushed and turned away without answering. 'I'll hear this from her then,' he said and strode towards the door.

'Before you dash off after her, Yates, you should see this.' Venables pulled from his pocket the note about the escapee. 'Nobody's completely safe, wherever they are, whoever they're with.'

Graham had turned pale on reading the few lines. He threw the paper onto his boss's desk. 'Does Elise know?'

'She does; and she knows we'll be keeping an eye on all concerned. Including you. Winters blamed you for grassing him up. I owe you a belated apology. You were right about him all along.'

Graham stood for a moment digesting that with his blood boiling then, without another word, he left the office.

Elise had made it as far as the Baker Street Underground station when she heard her name yelled by a familiar voice. She turned around and saw Graham haring towards her, waving his cap to gain her attention.

When he saw her stop and smile, waiting for him to catch her up, he slowed down. As he approached, he smoothed his hair and kept the cap in his hand.

'You've spoken to the major.' She broke the ice, reading from his strained expression what was bothering him. 'I haven't been dragooned into anything, Graham. In fact, your boss did his best to put obstacles in my path. But I know what I want to do; I've hoped for such an opportunity.'

'You don't know what you're saying. You've no idea what you're getting into. Opportunity?' He snorted. 'I don't think you want an opportunity to die, do you?' He clutched her hands firmly with fingers that were lightly vibrating. 'Listen, there's something I've been meaning to ask you, and I know this is a very bad time and hardly the place but it won't wait now.' He cleared his throat, but before he could speak she placed her gloved forefinger against his lips.

'Don't say anything else, please. I want to go home to France ... to what's left of my family.' She moved her fists to her heart. 'It's an ache I have in here. And I'll fight for that opportunity to live and die with them if that's what it comes to.' She gazed at his dear features. 'I love you and Faith; you've been the best friends to me. I'll never forget either of you or how you helped me settle into life in England.'

'It's Hawkes, isn't it? You've fallen in love with him.' Graham plunged his hands into his pockets and dropped his chin to his chest. 'You know it's just an infatuation ... because he saved your life you think you love him. If I'd been there I would have done the same for you.'

'I know.' She cupped his face, raised it so they were gazing at one another. 'I know you would.' She sighed and let him go. 'It's a funny thing – love – a bit like trouble.' She remembered Nathan telling her trouble couldn't be predicted but just landed on you without warning. 'It turns up when you're least expecting it. Haven't really got time for it ...' She smiled wistfully. 'I'll always want to keep in touch with you all. Would that be all right?'

He nodded then gestured as though he might have more to say, but after a moment's silence he turned and walked away.

The Tube platform was packed. Graham elbowed a path to the front to be one of the first to cram onto the next train heading for the East End. He couldn't – wouldn't – give up. Elise had become the most important person in his life. If she went away ... was killed, he wouldn't be able to bear it. He'd want to die himself. If he couldn't change her mind, he'd put himself forward for recruitment as an agent. They wouldn't deny him when he was already halfway there. *If you can't beat 'em join 'em,* the phrase danced devilishly in his head. In France he'd stick close to her, be able to protect her.

In his pocket he had a diamond ring in a velvet-lined box. Not that he thought Elise the type to be swayed by an expensive gift. He simply wanted to prove the strength of his love in some way. And he didn't know what else to do. He drew the box out and raised the lid, glimpsing the sparkles as the light caught the stone. A warm wind hit him from the tunnel.

He spotted the train's lights in blackness just as the box was snatched from his hand and an almighty shove in the back knocked him off balance.

A woman screamed and people pushed forward to try to see what had happened. The fellow behind, with odd, henna-coloured hair, hunched into his coat and barged against the flow towards the exit.

Chapter Twenty-One

'I'm going to be away for a long while during my next posting. So I want to say a proper goodbye to you this time.'

Clover upended the iron onto the table. She looked up from hot cotton at Elise, who'd entered the room holding her suitcase. In the year since she'd left the factory and joined the nursing yeomanry they'd got used to seeing her like this, framed in the doorway, dressed in her uniform with a brown leather valise in her hand. Clover knew in her heart that this parting would be different. She'd grown to know and love her French sister and already her heart was breaking at the thought of losing her after such a short acquaintance. Neil was folding his newspaper and casting his eyes between his wife and sister-in-law. He got up from the armchair as the suitcase was put on the floor for the final goodbye. Clover came first to embrace Elise and kiss her forehead.

'Wherever you go, make sure to take good care of yourself,' Clover said huskily.

'I will.' Elise knew her big sister had, of course, picked up on the fact that there was more to it than what had actually been said. Probably, Clover had known for a while that her service in the nursing yeomanry wasn't what it was supposed to be. But she never asked a question and kept her thoughts to herself, and maybe to Neil.

Neil embraced her and when he let her go the trio stood quietly. It was the only occasion there'd been an awkwardness between them. Even when she'd first turned up she'd slipped into this family like a missing piece of a jigsaw puzzle. This afternoon had brought tension and an unspoken sadness.

'You'll write if you can, I know,' said Clover.

'I will.' Elise knew she wouldn't and so did they. 'Would you give all the little rascals a cuddle from me when you go to see them at the seaside?'

'Of course. Now we've the Brownie camera we'll be able to show you some photos when we all next get together...' Clover's voice faded away. 'Until then, know we'll all be thinking of you. Every day.'

'I'll be thinking of you. I love you all . . . everyone ... tell them that,' Elise said and picked up her case, not looking back as she left. The glitter in her eyes remained hidden.

'Well, you could have let me know you were coming.' Faith dropped the *Radio Times,* jumped up from the chair and rushed to her unexpected visitor. 'Bloody hell! You look fit and well.' She'd felt her friend's solid limbs during their lengthy hug. 'Those nursing yeomanry people are putting you through your paces then.'

'Always,' said Elise and drew Faith back into another embrace. 'I've missed you.'

'Same goes...' said Faith, raking a hand through her long fair hair while grinning from ear to ear.

'Got time for supper, dear, or is it another flying visit?' asked Mrs Yates.

'Supper would be lovely, thank you.'

'You'll stay over then?' asked Faith in delight.

'If you'll have me.'

A quiet ensued and Elise knew they were all thinking of the bedroom once known as Graham's room, now known as Elise's because there was no Graham. Hadn't been for over a year, other than in their hearts and memories.

'Let's go for a walk along the beach.' Faith attempted to sound cheery. 'It was gusty earlier but it's calmed down now.' She gave a whistle and a brown terrier padded in from the garden and straight to his mistress's feet. 'Yes, you can come along, Kirk.' She rubbed the dog's head. As a pup he'd been called Dunkirk but the name had been shortened as she said she'd felt a fool yelling that out on the beach and making people stare.

'You youngsters go and stretch your legs then. We'll have supper a bit later. Your father might be back from the boatyard by then,' said Mrs Yates. 'It's stew so it'll keep.'

The sea was easy and the beach quite empty as people packed up rugs and chairs and went to find some dinner. Wafts of savoury aromas tantalised them as they strolled past cafés and restaurants. At intervals they stopped to throw bits of driftwood for Kirk or to skim pebbles over the still surface of the water. They paced back up the beach and sat down to one side of a seaweed-strewn patch of shingle with the sea wall warming their backs.

'How have your mum and dad been?' asked Elise.

'Up and down. Dad flies into a rage every so often. Says he's going to London to complain about the way the police investigation was handled. Mum manages to calm him down.'

'I understand how they feel. I miss him,' said Elise simply. 'So much.'

'He'd be glad about that ... in a nice way.' Faith leaned to fondle the dog's silky ears as it stretched out at her feet.

'Have the police been in touch with any news at all?' Elise had been tortured by a thought that a vengeful Toby Winters might have been involved in Graham's death. She'd told herself she was being daft; the traitor would have been fleeing for his life, not hanging around in London. She'd not found out much from Venables other than that the escapee hadn't been apprehended and was believed to have been smuggled out of the country.

A witness had come forward. The woman reported getting a glimpse of a jewellery box in the victim's hand. She'd said she was craning her neck to be nosy and see what was sparkling inside when it was snatched by a fellow with reddish-brown hair. The jostled victim had toppled off the platform and the thief had made a swift getaway in the ensuing pandemonium. Toby Winters had fairish hair. Yet Elise had come to know that man and believed him capable of anything. And getting hold of a wig wasn't difficult.

'Nobody's been arrested yet; I doubt they will be after all this time,' Faith said flatly. 'The inquest's over and done with. We've been told theft was the most likely motive. The rest just dreadfully bad luck. Doubt they'll catch the bastard now.'

A receipt for an engagement ring had been found in Graham's pocket, indicating he'd been heading to the East End to propose to her with it before his fatal accident. Elise drew in her knees, crossed her arms and rested her chin on top of them.

Faith gave her friend a cuddle. 'Graham thought the

world of you. He wanted to marry you and wouldn't want you to feel guilty or sad.'

'I do though.'

'Life's so bloody unfair.' Faith tilted up her face to the rays of the setting sun. She wouldn't ever ask her best friend what her answer would have been had her brother arrived in Silvertown and popped the question. That wouldn't be fair. 'Couldn't 'arf do with a nip of Scotch right now,' she said on a wicked giggle.

'Don't you dare.' Elise sat up straight and nudged her in the ribs. 'Have to make do with one of these.' She withdrew some cigarettes from her pocket, and when they were both leaning back smoking, Faith resumed their conversation.

'I stayed on the wagon even after it happened. Couldn't drink, what with Mum and Dad keeling over in grief. Had to take over for a while, and I'm glad I went back to work as well.'

'How's the gang doing?' Elise was already aware Faith had got her old land girl job back.

'Bermondsey's gone back home. Got knocked up by the greengrocer in Ramsgate. He's in his forties, married with two kids.' Faith started to chuckle. 'His wife came round to the farm and things turned nasty. Didn't bring any rotten tomatoes with her, but insults were flying about, I can tell you.'

'*Mon Dieu!*' Elise exclaimed while shaking her head in a mixture of amazement and amusement. After a while she said, 'I can help you out with money now you've lost Graham's pay.'

'No, it's not that bad, love.'

'You don't have to tell your mum and dad about it. And you've fed and housed me more times than I can count—'

'No,' Faith interrupted and tilted her head to rest against Elise's. 'You're a bloody beauty for offering but Graham's boss has worked out a pension arrangement. The money's started coming through. We're all right now.'

'Been out on the *Belle*?' asked Elise after a pause.

'A bit.' Faith got up, and cigarette in mouth stretched her arms over her head. 'But the old girl needs a few repairs so we've been using her less lately.' She dropped her dog-end and used her shoe to grind it into the sand. 'Now we're getting back on our feet we'll get her properly patched up soon. Most of it me and Dad can do ourselves, anyhow. I'm a dab hand with a paintbrush and a smoothing plane.'

'Us Dunkirk Club girls can turn our hands to anything.'

There was a pause, then Faith said expectantly, 'Speaking of turning our hands to things ... ?'

'Don't ask.'

'Righto.' Faith chuckled. 'Got used to those sort of answers with Graham. When will we see you again?' Her tone had become quiet and serious.

'Don't know, *cherie*, but if I can, I'll keep in touch. Promise.'

'Don't forget where I am and that Dunkirk Club girls stick together. Anything you need ... anything at all ... just ask.'

Elise hugged Faith then gazed out to sea. The sun had set and a breeze blew in off the water.

'I'm about ready for your mum's stew,' Elise said. She linked arms with Faith, and with Kirk padding alongside, they started walking back.

'You two worked up an appetite,' said Mrs Yates, clearing their clean plates.

'Thank you, it was delicious,' said Elise and sat down in a fireside chair while Faith twiddled the knob on the radio. She tuned it to the BBC French service and after the chords of Beethoven's Fifth Symphony died away a solemn voice intoned, *'Ici Londres.'* Elise knew the staccato introduction to the musical piece was Morse code: V for victory. She imagined she was the only one of them who did, although many months ago, prior to her training at Beaulieu, she wouldn't have known it either. The 'personal messages' started and they listened eagerly. Faith had improved on her schoolgirl French with Elise's tutoring and some of the riddles she could translate herself. Their meaning remained a mystery to all present though.

'I don't know why you bother with that double Dutch, Faith,' said Mrs Yates over a shoulder.

'It's not double Dutch to some people, dear,' said her husband who'd come downstairs, washed and changed ready to go out. 'If we were able to decipher it, so might Jerry.' He collected his hat from the peg and put it on. 'Right, just off for a swift half then, and will see you all later.'

'Swift half, my eye,' muttered his wife as he went out, but she continued humming. She dished up the girls' slices of apple pie then poured custard on top of each. She handed them their puddings which they ate, seated comfortably in the armchairs while she made herself a cup of tea.

'I listen to this every night,' said Faith. 'Won't stop until this war's over.'

'I pray to God it is soon,' rumbled Mrs Yates.

'Amen to that,' said Elise.

She'd slept here in this room many times, but knowing she might never do so again brought sharply into focus the first night spent in her Broadstairs' sanctuary. She'd felt like a drowned mouse that day: small and timid.

Elise felt differently now, but just as she had then she sat down on the chair by the window and gazed out, wondering what tomorrow would bring. The dusk was down, darkness not yet complete as the days were long. The sparkles were on the sea. Only a few lights from the harbour pricked the darkness.

She could still back out, say she wouldn't go. She could remain here, cosy and safe. And heaven only knew she owed this sad family, who still welcomed her into their hearts, so very much. She knew and so did they that if Graham had never met her he'd still be alive.

This rotten war had ripped apart so many families and would continue to do so until the sound of Beethoven's V for victory signalled dancing in the street, not a man spouting riddles in a posh voice. From the moment Major Venables sent her a brief message that all was received correctly from France, her fate had been sealed.

She gazed out to sea towards her homeland. All being well, that's where she would be tomorrow night. And she would find out what had happened to Luc and Nathan, or die trying.

'This can be a tricky time, waiting for the off. Try to relax.' The smartly dressed woman offered her pack of cigarettes and both of the people with her took one. A match was struck and the middle-aged fellow politely indicated the young woman should go first. She bent her head to the match, her black hair sweeping her face. He then availed himself of the flame before it was extinguished.

'Now, let me make a final check of your clothing.' The

older woman beckoned the younger into a separate room. The man sat down at a table and puffed on his cigarette while awaiting his turn to be searched for stray items. British coins, bus or theatre tickets – any small, easily overlooked thing could betray their true identities if they were apprehended and searched.

He counted through the creased French money he'd been given – no new banknotes that might arouse suspicion as having been collected from a foreign bank. While shuffling the limp paper into a pile, he listened to the *messages personnels* being broadcast, knowing one of them would alert his French contacts to be ready for his arrival.

'Clean as a whistle,' the older woman said and patted Elise's arm. 'You're wearing your French dress?' She had glanced at the couturier's label in the garment before straightening the collar. 'Nice touch.'

'It's rather tight on me now.'

'You look fine. Very pretty. Send him in next would you?'

Elise did so and the fellow got up, barely making eye contact, and disappeared into the room. They'd been encouraged not to get to know one another, or even talk much. He would accompany her to France in a Lysander aircraft but remain a stranger.

She stubbed out her cigarette in a full ashtray on the table. About to sit down, she heard the drone of engines and turned to the large windows overlooking the runway. She watched a small squat aeroplane land and taxi to a stop. The pilot climbed down a ladder attached to the fuselage and started towards the building. He smiled at her as he came in then disappeared elsewhere to be briefed.

Elise sat down and listened to the messages, guessing, as had her companion, that one of them would refer to her imminent arrival. Were Luc or Nathan listening? Things had gone quiet their end a long while ago. She hadn't found out about it until recently. She'd been at Beaulieu training and preparing for this day. Eventually, she'd been informed that contact had been broken. It was made clear that she wouldn't be put under pressure to carry on if she didn't want to. She imagined Venables and his cronies still hoped she'd go or they would have brought this up before she finished her training. She wouldn't allow herself to think the worst; long silences were to be expected. The people she loved were embedded in French Resistance groups and would move from place to place to sabotage, and to avoid capture.

'Right, let's take you to the aeroplane.' The woman in the civilian suit beckoned a steward who picked up the suitcases. They filed outside and got into a car that would ferry them to the aircraft.

Below, the Channel was shimmering beneath a full moon. It was a pretty sight but Elise was thinking her guts didn't like this first experience of flying any more than they'd liked travelling by boat. She'd got used to sailing though; had learned to enjoy the rock of the ocean. The pilot's voice crackled into her headphones, jerking her eyes away from the small window.

'Nice night for it.'

She looked up at the endless starry sky. *You should be more afraid than you are*, she told herself. Her heart felt fast and jumpy but apart from that she remained calm. Impatient, even, to be out of this rackety ride and on firm ground.

'Spotted them.' They'd been flying for about two hours when the pilot spoke again and jabbed a thumb to the left.

'You know about the corporal going back?' Elise waited on tenterhooks for her headphones to crackle into life. She believed Major Venables to be a shrewd individual but not a liar. He surely had stuck by his word.

'Been mentioned,' said the pilot. 'If he's waiting, he's welcome to hop on. Can't hang about though.'

The plane began its descent, bumping lower in stages, while the pinprick flashes of torchlight became clearer as their comrades guided them in. The landing was surprisingly smooth and she scrambled into action, pulling the suitcase from beneath the seat where it was stowed. The plane taxied then turned and returned to their reception party.

Her training kicked in and she did what was expected. Her travelling companion got down and was handed their suitcases. She grabbed the case of the man on the ground, stowing it on the fuselage before swiftly descending the iron ladder. The agent who was returning in the Lysander brushed past with a gruff 'good luck' and climbed aboard while the aircraft's propellers continued to whir.

Elise looked for her companion; it was too late to wish him good luck, he was already hurrying away across the field with his guide. '*Bonne chance ...*' She murmured it anyway.

Elise felt her arm gripped and a rough French voice demanded to know her name.

'Orpheline.' She continued to search for a sign of Nathan.

'You can ride a man's bicycle?'

She almost laughed hysterically. Of all the things she'd been taught, none had been as mundane as riding a man's bike. 'Of course,' she answered the Frenchman in his own tongue.

'Are you alone? Is anybody else here?' She hung back as he started across the field at a rapid pace.

'Only Nazis will be here if we don't hurry.' He grabbed her arm and pulled her along. 'Come, we have to meet others. It's not far; a comrade will journey with you some of the way to Lille when you are ready to go. Until then you can remain at my house. It is safe and there is much to do.'

She couldn't trust this stranger yet and daren't give in to a desperate need to ask direct questions about her brother and Nathan; it would risk jeopardising all of them. Her personal battle to find them would be fought secretly.

'You can use a gun?'

'*Certainment.* I was told you would supply one.'

He produced a pistol from his belt and some ammunition and gave it to her. With that dragging on her pocket, they set off along the shadowy lane then halted by a break in the hedge. From behind the bushes he produced a large bike and wheeled it to her, securing her case on the back of it, before retrieving his own machine.

Moments later, they were on their way, Elise behind her guide, while to one side of them the Lysander soared into the sky.

Chapter Twenty-Two

Mathilde hadn't spoken to Luc in a very long while. It was a mixed blessing. For his own safety and hers, she didn't want him to come back. It didn't stop her longing to know how he was. She doubted she'd find out by opening the door. Somebody was outside but it wasn't her grandson. The moonless night might spur his visit, providing the cover he'd need, but Luc wouldn't change his signal. His sequence of taps was his calling card and that wasn't what she'd heard.

She turned down the lamp and peeped from behind the curtain. If something had happened to Luc the British Tommy might bring news of it if he were still at liberty in France. He'd seemed a decent sort and she felt mean for hoping he'd not made good his escape to England. Luc needed a friend and she doubted he'd find a better one.

She opened the door a fraction and squinted through the aperture. Nothing. Her fingers stretched for the rolling pin placed within reach. Then a dark head turned quickly and Mathilde received a glimpse of a ghostly visage, so eerily familiar, that she smothered a gasp and almost swooned.

'I didn't mean to scare you, Grandma.' Elise pushed

inside and hugged Mathilde. 'I've missed you so much. You are well?'

'But ... you're in England ...' Mathilde spluttered. 'They told me you'd escaped.' She fought free of her granddaughter's fierce embrace. Despite her shock, she checked outside for snoopers before swiftly locking the door. Once done, they stared at one another, momentarily paralysed by emotion, then Mathilde grabbed the girl and rocked her in her arms as she had when comforting Elise as a child.

Finally, they broke apart and Elise said, 'I did get to England. Who told you about it? Have you seen Luc?'

'Yes, he said you were safe.'

'When was that?' Elise asked urgently.

'In a moment we will speak of it. Sit down, my love, let me look at you.' Mathilde turned up the lamp and held it close to Elise's chin. A buttercup glow lit up a hauntingly beautiful face. It was as though her daughter Sophie sat on the stool. 'You look older ... so much like your mother that you gave me a fright.'

'I'm twenty-one now, Grandma.'

'You've turned into a woman in those lost years.' Mathilde's smile faded. 'Did you come back by boat?'

Elise was on her feet again and placing a finger on her grandmother's lips. 'Hush, no questions then I shan't have to tell you lies.'

'Oh, Elise.' Mathilde put the lamp on the table and cradled her jowls, shaking her head in despair. 'What have you got yourself into?'

'Freeing France, that's all.'

'You shouldn't have come here, my love. The Gestapo have been asking questions.'

'Recently?'

'No, a year or more ago. But it wasn't the first time they came. They were eager to interrogate you and Luc about what your father did. You know Sidney's dead, don't you?'

'I guessed he was.' Hearing this blunt confirmation was hard to bear and Elise sank down onto the seat once more.

'He took his own life... shot himself.'

Elise dropped her chin and quietly wept. 'I'm glad he denied them the chance to do it,' she finally said.

Mathilde placed a comforting hand on her granddaughter's bowed head.

'When did you last speak to Luc, Grandma?' Elise wiped her wet face on her sleeve.

'It was the same day the Nazis paid a visit. What a wretched coincidence that was. Thankfully they got away unseen.' Mathilde paused. 'Luc didn't come back here after that. I've noticed him a few times since on market day or sitting by the stream. Once he knows I've spotted him he disappears. He does it for me so I won't worry about him.' She sighed. 'I worry more though in case the Milice catch him loitering. He's not been back for so long that I often go here and there searching for him. A glimpse would be enough to know he's all right.'

'Have the neighbours asked you about him?' Elise was alarmed by her brother recklessly hanging about like that and risking arrest.

'Nobody would know him. He looks thin and shabby. I hardly recognise him myself beneath his hair and beard.' Mathilde demonstrated its bushiness with her hands. Luc Bouchard had always been a handsome well-groomed boy who caught the local girls' eyes. He couldn't have used a better disguise when making a visit to his old stamping ground.

'You said "they" turned up?' Elise had picked up on something interesting. 'Luc didn't come here alone then?'

'He was with the British soldier who took you to Dunkirk.'

'Corporal Hawkes?'

'He wouldn't tell me his name. I do know he was an escaped prisoner of war hoping to get to England. He seemed nice.' Mathilde noticed her granddaughter's shining eyes. 'You like him?'

'I do, Grandma. I hope he's safely home by now.'

'I'll find you something to eat and you must stay here. The landlord has let your cottage to another tenant.'

'It doesn't matter,' said Elise, although the loss of her childhood home was a wrench. 'It's understandable – no rent's been paid in a long while.'

'He packed up your belongings and brought them to me in a few boxes, clothes and pots and pans and so on.' Mathilde comforted her granddaughter with a hug. 'A new beginning is what you need.' She paused. 'People think there's a family rift and you've gone away to escape the trouble your father caused. But enough time has passed. Blood is thicker than water and nobody will be surprised that you have returned to the bosom of your family. If the neighbours gossip, so what?' She shrugged. 'As for the Gestapo officer ... I can hide you if he comes snooping. After all this time I hope he'll not bother me again.' Having made her plans, Mathilde tutted in vexation. 'I've missed you dreadfully but at least I had the consolation of believing one of us was safe. Why did you leave England? Were the Coopers nasty to you?'

'No! Not at all. They are fine people. Now listen ...' Elise stood up and cupped her grandmother's soft cheeks. 'You won't need to hide me. I can't stay long. I have somewhere to go. Have you any idea where Luc might be? Did he mention other partisans?'

'The priest at Hazebrouck is a friend. Luc and your corporal have met up with him on occasion.' She gazed forlornly at Elise. 'I think you know more about the local Resistance than I do. Are you working for the British?'

'I'm fighting for France, Grandma, just as you and Grandpa did last time. Please don't ask me more than that.' She moved towards the door; her grandmother wasn't satisfied with her explanation and it would be better to go than face an interrogation. 'I'll come back and see you again if I can.' She held the older woman's hands as they sprang towards her to stop her leaving. Elise brought them to her lips. 'Je t'aime,' she whispered.

Mathilde muffled a sob as her granddaughter's figure melted into the darkness. With a heavy sigh, she dropped the curtain back into place and sank down onto the stool. She remained quite still, enveloped in a faint scent of lavender that provoked another memory of her daughter Sophie and times she'd rather forget.

When Mathilde had fought for France in the Great War she'd been twice as old as Elise. She'd had a husband and a daughter. She'd had a family life. Her grandchildren had not yet tasted the joy of having their own families, their own hearths to settle at. They might never have those things with the risks they were taking.

Her pride in them was boundless, but bittersweet.

Elise had skirted the hedges and arrived back at the point on the fringe of the woods where she'd concealed her bicycle. She'd not wanted to leave it outside the cottage and advertise the fact that Mathilde Bouchard had a visitor.

She wheeled it, turning it in the right direction. Her foot was raising to mount it when a hand was clamped over her mouth and she was jerked off balance, resulting in the machine thudding to the ground.

She kicked backwards, her shoe making hard contact with bone and grabbed for the pistol in her pocket. A larger, stronger hand covered hers, preventing her drawing it forth.

'When I said I'd come and find you, Elise Bouchard, this wasn't what I had in mind,' said a sardonic cockney voice. 'You're a long way from Silvertown and a whack in the shin isn't the welcome I've been dreaming about.'

Elise slowly relaxed, but her gasping breaths kept her breasts lifting and falling against his imprisoning arm. Her expression, unseen by him, had softened in joyous disbelief. 'What were you dreaming about, Corporal Hawkes?' she asked huskily.

'The day this would get to the right place.' He raised a fist, opening his fingers in front of her to liberate the kiss she'd blown him years ago.

He let her go and she whipped around to face him, barely hesitating before hugging him tightly. 'I've not stopped thinking about you, Nathan.'

'I've not stopped thinking about you either,' he said and held her against him. 'But why in God's name have you come back?'

His sultry tone had been replaced by exasperation. She didn't answer. She found his mouth in stubble, first with her fingers then she pressed her lips to his. They tasted salty and hard as they ground on hers and a hot, growling breath entered her mouth.

She made no objection when he took her to the peaty ground with him beneath the trees and kissed her passionately, again and again, until her mouth burned and throbbed and her cheeks were tingling from scraping bristles. He lifted his head to gaze hungrily at her and instinctively she entwined their legs.

'That was worth waiting for,' he said and the next kiss he gave her was tender.

'Is Luc here with you? Close by?' She gazed excitedly into his eyes, bright as stars in darkness. Then they were lost beneath his lashes as he closed them.

Inaudibly he cursed because he knew the moment to love her right here and now beneath the trees had been lost. She'd ask again about her brother and he had to tell her. He'd lied to women before and it had never seemed to matter much. But this time it would. He drew them both up until they were kneeling, facing one another.

'Where is Luc? How did you know I'd be here?'

'I didn't. I came to speak to your grandmother. I guessed you'd pay her a visit though as soon as you could. Perfect timing.'

'You heard the broadcast about my arrival, didn't you?'

'Yeah, we heard it.'

'Grandma told me about the priest at Hazebrouck. He's trustworthy?'

'He was ... now I can't be sure. The Gestapo came and took him. He was betrayed and might break under interrogation,' said Nathan. 'He knows our names, where we've been, what we've done. We fought our way out of the church but Luc was injured in the raid.'

'Is that what you came to tell Mathilde?' She grabbed his shoulders to hurry his answer.

'Your brother doesn't want her to worry about him. He wants her to think nothing's wrong.'

'It is though, isn't it?' she said anxiously, and her hands fell away from him. 'Luc's been captured too, hasn't he?'

'No. We both got away,' he said and swept a thumb over her cheek in reassurance. 'This happened months ago. Your brother refused to go to hospital.' Nathan added, 'I can understand why with a gunshot wound: he'd be arrested, questioned, sent away to a camp ... if he's lucky.'

'Is he going to die?' She forced the question out and sank back onto her heels.

'I don't think so, but he's weak and feverish. And argumentative as hell.'

'Where is he?' Elise scrambled up onto her feet. *Weak and feverish* wasn't so bad. She'd nurse him and make him well again. 'I have to go to him now.'

Nathan wanted her back in his arms but with a groan of frustration was soon standing beside her. 'He's not far away. A friend has him hidden in the attic of his house. A doctor comes to him but there's only so much he can do with limited equipment and medicine. Luc lost a lot of blood.'

Elise felt her spirits plummet again but she hoisted the bike upright, eager to get going.

'Why did you come back, Elise?' He held onto the handlebars, stopping her moving the bike into the open.

She remained quiet for a moment, although tempted to say she'd no choice because every day spent in England had brought with it feelings of guilt for having run away and stolen his chance of freedom. There was no time for unburdening herself or for apologising for having squandered what he'd given her. 'I had to, Nathan,' was all she said. 'Please, take me to Luc. I must see him tonight. Then I must go to my lodging in town. I have to find work and I have an important meeting arranged ...'

'With a British agent?'

She nodded.

'Where?'

'In a café ... Rue Vincent.'

He nodded, digesting that. 'Ever ridden crossbar?'

She smiled wistfully. 'Of course. Luc would pedal and give me a ride. We only had the one bike between us. Then Papa sold it to buy his ferry ticket to England – that was the last time he left France. I was twelve. I wish he'd stayed there and never come back.'

'I expect he had to come back, same as you did.'

Having settled himself on the saddle, Nathan helped her hop up and then pushed off with barely a wobble and without a squeak betraying their progress along the black lane.

'If we're stopped have you any documents?' Nathan spoke quietly into her ear.

Elise nodded.

'Forged in your own name?'

Another nod. 'How about you?'

'Father Pascal got ours from somebody he knows. Luc was using an alias but Louis Marron's wanted after helping two British POWs escape. Your brother goes by his real name now with new papers.' He shrugged. 'I'm Alain Roche, according to my identity card. The forgeries have passed muster when we've shown them.'

'Have you any money?'

'Not much. We've kept ourselves fed from casual labouring on farms and the railways. Luc's driven a tractor and a lorry. A few factory foremen have taken a risk on us because they're patriots. The most helpful fellow is a railwayman. He's a shop steward type ... Commie I wouldn't be surprised. One way or another, we've got by and managed to cause Jerry some headaches at the same time.' He chuckled at the memory of the havoc they'd created with their shop steward compatriot. 'Railway tracks kept buckling when we were around. And a load of flour and sugar went missing on its way to German barracks.' He paused. 'Trouble is ...'

'The trouble is, if the priest talks the circuit will collapse or be infiltrated by enemy agents.' Elise voiced his concerns for him.

'That's about the size of it,' Nathan grimly said. 'Did your grandmother tell you the Gestapo have questioned her?'

Elise gave a nod. 'She thinks enough time's passed for my father's crime to be old news.' Elise tightened her arms about him and he leaned to press his lips to her forehead. 'Have you been lying low since the priest was arrested, Nathan?'

'Yeah. We've been careful. Father Pascal's got the gift of the gab. He might eventually talk himself out of detention.'

'He'll need a silver tongue to persuade those devils he didn't know the local Resistance were camped in his church.' She paused. 'You have to assume he will break. You and Luc will need more papers, or to move somewhere you're not known.'

'Luc's not yet up to a journey and forgers are hard to find.' Nathan jabbed his head at a building emerging through pre-dawn mist. 'We're almost there.'

She squinted at a house with an attached single storey annexe. On a post hung a tavern sign. They passed through the open gate and Nathan brought the bike to a stop by an outhouse with a truck parked close by. A small dormer window in the main building leaked a muted light.

'Luc's awake by the looks of it.' He helped her down.

'Wait here while I put this in the shed. Then I'll take you to him.'

Nathan had a key to a side door. Once inside, they ascended a flight of stairs to a low doorway he had to stoop to enter. The room was compact, with sloping eaves and few items of furniture. A smell of stale blood and sweat hung in the air. Elise rushed to kneel beside the narrow bed and slip her arms about Luc. Beneath the cheek she'd placed on his blanketed chest she could feel his rapid breathing. 'I've missed you,' she whispered. 'You'll soon be well again now I'm here to look after you.'

'We heard about a female British agent coming.' Luc stroked her hair and sighed. 'When you didn't arrive I hoped it wasn't you, Elise. But I'll look after you.'

'I know you will,' she said although doubting he could look after himself at the moment. 'I was delayed. I was sent to assist a circuit in the Free Zone until another operator turned up. She was one of the girls I trained with in England.' Their reunion was brief. Elise had been impatient to resume her journey towards Lille.

Luc raised the backs of his fingers to sweep over her cheek. She smelled the sickness on his skin but grasped his hand and brought it to her lips. She was about to ask if he was improving but it seemed a stupid thing to do. His wan face and feverishly gleaming eyes told their own story. As did the bandage wound about his bicep, stained with blood and pus.

'The bullet was in there too long.' Luc had noticed the direction of her gaze. 'The wound got infected. We couldn't find a doctor to help at first. Everybody's scared.' He struggled into a seated position, his teeth gritted against the effort. 'Just my luck! Same arm as before and almost the same place. I got shot that day, you know, after I left you. Grandma patched me up and I made a good recovery. I couldn't risk going to her again, not after we nearly bumped into the Gestapo. They've been questioning her—'

'She told me all about that.'

'You've seen her? How is she?' he eagerly asked.

'She's well. And thinking of you. The Gestapo haven't returned since.' Elise could see she had given him some relief; he closed his eyes and relaxed against the pillow.

'The doctor will be back when it's light. He'll sort me out with some jollop.' Luc used Nathan's slang word for medicine. 'The fellow has promised to get proper stuff from the hospital.'

Nathan had seated himself on a rickety-looking chair close to the door. He had his elbows on his knees and his head lowered to his clasped hands while listening to brother and sister attempting to conceal their anxieties from one another. Luc was first to give up on the charade. His temper flared without warning, bringing Nathan onto his feet.

'You shouldn't have come back, Elise.' Luc swung his legs over the side of the bed and stood swaying in front of her. 'If I'd known you'd do this I wouldn't have got a message to you in London. All I wanted was for you to know I was alive.'

'Don't upset yourself, *cheri*.' She addressed him calmly, trying to make him sit down. He squirmed away and was forced to hold on to the chest of drawers for support as his head swam.

Nathan took over and gripped Luc's shoulders, stilling him and forcing him onto the mattress. 'Settle down, or you'll knock the wound open again.'

Luc sulkily shrugged out of his grip but did sit down, muttering to himself.

Nathan drew Elise away. 'He gets like this with me too. He's bored and frustrated that he can't do as much as he used to. Maybe it's best if you leave. I'll see you back.' He glanced at her brother, moodily watching them. 'Where are you staying, Elise?'

'A guest house in Rue Nord.' She gazed at him. Where do you sleep?' She could see only one bed. There wasn't really room for more than that. Apart from Luc's bunk there was a chair and a chest of drawers. On its top was the remnants of a meal on a tray. The rug on the floor looked threadbare and the boards surrounding it black and wormy.

'I kip in the shed. It's more comfortable than it sounds. There's a bunk and a water tap in the yard for washing. Probably not so good in winter when everything freezes. But we'll be gone before then. Being outside has its advantages: I'll know early if we get a visit from Fritz.'

They continued to gaze at one another. 'Want to see my humble abode?'

She nodded and blushed. He smiled and took her hand.

'I'll come back and see you soon, Luc,' she said then let Nathan take her outside into a day as yet unbroken by dawn light.

Chapter Twenty-Three

'Who runs this place? Can he be trusted?' Elise could hear noises coming from the tavern as pots and pans were put into action for breakfast.

'A middle-aged fellow and his wife. They're a bit surly but we don't see much of them. We deal with their nephew. Theo lodges with them. The priest put us in touch with him. He's the fellow I told you about. He's got a useful position on the railway and is permitted the use of a truck.'

'The shop steward type?'

'That's him. A lot of those people have joined the Maquis, especially in the south of the country. Theo heads his own circuit but I think he'd like to see the back of us now.' Nathan paused. 'Something big's brewing and nobody wants it messed up. Last week the doctor was about to pay a visit when he spotted two Nazi officers at the bar. Thankfully the Krauts were too drunk to make much of the car stopping then driving off. It was a close shave though and rattled everybody.'

'I'm not surprised.' She frowned. 'How long have you been here?'

'A few months. Before that we were holed up in a barn

near Amiens and a different doctor was seeing to Luc. He removed the bullet but we couldn't stay there with your brother running a fever. We managed to get a message to Theo. He picked us up in his truck and brought us here.' He paused. 'There's a radio in the main house. Every family that has one hides it and tunes in to the BBC French Service.'

'Who deciphered the message about my arrival?'

'Theo's contact. I questioned him about it. I wanted to know where you'd be dropped and who you'd be meeting. He said he didn't know but I reckon he did.' Nathan paused. 'The fiasco at the church has put everybody on edge since the priest was arrested. There's no trust.' He gave her a bleak look. 'I wanted to be there to put you straight back on the plane.'

'I arranged for you to have a place on the Lysander and be taken home. My boss said he'd send a message in advance to arrange it but I can see now why you weren't there. We put down a long way from here. The pilots avoid landing in occupied France where possible.' She sighed. 'I've kept hoping that you'd manage to escape under your own steam somehow.'

Nathan shrugged. 'It wouldn't have mattered if I'd made the landing site or not. I wouldn't have got on the plane without you. Would you have gone back with me?'

She avoided his eyes while shaking her head and continuing to brood on the close shave they'd had with the Nazis. Luc might be able to defend himself with a gun but a physical fight would be difficult. 'Those German officers might come back. You should move on.' She lifted her head from his chest and placed a kiss on his lips. 'What time is it? I want to see Luc before I leave.'

She'd slept almost immediately after they'd made love in

the dark hour that preceded dawn. She'd woken to the feel of nude satiny skin beneath her cheek and a thin morning light. There was barely room for one person on the narrow bed on which they lay. But the space had sufficed.

He picked up his watch from the floor. 'Five o'clock,' he said, winding it then stretching his arms up to fasten it about his wrist.

'Was I asleep for long?'

'About an hour. That's all.'

'I should get dressed,' she said. 'And get going.'

'I'll find us some coffee and something to eat. Luc'll want breakfast. Nothing affects his appetite.' He eased away from her and rolled off the edge of the bunk to stand up. She plumped the pillow behind her head and watched his lean buttocks disappearing inside his trousers, then the muscles in his shoulders undulating as he shrugged into his shirt.

'I want to ask you something, Nathan,' she said while he did up buttons

He turned back, noticing that she looked serious ... and shy. She was sitting up and had the blanket gripped beneath her chin. He gestured that she should go ahead, although he had an inkling of what was to come.

'Are you married? Or engaged? A sweetheart in England ... somebody you've left behind and haven't seen in a long while?' Her voice died away. 'Have you any children?' She felt ashamed for not having brought this up hours ago, before they'd kissed again and her need for him and his comfort had obliterated every other thought in her head. Yet had she done that, and whatever his answer might have been, what would have been hers? She loved him more than ever now.

'Do I seem the type to mess around behind my wife's back?' He continued doing up buttons.

'Is that what this is – a "mess around"?'

'You know it's not.'

'I don't know. When we met, we spoke of special people... you asked if I had a boyfriend. I told you my dad wouldn't let me. You didn't deny having somebody special when I asked about your loves.' Her teeth savaged her lower lip. 'I wanted you to get home. I thought if you had children they'd be crying for you.'

He said huskily, 'Thanks, that was sweet of you. I'm not a father and not married or engaged either. I did have somebody. A girl I'd known since I was about fifteen. I told her I didn't want to settle down yet and was enlisting. She didn't want me to.' He began pulling on his boots and tying the laces. 'I joined up and she said we were over. I said all right then. She wrote to me in France a couple of times – before Dunkirk – to say maybe we weren't over. I wrote back that it would be best to talk about it when I got home.'

'You didn't get home.'

'I didn't need to, to know it was over for me. If I'd ever loved her I wouldn't have left England. If I didn't love you I wouldn't still be in France.' He hunkered down and took her hands in his, placing his lips to her fingertips. 'I knew straight away at Dunkirk... Did you?'

'Yes, I knew. What's her name?'

'Does it matter?'

'Yes...'

'Laura. I expect she's met somebody else now. I hope she has and she's happily married.'

'So do I,' Elise said in a voice weakened by the intensity of her relief. But she had a confession of her own to make. 'I met somebody in England. He was the best friend to me...

So is his sister. She's the girl on the boat that took me across the Channel.'

'I'm glad you had friends around you. What're their names?'

'Faith and Graham.'

'Are you telling me he's special to you?'

'He was . . . very special, but not in the way you are. Then he died.'

'I'm sorry to hear it, Elise, truly sorry.'

'Graham loved me. He didn't try to seduce me, or even properly kiss me. He taught me to dance the waltz and foxtrot . . .' Her voice died with her smile. 'Graham wanted to marry me. I thought you should know.'

'I'm glad you told me,' he said and leaned to kiss her gently on the lips. He'd known she was still a virgin last night but her desperate honesty was another reason why he adored her and would never lie to her.

'It's my fault he died. If he hadn't fallen in love with me it wouldn't have happened.'

Nathan settled down to sit on the floor beside her. 'What d'you mean?'

She told him about the tragedy and when she'd finished, she remained quiet for some time wondering whether to add to it her suspicions about Toby Winters' possible involvement. But she wasn't sure she believed that herself, and it would open up a complicated new story she presently hadn't enough time to tell.

'That's God-awful luck for Graham, but it's not your fault, sweetheart,' Nathan eventually said.

'I wouldn't have married him even if he'd had a chance to ask me.' Her hands covered her face and from behind them she sighed, 'I feel wretchedly guilty.'

'It's this damned war makes everybody feel like that.' He pushed his fingers through his hair and let his own demons creep back. 'Wilmot didn't get off Dunkirk beach. He was caught in machine-gun fire. Evans was with me when we made a run for it. We were captured two weeks later, holed up in a bombed-out building. We were out of ammo so couldn't put up a fight.' His guts would writhe when he brooded on the wretched humiliation of coming out, hands up, to be greeted by smirking Nazis. 'We were detained for a work party but would've ended up in a camp in Germany if your brother hadn't helped us escape. He recognised us out on the road ...' It was a memory to put a smile back on his face. 'Luc was driving an ambulance and I thought our prayers had been answered. Turned out Evans would've been better off left where he was.'

'Was he badly injured?' She prompted him to finish the tale.

'He was, and only half-conscious when we scarpered. The Krauts would've put him in an infirmary. I thought I knew better, and took him with us. He didn't make it.'

'I think you did know better. He would've wanted to die a free man. I expect he'd thank you if he could.'

'Maybe ...'

A quiet followed until Elise asked, 'How did you both stay on the run? They must have been after you.'

'Your brother was already involved with Father Pascal. We dumped the ambulance and went to the church. Would've been done for if the priest had refused to shelter us. It was only a matter of time though before the Gestapo put in an appearance. As luck would have it, we were out that first time they turned up.'

Inwardly, she thanked the Lord he'd not been lying low

inside or he would have been captured ... possibly killed within days of his escape. And Luc too.

'We were on a horse and cart taking weapons to Theo. His lot was planning to blow up a fuel dump.'

'You and Luc managed to steal German arms?' She sounded in awe of their achievement.

'They weren't German,' he chuckled, 'they were ours. Most had been caught in trawling nets or washed up on the northern beaches after Dunkirk. God bless the fishermen for cleaning and hiding them.'

Elise listened to him praising her patriotic countrymen with a proud smile on her face.

'The salvage had been finding its way to the church to be stashed. We thought Father Pascal had lost his marbles on the day he levered the lid off a tomb saying he had something nice to show us.' Nathan remembered how he and Luc had laughed themselves hoarse at the unexpected sight that met their eyes. 'So off we jolly well went on a horse and cart with two dozen Lee Enfield rifles and four Lewis machine guns hidden under some sacks of spuds. Luc did the talking and I played the part of the strong silent type.' Nathan might have affected to act dumb and dozy but he'd kept his eyes on the cargo and the pistol within reach under the seat. They'd been stopped at a checkpoint by a soldier, but thankfully the sullen youth had barely bothered with the vegetable sacks.

'After we dropped the guns off, we took back the horse and cart and spuds to the farmer who'd lent them. We were walking back when we heard a commotion coming from the church.' He paused. 'We kept out of sight and watched Father Pascal arguing with a Gestapo officer while soldiers ransacked the church. He got away with it on that occasion.'

Elise felt her heart pumping with anxiety as she listened to the tale. 'Did you go back there?'

'Yeah. After dark when the coast was clear. Father Pascal couldn't risk the network he was putting together falling apart.' Nathan shrugged. 'We understood his reasons for wanting us gone. If the Gestapo had come back and searched again they might have found the other guns and the newly dug grave. We travelled south in the hope I'd get out through Spain. Didn't happen, and after that I decided I'd stay and fight.'

'You're a good man, Nathan.' She cupped his face with her hands. He didn't need to spell out that Private Evans was buried in the churchyard in his British army battle-dress. 'We owe it to everybody who won't go home to carry on fighting.'

After a brief silence he asked, 'How are you feeling this morning?'

'Very well, thank you.' She sat back with a bashful expression.

Her formality made him half smile. 'Happy?'

She immediately nodded, prompting him to stroke her blushing cheek. 'I love you, Elise; I know we hardly know one another but I love you and want to marry you. You can trust me, y'know. I won't ever let you down.'

'I do know. I love you and want to marry you,' she said. 'At first I thought it might be a crush because I was only seventeen and you acted like my knight in shining armour. But all these years later I still feel the same ... even more in love after last night.'

Her face became rosier and he drew her into his arms. 'So do I,' he whispered and closed his eyes, breathing in her summer scent as he had years ago when they'd lain together beneath the stars, hearing the Messerschmitt heading for Dunkirk.

'I really should be going soon.' The brightening morning alerted her to time passing.

'Right.' He pushed himself to his feet. 'I'll find us all something to eat then.'

She was glad he'd understood her need for privacy. He might have caressed almost every inch of her with his hands and mouth, but she would have felt embarrassed dressing in front of him as he had blithely done in front of her. Elise got out of the cosy nest where she'd fledged into womanhood and started pulling on her clothes. By the time Nathan was back she'd pumped water from the standpipe outside into a tin bowl and used the edge of his sheet to wash and dry herself.

The croissants were warm and sweet and the coffee strong and aromatic. He pushed one of the boiled eggs towards her and broke the top off his own.

'I don't know how you've avoided arrest when you can't speak the language.' She stabbed a piece of croissant into a golden yolk.

He answered in French that he indeed could speak the lingo.

'Your accent is diabolical, Nathan. Worse than my dad's and that's saying something.' She tutted.

'Do you know what happened to him?'

'Grandma told me.' Before he could commiserate and bring tears to her eyes she said, 'Did you give up on trying to escape and stay for Luc? To help him?'

'Partly, but he's helped me equally. Without him doing the talking I'd never pass myself off as French.'

She pushed away her empty plate then yawned and

stretched, wishing she could stay here in this little place. Later on it would be a beautiful day, she reflected, while watching dust motes dancing in the bright atmosphere striping through the window.

'Are you meeting the agent who came with you from England?'

She shook her head. 'He went in a different direction. Another courier travelled with me part of the way here. So much has changed in France.' Elise recalled her stomach twisting in knots every time they'd spotted enemy soldiers on the streets. And the French Milice were equally to be avoided. She hadn't been stopped so far to show her papers. Her travelling companion had encouraged her to keep calm when it happened and to flirt if need be.

A Nazi officer had been strutting about in the train carriage and had taken rather too much notice of her after her comrade got off. To avoid his amorous glances, she'd pretended to be asleep and had planted her feet rigidly in front of the wireless set beneath the seat. When she'd alighted at Lille carrying her luggage, her admirer had got off as well and started to follow her. Knowing the backstreets better than he, she'd given him the slip before collecting a bicycle from the appointed spot in an alley behind the High Street. The butcher's boy had emerged from the yard of the premises and wheeled it to her. He'd disappeared back inside the gate without saying a word.

'Have you got a description of this new colleague?' Nathan asked.

'He's in his early thirties, wears glasses and has brown hair and a thin moustache. Codename Marcel. Have you had dealings with him?'

'The name rings a bell. Luc might know more. Sometimes

when he's talking to Theo in French I can't keep up with what they're on about.' He gazed at her. 'Will you tell me your code name?'

'Orpheline. If I can't trust you, Nathan Hawkes, then I really am doomed.'

He repeated the name. 'Suits you.' He remained quiet and thoughtful then said, 'Tread very carefully with these people, won't you.'

'I'll never completely trust them. I doubt you and Luc completely trust the priest or the wireless operator.' She frowned. 'What happened to him on the day you were raided?'

'He'd already gone... needed elsewhere.' Nathan thought that fellow was either a jinx or a wrong 'un. He had fled one raid unscathed, then escaped another. Possibly a simple coincidence but he wasn't sure he believed in those any more. He was about to share his suspicions with Elise but instead shot to his feet and drew a pistol from his pocket.

'Car's coming.' He strode to the door to peer around its edge.

A dark saloon was approaching along the lane; recognising it, he relaxed and the gun was returned whence it came. 'It's the doctor, come to see to Luc.'

'I'd like to speak to him before I go.' Elise put her empty coffee cup down on the breakfast tray and together they went into the house.

The doctor was a stout man, aged in his mid-forties with a ruddy face and a sparse head of hair. He was startled enough on seeing a stranger with his patient's English friend for some of the colour to drain from his cheeks.

'Who is this?'

'Luc's sister.'

The fellow frowned on discovering more people were complicit in this. He continued unpacking some antiseptic and bandages from his case. Leaving those on the bedside chest, he hurried towards Elise. 'Your brother needs hospital, Ma'mselle,' he hissed in rapid French. 'You must tell him I cannot help him any more. The flesh is not healing as it should . . .'

'What are you whispering about?' Luc was on his feet and taking wobbly steps in their direction. 'I might have a rotting arm but I'm not deaf, you know.'

The doctor flapped a hand at him to return to the bed for treatment. He cleaned the angry-looking wound and put on a fresh bandage but continued to spear significant glances at Elise. He seemed in a rush to leave and was soon packing up his equipment.

'Make sure those dressings are burned on the fire straight away. Nobody must know I've been here,' he said before closing the door.

Elise hurried after him, knowing he wasn't exaggerating Luc's infection. The foul smell in the room had been more evident when the wound was unwrapped. 'Thank you for everything you've done for my brother.' She'd halted him before he could descend the stairs. 'Is there a private clinic he could go to? Somewhere out of the way with a sympathetic doctor like you? I will pay.'

'Hardly anywhere is private now, Ma'amselle. The Gestapo and the SS . . .' He gestured hopelessness. 'They are everywhere and not always recognisable until it is too late. I'm surprised you don't know this.'

She grabbed his elbow to stop him going. 'Where's the medicine you promised to bring?'

'I couldn't get any. I rarely work at the hospital; I work from a surgery. If I go too often they watch me like a hawk: what I do, what I use ... all logged. Penicillin is strictly rationed. The Nazis keep it for themselves. They visit the brothels and get diseased.' A smirk lifted a corner of his mouth: the closest he'd come to cracking a smile. 'I'll try to bring some sulfa powder next time.' He pulled free and continued on his way down the stairs.

Elise sighed and returned to the bedroom. Her brother seemed to have cheered up. He was smoking and taking sips of coffee. She was relieved to see him walk steadily towards her to give her a one-armed hug.

'Sorry for being ratty earlier.' He drew her to sit on the bed with him. 'How was it over there? Are Papa's family nice?'

'They are, and very welcoming. They asked about you, Luc.'

'Tell me about them.'

'There are lots of them; if I told you about them all I'd not finish talking until midday. But Clover is the eldest and her husband is Neil. I stayed with them and their two little children in Silvertown. We have a huge stepfamily of smashing people living in the East End, Luc. Isn't that wonderful?'

His agreement lacked enthusiasm. He offered her the pack of Gauloises but she didn't take a cigarette.

'I'll be back as soon as I can and tell you more about the Coopers.' She paused. 'There is something else before I go. I've a rendezvous with somebody called Marcel. Have you had any dealings with him?'

Luc repeated the name, looking thoughtful as he inhaled smoke.

'He wears spectacles and has brown hair and a thin moustache, aged about thirty.'

'It could be the fellow Theo was with. He was wearing a hat and I barely got a glimpse of him before they drove off. But I think he resembled your description.' He looked at Nathan. 'Have you told Elise about the job coming up?' On receiving a nod, Luc added on a chuckle. 'We'll light up the sky for miles around – as far as Dunkirk – on the night the rubber factory goes up.' He noticed a look pass between the other two people in the room.

'If you're thinking of leaving me out of it, you can think again,' he said forcefully. 'It was my idea. Don't worry, I'll be fit as a fiddle by then, you wait and see.'

Chapter Twenty-Four

'Go back before they see you. And take this. Give some money to the doctor, it might persuade him to make more effort to get Luc's Penicillin.' Elise passed a handful of francs to Nathan.

His eyes widened on the bundle of notes.

'Our friends in London are generous,' she explained, having read his surprise. She pulled him into a shop doorway and put her arms around his neck. 'Kiss me . . . they've noticed us.'

Two soldiers patrolling the street had begun to take an interest in the courting couple. Their lewd encouragement was carried across the road on the autumn breeze but they continued towards their comrades stationed about an armoured vehicle.

'Go back, Nathan, please.' She'd unsealed their lips and was adjusting his cap brim in a way that looked playful but was designed to shield his features before they parted.

She'd not wanted him to accompany her to her lodging, knowing his solo return journey would leave him vulnerable if stopped and questioned. He'd said he'd avoid the road and use the canal towpath. She'd succumbed to his argument, wanting to keep his company for as long as possible.

Beneath the rising sun, they'd flirted and laughed like the lovers they now were. She'd ridden on the crossbar again but on approaching the outskirts of town they'd concealed the bicycle in vegetation beside the canal. The remainder of the journey had passed quietly as they strolled arm in arm and drew out the minutes they had left. They both knew that if fate turned against them this could be their final parting.

'Your brother's right. You shouldn't be here doing this, Elise.' Nathan glanced at the jealous soldiers. 'You would have been better off never leaving France, never getting involved with the British. I didn't get you away for you to come back before the war was over.' His tone was harshened by his anxiety for her safety.

'I didn't only come back for the British. France is my home ... where my grandmother is. She brought me and Luc up after our mother died. What happened to my father – I haven't forgotten about that either. I can do without revenge but I'll have our freedom.' She made herself calm down. 'You British don't understand. You've not been invaded. There'll be no victory – not for the Allies, anyway – until France is won. That won't happen if people like me who want to fight are told not to.' She dropped her eyes away from his. 'Sorry, but that's how I feel.'

'I think we've just had our first row. Must be true love then,' he said drily and raised his eyes heavenward. 'I'm damn well worried about you, Elise. Can't you see that?'

'And I'm worried about you, and everybody else living here, terrified in case they do or say something that brings the Gestapo to their door.' She paused. 'And I'm worried about my stepfamily. You won't recognise the East End when you get back home. There are bombsites everywhere... streets full of ruins.'

He expelled a sigh. 'We heard all about London being blitzed. I hoped it wasn't as bad as I imagined.'

'It's worse. And I don't want to argue, but it's not just about us...' She noticed the soldiers were on the move and quickly went to the guest house and pushed open the door.

He clasped her hand before she could disappear inside. 'When will I see you again?'

'I don't know... not for a while. Now go... please.'

She briefly touched her lips to his cheek before entering the house.

'Je t'aime. Bonne chance...' She faintly heard his gruff broken French.

She turned and put her palms against the door and her face close to the panel. 'Je t'aime. Bonne chance,' she returned him a whispered farewell. She remained still until the ensuing silence satisfied her that he'd got away without being stopped. Only then did she climb the stairs to her room.

'I was expecting you to sleep here last night. I don't give refunds.'

'I don't want a refund, Madame. I stayed with a friend.'

'Ah...' The woman winked, and withdrawing her head from around the door, she fully opened it and entered the room. 'Handsome, is he?'

Elise allowed her coy smile to answer for her. The loose floorboard she was standing on would have necessitated a fuller explanation, had Madame noticed it. The case containing the wireless and her pistol were hidden beneath her feet.

'Shall I help you unpack?' The older woman was craning her neck to see what the valise on the bed coverlet might contain.

'I can manage, thank you.' Elise lifted the lid, displaying her few plain garments to douse any further curiosity.

The landlady was a plump woman of about fifty with frizzy auburn hair and a pair of darting eyes fringed by spiky black lashes. It was early morning, yet she had already applied make-up and had startlingly crimson lips. Presently they were pursed as she ruminated. 'You seem familiar,' she eventually said.

'I used to live around here but moved away a few years ago.' Elise managed to sound as though she were enjoying their conversation instead of being keen for it to be over. 'When younger, I worked for Madame Laurent.'

'Ah, now I know you. Little Mademoiselle Bouchard. I would see you darting about delivering the dress boxes.'

Elise smiled. Those days, mundane at the time, now conjured up a sweet nostalgia.

'You look all grown up. I don't see so much of your grandmother.'

'She doesn't go out much any more.'

'None of us go out much any more,' said the woman darkly. 'I heard what your father did ... when the Boche first came.' Her spidery eyelashes briefly concealed an eye in a wink. 'I like patriots. I liked Sidney.'

'Thank you,' said Elise, guessing Madame had known her womanising father more intimately than her words conveyed. 'Has Madame Laurent taken on another assistant, do you know? I might apply there again for work.'

'I can't say for sure, dear; I look in the window but never go inside. That place is too expensive for me.' Her expression became speculative. 'Fine clothes though, so if you should get your job back ... how about a discount for friends?'

Elise carefully removed her foot from the springy floorboard so it wouldn't squeak. She accompanied the sly-eyed woman to the door. 'I'll see what I can do, Madame,' she said.

After the landlady had gone she locked the door and began to set up the equipment on her bed, unravelling the radio aerial and poking it discreetly outside her window to improve the signal. She opened her notebook and found the codes to inform London of her arrival in Lille for her next rendezvous. It wasn't necessary to look from the equipment to the page. She knew the verse by heart. Her fingers began tapping in fast irregular rhythm while her mind remembered poppies between crosses in Flanders Fields.

At mid-afternoon the café was barely half full, which was a blessing and a curse: few people to eavesdrop but no camouflaging bustle either. Elise had spotted some Nazis sitting at a table before she'd fully entered the place. Going out again would have appeared suspicious, since she'd clashed eyes with one of them. She proceeded inside towards a bespectacled fellow with light brown hair and a neat moustache. He looked about thirty and she prayed he was Marcel. She was thankful he'd picked a window table to make himself conspicuous to her. On the other hand she was keen to know why he'd not intercepted her outside in the street and saved them both this ordeal. For the benefit of the uniformed men lounging in chairs a few yards away she'd given him a wide smile and pecked both of his cheeks.

'The weather's warmer than expected,' she murmured, briefly fanning her face with a hand as she sat down and manoeuvred the case beneath the table.

'A glorious Indian summer,' he rumbled in response. He took her fingers and brought them to his lips, playing his part in the charade. He'd politely half risen from his chair but settled back down.

She gave a tiny nod, letting him know his greeting matched her expectations.

Elise reclaimed her fingers and gave an order for coffee to the hovering waiter. When it arrived, she stirred in sugar with a hand that shook slightly.

'You're nervous?' Marcel quietly asked.

'Aren't you?' They continued to smile as though their thoughts were on intimacy rather than espionage. She hoped her suitcase had given the impression they were off somewhere romantic.

Simultaneously they stared out of the window as a car screeched to a halt and men in black uniform flung open the doors. A youth emerging from the bakery was manhandled towards the vehicle. It was the first arrest Elise had witnessed and it alarmed her, reminding her of the day her father had been marched away to his death. The soldiers pushed back their chairs and went out, strengthening her mean relief that none of them were here for her.

'Do you know who he is?' She felt desperately sorry for the youth being driven away.

Marcel shook his head. 'He could be related to somebody they're holding.' He turned from the window and leaned back in his chair. 'What in God's name is F Section thinking of, sending somebody as pretty as you?' Marcel sounded half amused, half annoyed. 'You've had the attention of every man in the place.' He jerked a nod at the proprietor behind the counter. Aware he'd been spotted, the fellow averted his eyes and went back to polishing glasses.

'I can do my job,' she said coolly. 'Can you do yours? *Mon Dieu*,' she hissed. 'What were *you* thinking of, not meeting me outside?'

'The Nazis followed me in. I couldn't turn tail and give them something to think about. Didn't they teach you about hiding in plain sight at Beaulieu?'

Elise ignored his arrogant manner, thinking she wasn't going to like Marcel very much.

'You match your description but please confirm your codename.'

'Orpheline.'

'Well, Orpheline, is this what I think it is?' He nudged the case with his foot.

'It is and I need it back very quickly.'

'You have a code to use?'

'Of course. Don't you?'

'Oh, yes,' he said. 'If they break mine it's good to have a backup in an emergency.'

'Let's hope they don't, or we'll both be in trouble.'

They continued to speak in French. Marcel had a passable accent but slipped up every so often as Major Venables had when conversing with her in his office. Marcel had received the benefit of an expensive English education and had studied languages, would be her guess.

He crossed his arms and said, 'I know you've been briefed about the rubber factory job.'

She sipped coffee then shook her head. 'You're supposed to put me in the picture about that.'

'Am I now?' He gestured impatiently. 'Little wonder

things go wrong when you Baker Street Irregulars can't get a simple act together.'

She'd heard the expression used before to describe Venables' clandestine operatives, but she didn't rise to his bait. She idly watched passers-by.

He leaned forward and planted an elbow on the table. 'This is what I know: local Resistance are planning on stopping production for us. Our RAF boys dropped some explosives weeks ago. I don't have more details yet... dates and so on. I expected you to supply those.'

'Sorry. This is all news to me. Anyway, it sounds rather ambitious. How on earth will it be achieved?'

'Ah, now that's the thing. We've got a few employed on the inside. Fritz is getting wise to these tactics though; I'd put money on them having their own people planted in the factory. Identifying them won't be easy.' He finished his coffee as a couple of elegantly dressed women walked past then settled at the vacant table behind.

'Time for a stroll, I think.' He picked up his hat from the chair beside him.

While he paid, she dragged the case from beneath the table, cursing beneath her breath as a catch loosened and one side of the lid flapped open, exposing metal. Her heart started hammering against her ribs but she refastened it without mishap.

Marcel returned and took the weighty case, guiding her to the door with a hand on her elbow. 'Put your arm through mine, my dear, as though we're any old normal couple.'

'What's your cover?' she asked in English when they were strolling in sunlight and nobody was within earshot. On the opposite side of the road a Swastika flag draped the courthouse, stirring limply as though a little fight remained within. Further along, queues stretched outside the *boulangerie* and *boucherie*. People were shuffling along, impatient to buy bread or some meat. The shortages here seemed worse than in England.

'You ask a lot of questions, Orpheline.'

'I've been told to.' She turned her attention back to him. 'Have you been here long?'

'Long enough. I've been moved around to hook up with various circuits. My documents say I'm a shipping clerk. Which is pretty much the same thing I did in Aldgate before this damned war turned everything upside down.'

'You know the East End? Did you live there?'

'Thankfully not. And what's your cover story, Orpheline?'

'I'm applying for a position at the couturiers. I'm going there next to enquire about it.'

'Where are you staying?' he asked.

'A lodging house in Rue Nord.'

'Not with your family then?'

She glanced sharply at him. 'My family?'

'I heard you have a grandmother and brother living locally.'

'Who told you that?'

'Can't remember ... might've been the fellow I replaced. He told me F Section were sending a Frenchwoman before he went back to London to be debriefed. Something big's on the horizon. Know anything about it? My guess is the Allies are planning a major offensive to liberate France. What's your view, Orpheline?'

She didn't immediately answer, although she agreed with his theory. 'One step at a time, is how I see things. The bigger picture can wait. If this rubber factory is next on the agenda I'd like to hear more about it.'

'As you've kin in the area, would they provide a safe house in town if it's needed?'

Elise gave a derisive snort. 'My grandmother lives outside town and the poor love is going senile. She'll be in a care home before long. As for my brother . . .' She gestured disgust. 'He's no longer in the vicinity and if he was I'd avoid that good-for-nothing.' Elise pulled on her white summer gloves, hoping she had dampened his interest in her family. She wouldn't disclose anything personal until he'd proved himself absolutely trustworthy. 'Well, I have a job interview to get to.' She straightened her hat in a businesslike fashion.

'You'll get it on looks alone.' He cocked his head and assessed her figure with slow eyes.

She ignored his flattery and said, 'The wireless set – I want it back soon.'

'You'll get it when I'm finished with it, my dear. And one other thing . . .' He caught hold of her elbow. 'There's an English POW on the loose. Apparently he's turned renegade and joined the Maquis. He could be useful to us. Do you know anything about him? How to contact him?'

Elise removed his fingers from her arm. 'Can't help with that one, I'm afraid,' she said.

'I'll contact you at your lodging as soon as things get moving on the factory job. London want it promptly out of action.'

'I'll need the wireless back.'

'Yes, I heard you; rather in short supply, aren't they? Well, for us anyway. The Gestapo must be sitting on a stack of the damned things they've seized.'

Elise pecked his cheek in farewell. She noticed a smouldering gleam at the back of his eyes. 'Nothing personal, only to continue the game, in case we're being watched,' she said then turned and walked away.

Somebody was watching them; Nathan withdrew around the corner and lit a Gauloises. He rested his back against the wall of the Banque Nationale and watched Elise from beneath his cap brim. Once she had disappeared into the dress shop, he emerged from the narrow passageway and started to follow the man carrying the suitcase, now some distance away.

'Shhh ...'

Elise had awoken with a start as a familiar firm yet gentle hand covered her mouth.

'Nathan?' She yanked away his callused fingers but one returned to press on her lips.

'Quiet.' He struck a match so she could see him in the darkness. His face appeared all savage angles in a bulb of yellow before the flame died.

'How did you get in?' she whispered. Then followed it up with, 'You shouldn't have come. You'll be arrested for breaking the curfew.'

'Nobody saw me. I was careful ... used the window.' He sat down on the bed, holding her hands in his. 'I had to come, it's urgent. I've something to tell you about the man you met today.'

She digested that while shifting closer to see his eyes. 'Have you been following me, spying on me since I've been in town?' She sounded indignant.

'It's just as well I have been. I think I know him. He looks different with the moustache and glasses but I'm pretty sure we met him down south.'

'We? Luc knows him as well?'

He nodded.

She fought off the dregs of sleep fogging her brain to reflect on her conversation with Marcel. 'He knew about my family,' she said anxiously. 'I told him I'd no idea where Luc was. He asked about you; I pretended ignorance of an escaped prisoner of war. I thought it too soon to open up.'

'You were right to be cautious.' Nathan brushed a grateful kiss on her lips. 'What else did he talk about?'

'The rubber factory. He asked me what I knew. Nothing, I said. But he knows everything apart from the date it'll happen.' She urgently squeezed his fingers. 'Who is he, Nathan? He's sending me a note to arrange another meeting and return the wireless. I didn't want to give it to him but a message came through sanctioning it.' She frowned. 'Do you think he's a double agent?'

'I'm not sure. It's possible he's working for our lot and didn't let on to us about it. My gut tells me something's wrong though.'

'I'll have to carry on as normal,' Elise said. 'If he is a double agent he'll have me picked up if he thinks I'm onto him.'

Nathan cupped her face and rested his forehead against hers. 'I hope I'm mistaken about this. Let him think you trust him. That way he'll let things ride and try to prise information from you.'

'He is inquisitive, but that might be his way of protecting himself. He needs to be able to trust me equally.'

'That's true. I'll find out what Theo knows about Marcel. You have to stall him; try to delay meeting him again until I get a message to you.' He said comfortingly, 'Perhaps I'm wrong. After you went into the dress shop I followed him back to a hotel. He didn't stop and talk to anybody.'

'You shouldn't be taking these risks! I wanted you to go home to England. You're not safe here in France.'

'Neither are you,' he said harshly. 'I could throttle the people in London who sent you back.' He drew a small snub-nosed gun from his pocket and closed her fingers around it. 'Keep this with you at all times. It's fully loaded.'

'I have a pistol ...'

'These Liberators are small enough to conceal on your body. Single shot, ammo in the grip. Make it count.'

She took it. 'Thanks. I have this, and it's quiet.' She went to the dressing table and returned with her hairbrush.

'You're going to groom him to death?'

She whacked him on the arm with the bristles. But their amusement had soon faded and their wistful gazes clung together. They both knew that things had turned deadly serious. Only days ago they'd been lovers; now they were comrades in arms desperately watching one another's backs. 'See ...' She twisted and pulled from the silver brush handle a thin blade of about six inches long. 'I had this with me earlier when I was in the café. It can be used as a hatpin. You don't need to worry about me, Nathan.'

'I know you're smart; it makes you more of a target to eliminate as far as the Gestapo are concerned.' Their eyes clung together but they remained quiet for a long moment.

'Marcel asked about my codes. I didn't tell him anything. Only my handler in England knows those.'

'If he betrays you, you'll not receive mercy, Elise.' Nathan drew her up onto her feet and into his arms, his rough sleeves abrading her skin through her nightgown. 'Get the wireless back. Send your handler a message that you want Marcel checked out and you want to return to England until he is. For God's sake! If you love me you'll go back!'

'No!' She struggled free. 'I knew the dangers before I came. Training covered everything. None of us were spared the truth of capture. What was Marcel's name when you met him in the south?'

'We never found out.' Nathan dragged a frustrated hand through his hair. 'It didn't seem important to question him about it. Then it was too late and we couldn't question him—'

A sudden commotion outside and a banging on the door brought Nathan swiftly up to it, revolver in hand.

'It's the landlady,' Elise warned in a whisper. 'If I don't let her in she'll use her key.'

'Keep that Liberator handy,' he said in her ear. 'I won't be far away, I swear. Wait to hear from me.' His brief hard kiss stood in for his farewell as another demand for entry was heard. In seconds, he had climbed out of the window and Elise had slipped the gun beneath her pillow. She rushed to see if he'd got away. A moving shadow was all that was visible on the lower roof. The sound of a second dull thud told her he'd jumped again and landed on the ground. He had disappeared before she'd closed the casement and drawn the curtains. She inhaled deeply then opened the door, yawning.

The landlady stood outside with a candle sconce in her hand. She peered around the flame to see into the room.

'Have you a man in there?' she snapped. 'Another guest believes she heard two voices coming from inside.'

Along the hallway a flash of white nightgown then a door closing indicated who the snooper was. 'I talk in my sleep sometimes. My apologies if I've disturbed anybody.' Elise added to the illusion of having been woken up by rubbing sleep from her eyes. 'Please come in ... check ... if you'd like to.'

'No ... it's all right.' The woman's frizz of hair touched Elise's face as she leaned to whisper, 'You need to speak to me first. I don't charge much extra for ... *gentlemen friends*. But keep it between us, Mam'selle. You understand ... I have my reputation to think about.'

Elise nodded. 'But there's nobody here, I assure you.'

The woman drew back with a sniff and poked her tongue against the inside of her cheek. 'Well, good night then,' she said huffily.

'I got my job back with Madame Laurent and start in the morning.'

'Well, that is good news. There's a nice red dress in the window.'

'I noticed it,' said Elise, retreating inside and closing the door.

'The rent is due again on Friday but I can wait a few days until you get paid,' said the landlady in a mollifying tone.

'Thank you.' Elise spoke loudly enough to be heard through the wood. She went to the window and scanned the blackness. There was no signal letting her know he was still out there. But she knew he was.

She closed the curtains and checked the gun. It was fully loaded as he'd said. She put it back and settled down again, although she doubted she'd sleep, even with one hand burrowed beneath the pillow, curved around metal.

Chapter Twenty-Five

'Are you accusing me of being a collaborator? A traitor to my country?'

Theo was an ugly fellow at the best of times, sprouting wiry hair from face and pate, and being almost as wide as he was tall. In a fit of rage, his pockmarked complexion became mottled, and his eyes were canopied by puffy skin.

'Chrissake calm down,' Nathan said. They spoke in French and though he'd not understood all of Theo's rant he'd got the gist of it and its cause. 'I'm not saying that, but why didn't you introduce us to Marcel?'

'Two reasons,' snarled Theo and counted off on his thick fingers, 'First, I don't trust him; second, I don't trust you.'

'What? You don't trust us!' In his indignation, Luc scrambled off his sickbed and onto his feet reasonably steadily.

'Let him speak.' Nathan barred his friend with an arm to stop him surging into a fight he couldn't finish. If Nathan could be sure of anything lately it was that Theo would always be true to France.

'Seems odd to me that your wireless operator always misses the action.' Theo's half-closed eyes were swivelled between them. 'The priest you're so fond of ... he was let out yesterday. Why? Has he done a deal with them?'

Nathan and Luc exchanged a glance. They had their own suspicions about Cyclist, as they called the wireless operator they'd met at Father Pascal's church. And they hadn't known the Father had been released.

'The priest's a good liar,' said Nathan. 'And I trust him. Who introduced you to Marcel?'

'A message came from London that he would replace the agent going home. Marcel said and did all the right things.' His shrug indicated he'd had no reason for doubts. 'There's an easy way to find out if he's rotten.' He pointed at Luc. 'His sister can give him a false date for the factory job. We'll watch the place. If the Boches turn up we'll have our proof. If Marcel's a Nazi I'll execute him myself.'

'It's too risky for Elise to do that. She'd be arrested.' said Nathan. 'Did you tell him about an escaped POW?'

'Didn't need to. You're the worst kept secret around here. Even the local tarts know an English Tommy's joined the Resistance.' He smirked. 'Some of them are keen to meet you.' He gave Nathan a congratulatory thump on the shoulder.

Over the years Luc had appreciated Nathan's cool character. Once in a while he would let rip though and it was best to be out of arm's reach when it happened. 'I never forget a face. When Elise meets Marcel again I'll spy on them.' Luc took his turn at defusing things as Theo's joke fell flat. 'If I recognise him as well ...' He shrugged that the matter would be settled.

'You're not ready to be out on the streets inviting trouble,' Nathan said. 'And Elise shouldn't see him again until he's been checked out. I'll meet him. Give him the false date and we'll see what happens.'

'That's suicide,' Theo bellowed, stomping to and fro. 'If he's a traitor, he'll lay a trap. Once they have you, they'll find all of us. I'll deal with it.'

After Theo had departed, crashing the door shut after him, Luc exchanged a glance with Nathan. 'You're going after this Marcel, aren't you? For Elise.' He shook his wounded arm in frustration, making himself wince in pain. 'But for this damned thing dragging me back, I'd do it myself. I'll shoot the bloody man, whoever he is.'

'There's still a chance he's on our side. But I won't let anything happen to her.'

'Have you fallen in love with my sister?'

Nathan didn't reply other than to say, 'Get some rest, Luc and start taking a double dose of Penicillin. I'll pay the doctor for another bottle. We'll be on the move again soon and you need to be fighting fit.'

Elise recognised one of the Nazis. He had followed her off the train on the day she arrived in Lille. Madame Laurent was serving him with a negligee. Another officer was lazily inspecting a pair of kid gloves. It would be Christmas next month. Perhaps they were sending presents to their wives. Or they might get leave and take the gifts home themselves.

She'd been spying on them through an aperture but a sudden noise made her swiftly and silently close the door. Her employer had rung the brass bell on the counter, to let her know her assistance was required. Instead of answering the summons, Elise snatched her coat and bag from the peg. She quit the stockroom where she'd been sent to catalogue rolls of fabric and dashed out of the side door into the unlit yard. It was almost six o'clock. She'd been lucky the men had arrived before closing time or she'd still be ignorant of this.

They'd been talking in German and although she hadn't understood a lot, one word had leaped out at her making her heart race. Madame Laurent had a better understanding of German, being on her second occupation. The French word for orphan, heard in a conversation between enemy soldiers would hold little significance for her, though, even if she'd grasped they were discussing a female spy. Fortuitously, the name didn't hold much significance for the junior officers either. They'd no idea that Orpheline was Elise Bouchard who worked in this shop. Possibly they'd overheard a British agent's codename when loitering behind a door, in the same way Elise had just discovered her cover was blown. She had to raise the alarm immediately and without arousing suspicion. Her boss, finding her gone, would assume she'd taken the liberty of finishing work a few minutes early.

Last week, Marcel had been browsing the shop's window display as dusk was falling. He had jerked a nod indicating he'd speak to her outside. He'd been empty handed; no wireless set to make the risk of an impromptu meeting worthwhile. But she'd been angry enough to go out and demand its immediate return. Not wanting to jeopardise Madame Laurent by asking him to bring it to the shop, she'd told him to deliver it to her lodging. He hadn't, and the longer he held onto it the more uneasy she became. Without a transmitter she'd been unable to pass her suspicions about him on to London. She'd not seen Marcel since and it had become clear why that was: whether intentionally, or through arrest and interrogation, Marcel had betrayed her.

It was vital to immediately quit her lodging with her

belongings then let Nathan and Luc know of this perilous development. A transmitter had to be procured from somewhere, and a message sent urgently to London, warning them of the breach so they could inform other agents to be on guard.

Having mounted her bicycle, she rode frantically through the gloomy backstreets towards Rue Nord. On reaching her destination, she scrambled off the machine, propped it against the wall and hurried inside. She heaved a sigh of relief at being out of sight, glad too that there was no sign of Madame. She'd no time to field requests for red dresses. She ran up the stairs, used her key and burst into her room.

An oil lamp had been lit and placed on the washstand, allowing her an immediate sight of her landlady sitting on her bed. Then she saw grey figures in the shadows. The soldiers were pointing machine pistols at her, causing her chest to suddenly constrict and threaten to suffocate her. Madame had her head bowed but looked up, giving Elise a view of her swollen, half-closed eye. Her make-up was smudged into black tear trails on her cheeks.

A movement by the window alerted her to somebody else being present. He wasn't in uniform, but in civilian clothes and she thought it must be Marcel, come to taunt her with his victory. When the fellow turned to face her she remained utterly shocked and motionless for almost a minute.

'Ah, Elise, Elise ... what have you got yourself into, my dear?' said Toby Winters in his cut-glass English accent. The silence sung into infinity. 'Would you prefer I call you Orpheline?'

She needed his mockery to antagonise her into action. Her chin lifted and she boldly walked closer. Toby rasped an order at the soldiers to stand down as a weapon jabbed into her, knocking her back.

'More to the point, what have you got yourself into?' She casually brushed away the sting in her shoulder and approached once more. 'A traitor to your country and a disgrace to your family. You'll hang for this.'

'A matter of opinion. They have to catch me first, and as Germany will win the war...' He shrugged his indifference, and taking her bag from her hand, emptied its contents onto the bed, idly picking them over. 'Good forgeries,' he said, having inspected her documents, then discarded them.

She was grateful for a small mercy: he'd stopped by the dressing table. The brush was on it, undisturbed. The bed, however, had been shoved aside to enable the floorboard to be pulled up. She didn't need to peer into the hole to know the pistol was gone. She'd seen he was holding a gun in each hand, hers and his own. The Liberator was strapped to her inner thigh but it was of little use. She'd be shot before she was able to pull up her skirt and free it.

'Looking for this?' Toby shoved the guns into his pockets and unsheathed the rapier. 'F Section need to up their game. Rather old hat this sort of thing.' He tossed the hairbrush down on the dressing table.

Through the noise of blood pounding in her ears, Elise heard the landlady start to sob. The woman didn't understand English but she had begun to digest the enormity of what had been going on beneath her roof. 'Let her go. She's done nothing.' Elise paused for a response but didn't receive one. 'I said let her go!' She came right up to him and stared into his eyes. 'For old times' sake, Toby. For me. Let her go.'

A gleam of lust appeared in his eyes, reminding Elise of the conversation she'd had with Becky Harding about this rapist. He'd tried to steal the child he'd fathered, and so had begun a battle with a foe deadlier than Elise had ever imagined.

Toby spoke in rapid German to the soldiers who escorted the landlady outside and closed the door behind them.

'Now what are we going to do about this?' He tapped a thumbnail in irregular rhythm against his lips. 'If you're sensible it won't be so bad.' He touched her face and his fingers felt hot on her ice-cold cheek. 'You've grown into your looks, I see,' he chuckled low in his throat. 'Only joking... you were a teenage beauty. I fancied you like mad you know. Being the gentleman I was – am– of course there wasn't much I could do about it back in England.'

'What do you want?' Elise twitched away from his touch.

'I think you know I'd love to hear all about your codes and your Resistance friends. Of course we're aware of the English POW and your brother.'

'Really?' She managed to sound bored.

'What's he to you, this Corporal Hawkes? Did he help you at Dunkirk?'

'How should I know? There were a half dozen or more soldiers that helped me. We didn't bother with introductions. Actually I was glad to see the back of the lot of them after I was on a boat.' She gazed at him. 'As for my brother, if you want to find him, look under a stone.' She gestured her disgust. 'I lost contact with him, selfish pig that he is. In fact I'm glad I don't have to put up with his whining.' She could see Toby wasn't convinced so said, 'Now it's your turn. I'd love to hear about your friends – one in particular.' An idea that Marcel's arrogant manner seemed familiar had been niggling at the back of her mind since she'd first met him. It had become apparent why that was. 'Who is he... a

Fascist chum? One of your sort? Public school dropout with a chip on his shoulder?'

'Very good.' Toby clapped mockingly. 'I think my sort still have the edge though on Silvertown scum, Cinderella. How are your sisters, by the way? And Becky?'

She ignored his insults and turned her back on him. A dark-coloured car had been parked outside on the opposite side of the road but in her haste to get under cover she'd stupidly overlooked its significance. Into her mind hurtled desperate thoughts of her brother and Nathan. He'd said he'd be close by. She prayed he was, and was aware of trouble having arrived in Rue Nord. She hoped he'd begun alerting members of Theo's circuit to make their escapes, and that he and Luc got away as well.

'I've been sent here to arrest you.' Irked at being ignored, Toby spun her about by the shoulder to face him. 'But if you cooperate in providing us with your codes and sending some messages to London for us, things will be better for you.'

Elise remained quiet, a look of contempt on her face. Inwardly, she felt triumphant at having destroyed her codes only yesterday. Had she not, the book would have been discovered with her gun. But she was confident she knew the poem off by heart and had the codes in her head.

'Don't be stupidly stubborn. If I hand you over you'll be squealing in no time.' He sighed. 'Let's chat some more about family then, while you think about it. How's my brother doing? And my son?'

She sat down on the edge of the bed. Picking up the cigarettes he'd emptied out of her bag, she took one from the packet and lit it with a match.

'Got one of those for me?'

She tossed the boxes over the coverlet without looking at him.

'You rather resemble my boy's mother. You're darker ... prettier ... but I imagine if we had children they'd look quite like Adam.' He lit up and took a lengthy drag.

'You're insane,' she muttered.

'Well, maybe I am. Better than being dead though. You'll long for that blessed state if you end up with Gestapo in Paris. Avenue Foch, have you heard of that hellhole? Only I can save you. Listen to me – Germany is the future now.'

'You're starting to bore me, Toby. *Ennui* ... I cannot bear it.' She gestured idly with the hand that held the cigarette. 'It wasn't something I associated with you. Excitement ... glamour ... yes. But not being bored.'

He dropped the cigarette and squashed it beneath his foot then pulled her off the bed, giving her a shake. 'France is finished. England is too. I can take you to Germany, protect you. A scapegoat can be found for this.' He jerked a nod at the door indicating the landlady as a candidate.

'Did you murder Graham?' She continued to draw on her cigarette, blowing smoke deliberately into his face so he'd let her go and move away.

He appeared agitated by that name cropping up. 'Yates was a troublemaker. I'm not sure I intended to kill him, just give him a thrashing for making life difficult for me. Spur of the moment thing. I needed money and there he was on the Tube platform, flashing a diamond ring. I knew it was for you. He didn't deserve you so I gave him a shove. He lost his balance.' Toby gave a careless shrug.

'Have you still got my ring?'

'God no! I pawned it in Cheapside the same day so I could

buy my way out of the country. Told the shopkeeper I'd been jilted.' His amusement faded. 'Was he a good lover?'

She heard the jealousy in his voice. 'Graham was a gentleman.'

'You're still a virgin?'

'You want to go to bed with me don't you, Toby? Take my virginity.'

'Of course ...'

He put out a fondling hand but she shrugged it off and stubbed the cigarette out in the ashtray by the bed. 'Send the soldiers away to keep things private. I'm a local girl with a reputation to keep, after all.' She gave him an acid smile. 'Then wait outside while I undress.'

'Tempting, very tempting, but I'm not a fool.'

'Neither am I. You're right. I don't want to die. And unfortunately I have little left to bargain with now you have my weapons. If I go with you, I want a promise from you that you'll not harm my brother or the English corporal.'

He crossed his arms, weighing things up. 'If they have any sense they'll already have left the area. The doctor's been arrested; things like that get around.' He gazed at her with hungry eyes. 'I'll stay while you undress. I'd like to watch,' he purred.

'I'm sure you would; but I'm shy. And you'd better be slow and gentle when you return.'

He ran eager hands up and down her figure in lewd pursuit of any concealed weapon. When they curved inwards and upwards on her legs, she arrested his hands. 'I said slow and gentle. Too soon for that, I think.' She moved his fingers to her breasts. 'Graham would stroke me, like this. That's all he would do. I liked it. Are you a good lover, Toby?'

He pulled her against him, kissed her ferociously until she tasted blood and felt the hardness at his groin.

'You'll soon find out.' He pushed her back, breathing raggedly. 'One minute and I return.' He pulled the blade from the hairbrush and pocketed it. 'Give me your key.'

She handed it over.

When he came back, she was in the bed with a pillow held modestly in front of her and an enigmatic smile on her bloodless face.

He started to undress, watching her with a savage intensity.

She watched him equally carefully, noting that one of the guns was brought with him and so was the oil lamp, and left by the bedside. She waited until the second he was reclining on the mattress beside her before rolling towards him and shooting him through the pillow to muffle the noise.

Chapter Twenty-Six

'I should've let you drown when I had the chance, you Nazi bastard.'

The imprisoned man struggled to twist around to identify his captor but the forearm choking him was tightened and a gun barrel ground deeper into his temple.

'Drop it on the floor,' Nathan snarled, having noticed him diving for his pocket. 'And remember I can pull the trigger before you point that Luger the right way.' The gun hit concrete and he kicked it out of reach.

He'd trailed Marcel from his hotel, ambushed him at gunpoint then frogmarched him into a derelict building.

'Whoever you are, you're mistaken about me.' Marcel licked his lips. 'I'm English like you. We can help one another. Are you SOE?'

'You know who I am; you've not forgotten that night any more than I have. I've been reminiscing about you saying you couldn't swim when we reached the river. Funny, you didn't mention that before we set out to cross into Spain. And there was nothing wrong with your eyesight either. You didn't need these to stop you tripping over in the dark.' He yanked off the spectacles and examined the clear glass before they went the way of the gun. 'Your Nazi pals made a mess of the timing, didn't they? Opened fire late: after we'd started wading across. That scuppered your chance to make a run for it and leave me a sitting duck. Reckon you gave them a bollocking about that, didn't yer, mate?' Nathan increased his stranglehold as Spitfire squirmed to free himself. 'Later at the cottage ... I wondered why they'd bother with a half-dead English pilot. They had the girl and the farmer to interrogate. But a double agent's valuable. They must've pulled out all the stops to save you. And that's my fault for bringing you back in the first place. Never mind, easily remedied.' Nathan hadn't thought about the girl with the toddler and the weeping farmer for a long while. Now he did, and wrath churned his belly. 'Paulette wasn't the rat; she was the scapegoat. You betrayed us all. Did they kill her, and the others in the circuit?' He loosened his grip to let the man speak.

'I don't know what you're on about,' he rasped. 'You've got me mixed up with somebody else.'

'You've never flown a Spitfire in your life. I reckon that RAF uniform you had on came off a corpse.'

'You're talking in riddles – what uniform?'

'Take off your coat and shirt. Let's see your right hip.' Nathan moved back a step to allow him to undress.

'No need for that, Hawkes, for obvious reasons,' said Spitfire, giving up on the pretence. 'You are Corporal Hawkes, aren't you?'

Nathan ignored the question. 'What happened to Paulette?'

'I don't know. I was in hospital for four months. Maybe she was executed. Not necessarily by us. You know what happens to those thought to be collaborators when they return home.' Spitfire demanded harshly, 'So what happens now?'

'Well, I could take you to Theo; you'll wish I hadn't. Or you could cough up the names I need. Something tells me you're not the only rotten apple in the barrel.'

'Won't do you any good, whatever I say. We've been watching the doctor. He was arrested last night. Orpheline's brother's laid up at the tavern. We thought you might be the invalid. She's trying to protect you all but you're amateurs,' he sneered. 'The British... the Americans... will never be a match for the Third Reich. You're on the wrong side of this, Corporal. Hitler will win and rule the world. You might as well give yourself up. POWs are treated preferentially in a camp.'

'Sounds great. And in my book, the amateur is the one on the wrong end of the gun.'

'Let me go. I'll give you a list of double agents you can send to London.' Spitfire started to barter, rattled by the other man's lazy sarcasm. 'I'll fetch the wireless. It's in my hotel room.'

A sudden shout of laughter emboldened him to yell for help. The Nazi officers escorting local women towards a brasserie didn't take much notice at first.

'*Hilfe!* Englander!' Spitfire screeched, then fought for his life as his captor dropped the gun to throttle him double-handed.

Nathan shoved the wheezing man forcefully out of the door and into view as the Nazis started drawing weapons. Gunshots and female screams followed. Before scooping the pistols from the ground and bolting for the back of the house, he glimpsed the traitor falling forward, clutching his chest. Having vaulted piles of rubble, he kicked open a door sagging on broken hinges. He was aware of pounding boots behind and a bullet chipped brick close to his face. He sprang, pulling himself up onto a boundary wall then swinging over it and jumped into the yard of an adjoining property. As he fell, he prayed that for Paulette's sake, Spitfire's paymasters had done a better job of finishing him off this time.

By racing across backyards and into alleys he brought himself again on to the street. Sirens wailed and headlights splintered the darkness as vehicles sped towards him. If he was seen running he'd invite pursuit; he slowed down, at intervals mingling with the citizens watching the unfolding drama. He tutted and shook his head along with the rest of them before striding on towards Rue Nord with a knot of fear for Elise's safety lodged beneath his ribs.

When close to the town's outskirts he started to sprint once more. He diverted across the road having noticed somebody he recognised skulking in a doorway. 'What in damnation are you doing here?'

'Looking for you,' Luc gabbled in relief. 'Elise is in trouble.'

They shrank deeper into the shadows as an armoured car and a motorbike roared past.

'They're looking for me as well,' Nathan said watching the vehicles disappear. 'Marcel's dead.'

'I was on my way to question her about him.' Luc hastily explained his reasons for abandoning his sickbed.

'What's happened? Where is she?'

Luc jerked his head to the corner of Rue Nord. 'Soldiers stationed outside the guest house. Gestapo must be in there interrogating her. Marcel must've betrayed her. All of us.'

Nathan's blood had started running cold the moment

he caught sight of her brother. He'd been dreading this news ... yet expecting it. 'He was a Nazi spy all right. The doctor's been arrested. Is Theo at the tavern?' He was hoping the big man was here in town where he could be of help.

'He's still at home. I couldn't warn him of this. I didn't know myself. There's no time to go back for him. Freeing Elise is all that matters.' Luc pulled a hunting knife and a revolver from his pockets. 'What have you got?'

Nathan showed Luc the two guns and a blade. 'No extra ammo. It'll have to do. How many of them?'

'Two troopers by the car and whoever's inside—' He broke off to excitedly say, 'I know him.' Luc had spotted somebody pedalling towards them on a bike with a basket on its front. 'He's Theo's nephew – works at the butcher's. He's a good lad. He's the one I told you about: shins up the telegraph poles and cuts wires for Theo. We can trust him to take a message.' Luc stopped the boy by the kerb. After a conversation lasting mere seconds the youth turned the bike around and pedalled quickly away, trailing an odour of gamey blood in his wake.

'We'll have to take the two troopers at the same time. No noise,' Nathan said.

Luc nodded.

'Ready for this?' Nathan knew if they were to have a chance of saving Elise her brother had to fight, ready or not.

Luc answered by rolling his shoulders without wincing.

They ambled into Rue Nord drawing attention with their slurred bawdy talk. The troopers contemptuously waved away the drunks to the opposite side of the street and continued sharing a crafty nip from a flask being passed back and forth. Seconds later it clattered to the ground and a woman walking towards them stopped and stared in horror.

Nathan put his finger to his lips and she tottered back the way she'd come, pretending not to have witnessed two bodies being bundled into a vehicle.

The landlady heard a movement in the hallway and opened her parlour door a crack, a candle flaring in her hand as the draught from the door caught it. She blinked her good eye; the other was already closed.

'Resistance,' Luc whispered.

The single word was enough; she pointed up the stairs. 'Second door,' she croaked with a sorrowful shake of her head.

'How many?' Luc asked.

The woman raised a single finger. 'More outside,' she hissed.

Luc thumbed at the street then drew the digit across his throat putting a fleeting smile on her face.

'Stay by the entrance and cover us, Luc. They'll have reinforcements here soon.' Nathan started taking the stairs quietly, two at a time, his gigantic shadow on the wall accompanying him. He passed the first door on the landing and hesitated to listen at the next. He tried the handle and felt resistance from the lock. Repositioning himself he booted the door then burst into the room with a pistol in each hand.

The fellow attempting to clumsily pull on his trousers was too slow in deciding whether to let them fall and grab for the gun on the floor. Nathan hit him in the face with the Luger, sending him onto his back.

Elise struggled off the bed and dashed to Nathan. He

enclosed her in one arm. The other remained raised, levelling the gun on the semi-conscious man.

'Where are you hurt?' Nathan had seen blood on her chemise.

'Most of it's his.' She started pulling on her clothes. 'I shot him.'

Nathan sent frequent glances at her bruised face and state of undress in between watching the man stirring. 'What's he done to you?'

'I wish I'd killed him.' She forced on her shoes with shaking hands then hugged Nathan again before swiftly collecting her weapons, and Toby Winters' gun.

'Wait downstairs, I'll finish this,' Nathan said quietly. She'd evaded answering him but it didn't matter. He knew.

She pulled him away as Toby Winters struggled to sit up. 'Leave him, he's no use to them wounded like that, and we've no time to lose.'

'I've time. Go downstairs!' He kept his eyes on the man on the floor. 'Your brother's waiting in the hall. I'll be there in a minute.'

He turned to her and their eyes held for a second before Elise went out. She'd endured more than a beating. If they survived this day there would be time later for the whole truth.

'Touching scene.' Toby Winters groaned as the bullet lodged in his upper chest made itself known. 'I take it you were the lucky chap who broke her in. Lying bitch wasn't a virgin.'

Nathan kicked him forcefully, lifting him off the floor and sending him back several feet onto the oil lamp that smashed and extinguished. Nathan followed to stand over him in the moonlit room. 'You're English scum as well, are you? If you're expecting Marcel to bring the cavalry, he's already in hell, waiting for you to join him.'

Toby settled back into a seated position beneath the windowsill with a hand clasped on his collarbone. Blood was soon seeping through his fingers, and his complexion took on a film of sweat. 'Of course, Elise won't have had time to tell you we're related.' He smirked. 'She offered herself in exchange for you and her brother.' He paused to suck in air. 'You want to know what happened, don't you?' He coughed a chuckle. 'Let your imagination run wild and you still won't come close. She's a beauty, isn't she?' He sighed nostalgically. 'We've got shared history, Cinderella and I. Stuff you know nothing about. Ask her if you don't believe me.' He cocked his head but the other man's silence was unnerving and prompted him to keep talking. 'I think introductions are in order as we've a mutual friend. You must be Corporal Hawkes ... your reputation precedes you.' He tipped an imaginary hat. 'Toby Winters. I won't bore you with the tangled mess of my relationship with the Coopers, but it does exist, I assure you.' His insouciance withered beneath the other man's icy despising. They'd both heard a vehicle braking outside. Machine-gun fire followed and was answered by a longer staccato burst that rattled the glass in the window. 'You don't have to kill me.' Toby sounded startled by the gun battle drawing things to a head. 'It'll be better for you if you let me go, Hawkes. I can make things easier for all of you.'

'Mayfair accent and a yeller streak ... might've guessed,' Nathan said with sour satisfaction.

'You've no need to kill me,' Toby whined. 'I'll be handed over to the SS ... face a firing squad before you will ...'

'I'm from Poplar, mate, we cut out the middleman,' said Nathan.

*

Having passed his nephew on the road and received a blurted message from the frightened boy, Theo had arrived within ten minutes at Rue Nord.

Nathan had emerged from the guest house seconds later to the sound of a whistle and the sight of a Sten gun sailing through the air towards him. Elise and Luc were already armed with weapons, grabbed from the back of the truck the moment their comrade screeched to a halt. The trio clambered into the vehicle where Theo remained at the wheel, revving the engine. They began firing at the advancing troops as Theo reversed at speed away from the soldiers barricading the top of the road. The truck's coachwork was holed with bullets by the time they'd skidded around the corner. Nathan could see Luc was wincing from the effort of holding and firing the weapon recoiling against his body.

'Where to?' roared Theo. 'Any idea? The tavern's no use now.'

'I know where we can go,' shouted Elise. 'Shake them off first then drop us by the bridge and keep going to save yourself. There's a place for us to hide close by.'

Chapter Twenty-Seven

The smell was the same: musty earth and stagnant water. The sounds were different. No summer footsteps and light conversation drifting down as people traversed to and fro. Elise doubted her brother was remembering those carefree times when they were children. His jaw was clenched against his pain and fever as Nathan settled him down onto the earthen ground.

They were huddled together in the dugout beneath the bridge; above their heads the timbers creaked and vibrated with the heavy traffic crossing it. Numerous vehicles loaded with troops and weapons were out in pursuit of them. The metallic noise reminded Elise of her final day with her father when the Nazi advance towards Dunkirk had seen them sitting together in a deadly atmosphere of foreboding. He'd known his time was up; Elise understood how he must have felt. There wasn't a chance of this place remaining undetected when the soldiers came back to thoroughly search the area.

'We have to move on soon so let's get this seen to.' Elise crouched by Luc's side. She tended to his wound while he rested his back against a wall of damp earth. Earlier she'd ripped a strip of material from her chemise. She dabbed away some of the mess from the weeping flesh and unrolled the fresh bandage over it.

'Move to where? Theo won't come back.' Luc sounded despondent. 'He'll be the first of us to be arrested. We're done for this time.'

'Theo's no fool. And I reckon he'll do his damnedest to come back for us.' Nathan sat down by them. 'He said he'd try to bring the radio if it's still in the hotel.'

'Is there a good chance of getting it?' Elise asked. If she could send a message to London things might not be so bleak.

'Theo's got people everywhere. He wouldn't offer if he couldn't deliver. A bombing raid would create a diversion and keep Fritz busy. Would your boss in London arrange something like that?'

'Possibly,' said Elise. 'But it takes time and we don't have any to spare.' She glanced at her brother then turned her eyes up, realising the noise of traffic was petering out.

Luc sighed and raised a hand to his sister's bruised face. 'You shouldn't have come back to France. Look what they've done to you.'

She removed his fingers from her tender skin. 'It doesn't matter, Luc ...' She stopped attempting to buck him up as Nathan pushed to his feet and drew her up with him.

He led her to the mouth of the cave where the sluggish water glistened like ebony oil beneath a weak moon.

Elise licked her parched lips. She could do with a drink of water and she knew the others could too. Venturing out of this hidey-hole to find a village pump or a friendly local wasn't wise, even if it did seem quieter. She was tempted to risk it to avoid the question coming her way. She broke the ice, although a thought of Toby Winters let alone a conversation about him made her feel sick.

'I heard the gunshot. Did you kill him, Nathan?'

His jaw clenched; it was more of an answer than his imperceptible nod. 'He said you knew one another.'

'It's not what you think.'

'I don't know what to think.'

'I imagine he said we were lovers in London. It's not true. I never even liked him. Now I loathe him.'

'Because he raped you back there?'

'And because he admitted to robbing and killing Graham Yates.'

Nathan closed his eyes. He'd dreaded hearing her confirm that Winters hadn't been bluffing about his depravity. Rage and hatred for the man who'd hurt her were bottled up inside. So were a thousand questions, but fighting to stay alive to untangle the mess was all he could do for now. And hold her. He enclosed her in his arms and rested his cheek against the crown of her head. 'I'm so sorry I didn't get to you sooner. I love you so much.'

'I love you.' She couldn't bear to hear the anguish in his voice and started to cry, muffling the noise against his shoulder. 'It's not your fault, Nathan.'

'I wish the bastard was still alive so I could kill him again more slowly. Was he lying about being related to you through the Coopers?'

A memory of the happy party times the Coopers had spent together in Silvertown made her sound wistful when saying, 'My stepbrother Jake was adopted by a posh couple when he was a baby. So was Toby ... they became brothers.' She rested her back against his chest then drew his arms around her waist. 'Jake thinks he knew you when you were kids.'

Nathan looked down at her upturned face.

'Jake Harding's his name.' She paused. 'He was abandoned by his mother and brought up in a Barnardo's home. He thinks you were there at the same time.'

'I do remember him at Stepney.' Nathan snorted in disbelief. 'We were pals. Small world, eh?'

'Jake thought you'd moved away from the East End.'

'I did for a while ... I heard my mother had moved to Manchester.'

'Did you find her?' She again tilted up her face to look at him.

'Nah. Found one of her cousins. Was told they'd no idea where she'd gone to when she left Manchester. They weren't a pleasant lot so I decided not to stick around and came back to London.'

'That's family for you ...'

'Family or not, I won't ever regret killing Winters, the ...' He silently spat the obscenity at the sky.

'Jake will probably thank you for saving him the job. He threatened to kill his brother himself.' She knew that statement begged an explanation, so while they stared out into the black landscape she told him all about the trouble that had pitted her against Toby Winters years ago.

'And was he the boy's father?'

Elise paused before answering. 'I think so.'

'Poor kid.'

'Family ties can be a curse as well as a blessing.' She sighed in a mixture of guilt and regret and turned back to face him. 'When it came to it I couldn't shoot to kill. I just wanted to get away and warn you the circuit was blown. It was stupid to do that. It gave him a chance to get his gun and hold it to my head. I'm a coward because I'm glad he's gone. He deserved to die for all the terrible things he did. I pray Graham can rest in peace now.'

'You're the bravest girl I know. Marcel, or whatever his name was, got what he deserved being shot by his own kind. He came from the same mould as Winters.'

The sound of heavy footsteps approaching made them swiftly draw back out of sight.

'It's Theo,' said Nathan having seen a squat figure breaking cover to splash towards them.

'What message will you send?' Theo was standing ankle deep in the stream as he triumphantly showed them the case he was carrying and handed over a bag of food. 'Will you go south and wait for a pick-up?'

With a groan Luc forced himself onto his feet to amble over.

'You won't get far with him in that state,' Theo rumbled a warning.

'We could make the northern coast in a day or two. Do you have a contact there?' asked Nathan. 'A friendly skipper to take us across the Channel?'

Theo snorted a negative. 'Roadblocks are set up every kilometre. The area's crawling with Boches by the Atlantic Wall and Forbidden Zone. There are batteries of defences set up right the way along the coast.' He swept apart two beefy arms in demonstration. 'You'll need a cover story and Gestapo passes to get anywhere near the sea.'

'You have to tell your lot to send the RAF to create a distraction, Elise.' Luc entered the conversation with a demand and helped himself to the bottle of wine Theo had brought, pulling the cork with his teeth.

'We can't wait, or rely on any help. Too many channels to go through, too much red tape to cut.' She gestured in frustration. 'We'll have to do this ourselves. And quickly.'

'Would your grandmother hide you while you recover?' Theo turned to Luc.

'She would, but I won't let her endanger her life.' Luc sank wearily down onto his haunches, nursing the bottle. 'Leave me behind ... you have to now.' He let his forehead rest against his fist. 'I know I'm holding you back and need a hospital.'

Elise crouched beside him. 'We go together or stay here together.' If Luc handed himself in he'd very likely be executed not allowed hospital treatment.

Taking the transmitter from Theo, Elise set it up on the riverbank, giving him the aerial to unwind. She knelt on mud beside the open case. 'I'll send some messages to London.' She glanced back. 'I can't promise any of it will work. We can only pray it does and be ready at the appointed hour. If I ask for arrangements for Friday night can your comrades create a commotion to help cover our getaway?'

'The rubber factory's overdue to be blown sky-high.' Theo growled a laugh. 'They won't be expecting it now they know the plot's been uncovered. They'll think we've given up on it. We'll throw everything at it. All the explosives might as well be used before they're found and turned against us.'

Baker Street, London

'Is Major Venables at home?' asked the female officer, scribbling furiously on paper laid out by the telephone.

'I believe he is.'

'He needs to see this right away. Fetch him would you?'

The younger woman in First Aid Nursing Yeomanry uniform dashed out of the office and down the steps of the building. In seconds, she was driving the saloon car at speed along the murky street.

Fifteen minutes later, Major Venables was striding into the office. He propped himself against the desk and frowned with great deliberation at the pencilled message. 'Did they say if any abnormality in stroke or frequency had been detected?'

'They don't think it was an imposter, sir. They believe it was indeed Orpheline.'

'Thank God. She's possibly still alive then,' Major Venables said. 'Have messages sent alerting those around Lille to lie low for now.'

'What about this, sir?' The female officer pushed the second message towards him. 'Should it go to the BBC? What does it mean? It's rather irregular, isn't it, to send a message like this?'

'What isn't irregular in this damned war?' said Venables. 'If Orpheline wants it sent then that's what we'll do. We have to trust she knows what she's doing. She's done everything we could have asked for so far, God bless her.'

Broadstairs, Kent

Mrs Yates upended the iron and frowned at her daughter, who'd shot up from her chair and gone to the radio to turn up the volume.

'The last message – did you hear it? I missed part of it.' Faith gabbled.

'You know I don't understand French as well as you, dear. Something about a bell. You know it's all gobbledygook on this station. Let's have on the Light Service . . .'

'Shh.' Faith raised a quietening finger and listened intently as the broadcaster solemnly announced he would repeat the previous message. He did, slowly, as though to ensure it would be correctly interpreted.

'Urgent girls' club meeting required Friday midnight. Same place. Bring Belle. Sorry,' he intoned in French before moving on to the next message.

'See, I told you it was nonsense,' said Mrs Yates, having listened along with her daughter. She tutted and flapped a tablecloth over the ironing board.

Faith had turned pale but she grabbed a pen and paper from the drawer and scribbled down what she'd heard. 'What day is it?' she asked her mother. Her mind was overwhelmed with a dreadful excitement preventing her concentrating properly on anything but checking her translation.

'Thursday ... and it's ten-thirty. Time your father was home. Where are you going, Faith? I didn't mean you had to fetch him, love.'

'I'm not, Mum.' Faith continued writing a separate note with a shaking hand then she pulled on her coat, and Kirk, knowing she was going out, padded to her side.

'Would you give this to Dad when he gets in?'

'What is it?'

'Just a note. It's important. Please give it to him.' She left the paper on the table.

'Where are you going?' On noticing Faith's strange expression, Mrs Yates abandoned the ironing and approached her daughter. 'Aren't you well? Oh, you're not going out for a crafty drink, are you? You've been doing so well, dear.'

'No.' Faith gave a wan smile. 'I'm not going out for that.'

Before she shut the door she turned around to gaze at her mother. 'I love you, Mum.'

Dunkirk

'Don't you know what this is?' Father Pascal tapped the emblem of two eagles facing one another then began waving the Gestapo pass beneath the Nazi officer's nose. The forged document was snatched back before it could be closely inspected. 'Oh, go ahead! Take a look, if you must, but this is an outrage . . . sacrilege,' roared the priest and crossed himself.

The officer by the hearse stood aside, watching while a trooper prised the lids off the two coffins in the back of the vehicle.

The waxy faced corpses of an elderly man and his wife were prodded by a gun butt and the priest exploded again in angry remonstration. 'Heathens! You have no respect for the dead, or the church. The Almighty will make you pay for this. Can you not see the disease in them? Tuberculosis. You fools.'

'I'm sorry, Father.' The officer shuffled backwards, cuffing his face in alarm and disgust. 'But checks must be made.' He waved at the guard by the barrier to let the vehicle pass.

Father Pascal jumped into the hearse beside the granite-faced driver. And off they went. On approaching a high coastal road that wound downwards towards a church graveyard, they stopped in a quiet spot. The men flung open the doors and bolted to the back of the vehicle. The coffin lids were again removed. From beneath the corpses emerged two people. Luc was assisted out, panting and gasping for air. Elise struggled out on her own, shivering from the ordeal of having endured dead flesh pressed against hers. Small air holes in the timber had barely kept them breathing in the suffocating malodorous space. When she'd recovered enough to do so, she muttered a prayer for the deceased who had saved them.

Nathan dropped down from the underside of the hearse and was soon on his feet, collecting the weapons that had also been strapped beneath the vehicle.

Theo had been driving but Father Pascal now took the wheel.

'*Vive La France. Bonne chance ... vite ... vite ... allez,*' was the priest's hissed farewell. In seconds, he was driving away and the three men and Elise started their stealthy descent towards the beach.

Chapter Twenty-Eight

'What time is it, Nathan?'

'Almost midnight.'

'Anything there?' Elise asked as he lowered the binoculars.

He shook his head and enclosed her in a hug. She had on his jacket for warmth but he could feel her limbs shivering in the November chill.

Luc was hunched in the sandy hollow in which they were sheltering. Elise knew his strength was failing and he'd find the dash to the water – should it come – arduous. But she wouldn't leave him behind. They'd agreed to stick together until the bitter end.

Theo crept back from where he'd been scouting the higher ground and dropped down to crouch in the dune. 'Boche sentries everywhere. I'll give covering fire when they start shooting.' Theo was brooding on his guilt for having allowed himself to be duped by Marcel and had frequently said he wished he'd been the one to execute the traitor.

Nathan gripped the man's arm in gratitude. He'd heard the patrolling troopers' voices and seen sporadic glows of cigarette tips. 'They'll be expecting an invasion up the beach not an exodus down it. With luck we'll make the boat before they spot us.'

'The beach is mined, and the sea, whichever way you run,' Theo bleakly reminded.

'It's a chance we have to take.' Nathan's eyes sought Elise's. They knew Luc, already wobbly on his feet, wouldn't be vigilant about where he stepped on their imminent scramble for the shore.

'You've done enough, Theo.' Nathan wanted their loyal friend to get away safely. 'Head back now or come with us.'

'I'll never leave France. I'll hang around here until you go. Use the torch again.'

Nathan flashed a beam towards the sea, but briefly to avoid its reflection being spotted.

'What's that noise?' Luc laboriously manoeuvred himself onto his knees to peer over the dune's lip. 'Sounded like a bell.'

Nathan used the binoculars again, taking a sweeping view of the ocean.

'A ship's bell; it's Faith! It must be,' Elise said excitedly. The faint noise had stopped. Her friend wouldn't draw more attention than necessary.

'No wonder I can't see her ...' Nathan growled a low chuckle. 'Bloody boat's painted black. Clever girl.' He picked up the torch and flashed a signal in response.

'Oh, she is marvellous,' said Elise in a voice throbbing with emotion.

Theo pulled Luc to his feet. They were all dressed in dark clothes, their faces camouflaged with mud but he warned, 'Move fast. They'll see you soon enough.'

'Give me a Sten gun,' Luc insisted.

It was handed over and Elise also picked up her weapon,

checking it again. 'What time is the factory due to go up?' she asked.

'Right about now,' said Theo, scanning the horizon. 'We'll wait for it.'

'We can't wait; Faith's already in danger,' Elise said. 'She can't hang about close to shore. If the boat's hit . . .'

'Elise is right,' said Nathan. 'We go now. The factory might not happen. The explosives might have been found.'

'Give my people a chance,' growled Theo. 'Without the distraction this is suicide. With it—' he gave a Gallic shrug '—suicide.'

Elise's further argument about moving immediately was drowned out by a distant blast. In unison they stared inland, delighted grins breaking on their faces as they watched a red glow spread into the sky. A commotion of voices was heard behind them as the Germans excitedly took notice of the sabotage.

Luc gave a hoarse chuckle. 'Well, I'm ready . . . let's go.' In a show of bravado he sprang onto the sand, landing with a grunt.

Elise was close to the water's edge when the first shots rang out. The two able-bodied men were supporting Luc between them but Theo let go to give covering fire.

Elise ran back to help although she'd had her first wonderful glimpse of Faith leaning to haul them on board. She'd heard her friend yelling she couldn't come closer or she'd ground the *Belle*.

They surged into the water, wading into the depths, pulling Luc between them. Once their skipper had hold of a groaning Luc, Nathan returned to join Theo, firing at the enemy.

Soldiers were advancing in a line down the beach. A mine detonated in a burst of sand and one of them fell.

'If I'm captured I don't want it to be for nothing,' Theo boomed. 'Go on ... clear off and good luck, Corporal.'

Nathan nodded and gripped the man's burly shoulder before wading out then swimming towards the boat.

'Get moving. Now!' he shouted the moment he had a hand fixed on an edge of timber.

Elise held onto his arm and Luc used what strength he had to cling to Nathan as Faith set off with bullets spraying water up at them. Nathan managed to haul himself up and over with their help, rolling onto the bottom of the boat. They stared back at the place where Theo had been last man standing. Some troopers were crowding around his fallen body. Others waded into the sea to continue shooting at the vessel disappearing into the darkness.

They all gave answering fire until there was nothing left to see but a burning sky above the disintegrating rubber factory.

'Better start bailing. We've been hit.' Faith rolled a bucket towards them and continued setting course.

Nathan used the bucket and Elise crawled along the boat towards Faith then jumped up and hugged her friend. 'I'm so sorry to involve you in this. I wasn't sure you'd understand the message or come ...'

'Why not?' Faith rubbed away the black mess on her friend's cheek then gave it a kiss. 'You'd come for me. Anyway, don't worry, love,' said Faith as Elise's tears flowed. 'Makes a change from listening to the Light Service every evening.'

'Thank you. I owe you one,' Elise said huskily.

'I reckon you do.' Faith chuckled. 'Never been so damned

scared. Worse than Dunkirk. And I didn't think that was possible.' She pulled a hip flask from her pocket with a trembling hand and upended it. 'Don't say a word to my mother about any of this ...' She shook the flask. 'I'll be all right again next week.'

'Got any of that to spare?' asked Luc who was stroking the dog lying in the bottom of the boat.

Faith handed him the flask. 'Keep bailing. And keep an eagle eye out for mines. Pretty sure I passed a few on the way over. Nearly had kittens.'

'This thing's hurting like hell.' Luc attempted to move his wounded arm and get onto his knees to peer over the side.

'Stop moaning, you've got your drinking arm.' Faith took back her whisky. 'So who are you?'

'Luc Bouchard ... and thank you, Ma'amselle for saving our bacon.' He chuckled to be using one of his father's phrases and fished out his cigarettes.

Faith lit him one of hers and handed it over after his soggy ones were discarded in disgust. 'My pleasure, M'sieur Bouchard,' she said. 'But we're not out of the woods – well, water – yet.'

'Put that out, they'll see it,' Nathan shouted as a faint red spot and smell of tobacco alerted him. He looked up at the sky.

Elise did too. They might be out of range of machine-gun fire from the shore but they weren't yet safe from an air attack.

They were over halfway to Broadstairs and frantically scouring the sea for mines when Nathan shouted, 'Here it comes ...' A Messerchmitt made a pass, trying to locate them in the darkness. 'The pilot'll spot the wake eventually,' he said and they picked up their guns.

'Is this jalopy at full speed?' asked Luc, sitting with his back against the boat's side, a Sten gun in his lap.

'It is.' Faith ducked as bullets splintered the cabin top.

Their answering fire sent the Messerschmitt quickly out of range. But they knew it would be back now it had a bearing. Elise pointed upwards as another aircraft headed towards them from the ghostly outline of Kent's white cliffs.

'Spitfire!' Nathan shouted and they gave a collective roar of encouragement as the British fighter engaged the Messerschmitt in a dog fight. A string of grey smoke on black sky was a final sighting of the German craft before it crashed into the sea, rocking the boat high and starting Luc off singing a feverish rendition of 'La Marseillaise'.

'Welcome to Broadstairs,' said Faith in her best cruise guide voice. 'We hope you enjoy your stay.' She sank to her knees, leaned over the side of the *Kentish Belle* and vomited into the sea.

Luc shuffled on his bottom to pat her back and when she stopped being sick he put his good arm around her, murmuring praise and thanks for what she'd done.

Nathan and Elise trudged up the beach supporting Luc between them. They settled him down against the sea wall while Faith ran towards the esplanade to fetch help.

Elise sat close by then reclined back on the damp shingle with a sigh that seemed to come from her core. Nathan lay down next to her.

Above their heads the Spitfire tipped a wing before disappearing inland.

Sensing his eyes on her, Elise turned her head to meet a look of pure love. Their smiles were barely there.

'You're home, Nathan,' she said and entwined her fingers with those caressing her face.

'Are you?' He tightened his grip on her icy hand. 'Will you stay with me, Elise?'

'Always,' she said.

Epilogue

8 May 1945, VE Day

'Not celebrating with your family?'

Major Venables spoke over a shoulder to his visitor.

'Maybe later. And you?'

'Oh, I dare say a dram or two of whisky might pass my lips at some point today.' He returned to his desk to resume packing up.

Elise came further into the office and closed the door. It looked different: no longer a threat now the dismantled equipment was in boxes around the walls. She noticed the desk drawer was open and a photograph of a woman – his wife she imagined – lay inside. She was tempted to take it out, ask him about it, and discover if this man did feel for somebody.

He placed a file on top of the photograph and gestured for her to sit down but she didn't. She occupied the place he'd had at the window and watched men and women in redundant uniforms dancing in the streets.

'How is your French brother, Miss Bouchard?'

'He's recovering well, thank you.'

'Good. I hear they can do marvellous things with prosthetics now.'

'He says he won't have one – he favours a hook. He would,' she said, wryly for herself.

'And is your corporal home yet?'

'His unit's still in Germany. But I've heard he's due back soon.'

'He was at the landings, wasn't he?'

'Yes.'

'Which beach?'

'Sword.'

'And your Cooper brothers are all safely home as well?'

Elise's expression softened. 'Yes, all safely back in Silvertown.'

'And that leaves you, my dear. You appear to be blooming.' He looked Elise Bouchard over: no sparky teenage girl now in a soggy mac but a beautiful, assured woman dressed in an elegant blue coat. 'Nice as it is to see you after all this time I suspect something brings you here.'

'I've come to say goodbye, Major Venables. But before I go back to France I'm curious for some answers,' she said.

'Ah ... not wise,' he said, continuing to load books into a box. 'You had your debriefing, didn't you? So my advice would be not to pick at the wound.'

'I have to if I'm ever to find some peace.' Her grey eyes bored into him. 'I hope you'll answer me truthfully.' She saw his mouth hardening but didn't let it bother her. It was too late for that. 'Did you allow Toby Winters to escape from detention then send me after him in 1943?'

'Come now ... what's brought this on?' Venables said gently. 'The war's over and nobody is more glad about that than me.' He pointed to the window. 'Listen to that:

the sweet sound of a nation putting the dark days behind them.'

'Did you, sir?'

He sat down behind his desk and met her eyes as squarely as he had on the day she'd come and begged him to send her to France. 'Extraordinary times call for extraordinary measures, Miss Bouchard. Had I not trusted you to be equal to the task I wouldn't have allowed you to go. I gave you every opportunity to refuse. Hoped you wouldn't of course. I had high hopes for you and you didn't let me down.'

'Why did you do that? You had him here! Out of harm's way!'

'We didn't have his associate though. His Fascist pal was wreaking havoc among our circuits. We knew his name but that wasn't much use to us.' He paused. 'We needed him flushed out into the open.'

'You mean Marcel?'

'Indeed I do, but he wasn't our Marcel. He was an impostor. Our agent was taken out shortly after he arrived in France. Poor chap was brutally interrogated and executed.' Venables drummed his fingers on the desktop. 'Those two were communicating on the transmitter you saw from early in the war, before Winters got himself into a silly spot of bother.'

'So I messed things up for you when I stopped him abducting my nephew?'

'Brought things to a premature head is how I'd put it. We couldn't pretend we didn't know the fellow was a fanatic after that simply to carry on feeding him false information.' He paused. 'But up until that point we did have ourselves a useful idiot.'

'You found another one in me soon enough,' she said.

'Hardly. You were our faith and hope ... Churchill's too

for he knew of it; every good wish went with you. You had a way with Winters ... got under his skin.' He paused. 'I didn't tell you this before: when he was in detention he asked several times to see you. Requests denied, of course.'

'Did Graham know any of this?'

'Some, not all; he had become emotionally involved.'

'He loved me, so he was expendable.'

'Every soldier is during war. Do you feel better for knowing any of it?'

'No, but I feel better for knowing you're guiltier than I am of his death.'

'I am. I sleep with ghosts as well, you know, far more than you can imagine.' He paused. 'You might not think so but you were one of the lucky girls. You came back. You have a life left to live.' He wandered back to the window and stared out. 'You and your band of Resistance fighters eliminated two dangerous traitors. Had you not agreed to work for us in France more of our agents would have perished. Of that I'm sure.'

She stared at his back. 'How many female agents didn't come home? Did I train with some of them at Beaulieu?'

'You did ... with some ...'

'Who were they? Tell me about all of them.'

He didn't turn to face her but a list of names flowed from him as though they played constantly in his head. When he stopped speaking, thirteen women had been identified and there was silence but for the revelry behind the windowpanes.

'Without you and people like you preparing the ground for us in France for the landings, the outcome would have been different. No dancing, no singing. Not in English anyway. Your heroism deserves recognition. I shall see to it.'

'Don't. I want no reminders shut away in a drawer.'

'So be it,' he said and pivoted slowly around. 'I'd do it again, you know. Would you?'

She used the back of her hand on her wet face and grimaced a negative before turning to leave.

'That's Miss Bouchard talking,' he said. 'What would Orpheline say?'

He perched on his desk contemplating the closed door and the faint scent of lavender. He took out his cigarettes. He lit up and pulled a whisky flask from his pocket.

'*Bonne chance, mon amie,*' he said into the silence, raising the flask in a solemn salute before taking a lengthy swig.

31 May 1945

'You said you wouldn't come back to France.'

He shrugged. 'Had to.'

'Why?'

'It's where you are.'

Elise smiled wistfully.

'And it's our anniversary. Have you forgotten? Five years since Dunkirk.'

'I've not forgotten. I try not to think about it now.'

'Easier said than done,' he said drily.

'Would you like tea?' She sounded calm despite her thrill and joy at his unexpected appearance in the open doorway.

'Got used to coffee for a while. Never liked it as much as a good old British cuppa though.'

She put the kettle on. He dropped his bag on the floor.

'Where's Luc? And your grandmother?'

'Out at the market. They'll be back any minute.' She

gave him a smile, subduing an urge to throw herself into his arms. It was too soon to be sure. 'Luc's getting married next year.'

'What?' Nathan chuckled and leaned back against the doorjamb, arms crossed. 'Who?'

'Two guesses. You have met her.'

'Faith ...'

'How did you know that?'

'I could see he'd fallen for her ... it's easy once you know.'

Their eyes held for a moment then Elise turned back to pour the tea. 'All our Cooper family are invited to the wedding.'

'Am I invited?'

'Of course. I'd love to introduce you to them. They all know about you, and Luc never stops talking about you.' She held out his cup of tea.

He took it, walked into the cottage to put it down then drew her into his arms. 'I still love you ... want to marry you, Elise.' He cupped her face. 'Do you still love me?'

She nodded. 'You didn't seem sure in your last letter. I don't blame you – things are different now between us. Everything has changed. I considered making sure it wouldn't ...' She eased free of him with a sob swelling in her chest. 'And I feel wicked and guilty for doing that.'

He comforted her again in his arms. 'Hush, don't cry. I was being a bloody fool. I'm sorry ... so sorry. I'm over it now.' He smoothed her black hair off her face. 'If you won't marry me, I'll just hang around anyway.'

She sighed. 'My dad was English, my mum French. It didn't work out well for them.'

He stroked her cheek and smiled wryly as he glanced up

at the cottage's whitewashed ceiling. 'D'you reckon they're watching over you?'

'Hope so ... I think of them all the time.'

'We'll show them how it's done then.'

She took his hands, kissed them, her heart breaking with her love for him. 'Are you sure you want to stay in France? Will you get fed up and go back to England? My dad would do that all the time.'

'I'm not Sidney Cooper.'

'Luc's moving to Broadstairs when he gets married. Faith visited him every day she could while he was in hospital and convalescing. She's going to be the best wife for him, the best sister-in-law to me. But I won't leave Mathilde on her own. She won't move to England. She's seventy and set in her ways.'

'I know. Did you go back to work at the dress shop?'

'No. I had some money from SOE. Madame Laurent didn't want the gossip, you know how it is. I grew up with that with my own mum. Nothing changes but the date ...' She regretted reminding herself of her first meeting with Venables. She'd used that phrase when persuading him to recruit her. She had the rest of her life to be grateful for, the major had said, the truest words she'd heard from him.

And she had this man and a yearning to make yesterday's impossible dream come true. 'My landlady is still a friend.' Elise half-smiled, remembering Madame sashaying along the street at a victory parade in her red dress – a gift bought at a good discount.

'Shall we go and see Father Pascal about our wedding?'

'I'd like that, Nathan,' she said. 'If you're sure. Are you?'

'Never been surer of anything in my life.' He kissed her. 'Will you show her to me now, Elise? Please?'

She took his hand and led him into the bedroom. The baby was sitting up in bed bouncing on her bottom in the cot.

Nathan gazed at the beautiful dark-haired child. 'She looks like you,' he said in a voice too husky to properly hear.

'Yes, she does. I wish it was different, Nathan ...'

'So do I, but it's not and I'm glad you didn't lie.' He drew her into his arms and they clung together, faces slippery with tears, until finally the baby cried for attention.

'What's her name?'

'Giselle.'

He repeated the name as though it were honey on his tongue. 'Let's see where life takes us, Giselle, shall we?' he said and picked up his daughter.

Author Note

The Special Operations Executive (SOE) French Section was set up in early 1941 and operated from 64 Baker Street, London.

British agents from all walks of life were deployed and sent to occupied France to gather intelligence and disrupt the Nazi war effort. The recruitment of women met some opposition; nevertheless the first trained female agent was in France by summer 1943. In all, thirty-nine were recruited. Some acted as couriers and wireless operators, others joined the Maquis (French Partisans) in active combat. Ambushing enemy troops and blowing up bridges and infrastructure was vital in assisting the D-Day landings that marked the start of the liberation of France, and Allied victory the following year.

The SOE Memorial at Valençay in France records the thirteen female agents of F Section and the First Aid Nursing Yeomanry (FANY) who never came home.

Acknowledgements

The following book was of immense help in writing *An Englishman's Daughter*: *They Fought Alone* by Maurice Buckmaster: a memoir by the head of SOE's F Section.